The Home Front

DW HANNEKEN

Ten|16
PRESS
www.ten16press.com - Waukesha, WI

The Home Front

ISBN 978-1-64538-127-3
First Edition
Cover Design by Laurette Perlewitz

The Home Front
by DW Hanneken

For information, please contact:

Ten 16
PRESS

www.ten16press.com
Waukesha, WI

To Mom.
For the idea, your support, and for your abiding love.

Prologue

Maggie Wentworth's eyes popped open, her chin resting on the edge of the bed, a cheek marinating in a small puddle of drool. She blinked several times to get her bearings, trying to recall the night before. *When did I go to bed?*

Lying frozen on her right side, Maggie examined the tapestry of her second-story bedroom. A dull morning light illuminated the farmhouse sanctum as she lifted her head and glanced at the clock on the nightstand. *Ten past eight?* At that hour, she knew her husband Erik would be busy in the fields.

Plopping her head back on the pillow, her attention was drawn to a nearby chest of drawers. Two generational wedding portraits sat in the corner – one black and white photo of her parents, Ivy and Big Jack, the other featuring herself and Erik. Both brides appeared content, the grooms proud. Two small photographs of her son Benny clung to the edge of the large beveled mirror – his baptism and the youngster's first birthday.

With the room awash in shades of gray, it marked the fourth straight day of clouds and possibly more rain. Slowly coming to life, Maggie pushed up onto her elbows and examined Erik's dirty garments scattered about the room. Nothing out of the ordinary. After five years of marriage, he still hadn't learned what the clothes hamper was for.

So what happened last night?

Maggie sat up, crossed her legs and took in a slow, deep breath. Stretching her arms up high, fingertips reaching for the ceiling, she winced at a sharp pain just above her left temple. Rubbing it, she felt an enormous lump beneath her thick brown mane – as if someone had surgically implanted a robin's egg under her scalp. She gently tapped the tender bump with an index finger, then noticed her forearm bore a black-and-green bruise. To make matters worse, she even donned the same blouse from the night before – crusted gravy stains splattered along one sleeve.

"Oh, God . . ."

The memories of that night washed over her like a strong gust of wind. The thunderstorm . . . the cold dinner . . . the argument . . . broken dishes . . . and finally, the beating.

Rolling onto her side, Maggie wondered why he would abuse her. She always wondered why. Curled into a ball, she closed her eyes and began to weep.

Moments later the bedroom door creaked, then stopped. It creaked once more, and stopped again. With her back to the entrance, she hesitated to turn around. Was it *he?* Had Erik tip-toed up to the bedroom to express a personal act of contrition, saying he'd had one-too-many the night before and didn't realize what he had done? Maybe he'd been too drunk to recall the incident at all. Another blackout, perhaps?

Mustering up enough courage to engage this creature of calamity, Maggie bit her bottom lip, took in a deep breath, and rolled over to face the beast. But instead . . .

"Hi, Mommy."

There in the doorway stood her four-year-old son, topless and in his underwear, his curly orange hair matted down to one side, the right thumb in his mouth and Mr. Chuckles the clown dangling from his left hand. Relieved, she felt a warm tingle deep in her solar plexus and smiled at the sight.

"Are you awake?" Benny slurred, his thumb still between his teeth.

She nonchalantly wiped her tears on the bedsheet and held out her arms. "Come here, sweetheart," she squeaked, forcing a smile. "How are you and Mr. Chuckles this morning?"

With rapid-fire steps, Benny sprinted toward her and leaped up onto the bed. "There were night monsters again."

"Yeah, I know. That was quite a thunderstorm," she said, hardly remembering the details while trying to ignore the memory of the fight with Erik. Hugging him, she could hear air exit his tiny lungs. "But you are a brave boy, aren't you?" Pulling back to look at her only child, Maggie once again dabbed at her eyes with the bedsheets.

"Don't cry, Mommy. Opa says the night monsters are only angels breaking rocks. You don't have to be afraid no more." He innocently wiped away a tear from her cheek with a soft, silky finger. Then more waterworks. More hugs. More kisses.

"Where's Opa now?"

"He's downstairs making eggs, and he sounds mad. He cussed three times!"

Oh my God! He knows about the fight. She could only imagine what her father saw in the kitchen that morning. For some time he had suspected trouble with their marriage. Several months earlier, he brought it up, but Maggie waved it off, telling him not to worry. She could tell by the expression on his leathered face he didn't buy it.

Pulling at her sleeve, she told Benny to run downstairs. "Momma will be down in a few minutes." Benny kissed her cheek and scampered out of the room, his little feet pattering down the hallway, then down the wooden steps.

Climbing out of bed, stinging pains danced throughout her body. A pinch on her ankle . . . a nip on her neck. Her hip ached as she limped across the room. Throbbing, head to toe. The pain all too familiar.

Maggie slowly removed her clothes – wincing periodically – and threw them into a tall wicker hamper tucked into the corner. Standing naked before a full-length mirror, she leaned forward to deliberate over her body. Who was this stranger staring back at her? She studied the reflection, thinking she looked nearly 45, despite celebrating her 25th birthday only a month earlier. *I'm hideous! No wonder Erik hasn't shown any interest in me for more than six months.* Turning sideways, Maggie saw a deep bruise on her hip and another on her thigh – she wasn't one to bruise easily. Honestly, the last thing in the world she wanted those past few days – those past few months – was to be intimate with him!

Her bloodshot eyes stared directly into her soul, and Maggie's breathing intensified by the second. With fists clenched, knuckles white, her fingernails dug deep into her palms. In the reflection, her stomach muscles became taut, she gritted her teeth and shook her head from side to side, trying to release herself from the grip of dark, debossed memories. She could sense the pain working its way from deep in her belly, up into her chest, to her throat . . . she wanted so badly to scream, but instead Maggie did what she always does – she swallowed hard and pushed it down, entombing the memory into the deep crevasses of her soul. Safe. Secure. Stockpiled. *How could I ever think I'd miss that barbarian?*

The sounds of thick, residual raindrops fell off an adjacent oak tree and landed hard against the steel roof of the farmhouse. *Ping, ping, ping-ping-ping.* The thunderstorm had abandoned them, but the July humidity loitered about and would likely stay for God only knew how long. In fact, the oppressiveness seemed to have only gotten worse. By the time she climbed into some slacks and pushed her arms through a long-sleeved shirt, the mercury already began to flirt with eighty degrees. Her hairline was low enough to cover the large bump on her temple and the sleeves would hide the contusions on her arm. As for the limp, she could only hope no one would notice.

Chapter One

The Letter

Downstairs, Maggie paused in the kitchen doorway to watch Big Jack clean the dishes in the sink. From the back, he appeared brittle and vulnerable. Hunched and bowlegged, his olive green trousers billowed as a thin black belt pleated them in numerous places along the high waistline. His white T-shirt rolled over his shoulders, bringing the short sleeves to his elbows. The bald spot on top of his head called attention to itself while framed by thinning silver hair. *When did he get so old?*

Looking around at the rest of the room, Maggie felt surprised at how uncluttered things appeared. Not spotless by any means, but tidy enough to wonder if Big Jack cleaned up. Or maybe Erik did it, before he went into the fields. *Right. Sure.*

The yellow linoleum floor looked the same as always – stained and worn – but not covered in mud from the wet boots he tracked in the night before. Maggie's knickknacks rested peacefully on the shelf above the kitchen table and were lined up right where they'd always been. Below the white cupboards stood four stainless steel containers, the words SUGAR, FLOUR, OATS and COFFEE etched on the sides. Clean pots and pans hung precariously above the stove on long hooks attached to the exposed white ceiling beams. Quite the contrast to when she was down there only a few hours earlier, everything was in its place.

As Maggie leaned up against the door jamb, those midnight hours washed over her . . . how the demon came home late – drunk as usual – and coiled tight. Little by little, the haze obscuring her memory peeled away like the soft skin on an onion. Just how much of her nightmare was real?

She remembered how, in an intoxicated fit of rage, pots and pans were thrown onto the floor. Several plants fell from their perch on the windowsill above the sink. And then the finale – Maggie felt a sharp blow to the back of her neck. And nothing more. Not 'til morning.

All of that, because the biscuits were cold.

Had Erik been home for dinner, he would have been able to enjoy those warm treats . . . pulling them apart, drowning them in butter and dunking them in hot gravy. Bread has been called the staple of life, and like Maggie's biscuits, families are also home-baked, and made from scratch. But as time passes, things get cold, dry out, and as a result, congeal.

Maggie turned her attention to the adjoining entrance on the other side of the room. *Strange . . . I'm sure he kicked that back door off its hinges.* Eyeing the door closer, she noticed a green housefly frantically bouncing against the screen as if tied to a piece of string. The insect's efforts to escape to the outside were not lost on her.

Next, she looked at the stove, where several hours earlier a tall cast-iron skillet held Erik's cold dinner and prepared to spill his venom. The conversation echoed in her head . . .

"This dinner is colder than a witch's tit!"

"I tried keeping everything warm, Erik. You said you'd be home for dinner, but when it got dark I wasn't sure what to do."

Maggie did her best to shake off the memory. No such luck. She remembered how things escalated, how after several choice words her husband pressed a handful of cold gelatinous gravy into her face. *"If this shit is so good,* you *eat it!"* She recalled how he shoved her head hard into the kitchen table, then kicking her legs out from beneath her, causing her to crash face-first into the floor. The source of the lump on her temple, no doubt. Contemplating those morbid memories, her hand unconsciously traced its way up along her shoulder, then to the base of her skull. *Oh, God. Oww!* She realized she wasn't breathing, then forced herself to inhale. The air in the kitchen suddenly felt heavy and thick. Maggie closed her eyes and let out a long, low moan. God did not answer.

"*Guten Morgen, Papa,*" she said, strolling into the room and taking a seat at the kitchen table.

"Morning," Big Jack said as he sprinkled Arm & Hammer baking soda into a frying pan and scrubbed stubborn egg yoke from the iron skillet.

Sitting beside her, Benny lost himself in his favorite pastime: coloring black and white newspaper photos with crayons. Local sweethearts Clara Meinen and Jason Beck had their engagement picture published in *The Dodge County Gazette,* and thanks to Benny, the groom-to-be sported a green mustache, the future bride a violet beard. Maggie spied a vase full of fresh-picked lilies in the center of the table, their scent filling the kitchen with a soft perfume. She rolled her eyes and picked up a card leaning against the vase.

Thought I'd let you sleep in. Enjoy the flowers!
E

Some peace offering. And that lone "E" always bothered her. *Why not finish the other three characters for chrissakes?* Just about everything Erik did bothered her these days. Maggie sighed and flicked it into the air like a pinwheel. Benny watched the note ricochet off the wall and land perfectly upright against his box of crayons, as if set there by a gentle hand. The young boy marveled at his mother, thinking it was a skill only she possessed.

"Looks like it rained again last night," Maggie said while reaching for her father's still-lit cigarette in a glass ashtray. "The crops will like that."

Big Jack said nothing as his arm pumped up and down with the Golden Fleece scrubber.

"Erik must be in the fields," she said even louder before tapping the long ash off her dad's Viceroy and bringing it to her lips.

"Better there than here."

Maggie froze before she could take a puff. *Oh God, he knows! Despite his bad hearing and the loud crashes of thunder, surely he awoke last night.* Big Jack's bedroom was right down the hall from the kitchen, so it would have been easy for him to hear the door being kicked in . . . the arguing . . . the dishes shattering . . . Maggie hitting the floor. *No one could sleep through that. Did Big Jack carry me upstairs?*

"With all this rain, the Old 40 has some standing water," Big Jack continued, making his last statement less worrisome and more practical. "So it's a good thing Erik's out there cutting a drainage ditch into the creek." Drying his hands on a dishcloth, Big Jack walked to the oven, pulled out a plate of eggs, sautéed onions and toast, then set it before her.

"I see you made your specialty, Papa," she said, relieved he seemed more like himself. "Your 'World Famous' eggs and onions."

"Don't you forget it. Hope the toast isn't too dry."

"Opa, you'll be a good mommy someday," said Benny looking up from his art project.

Maggie smiled through the pain.

"So, how'd you sleep last night?" exhaled Maggie, needing confirmation her father had no clue about the fight.

"Pretty good. Apparently there was another big storm? Benny told me about it when we got up, but I didn't hear a gall-darn thing."

Benny and Big Jack – the two men in her life who loved and appreciated her more than anyone else. Unfortunately, a nefarious creature loomed in the middle. *Push it down, Maggie. Push it down!*

"You look like you're all set, darling," said Big Jack. "I'm gonna head out to the barn and get to work on some projects."

"Can I come, Opa?" said Benny enthusiastically.

"Not dressed like that. Let's get you some proper workin' clothes."

Maggie watched as Big Jack led Benny up the stairs to change. A smile flashed in the corner of her lips as she thought about her dad. He still did what he could to help around the farm, albeit in small ways – like maintaining the equipment, looking after their few livestock, running errands and helping to cook. But his passion was Benny, the son he never had. They often climbed onto the tractor and toured the fields together, which made Big Jack feel connected to this place. Being a farmer was all he knew, the soil was in his soul, and the connection was amalgamated.

Although he tolerated arthritis in both knees and had trouble hearing, those inconveniences didn't prevent him from doing what he loved. A veteran of World War I with the *Imperial German Army*, Corporal Jon Mueller still carried French shrapnel in his hip, and on rainy stretches like this, the pain cut deep. But through it all, he never complained. Big Jack's spine was so kyphotic, Maggie now stood taller than him. Thankfully, a sense of humor kept him young and bigger than life. He always found unlimited enjoyment in the simplest of things, including burping and flatulence. Big Jack oftentimes reminded her of a 12-year-old boy, and Benny was quick to tag along, more playmate than grandson.

As she sat alone and enjoyed her breakfast, Maggie reminisced about baking Christmas cookies with her mother Ivy at that very table – the same one on which they also sewed her wedding dress.

Maggie grew up on this southeastern Wisconsin farm with her immigrant parents. They arrived from Germany in the early 1920s, after rejecting the rigidity of the *Weimar Republic* and its authoritarian grip. Their work ethic was as strong as their belief in God and love of country . . . in their case two countries: America and *das Vaterland.*

There were no brothers to muscle the land. Big Jack and a few neighboring farmers typically handled the autumn harvest. However, now in his mid-sixties and in less than stellar health, he trusted his daughter and her husband Erik to run things, just as he and Ivy used to do. That was, before his world came crashing down. Before Ivy's pneumonia.

Taking her last few bites of breakfast, Maggie noticed a small stack of mail on the far side of the table. Calling attention to itself from the bottom of the pile was a large manila envelope, an emblem in the upper left-hand corner read, *United States of America War Office.*

Wiping her mouth with a napkin and taking another drag from Big Jack's nub of a cigarette, she methodically slid the letter out of the envelope and unfolded it, just as she had done every day since its arrival three weeks earlier. She felt no need to read it top-to-bottom. Not again. Particular phrases became engrained in her memory:

Your commitment to your country is appreciated . . .

By enlisting you will help stem the tide of imperialism . . .

You will report for active duty . . .

Maggie turned the letter over, laid it face down on the table, closed her eyes and softly ran her fingertips over the embossing on the back. A number of characters were nearly pushed straight through the paper, as if typed on a Smith-Corona in anger. *This must be what Braille feels like.* With eyes still closed and her mind lost in the daydream, Maggie wondered about the person who typed it. A wife perhaps? A mother? Maybe a steady who recently learned her lover would be going off to war? Maggie asked herself if she could muster the same heartache? The same pain? A few years ago, sure, but on that hot July morning, after being brutally attacked by her very own night monster, she knew the true answer.

Chapter Two

The Last Day

Just after lunch, Arthur "Art" Kreiter drove his truck up the long gravel driveway towards the Mueller barnyard. The 1932 blue Ford pickup truck discovered a few wet potholes as it ambled closer, the water spraying out like a geyser each time a tire found a new crater. Overcast gray skies loomed, but for the first time in several days the rain sidestepped the farm, which counted for something.

Big Jack sat on the front porch with a glass of lemonade while Benny knelt beside him hand-cranking a wooden churn in an attempt to make homemade ice cream. When the boy's little arms would fatigue, Big Jack would take over and have Benny sprinkle rock salt onto the ice to ensure the metal canister of custard would thicken and freeze itself into a delicacy from the heavens. Making ice cream this way became a summer tradition for as long as Big Jack could remember, and it never got old for him – or Benny.

While the two "boys" were busy making their dessert, Maggie embarked on what she believed to be a far more practical assignment – collecting eggs inside their small chicken coop.

When Art pulled into the barnyard and turned the key, the motor from his truck refused to disengage. He pumped the accelerator three times, and the engine backfired loudly before cutting off for good. *BANG!*

"Hey," Maggie called, retreating from the flimsy coop with a basket full of eggs. "What's all the racket?" She brushed the hair out of her eyes and smiled at her neighbor.

Art swung his long, narrow legs out the driver's side door and stepped into a deep puddle. "Dangnabit! These boots are brand-spankin' new!" Like Big Jack, he was in his mid-sixties, but unlike his best friend, Art stood with a straight back, nearly six foot four, his short gray hair peeking out from under a weathered John Deere baseball cap. His face long, and carved by the Wisconsin weather. A scar from an old farming accident zigzagged across one cheek, stopping besides his left earlobe, and a deep dimple on his chin looked as if a seamstress sewed a stitch from the inside. Holding two large envelopes, he waved to Big Jack. "Another hot day!" he shouted towards the front porch. "But no rain. Thank goodness."

Big Jack returned the wave and yelled back to his best friend, "Pretty good, how are you?"

Maggie walked up to Art and laughed. "You know he didn't hear a word you said, right?"

"That old coot could go all the way deaf and I'd still come on out here to visit."

Maggie smiled. "So how are you, Art? Haven't seen you for a while."

"Feeling hale and hearty."

"You come to see Big Jack?"

"No, Erik, actually. Is he around?"

"Yes. No. I mean, he's in the back field cutting a drainage ditch into the creek."

"Good idea. All this rain makes me wonder if I shouldn't build myself an ark."

Maggie focused her attention on the two envelopes. Art noticed.

"So I have something for him, but I suppose you could handle it just as well."

"What are they?"

"Two applications for farmer assistance. One from the County Agricultural Agent and the other from the Manpower Commission."

"You think we need those Negroes helping around here this fall? I heard they stole at least a dozen of the Stecks' chickens last year."

"Aw, no one proved nothing. Rumors is all. Besides, with Erik leaving you're gonna need all the help you can get."

"It's mighty nice of you to think of us."

"Listen, Mags," Art whispered, leaning in. "You know I'm not a big fan of Erik's. Never was. But for your sake, I'm happy he's been able to work this place. I think the world of you, and I want to help out any way I can. Truth is, once Erik's gone, you and Big Jack are not going to be able to do it alone. So, fill out these forms and get yerself some *help*."

Maggie knew he was right. Sure, most area farmers and their families pitched in and assisted one another come harvest time, but with nearly every man between the ages of 18 and 45 either in the military or having moved to Milwaukee or Madison for higher-paying jobs, Maggie didn't have a lot of options. Even with some of the local teenage boys, they could not reap those 75 acres alone. The oats would be ready for cutting in several weeks, and the apple harvest would be close behind. Even if the war had never started, there wasn't exactly a considerable labor pool to draw from in Ramsey, Wisconsin, population: 300.

"Don't give me that face, Mags," Art said. "I filled the danged papers out, too. Let me tell you, those Jamaicans are hard workers. You'll see. Last year I had 'em on my farm and one can do the work of my three boys combined."

Maggie raised her brow. Art winced. The words slipped out before he knew he said them.

"I'm so sorry," Maggie said, placing her hand on his shoulder. "Jake was such a great young man."

"Doggone Japs," Art said, fighting back the memory of his son. "We gotta take them sons-a-bitches come hell or high water. And you better believe we will, too!"

Maggie rubbed his shoulder. "Of course we will."

"Oh, listen to me, bringing up my problems when you've got someone who's shipping out tomorrow. Here I should be consoling *you . . .*"

"Come on, Art. Don't worry about it. We've got each other, and Erik will be fine. So, give me those forms and I'll see to it they get signed and mailed in the next few days."

"Okay, sweetheart. They're all yours." He handed them over, took off his cap and wiped his forehead. Art's stiff brush cut stood straight up in salt 'n pepper gray and trimmed high above the ears. "By the way, you're gonna get heat stroke wearing that there long-sleeved blouse on such a muggy day."

"I'm alright," she said, subconsciously tugging at the sleeves to hide any bruises.

"Suit yourself." Art snugged the cap back onto his head and turned again to face the porch. "See you later, Big Jack. I have to run into town or I'd stay for a visit," he shouted.

"It's ice cream," Big Jack yelled with a wave.

Art forced a smile in Maggie's direction, tipped his cap, and climbed back into the truck. *Damn!* he thought. *Why does everything have to be so tarnationed hard on everybody?* He glanced up and took in a slow, deep breath. *Dear Lord, please don't let this beautiful young lady ever receive that Western Union telegram . . . like the one I got.*

He stopped short and choked back a tear as Maggie watched from the driveway. She wore the same pensive expression.

* * *

The evening draped the Mueller farm under a canopy of charcoal and white clouds. In the upstairs bedroom, Erik stood beside the bed packing his leather suitcase. At first glance, one saw a tall, handsome man with a square jaw, jet black hair, olive-tinted skin, hazel eyes and a sturdy, chiseled nose. A deep scratch found a home just under his left eye. Maggie's mark, from the night before.

Life as a farmer molded Erik considerably over his 29 years; his shoulders were broad, and his waist was thin. He sported strong, veiny arms and thick hands, and dirt found a perpetual home under his fingernails. Many voiced surprise upon learning his surname originated from Yorkshire, England and *not* the Eastern Mediterranean. Upon further regard, his physique appeared somewhat disproportional, with an upper torso a bit too long for his lower half. Despite this subtitle aberration, his crooked smile was usually all he needed to captivate the ladies – Maggie included. But these days she knew him more as Cheshire Cat than Casanova.

It had been nearly 24 hours since the "incident," and he hadn't said a word about it. In fact, Erik had been especially gracious to Maggie throughout the day. She wondered if it was more because he wanted to leave this life and less because he felt a sense of guilt for what happened the night before. *If he doesn't bring it up, I'm going to. There's no way he's getting off this easy.* It was a chance she had to take. Besides, Erik appeared sober, so she had that going for her.

"Benny's going to miss you," Maggie said, leaning up against the wall near the bedroom door.

"I told him I'd write every day, and he said he'd write me, too," Erik said, more focused on matching his socks than acknowledging his wife. "I suppose everything will come to me written in crayon."

Maggie pondered his words as he continued packing. *Who is this anomaly? Why do we share the same bed, but we're never intimate? Why does he abuse me, but then pick me flowers? Why does he say he'll write* Benny *every day, but not a goddamned word about writing* me*?*

Erik believed the true measure of a man was tied to how he provided for his family. Maggie often countered this ideology by saying it didn't matter where they lived – be it on the farm of her youth or in the basement of a brothel – she loved him regardless, and the concept of "home" was a state of mind. As long as they could be together, that trumped every other scenario. But none of that mattered to Erik, because living and working on his father-in-law's farm made him feel like a freeloading failure, a sentiment he wrestled with every day.

Maggie's best friend Audrey Stanton used the phrase "soul mates" when referring to relationships fraught with passion and intrigue. Maggie liked the sound of those words. Whenever the two of them convened at the Uptown Theater in their small township of Ramsey, Audrey would point it out and say Clark Gable and Loretta Young had it, as did Glenn Ford and Joan Crawford. That was real chemistry, and Maggie wanted it more than anything else. *Too much to ask? I did love Erik once. But now?*

Even when they were courting, the majority of people in town made it clear they didn't appreciate Erik. Perhaps it was his cockiness, a youthful arrogance reserved for the star quarterback of the high school football team, but not for a man of nearly 30. How many times had he argued with the locals? How many fistfights? Too many to count. Erik once locked horns with the three Lloyd brothers and paid the price with a broken nose and four loose teeth.

At first she believed few liked him because he hailed from northern Wisconsin, home to "simpleminded heathens," as she oftentimes heard the locals call them, but that was a hollow defense because nearly everyone in the area had been an outsider at one time or another. Dodge County in particular was made up almost entirely of German immigrants, most of whom settled in the area over the past 50 years.

No, Erik's swagger simply did not wear well in a community that went to great pains to embody stoicism. The locals preferred to present themselves with an old-fashioned modesty rooted in community and personal values. People here were proud and confident. Erik – he was vehement and pretentious.

By contrast, everyone adored Maggie. Call it innocence by association. Big Jack and Ivy became the community's altruistic icons, and it rubbed off on their cherished daughter. Ivy used to make meals for area migrant workers and even sewed birthday presents for their children. Big Jack always assisted with a neighbor's harvest if they took ill. Ivy made tapestries for the church. Big Jack helped to build that church. And at every event, every shared meal, every barn raising . . . Maggie tagged along, helping in whatever way she could.

So there she stood, helplessly watching from the doorway as her frosty husband rolled up his slacks as one would roll up a towel, then he balled up three T-shirts in a clump, some socks were tossed in, unmatched, as were several pairs of boxer shorts. Finally, she could bear it no more. "Why are you doing this, Erik?"

He played dumb. "I have to pack, Mags. Imagine how stupid I'd look showing up to basic training with just the clothes on my back."

"Why are you doing this!" she repeated, with the exact same timbre.

Erik's shoulders dropped and he tossed her a peeved glance. "Oh come on, we're gonna go through this again? Now? I'm shipping out tomorrow for chrissakes."

"And after these many weeks, you still never gave me an answer. Why would you leave us? Why would you leave Big Jack and your only son? And why do you . . . why do you . . ." Maggie paused for a moment, tapped her teeth and let out a submerged breath. "Why do you *hate* me so much?"

With her back against the wall, she slid to the floor, wrapped her arms around her knees, and bowed her head. Hunched into a ball, she poured years of emotions into her tears.

"Oh, come on, Mags," he said walking towards her, showing a rare sympathy. He reached down to help her up, but she wasn't budging. "You know that's not true." He then changed his grip to get a better hold of her, and she winced as pain shot up her bruised arm. He quickly released her. "Oh, sorry. I forgot . . ."

"Do you honestly believe I can't feel your contempt for me? What kind of animal are you, anyways? What kind of person could do this?" she cried, pointing to her bruises. "How can you hurt someone and then stand here and say you care about them?"

He stood debased, trying to find the right combination of words. "You know, I had one too many at The Wonder Bar last night. That's all. It wasn't me."

"Oh, so you're going to blame it on the booze again, huh? Tell me, why is it every time I see other people who've had 'one too many,' they're always living it up? They sing. They dance. They're in their own happy little world. But *you* . . . you spit venom and say the world isn't fair . . . that you're living under a cloud. No, you break cups, dishes, you break bones . . . you break *hearts*!"

Erik sighed as if to say, *Okay, okay, let it all out.*

"How can you blame the same cheap booze that makes everyone else happy?"

"Look, I do care for you and Benny, and Big Jack, too. I'm *doing* this because I care. Don't you see that?"

"How does that make any sense?"

"If I didn't care, would I work like I do? If I didn't care, would I put food on our table every night? If I didn't care, why would I have bothered to carry you up to bed last night – and let you sleep in? But you forgot about that, didn't you? Never said one word about it all day. I even picked ya some fresh flowers – and this is the thanks I get? An interrogation?"

Maggie sat flabbergasted. "Are you serious? That's how you show your love and affection – by getting drunk, knocking me unconscious, and then carrying me to bed because you *felt bad?* Well, forgive me for not bowing down to His Majesty and kissing your ring! My God, I'm starting to think you've lost your mind."

"You asked me why I enlisted. Have you forgotten it's my duty? It's my responsibility as an American?"

"Oh, don't give me that. *This* is your duty," she said, pulling herself to her feet and pounding her chest. "Your family is your duty. This farm is your duty. What about that?"

"So I'm risking my life to go fight the Japs – or maybe even some of your German relatives – and you want to make me feel guilty? Are you kidding? How much longer can I sit by and watch innocent G.I.s get killed without helping?"

"But you *are* helping! Why don't you see that? You help by growing crops for those soldiers, and . . . and by helping here on the home front."

Erik stared into her eyes. Sure, she was right. So what? He wore that same expression one gets when dealt a Royal Flush in poker. He knew he would win, no matter what hand she played. He knew because in the end, he always won.

The war in the Pacific had been raging for two-and-a-half years, and Erik watched the newsreel footage of the Normandy landings just a month earlier – how the Allies stormed Utah, Omaha, Gold, Juno and Sword Beaches. He was exempt from initial conscription due to his status as a farmer and caregiver to Big Jack and Ivy, but when he enlisted a month ago – all bets were off. As long as a fella passed the physical, Uncle Sam didn't care what he *used* to do, only what he would become. And in less than 24 hours, he would report to basic training at Camp Hixon, just outside St. Louis.

And I'll be free. Free of this life. Free of the farm that isn't mine. Looking at his wife, Erik studied her expression with passive indifference, then cracked half a smile and wiped the tears from her cheek. "You'll be alright." He then walked back to the bed and resumed packing.

Maggie let out a grieved sigh. *Is this what it's like when love dies? Or is it love at all?* She was thrilled to see him go. She was furious to see him leave. She didn't care if he ever wrote one letter. She would check the postbox daily.

Much like the human resolve to live, love also wants to persevere, probing for whatever it can latch on to. For Maggie, that once-bright flame became little more than a dying flicker on a spent wick. For Erik, the light burnt out soon after he lost the family farm to his brother.

Being naturally stubborn and resilient meant Maggie would not go down without a fight. Still, as time passed she found herself going through the five stages of grief. Denial greeted her one day, anger the next. She bargained with God and then would get depressed. But there in the bedroom, on the eve of her husband's departure to the U.S. Army, were the first signs of acceptance. *Why do I even fight it? Why push back?* The truth became apparent, and Maggie finally yielded – she was no longer in love with him.

Wiping her wet eyes on a shirt sleeve, Maggie watched Erik close the top of the suitcase and secure the two leather straps which coiled around the bag. Looking at her, he cracked that coy smile of his. "Well, I'm all done."

Maggie took in a slow, trembling sigh. *You're not the only one.*

Chapter Three

Shipping Out

For the second straight morning Maggie woke up alone. *I suppose I'd better get used to it.* Erik had slept on the davenport down in the living room, complaining of a sore back.

As the scent of fresh coffee, fried bacon and burnt toast floated up to her room, Maggie climbed out of bed and shuffled over to the window, her body still sore but better than 24 hours earlier. She noticed a light mist on the window. *Will we ever see the sun again?*

Placing her aching head against the soothing, cool glass, everything in the barnyard appeared monochromatic, like a Charlie Chaplin movie – the earth black, the sky gray. In stark contrast with the lunar scene below, a white cat tip-toed from the barn towards the house, zigzagging to avoid the water-filled potholes. It passed by the rusty hand pump, the Mueller's tall wind turbine, underneath Benny's tire swing, and ultimately, the feline curled up beneath a wheelbarrow parked beside Maggie's victory garden. She enjoyed that small patch of earth and found solace there. The cat, too.

While observing the scene outside, Maggie noticed her breath had fogged up the glass of the windowpane. Stepping back, she took her index finger and outlined a round head, and with three quick taps she made two eyes and a nose. Then after careful consideration she gave her new friend – a smile.

Downstairs, Erik finished cooking breakfast while Big Jack sat at the kitchen table enjoying a cigarette and a hot cup of coffee while reading *The Saturday Evening Post.* Sitting beside him, Benny enjoyed a bowl of hot oatmeal.

"Hi, Momma," said the boy, his mouth full of food.

"Morning, sweetheart. I see you're enjoying your breakfast."

"Opa added honey! It's good."

Walking up behind Big Jack, she kissed the top of his bald spot.

"Morning, hon," he said without taking his eyes off the magazine.

With a spatula in hand, Erik glanced up from the stove. "Looks like it's gonna be a great day." Maggie glared at him before filling a cup of coffee from the stovetop. Erik stumbled. "What I mean is, um, we got more rain last night, so it's good I got that standing water cleared out yesterday."

Big Jack removed his reading glasses and set the magazine in his lap. "So what's the plan, Erik? When does the bus come?"

"A little after noon," Maggie answered, her eyes still fixed on her husband. "He's all packed."

"Yep. I should be in St. Louis by nightfall. Probably have a crew cut before the sun sets."

"You get yerself some of them Japs! Says in this here article that they want to dominate the world. The Germans, too. So goddamn sad to see how upside-down everything is back in *Deutschland.*"

"Well, I'm more worried about *your* world," Erik said. "You and Maggie and Benny . . . I feel like I'm leaving you in a lurch."

Maggie's eyes got wide as she was taken aback. *Are you serious or just trying to make me cross?* It marked the first time since his enlistment that he had shown any reverence towards the family.

"Oh, don't worry about us," said Big Jack. "We'll get some of them kids from town to help with the oats and the apples, no problem. We may even apply for help from the Manpower Commission. Maggie got the paperwork from Art Kreiter just yesterday."

Erik whirled around in complete consternation. "What? Niggers? No sir-ree! I won't have any blackies working my fields!"

For weeks Maggie had been doing an exploratory to find something, *anything* that would provide her some leverage. Finally, she found a chink in the armor, and she took full advantage, feeling like a kid at Christmas.

"Oh . . . I don't know, Erik. I hear some of those Negroes are as big as giants, with hands so large they can pick three apples at once."

He slammed the frying pan against the stove. "Goddamnit! I *forbid* you to apply for that Commission bullshit! All they do is send you a bunch of slackers anyway."

"Do you mind?" she said pointing to her son.

Erik couldn't have cared less about his language. "Know what else? They've got sticky fingers! Last year, Jerry Willis had them working on his farm, and they stole a pig! His wife even had her wedding broach taken!"

Maggie kept pushing his buttons. "I don't believe any of it. Everybody knows she's a drunk. She probably sold that broach for a bottle of whiskey." Maggie saw the steam building up behind his eyes and couldn't have been more delighted. "We may have to hire a dozen of them Negroes . . . maybe more."

With fire in his eyes, Erik pointed the spatula at Maggie. "So help me, Mags, if you go over my head on this, I swear . . ."

"You'll do what, Erik? Huh? Go AWOL and return to this place you *love* so much? The place you can't bear to leave? Maybe you'll come home with all your training as a soldier and *kill* the migrants? Perhaps you can wage your own little world war right here in the kitchen. You seem to be pretty good at that!"

Erik took a deep, angry breath. "No niggers will be working my fields, and that's final!"

Big Jack raised his hands. "Whoa, whoa, whoa . . . don't get your bowels in an uproar, Erik. We don't know what kind of help we'll need. Or how much. If anything, we'll probably get us a bunch of Mexican folk."

"I'm warning you, Mags," Erik said, waving the spatula like a maestro conducting an orchestra. "Don't. You. Do it. I'm serious!"

Maggie's lips slowly curled into a smile. "Why don't you let us worry about that."

Erik slammed his fist on the counter. Glasses and dishware in the nearby cabinets rattled in a crescendo. "I don't need this. Not today!" He wiped his hands on a dishtowel, threw it hard onto the floor and stormed out of the kitchen.

"What's gotten into him? Jeez," said Big Jack as he learned back in his chair, opened the magazine and began reading again.

Standing by the sink, Maggie took in a slow, deep breath, stared out the window and looked off into the horizon. To the left of the barn, she could see her apple orchard silhouetted by a painted sky – broad strokes of orange, pink and gray intensified by the second. She leaned forward to take a closer look, and to her astonishment, she noticed for the first time in more than a week the clouds were finally breaking their stranglehold on the farm and the "prodigal" sun appeared as a bright ball behind the orchard. Erik's earlier prediction appeared to be coming true. *Looks like it's gonna be a great day!*

* * *

A little before noon, the cars began rolling up the driveway. Officially, some 40 well-wishers came to see Erik off. Unofficially, they wanted to show their support for Maggie, Big Jack and Benny. They knew it would be a challenge for the trio to run the farm without any outside assistance. Little did they know what kind of help would soon arrive.

During the festivities, Erik reveled in the attention while Maggie worked the room – handing out the small sandwiches made for the occasion. She stayed steady, all while forcing a smile and thanking her neighbors for their offers of support.

Erik weaved in and out of the group of well-wishers like a famous movie star at a Hollywood premier. He moved from the kitchen, to the parlor, outside onto the porch, shaking hands and sharing stories all the while holding Benny in his arms. His son was too young to understand the severity of what was going on and thought his father would be back in maybe a day or two.

At one point, it dawned on Maggie that her boy was the same age as she when the Muellers immigrated to America. She reflected on how she used to lie to her classmates, telling them she saw the Statue of Liberty from the deck of her ship, knowing full well they actually disembarked through the Port of New Orleans. In truth, Maggie didn't remember many details about the trip, nor did she recall how they ended up in this land of contrasts – where the cold winters seemed to never end and the summer sun blazed hot enough to fry an egg on asphalt. Her mother used to reminisce about old Germany and tell her how the rolling green Wisconsin hillsides reminded her of home. Maggie only remembered seeing black-and-white photos, so she had to take her mother's word for it.

To Maggie, Ivy was a saint who always put others first. She had taught her daughter how to sew, garden, cook, can vegetables and how to be a proper lady, despite the dirt beneath her fingernails.

"In Kraft ist Schönheit." (In strength, there is beauty.)

Ivy passed her big brown eyes on to her daughter, along with a crooked smile and the same cowlick in her upper right temple. Many pointed out the striking resemblance to Barbara Stanwyck, which Ivy always took as a blushed compliment. Even if she tried, her natural good looks could not be camouflaged behind ruffled aprons or baggy overalls. "Your mother doesn't just clean-up good, she dirties-up good,"

Big Jack would often say about his wife's translucent beauty. This picture of pretty stood tall, with curvy hips and a confident bearing. Most days Ivy greeted the morning with a clean cotton blouse tucked into a pleated skirt. She preferred ribbons to scarves – especially yellow silks – believing those ribbons looked best against her thick, brown mane. Her smile was disarming, her demeanor quiet. This shy beauty relished her role as a farmer's wife, and everyone liked her the instant they met. Always the voice of reason, Ivy had an altruistic knack for defusing even the most volatile situation, and that only reinforced Big Jack's deep-seated love for her.

Because of complications during Maggie's delivery, Ivy could bear no more children, so she doted on her only child. In his own way, Big Jack also lavished her with affection. Both taught Maggie the skills normally reserved for the boys in a farm family. Big Jack had her sitting behind the wheel of a tractor before she knew her ABCs. As a young lady she learned to prep the fields, harvest crops by sickle, shock oats, prune apple trees, help a cow give birth, and when necessary, put one down with a pistol. Big Jack loved her dearly and would often brag that by the age of 14, she could drink three shots of blackberry brandy and iron a straight pleat into his Sunday trousers.

Farming was in the Mueller's blood. She understood why people called it "the toughest job you'll ever love." But Maggie was about to see just how much she really loved it without having a husband around to help.

As Erik's departure time approached, he handed Benny to Maggie and went upstairs to grab his suitcase. With as much stealth as he could muster, Big Jack haphazardly passed around small shot glasses of his homemade brandy for the send-off.

"How many have you had already?" Maggie asked her father.

"Nichte viel." He laughed deep and loud, a common occurrence after consuming one too many – when his English slipped into slurred German and his voice rose in sonority.

As Erik came down the steps, the guests all raised their glasses and sang, "For He's A Jolly Good Fellow." Big Jack was the loudest of the bunch, his German accent obvious to the group. *"Für he iz eh jolly guuut fellow!"*

Maggie silently mouthed the words, pretending to sing.

Visibly moved, Erik invited the forty guests out to the road to see him off.

Those looking down County Highway CC could see waves of heat roll over the asphalt as they squinted their eyes against the blazing sun. The air felt thick and still, and the July humidity hit everyone with a vengeance, as if to make this special occasion even more miserable. Finally, one of the youngsters yelled, "I see it! I see the bus!" That's when the glad-handing began. A slap on the back here and a wish-him-well there.

"Don't shoot my cousin!" someone barked.

"Get some of the bad guys for us," somebody else snapped.

As the Trailways bus ground to a stop before the assemblage, everyone said their final goodbyes – everyone except Maggie. Erik leaned forward and whispered in her ear.

"You know I have to do this, right?"

She stood silent.

Someone in the crowd yelled, "Kiss her, you old goof!"

Wearing that cocky grin of his, Erik took Maggie in his arms and dipped her. As his lips drew close, she wriggled out of the grasp and fell onto all fours, then bounced up and ran the long driveway toward the house, sobbing. Her best friend, Audrey, chased behind.

"I guess it's just too much for her," Erik said, embarrassed. "You know women!" Next, he reached down and hoisted Benny high into the air, then set him down and shook the boy's hand much the same way two men would bid farewell.

"Goodbye folks. And thanks for the send-off. I'll never forget this!"

Erik clicked his heels to attention, saluted with his left hand and stepped up onto the bus where he disappeared into a mass of passengers who were off to adventures of their own. Within seconds, the bus was no more than a distant blur on the horizon.

Back in the kitchen, Maggie sat at the table and buried her face in a handkerchief as Audrey set a glass of lemonade at her elbow.

"So," Audrey said, pulling out a chair and squeezing her best friend's arm. "You want to talk about it?"

Chapter Four

In The Crosshairs

Two American snipers sat cleaning their rifles in the steeple of Saint Rita of Cascia, a gothic church named after the Augustinian nun Rita Mancini. Married at the age of 12 to an abusive Italian farmer, Rita became the *Patron Saint of the Impossible*, so it seemed fitting on this warm Saturday morning in July, two American boys would undertake a nearly impossible mission of their own.

They had intercepted a report that a train carrying some of Hitler's most elite fighters would roll into the small village around noon, and Joe Brandish and Vince Weber prepared to unleash a surprise attack from on high. Situated directly across from a cobblestone square and overlooking the train depot, the old Italian church provided them the perfect vantage point. They had no air support and no radio. Having snuck in the church the night before, they were on their own.

The village below presented itself in picture postcard fashion: The main street was made up of charming red brick buildings, each storefront featuring hand-painted signs on glass advertising everything from baked goods and candies to cured meats, fabrics and tools. Awnings hung over cobblestone sidewalks, small apartments sat above each store, their windows of true divided light looked out onto the streets below.

The unsuspecting villagers went about their everyday business – no different than any other Saturday. An elderly farmer and his wife rode a horse-drawn wagon, bringing squash, beans and asparagus to the town market. A café owner stood in his doorway sweeping dirt and dust into the street. A young mother pushed her newborn baby in a stroller past the local tavern as the proprietor tipped his hat and set a bowl of milk next to the entrance for three thirsty kittens. In the distance, the whistle of a train announced it would soon be "Go Time." Both Brandish and Weber loaded their rifles, looked at one another, and took in a slow, steady breath.

"So, you ready for this?" asked Joe.

"Hell no. But I'm willing to do it," said Vince.

Their preferred targets: German officers, providing they could tell their rank from so high above the ground. They knew it could very well be a suicide mission, but they saw it as a calling – one they gladly undertook.

As the train haltingly rolled into town, a rhythmic bell rang from the engine. *Ding-ding, ding-ding* . . . Smoke billowed from the stack as the cars ground to a stop, the screeching of the wheels giving way to a loud belch and a long plume of steam stretching up and over the tender.

The two snipers watched as the doors slipped open and hundreds of Hitler's best and brightest tumbled out into the daylight. There was a certain nonchalance to the entire event – an ethereal element – with many of the Germans laughing, smoking cigarettes, and squinting upwards as the bright sun beat down on their heads. One of the officers blew his whistle, and the soldiers stepped off the platform, tossed their cigarettes aside, and fell into a tight formation in the middle of the road.

Joe nudged his friend. "There must be a couple hundred of them. That's more than I expected."

Kneeling with his rifle at the ready, Vince nodded, but said nothing.

Shocked and confused, the locals got to witness what had to be the most peaceful invasion of the war. As the soldiers settled in, an officer called out in German and the group snapped to attention. He then blew a short blast on his whistle, snapped his crop against his thigh and ordered, *"Marschieren Sie!"* The group forged ahead in unison, and with every step moved closer to the church, all while singing one of Germany's most popular songs, "Lili Marleen."

The time had come. From high above the street, the two rifle barrels extended downward from the steeple, and in a matter of seconds the guns began to pop ammo around the station yard.

"*Autsch!*" a captain with Rommel's Afrika Korps cried as he took a shot to his back. A private standing next to him took another to the calf and one to his head before stumbling backward. Another soldier pointed up at the bell tower.

"Waffe! Waffe! Waffe!"

Bodies dashed left and right as both soldiers and town folk bolted for safety.

"Schützt euch!" (Protect yourselves!)

German soldiers dove for cover behind flowerpots, water barrels, and even an old mule tied to a post. The two gunners in the tower continued their spray, accidentally hitting several locals in the barrage. A baker emerging from his store took a shot in the thigh, the loaves of bread he'd been carrying spraying out of his arms. A bullet found a ten-year-old boy as his leashed dog relieved itself on a tree. And one errand shot hit . . . Maggie Wentworth as she walked across the road with two pounds of coffee and a bag of flour.

"Ow!" she cried, looking down at a red welt on her forearm.

"Get down!" someone shouted to her.

"*Schnell. Schnell!*" a German officer cried nearby.

Maggie stood frozen, directly in the line of fire, looking up at the tower and then at her arm. Against the bright blue sky, she saw the gun barrels and heard the pops of two BB guns. Indeed, she had been struck not by an American M-6 rifle, but by a Daisy Red Ryder.

Without warning, she was tackled from behind and wrapped in the arms of a stranger. "Get down, *Fräulein!* You could get killed," the rescuer with a German accent remarked. Both fell to the ground next to a large pot of petunias.

"What are you doing?" Maggie said to the ghostly figure. "Let go. I'm fine."

"Quiet. You don't want to draw their attention. Any sudden move and next thing you know you'll be toes up."

"I'm sorry, but you are mistaken," she said struggling to sit up. Looking down at her waist, she noticed his arms were still around her. "Um . . . if you don't mind, I think I will be fine without the bear hug."

"Come now, *Fräulein,*" said the German. "If you got shot, I could never live with myself."

"Too late."

The German released his grip and sat up beside her in a panic. "What? What do you mean? You are hit? I have medical training . . ."

Maggie decided to have fun at the gullible German's expense. He clearly did not know the snipers were using BB guns and his concern went to a whole new level. "Yes, I've been shot. In fact, I'm getting very lightheaded."

The German seemed frantic. "Where is it? Where? Let me see . . . I don't see any blood. Where are you hit?"

Maggie proceeded to raise her elbow over her forehead, as if to nearly faint. "I don't know if I will make it."

"Just tell me where you were hit," he pleaded with her. "Please . . ."

"Oh wait. Hold on a sec," she said, taking a deep breath. "Okay, I think I'm getting better. Yeah, it passed."

The POW looking confused. He examined her neck, her back, her head.

"I believe those snipers are using America's new secret weapon. It's a bullet that is only effective on Germans. If an American gets hit it only causes a red welt. See?"

As Maggie held her arm up and laughed at her own little joke, the German gave her a puzzled look. "I don't understand. How is that possible?" Maggie smiled coyly, but before she could explain and offer a soft apology, the answer revealed itself via shouts from the middle of in the street.

"Goddammit!" yelled an American guard stepping out from behind a wooden flatbed wagon. "It's two kids with air rifles! I hope you two little shits had your fun," he shouted with piss and vinegar. "Now you git yore britches down here before we blast you with *real* bullets."

Turning his attention back towards Maggie, the German seemed slightly embarrassed and tried to recover from his overprotective efforts. "So you were not hit with a real bullet?"

"You sound disappointed."

Twisting his mouth into a tight nub, and knowing he had been played, the German cocked his head slightly. "So tell me, funny girl, what makes you so sure those snipers are not trying to shoot Americans? Perhaps they are fellow Germans who have been sent to rescue *me* and my comrades from the American clutches."

Maggie could not help but smile at his effort to save face, and for the first time she leaned back and studied him. *He's an interesting one.* Late 20s, maybe 30. Tall. Fit. Tan complexion. Obviously confident, and undoubtedly brave. His hair sandy brown and slicked back, with a few stray bangs waving in front of piercing blue eyes. Despite the grit and grime on his facade, he was about as handsome a man as she'd ever seen. Those two cute dimples in the corners of his mouth, those bright white teeth. She wondered how much battle he had seen. How much of the war. Did he kill many people? Her mood shifted from playful to flirtatious.

"I must say, I can't think of a better welcome," the German continued, now half laughing to himself.

"Whatever do you mean?"

"Well, if your G.I.s fight us with pop guns, we may stand a good chance after all."

My God, he's tempting. Is it the smile? The eyes? Perhaps his sense of humor? Whatever it was, Maggie felt a level of comfort with him. Yes, he was the *verboten* enemy, but still, there was something about him . . . Suddenly, the surrealness of the moment hit her. He was a real German soldier. *A POW!*

"This is all a bit overwhelming. Tell me why you are here," she asked.

"To work. We're going to do the jobs many of your men left behind. Maybe fix roads, cut down timber, harvest crops . . . At least that's what they tell us."

"I must say, your English is very good," she remarked, batting her eyes.

"So is yours," the German chuckled.

Just then, the front door of the church cracked open across the road from them, and two freckled faces peeked out. The gathering crowd let out a roar of anger.

"My God," Maggie said as her attention was pulled away from the POW's magnetic presence. "That's Joe Brandish . . . and little Vinny Weber."

The American guard in the street looked at them with fire in his eyes. "You! You damned troublemakers!"

He spat toward the platform and proceeded to walk towards the boys, but before he could unleash a father's discipline, the town's top law enforcement officer Sheriff John McGee came running through the crowd of people gathered outside. "Move! Move out of the way!" he said while carving his way through the masses like a hot knife through butter. He then stopped short and turned to the American guard. "What's going on? What have we here?"

"It's these two," said the tall and muscular centurion. "They shot at the POWs from the church with their BB guns. Scared the living hell outta folks."

"The church?" The sheriff looked incredulous. "*From the church?*" He turned to the boys. "Step forward!" The 13-year-olds lumbered up to the sheriff, their faces drawn, their eyes mere slits. Sheriff McGee was a short, stocky fellow who always seemed to be pulling up his navy blue trousers and tucking in the one-size-too-small button-down white shirt. This moment was no exception. He wore a thin mustache, had a wobbly double chin and was bug-eyed. The black necktie, its short point resting four inches above his beltline, danced left and right as he talked. Upon hearing the news about the wannabe assassins with pop guns, he squinted his eyes and grabbed them by their collars. "Think you're sooo smart, huh fellas?"

A growing crowd of locals motioned toward the POWs, most of whom had been sequestered into a tight group by a handful of armed American guards – like cattle being readied for the slaughter.

"Okay, so we know who the snipers are, but who are these men?" someone yelled from the crowd.

"Yeah. What the hell's going on here, Sheriff?" shouted another.

"Are these really *German* soldiers?"

McGee shook his head. "Don't you folks ever read the papers? These are the German POWs who are gonna be staying at the prisoner of war camp just on the edge of town. You know, in the old Kaston Ballroom?"

Blank stares.

"There was a town hall meeting about this fer goodness sakes."

Still, bewildered looks.

McGee took in a heavy sigh through clenched teeth. "You all just need to break it up now, okay? Go about your business! Everything's under control. I'll handle everything from here."

There was a biblical nostalgia to the entire scene, as if the mob on the street were lobbying Pontius Pilate for a crucifixion. Only they didn't want revenge on the juvenile sharpshooters as much as they wanted retribution for the surprise attack of German combatants. The anger was palpable. More shouts. More catcalls. More demands for justice. The two boys played Barabbas in this conflict.

Out of nowhere, someone threw an apple at the POWs, but it found McGee's shoulder instead. Small pieces of fruit splattered onto his face. "Jesus, Mary and Joseph! Who threw that, huh?" The sheriff took his attention off the boys and looked at the crowd of locals. "Who did that? Come on, who else wants to go to jail."

"She did it," yelled a strange voice from behind the mob in the street. "It was her."

The large crowd turned around to face the distant voice. Murmurs floated about as heads cocked left and right to see who made the accusation. The sheriff went to investigate and the crowd parted like The Red Sea. "Who said that, huh? Who was it?"

"Over here, officer. Yeah, it was her," said Maggie's new friend, the German POW. "I saw her do it. She has a good arm, that's for certain. Maybe she could play for your New York Yankees."

"Have you lost your mind?" Maggie said to the German, punching him in the arm. "I did no such thing."

McGee looked her in the eyes. "Maggie, what in God's name is he talking about?"

"Honestly, Sheriff, I have no idea!"

"Now, now, *Fräulein*. There's no need to deny it," the German said to Maggie. Then turning towards the sheriff, he put his arms up in surrender. "To be honest, sir, it was *both* of us. We both threw pieces of fruit. So, I think you have no choice but to throw us *both* in jail . . . together."

Maggie began to laugh at the absurdity of it all. "My God, Dale. This one must be shell-shocked."

"Come now, *Fräulein*. Don't protect me. Trying to take the blame all yourself is admirable, but I believe we should both confess and maybe the judge will take that into consideration at sentencing."

Getting increasingly agitated, the town sheriff inhaled deeply and looked Maggie in the eyes. "If this isn't the end all, be all . . ."

Maggie began laughing so hard, she could hardly talk. "Come on,

Sheriff. You've known me forever. I did no such thing." Her laughter was born out of the appreciation for the game of revenge the German was playing on her. "Seriously, I didn't throw a thing. And neither did this man."

"Then stop wasting my time!" Sheriff McGee snapped as he spun around on his heels and marched back towards the two boys, who for the time being were being detained by the American guards. As he walked towards the youngsters, he began ranting to himself. "Uninformed townsfolk, who don't read the papers . . . two crazy boys shooting BB guns . . . someone throwing garbage at a law enforcement official . . . I've got better things to do than to be part of these shenanigans." As he returned to secure the boys, he turned towards the crowd. "Okay, folks. Here's the deal. You all need to relax and go about your business. I'll deal with these two troublemakers in short order. In the meantime, go read the papers why don't you! These boys seemed to know the POWs were coming today. Isn't that right, fellas?"

The boys looked down at their shoes. "Yes, sir."

"So everyone go on home or go about your chores or whatever it is you need to do. We need to break it up."

As the crowd began to disperse and the sheriff marched the boys past the Germans, he paused before one of the American guards. "Sorry you fellas had to put up with this nonsense."

A tall lieutenant squinted. "Yeah, well, these little shits are damned lucky we didn't pump them full of hot *lead*!" The boys looked ashamed as they shuffled along the sidewalk.

Maggie turned her attention back to the POW. "Okay, I guess I deserved that."

The German POW gave her half a smile.

"So what would you have done?" Maggie asked. "If he really tossed us in jail, I mean?"

"Are you kidding?" asked the POW. "I would have *preferred* being locked up with you."

"Well, aren't you fresh?" Maggie said, fawning over him.

"Oh don't flatter yourself. You just smell better than my comrades, that's all."

"That's all?" asked Maggie, fishing for more compliments.

"Of course," said the German trying hard to not reveal his infatuation. Too late.

Maggie laughed bashfully at the compliment. "So tell me, how is it you speak such good English?"

"Well the thing is, I spent a lot of time here in your Midwest prior to the war. In Chicago, mostly."

"Really? Why on Earth were you in the Midwest?"

Before he could answer, an American guard walked up and barked. "Hey you! What the hell are you still doing over there? You know the rules. No fraternizing with the locals! Get back in formation with the others." He used his rifle to push the German back into the street. The POW walked backwards, still facing Maggie. The prisoner motioned for the guard to wait. "Please, stop. I must get her name."

"Move it, pal!"

"What is your name?" he shouted out from the middle of the road. "Please tell me!"

The guard pushed him again while another guard blew his whistle. Soon all the POWs followed their commanding officer's lead and fell into formation, only this time with more trepidation. Some looked up at the surrounding buildings and trees, wondering which one held the next sniper, perhaps one with a *real* rifle. But the lovesick German couldn't have cared less. His eyes locked on Maggie as he cupped his hands and shouted, "Hope to see you again, *Fräulein!*"

Maggie smiled bashfully as the POWs marched out of town. Then bending over to pick up the coffee and various sundries which had spilled at her feet, a pair of shoes stepped in front of her, nearly crushing her white gloved hands.

"And what was *that* all about?"

"Audrey! Well . . . hello to you, too," said Maggie looking up at her friend while trying not to feel embarrassed.

Audrey Stanton towered over her and looked down at Maggie the way a teacher eyes a student caught cheating on an exam. Tall, fair-skinned, with beautiful flowing red hair, Maggie's best friend always dressed impeccably, regardless of the occasion – and this day was no exception. She donned a soft green day dress, with Peter Pan collar and a full gathered skirt cinched in at the waist by a white belt. Red gloves matched the oversized red sun hat. A set of pink earrings, double strand of pearls and a white handbag complemented the ensemble.

"Come on, answer the question," Audrey said.

"Some kids trying to be heroes, I suppose. Thought they could shoot the German prisoners with their air rifles. Can you believe it?"

Maggie's best friend smiled and shook her head. "Not the young boys, but that *POW!* I saw the way he looked at you. I saw the way *you* looked at *him*. I was ten feet away the whole time."

"Don't be ridiculous. Now if you don't mind helping me with these groceries . . ."

"Uh-huh." Audrey picked up the bag of coffee and helped Maggie to her feet. "Fine. So if you don't want to tell me about him, at least come with me to get some fabric. I have a dress to finish today."

Pausing for a moment, Maggie said. "Sure. Big Jack's babysitting Benny, so I've got some free time."

As they walked across the street from the town square and entered the general store, a tiny metal bell announced their arrival. Before them sat a potpourri of staples and everyday foodstuffs. The goods for sale were divided into three sections; the left third of the store featured large wooden barrels and sacks of flour, oatmeal and dry crackers. A small weighing station sat next to jugs of molasses, vinegar and kerosene. *Marvel* comic books like *Captain America* and *Terry-Toons* were stacked neatly on the end caps. Nearer to the checkout counter were heavy glass jars full of multi-colored hard candies, boxes of Milk

Duds, Pixy Stix and candy cigarettes for the kids. In the middle third of the store, numerous wooden bins were filled with hats and scarves for women, work pants for men, stacks of T-shirts and Jockey underwear all neatly folded and sorted by size. Socks, work gloves and bib overalls rounded out the hoard. On the far right side of the store – where Audrey set her sights – sat fabrics and upholstery. Before the war it was a seamstresses' nirvana. But in the past few years, at least half the textiles were discontinued or used by the military. Audrey would take what she could get.

"Hello, ladies! Welcome," said Dan Skilling, the round-faced storeowner who looked up over his bifocals while taking inventory. A brown leather apron partially covered his pressed white shirt, a red bowtie wrapped snugly around his thick neck. He held a clipboard in one hand, a pen in the other and looked at Maggie and Audrey inquisitively. "So what was all that racket outside? I heard a lot of shouting."

"Boys being boys," Maggie said nonchalantly.

Audrey turned to look out the front door and back into the street. "I swear, I'll never get used to the idea that real German soldiers are just outside of town while our boys are over there fighting." She pushed the hair back from her face and tucked it under her hat. "It just doesn't seem right."

"How is this even possible?" asked Dan, now removing his glasses.

"It seems Churchill has a problem," said Audrey. "Too many prisoners to handle, so . . ."

Dan's wife, Dolores, came over to interject herself into the conversation. Short and stout, like her husband, she wore her blonde hair in a bun so tight, it appeared to tug at the corners of each eyebrow, giving her a perpetual look of shock and surprise. Her reading glasses hung around her neck by a thin metal chain. "And we said *we'd* take them?" she asked, waving a pincushion around as she spoke. "Roosevelt agreed?"

"FDR was all for it, apparently," said Audrey.

"Heavenly days," Dan said. "It just don't seem right. Look at Maggie here – her husband shipped out – what, maybe three weeks ago? And now they're sending Germans to us? It's crazy. It's like we're horse tradin' our men for theirs." He turned to Maggie. "I swear, I don't know how you do it."

"Do what?"

"Put up with it all. And now with your husband gone and you runnin' the farm."

"It's more than a person should have to endure," Dolores added.

Maggie shrugged her shoulders and inhaled deeply. "Oh, I don't know. It's not that bad. Although sometimes I do feel like I need some time off. Just to get away for a spell."

Audrey nodded in agreement. "I should say so. If I can ever get her off the farm, we're going to spend a night or two in Milwaukee. Staying at the Pfister Hotel, going to enjoy some fancy dinners and maybe take in a show at the Pabst Theater – just two lonely ladies hitting the town looking for fun and adventure."

"Ooooh, how decadent," Dolores said.

"Yeah, well that's *if* I go," added Maggie.

"Whaddya mean '*if* you go'?" asked Dolores. "Who wouldn't want to go on such a wonderful trip?"

"Thank you, Dolores! I've been saying that for weeks," said Audrey, spreading her arms wide to make her point. "I gave her the trip for her birthday two months ago, and she still hasn't committed to going."

"It's not as if I don't want to go. It's just that it's hard to get away is all."

"Well, you know you deserve it," said Audrey.

"Can we change the subject?"

"Big Jack will take care of Benny. We'll go right after harvest," announced Audrey, ignoring her friend's request.

Dolores's eyes lit up. "Hey, I'll take your place if you don't want to go, Maggie!"

"*You*?" said Dan, setting the clipboard on a stack of shoeboxes.

She turned to her husband. "You never take me anywhere. And I ain't never stayed at the Pfister Hotel, that's for sure."

"And who will mind the store?"

She giggled and waved a hand. "Don't be such a fuddy-duddy. I'm only joking."

Audrey grabbed Maggie's arm and leaned close. "So, are you in?"

Maggie glanced from one face to another, anticipation in the air.

"Because I'm not going to waste my time making you a killer-diller outfit if you back out at the last minute," added Audrey.

"An outfit? For me?"

"For you."

Maggie grinned. "In that case, I don't know how I can refuse! But you're right – it'll have to be after the harvest."

"Deal!" Audrey gave her a hug before turning to Dolores. "So, about that silk . . ."

"Sorry, just because you're the best seamstress in the county doesn't mean you have any pull with the U.S. Army. Believe you me, I try to get silk in here once a week, but it's all being used for the war effort. Probably been turned into parachutes by now.

Audrey looked up at the ceiling, thinking about her options . . .

"I do have some other fabrics that are almost as nice," added Dolores. "Let me show you what just came in . . ."

Chapter Five

Stalag Ramsey

Situated on the outskirts of town, "Camp Ramsey" looked more like a fenced-in schoolyard than a maximum security internment facility. The entire footprint ran the size of two football fields positioned side-by-side, with a hundred white canvas tents flanked to one field, and an open, grassy courtyard on the other. Smack-dab in the middle of it all stood the former Kaston Ballroom, a stocky brick building once known as Dodge County's most popular dance hall. Benny Goodman, the Dorsey Brothers, Lawrence Welk, and Woody Herman all played there, and fans from throughout the county would pack it full every time the famous bands rolled into town.

But the music lovers who once "cut a rug" and did the "shim-sham" were long gone. The dance floor found a new purpose as a makeshift dormitory and mess hall . . . for German POWs.

The building itself couldn't have been designed any better for the American military: In addition to the outdoor tents, the spacious ballroom held another 50 cots on its hardwood floor; a separate dining room connected to the old dance hall; a large kitchen sat in the rear, and the military administrative offices lay upstairs. Outside and snuggled up close to the main building stood two smaller structures built by Roosevelt's CCC – one served as living quarters for the American guards, the other provided storage. In the courtyard stood a tall flagpole – Old Glory flapping in the wind.

Notably, the exterior of the camp lacked barbed wire fences, machine-gun posts and guard towers. Simple and primitive, the perimeter consisted merely of two parallel rows of snow fences, each no more than four-feet high. Unwound from large spools, they were constructed of thin wooden pickets, connected to one another by thick wire and secured to the ground by metal stakes. Despite these archaic measures, armed guards blanketed the grounds, along with the even more intimidating threat: military dogs.

It was mid-morning, the Germans' first full day at camp. Once part of Field Marshall Rommel's elite Afrika Korps, these POWs comprised a mix of officers and enlisted personnel – some as young as 15 and others as old as 50. Under a bright blue sky, they milled about the grassy courtyard and seemed to relish their new surroundings. Grateful to be out of the line of fire, the majority clustered together smoking cigarettes and playing jokes on each other while still wearing their German *Bundeswehr* military-issued shorts from the day of their capture – high socks and tattered uniform tops. Another thing they all had in common: the letters "PW" stamped on the backs of every shirt and under the front pockets of their pants.

Sergeant Allen Keller approached with a whistle between his teeth and a chip on his shoulder. The American guard stood six-foot-five with broad shoulders, a barrel chest, Popeye-like forearms and a chiseled chin. To the Germans he was a biblical giant.

"Okay, gather 'round. Gather 'round," he barked. Many of the POWs did not understand English, but they all recognized an order when they heard one.

Next to Keller stood camp commander Colonel Mark Raymonds. He looked older than his 45 years. Tall and lanky, like a walking beanstalk, Camp Ramsey's *commandant* wore wire-rim glasses and donned longer hair than most officers. Parted on the side, his mane struggled to stay put under the combined forces of a receding hairline and a stiff breeze. Raymonds – a martinet who rarely bent the rules – happened to be a native Wisconsinite, so he relished this particular assignment.

Standing next to the commander, Private Kleist tried his best to translate in German with the same sense of commanding authority. Much of the emphasis was lost in translation when the diminutive Kleist echoed the commander's words.

"Let's go! Come on! Everyone line up in formation," yelled Keller.

At the urging of the senior-most German officer, the former pride of Hitler's army mingled into respectable alignment in the shadow of the old dance hall. They looked like misplaced chess pieces – chipped and tarnished – each of varying heights and all in desperate need of some polish.

With a voice deep and resonant, Raymonds addressed the prisoners:

"Welcome to your new home. The United States is happy to have you as our guests. In following with the rules of the Geneva Convention, we will provide you with food and protection for as long as this war wages. Furthermore, we will do our best to provide medical care, healthy activities, Red Cross packages and mail – when and if it arrives.

"While here, you will be required to follow the rules, cooperate with my men, and do as they say. As prisoners of war, you will be used to help the Allies win this war that *you* started. To that end, most of you will be put to work on area roads, at local farms, and in nearby canneries. Much of the food you harvest and package will be fed to our boys overseas, so when this war is over you can tell your children and grandchildren you helped win it – for America.

"Rest assured, we will keep you busy, and it will be in your best interest to cooperate. Who knows, you may even like Wisconsin, one of the most beautiful places in these United States."

As Kleist translated, some POWs began to lose interest in the speech, instead looking around at the surrounding woods and up at the random cotton ball-like clouds which floated gently overhead. One German elbowed a friend and nodded skyward towards a large hawk which rode the thermals with its wings silent and steady. The prisoners wore the faces of men tired of the fight, men who had seen enough death and destruction. Now safe, even if so far from home.

"You will soon learn I am a tolerant man, I will be fair and treat you with dignity and respect," Raymonds continued. "But make no mistake, I can come down hard and I will do so if the situation warrants. You probably have noticed you are walled-in by simple picket fences, and it may appear tempting to hop over and make your way into the woods, but bear in mind you are exactly 6,000 miles from Berlin. That's quite a long hike.

"My guards, while armed, also have the support of highly trained and highly intelligent canines who might just persuade you to stay put until that ugly party in Europe comes to a close. To further reinforce my point, I provide you with a small demonstration."

He then motioned toward one of the smaller buildings, where a guard opened a door and a man dressed in gray padding and a football helmet stepped into view – his clothing so thick, he more waddled than walked. Following behind him was a uniformed American soldier with two large Airedales in tow. As the man in pads stood waiting in front of the Germans, the dog handler positioned himself a good 20 feet away. The Airedales sat on either side of their master while he unhooked their leashes. The two lean and muscular canines panted, their tongues hanging out in an effort to stay cool in the summer heat. If one didn't know better, they appeared as friendly as any house pet. There they sat, unencumbered – until their master yelled, "Kai-up!" and pointed to his padded colleague.

At that command, the dogs bolted toward their target and hit with such force, they knocked him off his feet and he landed hard onto the ground. "Oof!" Soon cotton stuffing wafted into the air as the dogs began tearing his padding to shreds. What started off as ten rows of POWs in perfect alignment quickly became a tight herd of terrified sheep as the Germans instinctively pushed backwards and clustered together in uneasy trepidation.

The American in gray padding let out a yelp as one of the canines finally penetrated his thick armor.

"Kipsie kai!" the dogs' master yelled. "Kipsie kai!"

Both dogs withdrew from their victim and patiently sat down beside him, as if awaiting a treat. The man in the padded suit stood up, wobbled a bit, and removed his leather football helmet as sweat rolled down his face.

"That's the last time I volunteer for *that!*"

"Do you see what you are up against?" Raymonds declared while looking over his command. "And you won't have the advantage of such padding! We won't be feeding you that well."

Nervous chuckles could be heard, but one German in the front row was not amused. "Are we supposed to be afraid of these billy goats?" he spoke in broken English. "In *Deutschland* we have dogs much more fierce than these. Ever hear of a Doberman Pinscher?"

Without hesitation, the canine master yelled, "*Collar, collar veer*," pointing to the prisoner.

The dogs took off, targeting the cocky German. General pandemonium set in as hundreds of prisoners scrambled for safety. The mouthy POW also took off in the mad dash, zigzagging left and right through the crowd, pushing his comrades out of the way as he desperately sought some kind of protection.

There it is! The flagpole!

In the nick of time, he leaped high, grabbing the flagpole's crossbar nine feet off the ground, before chinning himself up and curling his legs high while the dogs barked and nipped at his heels. Using the halyard for leverage, the German got one knee onto the crossbar, followed by a foot and eventually clambered higher, balancing precariously out of harm's way. His fellow POWs settled down and laughed as the dogs barked and jumped at the missed meal standing above them and out of reach.

"Okay then, you are free to relax for the rest of the morning," the commander shouted to the prisoners. "Lunch will be served in exactly one hour." Leaning into Keller, he said, "I couldn't have scripted that any better. Leave that POW up there until 1600 hours."

* * *

At Camp Ramsey, the German officers got to sleep inside the comfort of the ballroom, along with 20 non-coms who, through the luck of the draw, avoided the outside elements. The majority of the prisoners, however, slept outdoors in the tent city. Each waxed canvas shelter contained two cots, the obligatory dirt floor, and had an affinity toward attracting Wisconsin's unofficial state bird: the blood-thirsty mosquito.

On this particular night, however, all of camp prisoners packed into the spacious hall to kill time and even learn a new hobby, compliments of the nearby YMCA in Hartford – the camp's main supplier of playing cards, magazines, musical instruments, sports equipment and phonograph records.

German POW Adam Klein was one of the lucky ones assigned to an indoor cot, and he used his time to perfect the art of working a yo-yo. While sitting on his makeshift bed and struggling to keep the toy's string from knotting up, he thought back to his encounter with Maggie a day earlier. If only she had given him her name. *Who was that beauty? I hope I get to see her again.*

Before Klein could get the yo-yo to bounce back up, a loud whistle filled the hall. Once again the towering Sergeant Keller returned, this time with four other American soldiers all carrying white file-sized boxes. They climbed the five steps up to the elevated stage and took their positions behind two long tables. As the four guards began unpacking the boxes and stacking pamphlets in neat rows, Keller addressed everyone in the tall and airy ballroom.

"Your attention, please. May I have your attention!" The room got quiet as all eyes focused on the tall non-com from Oklahoma.

"Achtung!" Kleist squawked, doing his best to match Keller's tone.

"We are going to pass out some information about the details of your stay. It's written in German and better describes your duties as detainees and exactly how you will be compensated for your work. So let's start a line on this side of the stage and we'll hand out the materials as you come up. Come on! Let's go. Line up!"

The pamphlets outlined the operation and how the POWs would be employed at local canneries, lumberyards, with road crews and on area farms. It further described how they were to be paid in U.S. military free-market wages. Specifically, the average POW would be compensated 80 cents a day in canteen coupons, with the remaining wages going toward camp operations. Some prisoners could even put a portion of their wages into a government savings account, which they would be able to withdraw at the end of the war.

On a cot next to Adam sat Heinrich Richtor – the same man who'd had the run-in with the Airedales earlier that day. Perpetually disgruntled, he was of medium build, slightly taller than Adam, with hair parted to the side like a blond Adolf Hitler. His forehead oily from sweat, the face acne-scarred – like the skin on old fruit – his eyes were bloodshot and set deep, the pupils small and beady. His hands were soft, like a child of privilege, but the fingernails were chewed well beyond the tips. Heinrich was a walking bad temper with tiny teeth and a large chip on his shoulder.

Ever since joining the POWs at the holding station in New York Harbor, Heinrich took issue with his countrymen for losing their fighting spirit, accusing them of "hiding behind the Yankee apron."

Rumors circulated that the edgy Nazi patriot had been in the SS, and he did his best to perpetuate that rumor. Not one of his comrades could recall seeing this malevolent scorpion ever crack a smile.

As the line of POWs began to form near the corner of the stage, Heinrich groaned aloud, chewing on a thumbnail. "Can you believe this shit?" his voice snakelike. "It's obvious they are trying to soften us up. To get us to *love* America – all for a slave's wage."

Against his better judgment, Adam engaged him. "What makes you so sure?"

Heinrich stopped biting his thumbnail and stared Adam up and down. He squinted his eyes in both shock and disgust that someone would actually react to his dogmatization, much less dare to challenge his point of view. "Are you blind? Listen to their propaganda. Look at what they are feeding us."

"The lunch was quite good. Dinner as well," said Adam, trying to lighten the mood.

Heinrich saw no humor in any of it. "Beyond the food, you fucking *Dummkopf!* They are also feeding us hype, trying to indoctrinate us with their little toys and games and magazines to read. Each and every one of us are like schoolboys being bribed with candy. But I am a German and will fight every last one of them, even on *these* shores!"

"Pissing on their crops will not do much good," said Adam.

"Well, keep your eyes open. Look for opportunities. And whatever you do . . . do not get in my way."

Heinrich then spit a piece of his extracted thumbnail in Adam's face, snatched the yo-yo from his palm and smashed it on the ground before storming off to stand on the other side of the hall. Adam sat speechless. Other prisoners who heard the exchange simply looked away.

"This entire social experiment," Adam whispered to himself, "is getting very interesting!"

Chapter Six

One Of The Boys

"That's a lot of poop!"

Benny stood in the doorway of the horse's stall, watching in amazement as an almost endless stream of feces flowed from the mare's rear end. With Bucky's tail lifted high, the Mueller's large workhorse paid no mind to her small audience. Standing beside the dark brown beast, Big Jack took great care to reach for the manure with a rusty metal shovel and scrape it towards him. Then, she urinated as well, the liquid splashing on the concrete floor.

Benny could only stare and plug his nose. "Eeew!"

"You get used to it, boy."

"Why are you reaching for the poop, Opa?" he asked in a raised pitch. "Why don't you just stand behind Bucky and scoop it up?

"Let me tell you something, son – never, *ever* step behind this horse. She'll kick you into the next county."

"But you stand behind her when she's hooked up to the wagon."

"That's at a safe distance. You may have noticed I never get directly behind her, ever."

"Is that why you call her Bucky?"

"You catch on quick, little man."

Big Jack filled the shovel with a soupy mixture of urine and old feces, then dumped its contents into an empty shoebox. Suri, Big Jack's other workhorse, let out a loud whinny from the next stall.

"I think Suri wants you to use her poop, too," Benny giggled.

With the box now full, Big Jack put on the lid, tucked the shoebox under his arm and gave Bucky a thick carrot from his pocket. While patting her on her strong, powerful neck, the tall black horse crunched loudly. "There you go, girl."

Benny studied his grandfather, and smiled at his affection for the animal.

Snapping out of the moment, Big Jack looked at Benny. "Okay, son, you ready to have some fun?"

The youngster's eyes got wide with anticipation as his grandfather prepared to demonstrate the basics of his favorite practical joke.

They both walked to the other side of the barn, where Big Jack had cleared things off his workbench. In front of them, sunlight streamed in through a dirt-streaked window, illuminating the spot where old hand tools were piled up to one side. Next to them sat several empty coffee cans and glass jars full of nails, screws and washers of every possible size. Just below the windowsill hung a hand drill, a rusted handsaw and several screwdrivers on chipped pegboard. And in the middle of the workbench, lying in wait, was a large piece of bright red wrapping paper and thick white ribbon. Using a pair of scissors and a roll of Scotch tape, the metamorphosis began.

"Watch and learn, boy. Not even Gimbels can gift wrap a box like this."

Benny stood in quiet wonder as his grandfather cut a three-foot piece of wrapping paper. With his little tongue poking out from the corner of his mouth, Benny balanced on an upside-down metal bucket, his elbows propped on the workbench. Paying particular attention to the folds and pulling the corners taut, Big Jack transformed the box of horse manure into a gift worthy of a wedding registry.

"Okay, Benny, now give me your finger."

The boy obliged with his tiny digit as Big Jack tied the beautiful white ribbon into a symmetrical bow.

"Perfect!" exclaimed Big Jack.

"Perfect!" mimicked Benny.

Just then, the horn on Art Kreiter's pickup truck announced his arrival outside in the barnyard.

"He's here!" Benny announced with an almost hyper-intoxication.

They both scampered out of the barn, the gift-wrapped present in hand.

"Where are you two off to?" yelled Maggie from an upstairs window. "You've got chores to do."

"Quick errand into town," Big Jack said while he and Benny climbed inside the cab of Art's truck. "Back after lunch."

"Yeah Mommy, we have a box of p – " his voice cut off just as Big Jack slammed the passenger door shut.

As they turned onto the county highway outside the farm, Art looked over at Big Jack and said, "So, looks like you got it."

Big Jack held up the package. "Oh, we got it alright."

As the stench from the manure and urine mélange filled the cab, Art twisted his nose and said, "Whoa, about the only way your horses could have shit that bad is if you fed them shit."

Big Jack and Art laughed like giddy schoolboys.

Benny grimaced. "Can we roll down a window, Grandpa?"

Best of friends, Art and Big Jack had known one another for nearly 30 years. Both farmers, both immigrants – Art from Austria, Big Jack via Germany. In fact, it was Art who coined Jon Mueller's nickname many years earlier, having earned it not for his physical size – he hardly stood five-foot-seven – but for his victory in a hand of *Pochen*, the German version of poker. As the night's top winner, *Big Jack* took home a pot of $25 from his fellow townsfolk on nothing more than a bluff. Art blurted out the nickname, and from that day forward it stuck.

Winding down the highway several miles from the farm, the three pranksters pulled the blue pickup truck onto a gravel frontage road and parked out of sight, behind a cluster of tall shrubs which grew adjacent to County Highway 36. When they climbed out, Big Jack turned towards Benny and presented the gift-wrapped package. "Okay, son, so we want you to cross the road, place this on the opposite shoulder and then come join us behind the bushes. You got that?"

"You mean it? Me?"

"That's right. It's your day to shine."

Benny was slack-jawed.

Looking left, then looking right, the proud youngster darted across to the road, gently rested the box onto the gravel shoulder as if the package were made of crystal, and then sprinted as fast as he could to meet his grandfather and Art behind the thick hedge.

"Now what do we do?" asked Benny, more out of breath from the excitement than from the short sprint.

Cracking open a lukewarm Schlitz from his wicker fishing basket, Art said, "We wait."

"Yeah, we wait," repeated Big Jack, unwrapping a liverwurst sandwich from wax paper.

We wait.

A better vantage point could not have been found on that meandering road. The woody vegetation of buckthorn, tallowtree and bluewood acted like a two-way mirror; the shrubbery thick enough to hide a corn combine, but not so dense as to block their view of the road. And because the highway curved towards them in a long hairpin, they could easily see vehicles coming from either direction. The trunk of a tipped-over maple tree made the perfect stoop, so there the pranksters sat until Benny saw the first car approach.

"Look! I see one!" yelled the youngster.

But the gray Ford Standard took the sharp curve too fast. With wheels screeching and dirt kicking up from the shoulder, it kept on going and soon disappeared into the distance. Benny dropped his shoulders.

"Patience, son. Patience," said Big Jack as he popped open his own beer and offered a sip to Benny. The boy took three big gulps while Big Jack playfully ruffled his hair.

A few minutes passed when Benny saw another car approach, this time from the opposite direction.

"Look! Look!" he declared, pointing to the new mark on the horizon. "Here comes one from that way!"

"I've got a feeling about this one," said Art. But as the car came closer it, too, shot past the red souvenir without abating.

"Aw, shucks!" yelled Benny, slapping his knee. But not a second later they could hear the tires skid on the asphalt as the vehicle came to an abrupt stop. Pausing for what seemed like an eternity, the automobile backed up with a loud whir.

"He's coming back!" proclaimed Big Jack matching Benny's enthusiasm. "We may have a fish on the line, fellas!"

Benny let out a loud shriek. Art grabbed the youngster and covered his mouth.

"You gotta keep it down, son!"

As the black Cadillac backed up and stopped next to the gift-wrapped package, a finely-dressed man in a wool suit stepped out and studied the mystery gift. *How could such a perfectly wrapped present have found its way to the side of a county road? Did it fall out of someone's trunk? Was it accidently left on the roof of a car and finally fell as they hit this hairpin curve?* The driver wore an expression that clearly read, "This must be my lucky day," as he quickly snatched up the box, jumped into the car and escaped with a screech.

With tight emotions too powerful to contain, the three jokesters exploded with laughter. Proud of themselves, they walked out from behind the hedge, stood in the middle of the road and watched the car as it made tracks towards town.

"Either that guy's got a bad cold or his sense of smell ain't right," said Art with both hands on his hips.

"Hold your horses," Big Jack chuckled. "It'll hit him any second now."

Just then the Cadillac's break lights illuminated, and the car momentarily skidded out of control, barely missing a large oak tree as it pulled onto the shoulder and stopped in a cloud of dust. From a distance, they could see the driver-side door burst open and the motorist shot out of the car with the package in his hands. He ran to the rear of the vehicle, and in an attempt to toss the box into the ditch, he slipped and fell backwards – the now soggy box spilling its contents onto his chest. While the three pranksters could not hear the specifics of his cussing from where they stood, the breeze helped float several words of protest their way. *Son-of-a-bitch . . . catch holy hell . . . Jesus Christ . . .* Upon hearing the distant barking, all three buckled over in laughter one more time. The driver did his best to wipe himself off, jumped back into his luxury car and sped away with a shit-covered tail between his legs.

After such a successful prank, a well-deserved reward beckoned. A triple chocolate sundae from Kitt's Ice Cream Parlor had Benny's name on it. As the truck flew down the highway towards Ramsey, Big Jack poked Art's shoulder and motioned for him to look at the boy sandwiched between them. Art leaned over the steering wheel to nonchalantly glance at the youngster, and he couldn't help but smile – but it did not come close to rivaling the expression on Benny's face. Lost in the moment, and with the fun-and-games behind them, the boy had a ten-foot-wide grin and a memory that would last a lifetime. He felt proud he passed his initiation and had unofficially been allowed into an exclusive club with his granddad. As the warm July wind whipped wildly though his thick red hair, Benny thought to himself, *This is the bestest day of my life!*

Chapter Seven

Dear Maggie

Postman Mark McCabe's motorcycle could be heard from a mile away – some days even further, depending on the direction of the wind. All the local farmers in the area knew his Harley-Davidson needed a new muffler, but most asked he never repair it, and he gladly obliged. Everyone liked knowing their mail had been delivered without having to leave the fields or exit the farmhouse to check the postbox. As the rooster signaled the day's sunrise, McCabe's loud V-twin announced a mid-afternoon delivery from the United States Postal Service.

Benny ran down the stairs and into the kitchen as Maggie sat at the table cutting onions and peeling potatoes and raw carrots for a stew. "He's coming, Mommy! I hear him. Can I get the mail?"

"Of course, sweetheart. Let's go," she said, wiping her hands on her apron and standing up from the kitchen table.

With the screen door on the back porch slamming shut behind them, mother and son hiked down the long driveway just as McCabe pulled up.

"Sorry I'm late, Maggie," he shouted over the idling engine. "I had a flat back in Sussex. Didn't have no inner tube, so I stuffed the tire with pieces of cardboard."

"Seems to be working."

"Cross yer fingers for me."

McCabe took several letters out of a worn leather knapsack from the attached sidecar, and thumbed through them.

"Tell ya what," Maggie continued. "If they're bills you can stuff them into your tire with that cardboard."

"Not a chance. They're all yours," he said with a smile while presenting her with the day's delivery.

Maggie bobbed and weaved her head to signal for him to place the mail in the postbox so Benny could retrieve it after he drove off.

"Oh, of course," McCabe said as he opened the little door and placed the mail inside. "You two have a great day," he said before tipping his hat and driving away.

"Up, Mommy, up," her son said while plugging his ears. Maggie hoisted the child and his little arm disappeared into the metal mailbox.

As they walked back to the house, the boy tried to read the names on the envelopes. Today's bundle included a best-wishes card from a neighbor; a plea to buy war bonds, her monthly bank statement – and a surprise!

"Hey, this one's got my name on it!" shrieked Benny.

"What?" Maggie stopped dead in her tracks and snatched the envelope from her son.

She couldn't believe her eyes. *It's from him!* Erik's first letter had finally arrived. Upon closer review, she noticed her husband indeed addressed it to Benny, and even wrote their address with blue crayon! She quickly collected herself and gave her son the impression it wasn't anything important.

"It's, um, from the bank, Benny. Don't worry about it."

The boy shrugged it off and threw a rock at a large crow which had perched itself on the white wooden fence that ran parallel to their long driveway.

As they got near the house, Big Jack stepped out of the barn. "Any mail today? I hear McCabe's motorbike."

"Just bills," Maggie fibbed as she nonchalantly snuck Erik's letter into the pocket of her apron.

* * *

Later that night, as the house fell quiet, Maggie sat cross-legged on her bed with Erik's yet-to-be-opened envelope resting face up on a pillow in her lap. She picked it up and reflected on her life since his departure:

- She had been strong all month long . . .
- The laughter flowed and love permeated throughout the house . . .
- In many ways, the family had never been closer . . .
- Most obvious: Benny didn't appear to miss "*Papa*" as much as she expected. Big Jack kept the boy busy, which also helped.

As Maggie held the letter, she thought about all these things and contemplated not even reading it. *If I open up this envelope, do I also open up old wounds? Perhaps I should just give it to Benny. After all, it is addressed to him. Then again, Erik knows he can't read too well and I'd do it for him. A futile attempt at humor, perhaps? Oh stop overthinking things and read the letter already!* She tore at the paper and took out a hand-written note.

20 July, 1944

Hi Mags:

So did you like the outside of the envelope? I thought Benny would appreciate that. Do you know how hard it is to get a crayon in camp?

Basic training has been a real grind. It seems all we did the first week was paperwork and push-ups. We're living in small tents. I share mine with Phil Haskins, a guy from Minnesota. I wonder if he isn't a fairy, considering the way he carries on like a woman and all. Even the way he gets dressed . . . Who puts on a sock, then their boot, followed by the other sock and then the other boot?

The chow here is nothing to write home about, but here I am writing home about it. He-he-he . . . Tomorrow we're going to be introduced to the heavy artillery – a Howitzer! They say the gun is so strong, your heart skips a beat when it fires a shell.

My commanding officer is a swell guy who just returned from action in Italy. He thinks this war is going to last many years and Hitler is the devil with a mustache. Us Yanks are making strides over there, but we're taking casualties, too. Same in the Pacific. Tell Benny not to worry, I'll be fine regardless of where my assignment lands me. I miss the little fella.

Okay, they're calling "lights out," so I better run.

E

Maggie sat motionless and numb. *That's it? It's been a month since you left, and this is all you write? Benny had already written you at least once a week. Did you even get those letters? And what about that darned goodbye? That dreaded "E." Where were the other three letters? The L, the O and the V?*

With eyes heavy, Maggie laid back, rested her head on the pillow, took a heavy breath and fell asleep with Erik's note on her chest.

At that very moment, several miles to the west, Maggie's best friend Audrey Stanton burned the midnight oil sitting at her sewing machine. It had been three years since Audrey Ross and boyfriend Bob Stanton tied the knot – three years since every eligible bachelor in the county shook his fist skyward and cursed the heavens that Bob had won and they had lost.

Audrey epitomized the expression "natural beauty." Tall, with shapely hips, long red hair and milky white skin, many told her she looked like Rita Hayworth. Privately, she believed she looked more like Lana Turner. Regardless of the likeness, Audrey had movie star looks and knew it. She wore a strong sense of confidence, but always had a sincere "thank you" and a matching compliment for anyone who would fawn over her – an approach which endeared her even to the competing eyes of other women who could have easily been jealous of her beauty. If not the best seamstress in the county, Audrey most certainly could have taught classes on diplomacy and poise.

Marriage proposals were not uncommon – one came after a chance meeting on the short train ride from Milwaukee to Madison. Another occurred – on bended knee – during a visit to her sister's in Minneapolis. Men saw her and would philander even in the presence of a wife or a steady. Maggie stopped trying to compete with Audrey back when the two best friends attended elementary school together. Some women are born with good looks, others were blessed with a great personality. Audrey had both, in spades.

Sitting in front of "Old Faithful," one of her three Singer sewing machines, Audrey stitched a straight hem on the edge of Benny's quilt. With her godson's birthday just around the corner, she wanted to create a special gift for the boy. She had chosen a circus theme, knowing how much Benny loved his clown, Mr. Chuckles, and how often he spoke of being a lion tamer when he grew up. Thinking back to that memory, Audrey shook her head and smiled. *What a little Dickens he is*. Then her mind wandered to other things. Not so pleasant things.

"*So Audrey, when are you and Bob going to have children?*" The question seemed to repeat itself daily, and as she worked on Benny's quilt she couldn't help but chew on the thought. Three years had come and gone for the Stantons, and still no kids. Sometimes Audrey wanted to scream. In fact, things had gotten so bad, when she saw friends shopping with their children in downtown Ramsey she would intentionally walk on the other side of the road because she knew the youngsters would provide a natural segue to her fertility – or lack thereof.

Everyone understood Bob traveled plenty as an insurance salesman, so she used his absences as an excuse. In truth, she wondered if the injury he had sustained at basic training two years earlier couldn't somehow be related? Gossipy townsfolk wondered as well.

Before securing his job with Northwestern Mutual Life Insurance, Bob enlisted in the Army – along with just about every other man who first heard the words "Pearl Harbor." But his discharge from the Army and his subsequent return back to Ramsey happened so fast, many didn't even know he had gone. Bob never talked about the incident, only to say something happened in a training exercise and he was lucky to have lived. Not even Audrey knew the details. He simply would not discuss it.

One night she got him drunk, all in an effort to unbosom the tale, but after two bottles of wine, he remained indomitable as Audrey passed out on the davenport in their living room. Some soldiers return home with Purple Hearts. Some have parades in their honor. Bob Stanton came home with a limp and a secret.

Ever since securing the job at the Milwaukee-based insurance company, Bob had tried to galvanize the idea of moving 40 miles east into the "big city," but Audrey wasn't having it. "*You're on the road all the time anyways, so what's the difference where we live? Besides, I don't want to move to Milwaukee. I love Ramsey. I grew up here.*"

In many respects, Audrey enjoyed her quiet time alone. Sewing was her passion, and she found her productivity went up when Bob went out. *If only people would stop it already with the questions about children . . .* Of course, she would love to have several of her own, but for whatever reason the stork had not paid them a visit. It didn't help either that with all his travel, their moments of intimacy were, well . . . *What are moments of intimacy?*

Audrey sometimes wondered if there was something wrong with her, or if her husband found comfort in the arms of other women. When her mind wandered with such vexing questions, she would dismiss them and dive into her work.

As the sewing machine whirred with the precision of a finely tuned timepiece, she fought off the heavy eyes and focused on a circus elephant standing on its hind legs. She twisted the fabric and adhered the animal to the body of the quilt with the steady hand of a surgeon. Her stitches were so precise, they looked to be drawn onto the fabric. As she continued working, her thoughts wandered to Maggie's recent encounter with the German POW. *Why did he flirt with Maggie and not me?* She began to analyze her feelings and came to recognize she was jealous. It had been a long time since someone flirted with Audrey, and admittedly, she missed the attention.

Letting out a deep sigh, she put the finishing touches on the elephant, who shared real estate on the quilt with a ringmaster, a dancing bear and a tightrope walker. But instead of putting these roving troupers under the big top, Audrey found a more suitable location: she placed these characters in the barnyard of the Mueller's farm.

Chapter Eight

Help Wanted

The summer cicadas announced their arrival as they filled the August air with their familiar buzz. Maggie knelt in the dirt beside her victory garden as dragonflies darted to-and-fro, while 40 feet above her a weathered gray wind turbine squeaked in the soft breeze with every rotation. Bumblebees went about their business, rebounding from sunflower to sunflower, taking whatever nectar they could find.

Maggie focused her attention on several weeds which propagated between her cucumbers and baby squash. She pulled, tugged, tore . . . some weeds were so resistant to her extraction, she wondered if someone in China wasn't pulling hard on the other end, creating a global game of tug-of-war. Winning the contest, she took out a large dandelion – root and all – and dropped it into the rusty red wheelbarrow positioned beside her. As she reached to uproot another malignant invader, she noticed a flatbed truck coming up the driveway. A white cloud of dust trailed from behind as the driver downshifted, grinding the gears while lumbering closer. Nearly a dozen Negroes bounced hard on the bed, and one young man nearly tumbled off the back as the truck hit one of the many potholes Erik had promised to patch prior to his departure. Maggie stood up and wiped the sweat from her forehead with a dirty gardening glove, unwittingly leaving a black stripe just above her left eye.

When the truck stopped in the barnyard, she squinted and watched a tall, slender Negro wearing a straw hat jump out of the driver's side. The rusty hinge on the door made a squeak, then a loud pop before he slammed it shut. As he ambled towards her, she observed that his dark skin and facial features nearly blended together, and in his hands he held some paperwork, which he used to fan himself.

"Are you Muggy Went-what?" he asked in an unfamiliar accent, a toothpick tucked in the corner of his mouth.

"Wentworth," she said correcting him. "Yes, I am Maggie Wentworth. How can I help you?"

"My name is Oku Manley," he said, extending his hand to shake hers. "I have been told we can find work here at your farm, yes?"

Maggie removed her glove and shook his hand – marveling at how white his teeth appeared through a wide smile. He then handed her the papers from the County Agricultural Agent, the primary resource for granting migrant assistance to area farmers.

Maggie quickly skimmed the paperwork. "Good heavens. Um, yes, I did apply a few weeks back, but I expected a letter or a phone call or something first. I really didn't think this would happen so fast."

"Sorry if dis is coming outta nowhere, Miss Maggie. Normally folks are contacted aheada time."

"It appears there are a dozen men in that truck, but I only have 75 acres. I could use maybe . . . six or seven, but can't afford to pay for many more than that."

Oku's smile went from ear-to-ear, revealing even more blinding-white teeth. This was welcome news to the stranger.

"We will be harvesting our oats soon, and then our apples," Maggie added. "I'm sorry, I wish I could hire them all."

"Even a few hires would be most welcome news, Miss Maggie. We can start any time."

"Golly, I really wasn't prepared. My husband is in the service, and Lord knows I could use the help." Rubbing the back of her neck, Maggie inhaled deeply, trying to take it all in. "Tell you what . . . let me go through this paperwork tonight, and if it all checks out, I promise to have an answer for you by tomorrow or the next day."

"Dat is most fair," said Oku. "We will return in two days."

Oku then looked around the barnyard and wore an uncomfortable expression.

"Is there something else?" asked Maggie inquisitively.

"Actually, yes. Pardon me for asking, Miss Maggie, but could we botta you for a drink of water? We have traveled far today and my boys would like ta 'wet their whistles,' as you Wisconsin folks sometimes say."

"Help yourself. The well is right there, next to the barn."

"Tank you. You are most kind."

Turning towards the truck, Oku then summoned everyone off the flatbed using a deep and booming voice, followed by a high-pitched whistle. The group of migrants, who had been very reserved up to this point, cheered loudly and headed over to the hand pump. Maggie studied them as they walked past. The men ranged in ages from sixteen to about 30. She also observed their tattered work pants and stained white T-shirts. *What must it be like to be part of 'the circuit,' and travel like they do?* As the migrants reached the pump, they laughed and playfully pushed one another for the first position in line.

"If you don't mind my asking," Maggie inquired, looking back at Oku. "I'm curious about the accent."

He smiled again and said, "Of course. Sorry about dat. I am from Kingston."

Maggie looked confused.

"Jamaica, mon. The island of Jamaica."

"Oh! Very good."

"Ever been?"

"To Jamaica? Heavens no. I'm lucky to get to Madison once a year, much less to an island getaway."

Oku didn't answer, he just smiled again, tipped his straw hat and sauntered over to the well to be last in line for a drink.

As he walked away, Maggie replayed what he had said to her earlier. "*You are most kind.*" A compliment! Something she hadn't heard from a man in what seemed like forever. Watching him stroll towards the group, she studied his broad shoulders and exceptionally narrow waist. He took slow, measured strides and walked with a strong sense of confidence. Oku's gray T-shirt had a dark line of perspiration running straight down the center of his back. The blue jeans appeared faded, dirty and worn, the back pockets torn off – but the dye had not faded equally to the rest of the denim – leaving two ghosted imprints where the pockets used to be.

Maggie prided herself on her capacity to profile people almost instantaneously. She likened it to a sixth sense. There was something about Oku she immediately liked. This visceral feeling reassured her, despite the claims about Jamaicans poaching from area farmers during past harvests.

As the migrants drank from the well and argued over who got to pump the rusted metal handle, Benny popped out of the screen door at the rear of the house and ran to Maggie.

"Are these your friends, Mommy?"

"They may help us on the farm in the next few months."

"They sure are dirty. How come the water doesn't clean it off?"

"They're just like you and me, Benny, only their skin is a different color. It's like you have red hair, and mine is brown."

Benny shrugged.

After getting a good drink – and a good soaking – one by one the Jamaicans headed back towards the truck. They more skipped than walked, and each politely thanked Maggie as they passed by. Lastly, Oku returned to her, wiping his mouth with the back of his wrist. "I like your garden, Miss Maggie."

"Thank you."

"But you'd get more sun if you let me take down dat branch," Oku said, pointing up to a maple that cast a partial shadow over a corner of her natural sanctuary. "Maybe I can cut dat down for you one day, ya?"

"Problem is, that branch is holding up my son's tire swing, so you'd have to take it up with him."

"What? Cut down my tire swing? No, Momma!" protested Benny.

Oku laughed. It was deep and contagious – one of those laughs which makes everyone else smile upon hearing it. "Oh right. Well, we can't do dat to the little man. Maybe someday I could sit in there and you could push me?"

Benny eyed him up, suspiciously. "You wouldn't fit."

"Yeah, yeah, I guess dats true. How about we hang a tractor tire from dat branch, instead? Den I could probably fit."

"A tractor tire?" asked Benny with a giggle. "That's funny."

"Tell me little man, how'd you get such orange hair?" said Oku, placing his massive hand on top of Benny's head. "I betcha eat a lotta carrots."

The boy smiled. "Carrots don't give you red hair!"

"Dey don't? I always taught dey did."

"Nooo!" insisted Benny with a giggle.

"Did ya know all da kings of England had red hair? Maybe you'll be a king one day."

"I'm not a king!" insisted Benny, his giggle turning into a laugh. "You're a silly face."

"A silly face? Ooo, does are fightin' words, little man. But I know betta ta not tangle wit you."

Benny pulled up his shirt sleeve to flaunt his tiny bicep. "Look! I've got muscles."

"Indeed you do," said Oku, feigning veneration. "If I ever need someone ta help me fix a flat tire on my truck, I'll ask ya ta hold it up while I take off da wheel. Is dat a deal?"

Benny laughed even harder. “I can’t hold up a truck.”

Turning his attention back to Maggie, Oku returned to the main subject. “So if everytin checks out, we’ll be back in two days, if dat’s alright, Miss Maggie. I’ll be here wit six of my best workers.”

“Do you have sickles?”

“Oh yes, we own sickles, no problem. We are very good at cutting and shocking oats. You can trust me on dat.” Again Oku tipped his straw hat, waved to Benny, then turned to walk back to his truck.

As the migrants all piled onto the flatbed and drove away, Maggie put her arm around her son, smiled and brushed the hair out of her face.

If only Erik could see us now.

MOVIETONE Title:
THE FIGHT FOR PARIS

(Newsreel Narrator): "We have recently received the inside story of the French Resistance fighting for the freedom of the capital. Right up to zero-hour, everything seemed normal. Even though bicyclists moved about, presumably awaiting their final orders. Paris was still firmly held by the Boche, but in no time the streets became empty and ominously quiet. The hush before the storm.

"Then it all broke loose. After four years of German rule, Parisians tore down signs and proclamations . . . and now at last, before the arrival of the Allies who were just outside the city – the people of Paris rose to wipe out this humiliation. This newsreel footage tells an amazingly vivid and dramatic story. Don't let the lack of official uniforms fool you; every man and woman in the underground operation had precise orders. This was a fight by the people, for the people.

"The Hotel de Ville was used as the headquarters for the Forces of the Interior, and in no time, those underground legions went into action. The Boche did, too. He had tanks and all the rest of it. But neither his superior equipment nor his much-vaulted membership in the "Master Race" stopped his being beaten by the people of Paris. These residents fought from street corners, from windows and rooftops . . . they fought for Paris!

"It was bloody, and there were many casualties, many dead and wounded among the people. If not for the women of the Red Cross, the death toll would have been immeasurably greater.

"The battle lasted several days. The great news is while the fight raged on, everywhere the Boche were being killed or captured. Quite a different

picture from 1940, when he goose-stepped into Paris. Now he's front-marched into prison. For years they've strutted in the streets of the capital. But now Fritz and Heinrich have surrendered, not to the overwhelming might of allied arms, but to the citizens of Paris!"

Chapter Nine

Into The Fields

The low morning sun illuminated the Wisconsin sky in soft hues of pink and orange, silhouetting a cluster of tall pines that bordered Jon Mueller's farm. Several landmarks and rich topography enhanced the expanse in every direction: to the north, a large grassy hill sloped gently downward towards the farmhouse, the same highlands Maggie remembers glissading down each winter as a little girl on a snow sled; to the south, everything appeared outstretched, including the land which housed the apple orchards of Pink Ladies and Winesaps; eastward, *Mueller Manor* was bordered by Big Jack's low, handmade stone fence, which ran parallel to County Highway CC, meandering around the bend. Beyond the country road, neighboring barns stood noble and vigorous, with accompanying silos protruded up from the ground like prairie dogs safeguarding their burrows. Finally, to the west, the Mueller property line followed a small creek, which snaked to-and-fro along their flowing fields of oats. An aerial depiction of the homestead – complete with their red barn and white farmhouse – could easily have been showcased on a postcard with the words: *AMERICA'S DAIRYLAND* imprinted on the front.

Outside Maggie's half-open bedroom window, a rooster let it be known a new day had arrived. Several mourning doves chimed in to provide backup. In the yard, a handful of crickets did their best to dominate the trio, but with each passing minute the nocturnal chirpers conceded to the daylight.

Maggie's alarm clock drowned out the rich cornucopia of sounds, and as she sat up in bed and rubbed the sleep from her eyes she could hear a vehicle advance up the driveway with deep reverberation. Maggie jumped out of bed and shuffled over to the window. Oku and his team had returned.

Scrambling to find her robe, she quickly trotted downstairs just as he knocked on the flimsy screened door in the back of the house.

"Yes, good morning," she shouted as she side-stepped into the kitchen, one arm in pursuit of a sleeve in her thin cover-up. Oku stood patiently outside the door as she tied the cloth belt around her waist. As expected, he stood before her with a larger-than-life smile.

"Hello, Miss Maggie! I am Oku. We met two days ago and I now come back wit my best crew. No problem."

"Yes, Oku. Nice to see you again," she said talking through the screen door, a bit exasperated. "Please, come inside."

Pushing on the wood frame of the flimsy screen door, Oku entered the kitchen while nervously stroking his straw hat. "So I am wondering if all da paperwork checked out? We are good to work today? You told me ta come back in a few days . . ."

"Um, yes, it's all good. I just didn't expect you so early. Everyone's still sleeping," she added with a heavy sigh. "Can I get you and your friends something to eat or drink or . . . ?"

"No, tank you, Miss Maggie," he said. "We already ate and are ready to assist in your fields."

"Maggie."

"I beg your pardon?"

"Maggie. Everyone calls me Maggie," she said, rubbing the back of her neck, caressing the kinks out.

"Yes, okay den, Miss Maggie. I will call you dat."

With an exasperated sigh, she ignored the blunder.

"We can git started anytime. We will work very hard and charge you by da man for da day's wages. It's all in the paperwork. We will only need you to show us where to cut."

"That will be easy, because the oat field is bordered on four sides – by the highway, a creek, a tall hill and some woods. Once the sun comes up fully, you will be able to see the boundaries much easier."

Sketching a crude map on a folded paper bag, Maggie pointed to where they should meet. "Follow this road to the west, and I'll meet you there in about 20 minutes. It's the best place to start cutting the oats."

"Dat is a fine plan. Tank you, Miss Maggie."

* * *

At that very same moment, Adam Klein was in a deep slumber when a loud whistle nearly bounced him out of his cot and onto the wooden parquet dance floor. Startled, he propped himself up on his elbows and got his bearings. Sergeant Keller had entered the hall, blowing that damned whistle of his and barking orders as he marched along the perimeter.

"Up and at 'em! It's time to get to work and help America win this goddamn war!"

Sporadic groans and the squeaking sounds from the metal-framed cots filled the chamber. The grumbling soon turned into mixed laughter as pillows got tossed from one cot to the next. Here awoke some of Hitler's finest, most feared fighters – men who wreaked havoc throughout Northern Africa and on the boot of Italy just six months prior – and as they slowly rubbed the sleep out of their eyes, not one of them would have imagined they'd be waking up in an old converted ballroom in the heart of America's Midwest. Yet here they rustled about like a group of Boy Scouts at summer camp.

Still blowing his whistle, Sergeant Keller advanced along the far wall and pulled open the long brown velvet curtains as he went. At each window's passing, a plume of dust kicked up so thick, it partitioned the brilliant morning light and made the sunlight appear glassy and tactile.

On the opposite side of the room stood a long but cramped serving window, which connected the hall to an ample and well-equipped kitchen. It was a narrow, cafeteria-style opening to a beehive of activity. Inside busy G.I.s frantically prepared the day's breakfast. Dressed in stained white aprons, these hash slingers cooked enough food to feed all 250 Germans, plus the 30 American guards.

In front of two stoves, two G.I.s amused themselves while stirring tall, steel pails of runny oatmeal, steam wafting up to the exhaust fan above. On a long table positioned beside them sat a stainless steel bin full of hundreds of pieces of toast, each lightly browned and smothered with a dollop of lard. Down the line, another G.I. culinarian precariously stacked cups next to several pots of coffee on a spacious metal cart. A bored private sat alone typecasting through a large container of silverware. At the end of the row stood three steel containers of lukewarm milk.

Unlike their American counterparts in German *stalags*, the POWs of Camp Ramsey enjoyed hearty meals every single day. In fact, they shared the exact same menu as their American guards. This not only stifled their physical hunger, but also lessened any cravings to escape the confines of their temporary home. When the choices included warm, home-cooked meals versus eating out of garbage cans in a strange land, the Germans found little temptation to escape beyond the flimsy fences.

After breaking down their cots and getting changed into their official work garb, the POWs loaded up their trays with food and sat at long rows of tables set up in the attached cafeteria and on the perimeter of the great room. Once all the inmates from the outside tents made their way indoors, the former dance hall quickly filled with casual conversation, periodic laughter and plenty of flatulence.

As the Germans ate their breakfast, Commander Raymonds entered, followed by his translator Corporal Kleist. Upon seeing the two of them step up onto the stage and walk to a center podium, the POWs' chatter quickly turned into hushed tones.

"Good morning, men," he said, followed by a screech of feedback from the microphone. "I hope this day finds you invigorated and excited, as you are about to embark upon a new kind of battle. A form of hand-to-hand combat that pits you against road tar, canning machines, stalks of corn and the like. Are you ready to see the sites and enjoy the beauty of this picture-perfect land we call Wisconsin?"

As Kleist interpreted, the energy in the room began to wane.

"You've been here awhile now, and it is time you got to work for these fine meals. Soon we will call you into groups and then gather outside in the compound for your assignments. You will have a break for lunch, which will be delivered on-site by our wonderful chefs . . ." Several distant cheers came out of the kitchen. ". . . you will then return to Camp Ramsey this evening in time for dinner."

Raymonds stepped off stage and Sgt. Keller blew his whistle to settle down the commotion. Reading from a clipboard he proceeded to call out, "Group A, Group B . . ." mispronouncing the likes of *Räthskeller, Schäfer, Wöllschläger* and *von Rothkirch.*

Upon hearing their respective names, each POW stood up, dropped off his steel meal tray and empty dishes, then timidly worked his way to the outside compound. The migration had all the qualities of a first day of school.

In the open courtyard, the newly formed cliques consolidated behind ten large troop transport trucks. Each congregation was made up of at least 20 POWs and a handful of American centurions. Group A and B would be adding new tar to Highway 20. Group C and D were going to the nearby Libby's vegetable plant to can, crate and ship beans, peas and beets destined for the European troops. Groups E, F and G – by far the largest contingent of POWs – were going into the fields.

As Adam Klein made his way outside to meet up with his crew, he took note of the perfect weather, with temperatures in the mid-70s and a slight breeze gently kissing his face. He was assigned to a group of eight POWs under the supervision of Captain John Lincoln, a short man who had a lazy eye and Corporal John Jennaro, a skinny Italian kid from New York who always seemed to wear a five o'clock shadow. Adam noticed one man in particular assigned to his group: the petulant Heinrich Richtor. As soon as the two made eye contact, the sun snuck behind the only cloud in the otherwise naked blue sky.

Holding a clipboard, Lincoln stood in front of Adam and said, "So Klein, I understand you speak English pretty well." Because of his lazy eye, Adam did not know if Lincoln was speaking to him or to someone else.

"Cat got your tongue, Sergeant?" Lincoln asked sarcastically.

"Oh, um, no sir. I'm sorry, I wasn't paying attention," said Adam, lost in his efforts to stay focused on the good eye. "Actually, I speak it well enough."

"It seems you do," said Lincoln, impressed. "How did you come to get so well versed in our language, might I ask?"

"I used to travel to America often. As a salesman."

Lincoln and Corporal Jennaro leaned in, both casting a suspicious expression upon the German. Adam knew they didn't believe him.

"Really, fellas, I've spent a lot of time here. I traveled to Chicago mostly, selling watches. The *Robert Mühle & Sohne* brand – better than *Swiss Bulovas*, if you ask me."

Lincoln and Jennaro both laughed in disbelief. To further his case Adam continued, "One of my best customers was Marshall Field's. Do you know it?"

"Marshall Fields? My mother's favorite store," said Jennaro. Dumbstruck, the corporal could only laugh as he walked to the back of the large truck and opened the tailgate.

With that, the soldiers climbed into the troop transport. Jennaro and a third guard, Private Mike Thompson followed the POWs inside and under the dark green canopy while Lincoln crawled up into the driver's seat and turned the key.

Chapter Ten

The Old 40

As Maggie's pickup rolled down the highway, she futzed with the radio dial until she heard a familiar voice: Frank Sinatra, singing "I Couldn't Sleep A Wink Last Night." She smiled, turned up the volume and recalled that magical evening several years earlier when she and Audrey met *Old Blue Eyes* at the Coronado Theater in downtown Rockford, Illinois.

At the time, it was commonplace for a movie house to host a stage show before the playing of a feature film. This skinny crooner had just begun to sing with the Tommy Dorsey Band, replacing popular front man Jack Leonard – the one Maggie and Audrey wanted to see. While Sinatra had not yet become a household name, on that particular night, right after the stage show and during the playing of the movie, he sheepishly approached the two friends and asked if he could join them in the back row. Maggie fell for him in an instant. Audrey thought him pompous. Most in the theater had never heard of him – yet.

As the song on her radio continued to play, Maggie's mood went from being worried about the migrants to happy and reminiscent.

At the intersection ahead, she could see Oku's flatbed parked on the side of the road, right next to the oat fields. With his truck half on the gravel shoulder, half in the ditch, she thought for certain his vehicle could topple onto its side if the pitch into the gully were one degree steeper, or possibly if a strong gust of wind hit it broadside. Standing to the rear of the truck and unconcerned for its well-being, Oku held court with his fellow Jamaicans. Waving his arms and pointing to the fields, he appeared to be making a game plan with his team as Maggie pulled up behind him in her red Dodge.

"You followed my map perfectly, Oku," Maggie said, climbing out of the cab and walking towards the group.

He just smiled that wide smile of his and chuckled.

"In the back of my truck are four more sickles and several spools of twine for bundling the oats. Feel free to pass them out to your team."

"We have sickles. But da twine – we could use dat for sure."

"Forgive me for needing reassurance, but tell me again . . . you have shocked and bundled oats before?"

"Oh yea, mon. Tree of us cut while da other tree bundle. My preference is to stand five bundles up to one shock, if dat is okay. You end up with more shocks but it dries da oats faster."

At that Maggie felt convinced he knew what he was doing. "We've always stacked at least six to seven per shock, but I trust you."

"You will see, Miss Maggie. We Jamaicans are true Midwestern farmers at heart. I tink we were destined to be here – except in winter. Dat cold air dries out my skin, ya know?"

Maggie laughed and pointed to the oats. "So remember, this field goes all the way to the creek, then west towards the other road. Sooner or later you will end up near the farmhouse. But you needn't worry about all that now, it'll take you quite a while to get it all done."

"Okay, Miss Maggie. We are so grateful for da work."

Just then, a caravan of four U.S. Army trucks approached, blasting past Maggie and Oku's team while ignoring the stop sign in front of them. The wind from their backdraft blew Maggie's hair forward, into her face and knocked the straw hat from Oku's head. Everyone watched with curiosity, having never seen trucks like these before. The large troop carriers were called *"deuce and a halves"* because of their two-and-a-half-ton capacity rating. Maggie could see into the open back as they passed and noticed German POWs sitting inside.

"Are we under attack?" Oku said jokingly. "I taught da war was on da other side of da world?"

"It's the German POWs. They are here in Wisconsin helping with the harvest."

"Hey, no fair!" he said with a wink. "Dat's competition for my guys, right? So we betta work extra hard so dat you keep us, right Miss Maggie?"

"You got that right," she said, playing along. "And remember, there are 30 acres of apples that will need picking soon. So don't let me down."

Oku let out a hearty laugh then turned to his group, clapping his hands like a football coach. "Okay guys, let's go. Let's go. There's a lot of work ta do and we have ta impress a beautiful lady in da process. Bobby and Michael, grab da twine out of Miss Maggie's pickup truck. Let's do dis!"

Maggie smiled at Oku and he winked back. She believed in him and his Jamaican helpers and looked forward to seeing if his "five-bunch shock" would be better than her traditional seven.

As she walked back to her truck, she noticed another large army transport truck rolling towards them, only this one approached at a much slower rate of speed. The brakes squeaked as the truck pulled over, just behind Maggie's pickup.

While the driver stayed in the truck to gather some paperwork, Corporal Jennaro and Private Thompson exited from the rear, rifles on their shoulders, and they lowered the tailgate for a group of Germans to depart.

One by one, eight POWs popped out of the back. The last to step into the sunlight: Adam Klein. When he saw Maggie, his face lit up like a child's on Christmas morning. Maggie recognized him instantly and wiped the hair out of her face, offering a confused smile.

By this time, Lincoln grabbed all the paperwork he needed and stepped out of the driver's side of the cab lip-hanging a cigarette. "Hello there, ma'am. I am looking for . . ." he looked at his clipboard, "a Maggie Wentworth. Might you be her?"

"I am," said Maggie, bewildered.

"My name is Captain John Lincoln, and was told I could find you here. We met your father at your farm. He told me you'd be parked on this road."

"Does this have anything to do with my husband?" Maggie asked. "Is he alright?"

"Oh, I don't know anything about that, ma'am. I'm here to drop off these German POWs to work your fields." Flipping through some paperwork on his clipboard, he continued, "You put in an order with the Manpower Commission several weeks ago, is that correct?"

"Yes I did, but I have my team right here," she said, pointing to the Jamaicans. "They were just about to begin cutting my oats, so there must be some kind of mistake."

"Pardon me for saying so, ma'am, but these Germans supersede blackies any day. Kind of the lesser of two evils, if you ask me. Besides, there's really no arguing with Uncle Sam."

Anger started to build up from deep in the pit of her stomach – more from the cockiness of the American soldier than from the obvious error. "Well, it seems he *did* make a mistake," Maggie snapped. "You need to send these Germans to another farm because I have things worked out here."

"Ah-huh, well, the thing is Ms. Wentworth, we can't do that. You see, I have my orders . . . and my orders are to drop these here prisoners off on your farm this morning and take them back this evening. If that's a problem, then I suggest you talk to our camp commander. In the meantime, I gotta put the *Krauts* to work."

Finding a confidence she hardly recognized, Maggie retorted, "Excuse me, Captain, but I was born in Germany, as was my mother, my father and just about the *entire* population of this whole county, so I would suggest you watch the derogatory tone about both the Germans, and for that matter, the Jamaicans. They are not *Krauts* and they are not *blackies*. Please refrain from saying so."

"My apologies, ma'am. It's just we're at war with many of them and, well, we tend to have a different perspective is all."

"You've made that quite clear."

Taking a drag from his cigarette, he continued. "Now let's talk about the situation we got ourselves in here. I hate to do this, but I'm going to order these *'Ne-groes'* back on their flatbed and have them scoot on outta here."

"First of all, you can't *order* them to do anything. They are not in the Army. Secondly, what do your prisoners even know about shocking oats? Do you have sickles? Or twine? Do they know how many bundles you need to set up a shock?" She could tell by the captain's face they didn't think this through. "Sir, please don't tell me you came here to cut down oats and you don't have anything to do it with."

The American guard studied her, not saying a word.

"Maybe your bayonets?"

Lincoln looked embarrassed, but pride forced him to stick to the script. "Perhaps we could use your sickles?"

Maggie became incredulous. "Are you serious?"

But Lincoln would not back down. "I'm sorry, but the migrants will have to look for work elsewhere."

Until now, Oku and his team had been watching quietly from the wings, but he suddenly came to life, showing a side that surprised Maggie. "You cannot be serious!" he shouted, approaching the American with a rolled up baton of papers in his hand. "I have da paperwork right here! You cannot do dis."

"Yeah, well I don't know where you got your paperwork, mister, but what I have is orders, and they stand."

"Hey, come on, mon," Oku said, taking a milder tone. "I got a family to feed, right? Dis is my life. I tink Uncle Sam's got it all wrong, mon."

"I would say *Uncle Tom's* got it all wrong," chimed in Heinrich Richtor, the cantankerous German. "I won't let some nigger get preference over me!"

"Keep it down, Heinrich. You don't have a say in the matter," insisted Lincoln.

"Who you calling nigger, you white-haired *Kraut*?" snapped Oku angrily to Heinrich. "Go back to Germany."

"Go back to hell," retorted Heinrich, his English equally raw to his statement.

"Stop it!" ordered Lincoln. "Both of you, I mean it."

Ignoring the captain, Heinrich kept at him, "Hey, did you know what God said when he made the first nigger? 'Oops, burnt one.'" Some of the other Germans laughed, but Adam was too transfixed on Maggie to even register the offensive joke.

"How about this," said Adam, breaking out of his trance and acting as an arbitrator. "So let's split the work detail. We get half the field and these migrants get the other half. We could have a race, winner gets extra portions at lunch."

Maggie studied him and actually liked the idea. *He really is something else.*

"You stupid sympathizer," chimed in Heinrich. "We don't take a back seat to niggers."

Oku had had enough. He marched towards Heinrich with a long sickle in his hand. Lifting it high, as if it were a Samurai sword, he swung the tool with ease in a strong, fluid motion. Heinrich ducked in the nick-of-time, the blade missing his head by fractions of an inch. Realizing he could have just then been decapitated, the auspicious German charged, tackling the Jamaican into the gravel shoulder besides

Oku's truck. Jennaro and Thompson quickly ran over to break them up, but before they could pull the two apart, several more Germans jumped into the fray and attacked the remaining Jamaicans. Chaos ensued.

Oku quickly got the upper hand on Heinrich, and with the strength of a superhero, literally picked him up over his head and threw him into the side of his flatbed truck. Heinrich landed with a hallow thud, the wind retreating from his lungs. Under a cloud of dust, most POWs administered headlocks and half-Nelsons, but few real punches were thrown – as they did not feel the passion to fight with spit and vinegar. As the American soldiers tried to break things up and pull bodies off the pile, three shots suddenly rang out, followed by the booming command, "That's enough!"

Everyone froze in place, then turned ever so slowly towards the sound of the gunshots. There stood Maggie, tenacious and imperturbable, heroically posed like a bronzed statue found in virtually every town square in America. "Stop this fighting right now! I mean it!" she said while holding a rifle that had been dropped in the fracas. With her heart pounding and adrenaline pumping, she was completely exhilarated.

This was not the same Maggie Wentworth everyone in Ramsey had come to know and love these past 25 years. Throughout her life, she had been more peacemaker than agitator – which seemed to be true of all the Muellers. This farming community had a hierarchy to it, and when it came to the pursuit of wisdom, astuteness and resolution, it was to this royal family everyone would turn. People would tell Big Jack and Ivy things they would never think to tell their own pastors. They were the neutral country. The adjudicators for anyone in need. Trust, reliance and an undercurrent of general goodness made this community tight-knit and strong. *"Without the sensibilities inherent in families like ours, utter chaos would surely follow,"* Big Jack would say on numerous occasions.

By birth and by circumstance, Maggie was equally admired. But ever since Erik's departure, she had become more phlegmatic, and fixated more on her own needs and those of her immediate family. During that summer of 1944, she set sail on a noble journey of self-discovery. She had problems of her own now – big ones. Add to that, ebullient change was happening swiftly across both oceans and on the home front. The mediators of the world were no longer esteemed or solicited; their points of view mere whispers of the minority. Those voices of reason had been replaced by a malignant ideology, which manifested itself in the death of millions throughout the world. The reign of the peacemakers had passed and it seemed the only way to win any conflict was to fight fire with fire. This poisoned thinking had even found itself into Maggie's tenets, and at that very moment, with rifle in hand, she could not have felt more alive – or more in control.

"Whoa . . . now let's be smart here, Ms. Wentworth," said Captain Lincoln, eyes wide, his expression aghast.

"She's got your rifle, Cap-'in!" observed Jennaro.

"Please, lower the gun and hand it to me," said Lincoln.

"I will if—" Two more shots rang out into the air. "If you help me solve this little dilemma and stop arguing about it."

The other American soldiers pointed their rifles directly at Maggie while everyone else stood frozen in place.

"Put them down, boys! Lower those guns!" Lincoln shouted to Jennaro and Thompson as he slowly walked towards Maggie. "We can work something out here. How about we take a drive back to the camp and have a little chat with my commander. We'll get to the bottom of this. Please, just hand me the gun."

Maggie squinted her eyes and studied the American. "Do I have your word?"

"Yes. Absolutely. We'll figure this out. I'll let the Jamaicans get to work, at least for today, and we'll go back to camp to chat with my commander. Deal?"

"Fine," Maggie said, turning the rifle around with a casual flip and handing it to Lincoln, butt-end first.

"Okay," said Lincoln to Maggie with a heavy sigh as he took back the weapon.

"Alright, everyone back in the truck," Jennaro announced.

"This is insane!" objected Heinrich, holding his stomach and trying to regain his balance from Oku's thumping. "You pansy Americans amaze me. Just shoot these niggers and get it over with."

"Shut up, Heinrich. Get back in the truck," ordered Thompson while cracking him across the head with the butt of his rifle. "You're the reason this whole thing started!"

The two adversaries split into their respective groups – the Germans slowly walking back to the their "deuce and a half" while Oku's boys moved up the berm and towards the crop line. Some walked, some limped, and both parties brushed the dust and gravel from their pants and picked up their hats.

Adam passed Maggie and smiled coyly. "It's a good thing you weren't in that church steeple a few weeks back, or us Germans would have been goners for sure."

Maggie smiled. "Perhaps that's true, but I may have made one exception . . . if I saw you." With that, she teasingly walked away.

Adam's eyes got large. *The attraction is mutual!*

Before he could say anything more, Jennaro ordered him back to the truck. "Nice try, Klein, but forget about that one."

Maggie walked up to Oku. "So, you alright?"

"Hey, I was just playing around with dat guy." Oku said.

"You have a funny way of showing it."

"Listen, if I really wanted ta hurt him, he would still be down."

Maggie squinted as she looked up at the tall Jamaican. "Well, I sure hope we can figure something out. I feel bad about all this."

"What did you do, Miss Maggie? Dis is da way it goes. I hope we can stay. If not, well, wit God's good grace we will be working someplace else. I am sorry I lost my temper. But dat guy . . ."

"That guy is a jerk! Just get started on the oats and hopefully you will make so much progress the commander will have no choice but to let you finish."

"Good tinking. We will start as soon as da Germans leave."

"Um, Ms. Wentworth," Captain Lincoln called as he stood next to her pickup truck nervously lighting another cigarette.

Maggie walked towards him.

"So can I trust you to follow us back to the camp without me worrying you'll mix it up with a different group of POWs? Because if that's the case, I'm going to need to put in a requisition for double the ammo."

Maggie took a moment to ensure he was actually joking. The corner of his mouth cracked, which confirmed her suspicions, and then she played along with a sarcastic edge. "Well, I suppose if you doubled your ammo allowance only then would it be a fair fight."

He laughed. "You know, you handled that rifle pretty well. My compliments to . . . your husband maybe?"

"Heavens no. My father gets the credit."

"Oh right. It's just you mentioned a husband earlier and . . . may I ask?"

"He's doing basic training right now, at Fort Hixon, in St. Louis. Then off to God only knows where."

"You must be proud."

"Yeah, I am. Proud of *myself* for getting along just fine without him."

Lincoln pursed his lips tightly and cocked his head to the side, realizing he had treaded into sensitive territory. Clearing his throat, he wisely changed the subject. "So, um, do you know where Camp Ramsey is?"

"If you mean the old Kaston Ballroom, yes, I know where it is. You're welcome to follow me there if you'd like," she said with a saucy bite.

He smiled, ignoring her cocky response. "Oh, and Ms. Wentworth, there's one more thing . . ." he said, offering her a cigarette, lowering his voice and leaning in. "I know you don't owe me, but . . . can I count on you to make sure this little incident stays between us?"

Maggie waved off his offer for the cigarette and studied him coolly.

"The thing is, if word got to my C.O. that I let my rifle fall into a 'civvy's' hands, well, it could mean garrison duties for sure."

"That all depends."

"On what?"

"For starters, you can cut the racist remarks."

"Done. My apologies."

"And second . . ."

"Yeah . . ."

"If you help me figure out a way to keep the Jamaicans maybe, just maybe, I'll bite my tongue."

She stepped into her truck and started the engine. "I'll follow you."

The time had come to settle this little misunderstanding.

* * *

Colonel Raymonds could not have picked a more ideal assignment with the Army. Born and raised in the neighboring community of Hustisford, he was savvy to the Wisconsin ways and even had friends in the surrounding principality. He ran a mechanic's shop before the war which boasted repairs for everything from automobiles and farm tractors, Harley-Davidson and Indian motorcycles, to wind turbines, hand pumps, and even and the occasional tricycle or child's teeter-totter. If it had at least one moving part, he affirmed his shop could fix it.

Originally stationed in Hawaii after the bombing of Pearl Harbor, the only action Raymonds ever saw was paper pushing. His commission at Kaneohe Air Base on Oahu lasted two years before he unexpectedly received orders to return to the mainland. At first he objected to his superiors and believed he could do more good fighting the Japanese from the Pacific, but when he learned he would be part of a select group of highly vetted camp commanders on the mainland, he felt honored. Furthermore, when he discovered the camp would be less than 20 miles from his hometown, well he was downright ecstatic, as was his wife.

Collectively, Wisconsin's POW camps housed more than 20,000 German, Japanese and Italian prisoners during the war. The military did everything it could to keep these camps inconspicuous, primarily to soft-pedal any hostility from local veterans and area families who may have a bone to pick with the "new residents." Fortunately for the Army, Camp Ramsey stood in the heart of a community made up primarily of German descendants, so the need for a camouflaged presence was unnecessary, and having a group of "old friends" move into the neighborhood was anything but precarious.

Impeccably clean, organized and systematic, Raymonds' reputation preceded him. Prior to the war, his happy customers often joked he cared more for his own tools than he did for their transmissions. This obsession carried over to his new profession as a camp commander as he placed everything on his desk at right angles; he waxed its cherry surface twice per week, not satisfied until he could gently push his cloth from one end and have it slide off the opposite edge with very little effort. One of the camp's privates was tasked with sponge-mopping the floor in his office once every other day and polishing his boots with a mixture of naphtha and turpentine every morning.

In keeping with this notoriety, Raymonds stood washing the windows of his second floor office when he saw Captain Lincoln's transport return to the compound, followed by a civilian pickup truck. As the main gate closed behind the two vehicles, Raymonds let out a subtle groan.

German POWs jumped out of the back of the large Army truck for the second time in less than an hour and several American guards came over to inquire as to why they had returned. As Maggie stepped out of her pickup, she turned to find Adam Klein standing right beside her.

"Hello again," Adam said.

"Ah!" cried a startled Maggie, jumping backwards and nearly falling back into her vehicle. "You scared me."

"My apologies."

"You are like the wind. *POOF!* – there you are."

"If I didn't know better, I'd swear you were following me," said Adam with a wide smile.

"Maybe I wanted to see where you made your living," said Maggie, pausing to look around.

"Well, here it is," said Adam pointing up to Colonel Raymonds' second story window. "I'm trying to work my way up to that corner office. I'll run this entire empire one day," he joked. "That much I promise you."

"Well, everybody's got to start somewhere," Maggie teased, brushing the bangs out of her eyes. As she looked at him, she almost forgot why she was at the camp. Normally, Maggie didn't like to disentangle knots in her regimented day. She preferred things in her life to mesh smoothly, without interruption – be it choosing the exact times to milk her cow, when to do the laundry, making Benny his lunch, tending to her garden, the best time to venture into town for icebox pick-ups, grocery shopping, when to pay the bills, and even choosing when to visit with friends. Maggie ran the farm like a tight ship and few things were more vexing to her than being blindsided by feeble obstructions. They tipped her equilibrium. This visit to Camp Ramsey would appear to be one such messy example, but this time, she was fine with it.

Adam continued in vain to flirt and playfully soften her hard shell, and she couldn't help but appreciate the flattery. *I forgot about those deep blue eyes . . . and that enticing smile . . .*

"So look at the two of us," Adam continued. "We've been shot at, we almost went to jail together, we've been in a fight together . . . you're shooting guns like it's America's Wild West. We've been through so much. We are both survivors, you know?"

"Or . . . maybe we're just lucky."

"I know I am," said Adam.

Maggie took in the compliment, then looked away for a moment. *Oh, he's good.*

"I think we've known one another long enough that perhaps it's time we took this relationship to the next level," added Adam, going down to one knee. "So, on bended knee, let me pop the big question . . ."

Oh Lord! Is this stranger really going to propose? Right here?

"Please tell me . . . what is your name?" Adam asked.

Maggie was blindsided and laughed out loud at the misdirect. "Ohhhh, um, sorry, I thought you were going to . . ."

"You thought what?" Adam knew exactly what she meant.

"Oh never mind," said Maggie slightly embarrassed. "So fine, if you want to know my name, then you're going to have to guess."

"Okay, but to warn you, I'm pretty good at this game." Adam then cocked his head, rubbed the stubble on his face and slowly began to reel her in with a soft smile. "Is it Rita? Heidi? Rosemary? Oh wait, Angela!"

As he continued to go through his litany of aliases, a whistle blew next to her truck. "Klein! What the hell! Get away from there," yelled Captain Lincoln. "Jesus Christ, you are relentless."

"Scheiße!" he said softly to himself. "Not again."

Maggie smiled at the timing. "I guess it'll have to wait."

"I suppose the next time I see you there will be an air raid?" Adam added.

"Now that would be exciting," Maggie replied as he stepped away from her.

At this same moment Raymonds came out and trotted down the steps of the main building. "Captain! What in God's name is going on here?"

Lincoln and Jennaro snapped to attention and saluted, then Lincoln struggled to find his words. "Well, sir, I regret to tell you that, um, we have a situation."

"A situation?" said Raymonds mockingly. "Do you mean how you came into an American prisoner of war camp with a civilian? No keystroke approvals? No clearance? No sense for whether or not she could be a spy? Or worse – a reporter?"

Maggie became increasingly impatient at the military protocol, and it showed when she let out a heavy sigh, saying under her breath, "Oh, brother."

"Sir, may I present Mrs. Maggie Wentworth," said the captain. "We were at her farm when we discovered the discrepancy."

Watching from the wings, Adam registered the name. *Maggie!*

Raymonds studied her with squinted eyes. "Perhaps you could shed some light on the subject, madam?"

"Um, yes, Commander, I can tell you the 'situation' is Uncle Sam made a mistake, plain and simple."

Upon overhearing her, Adam called out, "You tell them, *Frau Maggie*! You tell them who's boss."

"Please shut him up," barked Raymonds to Private Thompson, the closest guard to Adam. At that Klein quickly threw his arms in the air and apologized.

"Wentworth?" asked the commander, his attention back on Maggie. "Your name is Maggie Wentworth?"

"Yes," she said confused.

Raymonds gently took her left hand, examined the wedding band and looked at her curiously. "What is your *maiden* name?"

"Um, Mueller," she replied suspiciously. "What does that have to do with anything?"

"You're Big Jack's daughter?"

Maggie paused for a second and struggled between being impressed and concerned. "Why, yes. How do you know my father?"

"I've known Big Jack for 20 years. Good man. How's his health?"

"Strong as a mule," she said, warming up to the colonel. "Hearing is still bad, but . . ."

"I'm sorry for being short with you. Please, let's go upstairs into my office with Captain Lincoln so we can get to the bottom of this."

"I'd like that."

As they walked, the remaining Germans all hooted and hollered like school kids bidding goodbye to a classmate heading to the principal's office.

"You all better shut up!" barked Jennaro.

Upstairs in the commander's office, Maggie sat in a mahogany jury chair positioned directly in front of his desk. Captain Lincoln stood behind her.

"Now what seems to be the problem, Ms. Wentworth?" said the colonel while pouring her a glass of water and handing it to her.

Lincoln spoke up, "It's like this, sir . . ."

"I asked the young lady, Captain, not you!"

"Yes, sir," returned Lincoln sheepishly. "My apologies."

At this, Maggie chimed in, "Two months ago, Big Jack and I put in a request with the Manpower Commission *and* the County Agricultural Agent to get some field help . . ." Handing the commander her paperwork, she continued, ". . . and we got their approval for Jamaican migrants. Having already met them earlier this week and after sending them into the fields today, I am now being told to take German POWs? It doesn't make any sense."

"You have a problem with Germans, Ms. Wentworth?"

"Lord no! I was born in Germany. So were my parents. If you know my father, you already know this. It's just the Jamaicans had everything in order. They know what they're doing. They're experienced. They have all the right equipment . . ."

"Well, your paperwork is indeed approved. But . . ." Reaching back to take a sheet out of a dark brown folder in his desk, the commander pulled out his forms. ". . . so is mine. It seems you got approval from *both* agencies. Can't say I've seen that before."

"That's odd," said Maggie.

"May I offer a suggestion?" said the commander.

"Please."

"It says on the application you have roughly 50 acres of oats and another 25 acres of apples, both of which are in need or will be in need of harvesting soon."

"That is correct."

"And you have been assigned seven migrants from one organization and eight German POWs from the other."

"It seems so."

"Then let's have them work together. You will pay the same amount either way, because the Germans are compensated at the market rate, and the work will get done in half the time."

"Sir, if I may . . ." interjected Captain Lincoln. "They really shouldn't be working side-by-side. There was, shall we say, an incident."

"What? A fight?"

The captain looked down at his shoes.

"Oh for the love of Pete, it's not even 8:00 in the morning! Tell me, Captain, how on earth could you have been part of a skirmish on the first day, within the first hour of this operation?"

"Well, um . . ." Lincoln's voice trailed off as he struggled to find the right words.

Maggie stepped in to share a solution. "I have another idea . . . How about the Jamaicans work the oat fields? They seem to know what they're doing – unlike the Germans who arrived today with no tools and no experience." The commander wiggled awkwardly in his chair, a bit embarrassed. "And when the apples are ready, perhaps your POWs can work the orchard? That way they can still help but at the same time be separated."

With a heavy sigh, the colonel took off his wire-rimmed glasses, leaned back in his chair and pinched the bridge of his nose. "I suppose I could find something else for that detail to do for the time being. Tell me, when exactly do you think the apples will be ready for picking?"

"Not long. A few weeks," said Maggie. "The Pink Ladies first. The Winesaps can be harvested later in the fall. Both are hardy fruits."

He pondered this for a moment. "Okay then. That'll be the new plan."

"I think that is a great solution, Colonel," chimed in Lincoln.

Raymonds shot the captain a cold look. "Is there anything else I need to know, Captain? Something you failed to tell me?" inquired Raymonds.

Maggie turned around in the chair to look back at Lincoln, who had a wishful expression on his face. "There is one other thing, sir," Maggie said, causing Lincoln to grimace and hold his breath. "You should stop by our farm sometime and say hello to Big Jack. I'm sure he would like to see an old acquaintance."

"I will do that," said Raymonds as he stood up from his chair and extended his hand. "And thank you for your understanding with this obvious mix-up. We'll be in touch."

Maggie shook his hand, then turned towards Captain Lincoln, who closed his eyes and drew a heavy sigh. Maggie smiled at him coyly and stepped towards the door.

"I'll walk you to your truck, Ms. Wentworth," Lincoln remarked.

"And when you're done with that, Captain," said the commander, "report to the kitchen. You're going to be reassigned for a few days, just to ensure you don't make the same mistake twice."

* * *

A week or so passed without incident. The Jamaicans had success cutting and drying out the oats at a near record pace. On occasion, Maggie, Benny and Big Jack would interrupt Oku and his crew, delivering lemonade and homemade cookies while marveling at their progress. These visits were always affable and provocative. Maggie solidified her relationship with Oku and accredited his team as they proved their mettle daily in the scorching sun, their five-high shocks standing tall. Big Jack marveled at their skills as well and would often brag to his poker-playing friends about the gleeful Jamaican who worked his fields. Those fellow farmers would nod their heads as he told his tale, then tap the long ashes off the tips of their cigarettes, lean back in their chairs and remark coolly, "Well, just remember to keep an eye on your valuables. Can't trust 'em as far as you can throw 'em."

It wasn't long until the first Pink Ladies ripened in the south orchard, and it marked the first time both the Germans and the Jamaicans worked on the farm together – albeit in different fields and far apart from one another.

On the first day of the Germans' arrival, the Mueller trio drove to the far side of the orchard to check on their status. Maggie still had a bad taste in her mouth from that first encounter with the pompous American soldiers, but secretly liked the idea of seeing Adam Klein again. Big Jack was much too eager to meet everyone – the Germans more so than the Americans.

As Maggie, Big Jack and Benny pulled their truck to the side of the road, behind an Army Jeep and a troop transport, the POWs were in the middle of their lunch break relaxing under the shade of an apple tree. The American guards sat nearby enjoying liverwurst sandwiches and fresh fruit. The humidity made the air heavy, and the dust from the fields settled in their throats like a thick, oily film. The light westerly wind was but a tease and of little relief from the dog of a day.

Maggie and Big Jack stepped out of their pickup truck and told Benny to stay inside. He did as ordered, propping his elbows on the edge of the truck's rolled-down window. Upon seeing the POWs nearby, Big Jack immediately walked towards them, speaking in German as he approached.

"Hallo, hallo meine alten Kameraden," said Big Jack with arms open wide. (Hello, hello my old comrades.)

Dumbstruck, they all jumped to their feet to receive the American stranger who spoke in their native tongue so flawlessly. Jennaro watched suspiciously and walked up to Maggie. "Hello, Mrs. Wentworth. I'm Corporal Jennaro. We met a few weeks ago . . ."

"Yes, I do remember," she said sheepishly.

"I hope we can start things off on a more positive note this time."

"Thank you. I would like that." Pausing to look at the other two American soldiers, she added, "So what happened to the captain? They didn't find out about that little incident with the gun, did they?"

Jennaro laughed, "No, no, let's just say the commander wasn't too keen on you showing up at camp unannounced. The captain's been pulling KP duty for a while."

"Turns out your commander knows my father," said Maggie, pointing to him interacting with the Germans.

"Let me guess – the infamous Big Jack?"

"In the flesh."

Maggie, Jennaro and other American guards watched from a distance as Big Jack walked up to each of the eight POWs and enthusiastically shook their hands with two of his. In no time at all most were laughing right along with him as he talked wildly, arms flailing about.

"Pardon me for saying so, Mrs. Wentworth, but Big Jack's really not that big."

Maggie laughed. "Well, he's big-hearted, anyways."

"You know we have a strict policy against letting the prisoners mingle with civilians," said the corporal.

Maggie cocked her head and gave him a sour look.

"Of course, I'm sure exceptions can be made," he added, backpedaling a bit. Maggie smiled in gratitude.

At this point her father could be seen talking with Adam Klein, and the conversation appeared serious when Big Jack pointed up the gully to his daughter, then waved to her. "Mags, come down here," shouted Big Jack. "I want you to meet someone."

Her heart fluttered, but she feigned a heavy sigh and then looked at Jennaro. "Didn't you just say there is a rule against fraternizing with the prisoners?"

"Oh, I get the sense your father trumps even Uncle Sam in these matters," said Jennaro, toying with her. "You better go. Besides, Klein is harmless. And the guy speaks perfect English."

Maggie sheepishly walked to her father.

"This is my daughter, Maggie," said Big Jack. She shook Adam's hand half-heartedly. "This is Adam. From Bremen, just a few miles from where I grew up! His family knows the Franks, the Schultzes and even the Starks. I can't believe this!"

"Yes, *Frau* Maggie. Good to meet you . . . again."

Maggie sheepishly smiled and brushed the hair out of her face. "So what did you say to me in the town square? You used to work here?" inquired Maggie, struggling for something, anything to say.

Big Jack looked at both of them, a bit perplexed by the question.

"We've already met, Papa," admitted Maggie, noticing her father's confusion. "The day they arrived, actually. It's a long story."

Big Jack shrugged and seemed blasé about the details of their first encounter, but he, too, wanted to know why Adam was in America prior to the war. "So what's this about you working here?"

"I sold fine jewelry for one of Germany's best watch manufacturers. I used to drive all throughout Wisconsin to Madison . . . Milwaukee . . . Green Bay. But mostly my business was in Chicago."

"So you *were* serious when you told me that?" said Maggie, a bit surprised. "I never know with you."

Adam laughed. "Yes. In fact, I was in the Midwest nearly two years ago, after a sales run to Cleveland. I returned back to Germany and found the paperwork for my enlistment into the *Wehrmacht*, with only one day left to report. The letter sat there for nearly a month and no one had a way to contact me. When I arrived home you can imagine my surprise – I could hardly get word to my company. I had to leave the next day."

"Where did you get shipped off to?" asked Big Jack, genuinely interested in the German's tale.

"The short story is Africa. I served under Rommel. Most of us did," said Adam pointing to his six other comrades who watched the conversation with interest. "Now, here I am, in the same state where I had spent so much time prior to the war. It's crazy."

"That is crazy," said Big Jack astonished. "Well, we need to have you boys over to the house for dinner sometime. I know the camp commander over there, and I'll try to make the arrangements."

"Papa, this is not a vacation for these men," warned Maggie. "You can't just invite them over to the house for dinner. That's ludicrous." *That's great!*

"Eh," said Big Jack waving his arm as if it would be straightforward and easy.

Just then one of the German soldiers began to scream. *"Das ist mein Sohn Willie!"* he shouted and then bolted towards Maggie's truck. Benny had gotten hot and bored inside the vehicle, so he stepped out and reposed himself next to the passenger side door. When the German POW sprinted towards him, the frightened boy took off running in the opposite direction, screaming as he did so. The American guards saw the POW's pursuit and scrambled around looking for their guns. Too late.

The German had nabbed the child, who let out a loud shriek. Maggie took off running as well. Hugging Benny with all his might, the POW felt as if he had just found his own son in America's heartland. Tears streamed down his cheeks as he repeated the words, "*Meine Willie . . .*"

"Do something!" Maggie cried to Jennaro.

"Let him go," the corporal commanded.

The German only squeezed the boy tighter. "Stay away from me. Stay away," he said in broken English.

Benny screamed, "Mommy!"

Adam approached and with a calm and assertive sense, speaking to his comrade in German. "Micah, please, put the boy down. He is terrified."

"He's my Willie," the POW said. "Oh God, my Willie. Who knows where he is or if he is even alive?"

"He means the boy no harm," said Adam to the American guards. "Please, put the rifles down."

"Listen to me, Micah," continued Adam in German. "They have guns and will use them. Please do not put the boy in danger. Give him to his mother. She, too, is scared."

With tears streaming down his cheeks, the German father sobbed even harder. "My son. I miss him so. I will never see him again. I just know it. He is dead. I can feel it. He is gone forever."

"You don't know that, Micah. You have no way of knowing such a thing. Please, give the boy to his mother."

Maggie cried. She understood.

"I appreciate how you must feel, sir," said Maggie in her own flawless German. "I would not be able to live without my child. But please, let him go and we can talk. He is a fine boy and you are hurting him. He is scared. If you love your son, please let mine go."

The German seemed to loosen his bear hug on Benny.

"That's right. Please . . ." pleaded Maggie. The German slowly released Benny, who then darted into his mother's arms.

"I am so sorry," Micah said. "I am so, so sorry." He slumped to the ground, buried his face in his hands and sobbed. Two American soldiers approached, gently grabbed him under his arms and walked him over to the Jeep. He kept looking back at Maggie and her son, apologizing through his tears. "I'm sorry. And goodbye, *mein Kind Willie.*" The two guards set him into the open-aired Jeep and took him back to camp, leaving only Jennaro to tend to the German apple pickers.

Maggie went straight to Adam. "That was a great thing you did there, Mr. Klein. Thank you."

"You are a hero!" insisted Big Jack.

"Not really," said Adam, with eyes red and moist. Clearing his throat, he continued, "I, um, I've listened to Micah's homesick stories for weeks now and knew it was bad. Just not *that* bad. He is always showing people pictures of his boy. I suppose something just broke in him when he saw the youngster."

"Well thank you, anyway. You kept a level head," said Maggie, still somewhat curious as to why Adam also appeared visibly touched. *Could he have a family in Germany as well?*

"Now we *must* have you over to the house for supper," insisted Big Jack.

"Papa, that won't happen," insisted Maggie, her son in her arms, his face bashfully buried in her chest.

"We'll see," said Big Jack.

"Okay, time to get back to work," said Jennaro as he approached the group. "Sorry to break up this little homecoming, folks, but I can get in trouble if this row of trees is not picked clean before 5:00. And now I'm a man short, so . . ."

"Does your commander track your work so thoroughly?" asked Maggie.

"It's not the commander I'm worried about, but the owner of this here orchard. She's one tough cookie," joked Jennaro.

Maggie and Big Jack smiled.

"That is true," added Big Jack, playing along. "You don't want to mess with her. She's liable to grab a gun and start shooting."

Both Maggie and the corporal looked at one another and smiled. Jennaro winked and said nothing about their secret.

"Hey, that's funny," added Adam. "Because just a few weeks ago *Frau* Maggie here took a gun and—" Jennaro cut him off.

"You can share that story another time, Klein. Let's move it."

Adam looked puzzled at first but then understood it would be best to keep quiet.

Maggie, Big Jack and Benny watched the Germans as they got back to work. They had six ladders set up beside six trees, and each prisoner had a canvas satchel slung across his shoulder to hold the apples. Once full, they would carry the bags to a large metal wagon parked on the side of the orchard, pull a string at the bottom, and all the apples would tumble out into the multi-layered bin. They would then re-tie the bottom string and fill the satchel again. It was slow, tedious work, and at this pace it would surely take many weeks to complete the job.

Chapter Eleven

Dinner Is Served

Over the course of the next few weeks, the Germans picked the south field while the Jamaicans harvested to the west, and as each day passed both groups inched their way closer to the Mueller farmhouse. Due to their abutting proximity, the G.I.s started to use the barnyard as their staging point. It provided both the Americans' and the POWs' access to the Mueller's well when a thirst called, and a *biffy* when nature called. Big Jack was giddy at the prospect of having the Germans so close, even if it meant he'd only see them in the mornings when they arrived and in the late afternoon when they returned to camp.

Because of the now familiar routine, and the familiarity between the guards, the POWs and the Americans became increasingly lenient with each passing day. The prospect of an escape or someone sabotaging any operations became extremely remote. Some G.I. centurions actually formed friendships with the POWs and began to see the war at face value: the collective fault of statesmen with a grudge. For both the American soldiers and the POWs, the school colors slowly began to fade, and each respected their roles as brothers-in-arms. A prevailing sense of honor and love of one's country kept things loose and friendly. Even Heinrich Richtor, who carried an almost constant chip on his shoulder, seemed to soften his fortified shell – although one had to look hard to see it.

By this time, Captain Lincoln had rejoined the group as the Officer of the Watch and since his return, he went out of his way to be exceptionally kind to Maggie. His fellow G.I.s and even some POWs would rib him about it constantly. "*What kind of soldier lets a civvie steal his rifle? Especially a woman?*" Others speculated that deep down he had a high school crush on Maggie. Whatever the reason, she used it to her advantage.

Things got to be so comfortable between the two sides, it became increasingly rare for the guards to even carry their rifles into the fields, often leaving them in the transport trucks or in the Jeep. On this particular day, Lincoln and Jennaro stood next to Maggie's barn, pumping a cool drink of water from her well when they spied a very large rabbit nibbling on some tall grass, roughly 50 feet away.

POW Gary Hofstädter stepped out of the outhouse after his morning constitutional, and as he walked back towards the orchard, Lincoln yelled to get his attention.

"Hey, hey you – stay where you are!" Like many of the Germans, he had a functional grasp of English, so when Lincoln told him to stop, he did so as if about to step on a land mine. The German immediately looked left and then right, shooting the Americans a puzzled look.

"What is it?" he whispered loudly to the two guards. They both pointed towards the rabbit, who continued eating roughly 20 feet in front of him. He cautiously stepped away from the bunny and stood next to the Americans with his eyes fixed on the hungry creature.

"What is the matter?" asked the German.

"You're name's Hofstädter, right?" asked Lincoln.

"Ja," said the confused German. "So what – are you afraid of a *Kaninchen?*" he asked in broken English.

Ignoring his question, Lincoln said, "Were you really a sniper?"

"*Ja,* that is true," he said with a puzzled look on his face.

"I hear you bragging all the time, about how good a shot you are."

"It's not bragging if you can do it, Captain," said Hofstädter.

"Well, if you're so good," added Jennaro, "do you think you could hit that rabbit from here?"

"From here? Are you joking?" he laughed. "I could even hit it from that clothesline over there," Hofstädter said, pointing to Maggie's hanging laundry of shirts, pants and bedsheets which danced in the summer breeze roughly 50 feet further away. "I could even shoot that rabbit using your gun."

"Oh, funny guy!" said Jennaro. "Even with a sniper's rifle that'd be a tough shot."

"Do you want to put a wager on it?" asked the German confidently.

Jennaro said, "Are you kidding? We can't do that. We're American Army—"

Lincoln cut off his fellow soldier. "Hold on, Corporal. I think we can bend the rules here a bit." Looking back at the POW he continued. "What do you suggest?"

"Well," pondered the German, stroking his chin, "he looks like he'd make quite a good meal. How about if I shoot him – clean – me and all my comrades get to have him for dinner."

"And if you miss . . . we get a week's worth of everyone's smokes," bargained Lincoln.

"That would be a deal!" said Hofstädter, shaking Lincoln's hand.

"But only if you shoot him clean. Otherwise there won't be much left to eat," added the captain.

"I am confident I can take his head off even from another hundred meters."

"Okay then, so run over to the truck and grab my rifle," said Lincoln.

The confused German couldn't believe his ears. "I'm sorry. What did you say?"

"It's okay. Go fetch my gun. It's in the transport over there. Front seat. Passenger side."

"You want me to get it, and carry it back here?" said Hofstädter as he pretended to hold the gun in his hands and moved his index finger to simulate the pulling of a trigger.

"*Ja*," said Jennaro mockingly. "Go ahead! The captain said it's okay. We'll keep an eye on the rabbit for you."

"Okay," he sung with a shrug. With that, the German trotted towards the large transport truck parked on the opposite side of the barnyard, next to the orchard.

The weapon lay right where they said it would be, resting on the front seat of the cab. As Hofstädter returned with the rifle in hand, another POW caught a glimpse of him with the ordnance, then sprinted back into the orchard to tell the others. In no time, they all ran to the barnyard to see what was happening.

Hofstädter approached the captain, but when coming face-to-face with the American guard, he suddenly clicked his heels three times, stood at attention and began to spin the rifle very fast, like a baton. He twirled the gun clockwise around his extended arm and then tossed it in the air, catching it with his left hand, then in one seamless motion, grabbed it by the barrel and swung it behind his neck. Then with his right hand, he caught the butt and wheeled it in front of him, dropping it to the ground and then kicking it upward with his right foot. The rifle spun in the air a full 360 degrees before the German grasped it with one hand and presented it to the Americans in a display of showmanship reserved for a military color guard. Lincoln looked at the POW with a small twinkle of worry in his eyes. *If this German's sharpshooting is as good as his drill team skills, the week's rations of cigarettes might have to wait.*

By this time, the other POWs had arrived from the orchard, and they erupted with laughter and applause.

"Impressive," said Jennaro to Lincoln.

"That doesn't mean he can shoot," snapped the captain, trying to hide his admiration. Turning his attention back to Hofstädter, he added, "Okay hot shot, do you know what today is? It's put-up or shut-up day. And I can't wait to get a week's worth of your smokes."

Hofstädter had a reputation as a joker at Camp Ramsey, so most did not know what to believe when he would spin a tale about his service in Italy. He came from a different company than the others, and always wore a coy expression on his face, which made his stories that much more suspicious. The two things most everyone heard about Gary Hofstädter: Number one, he claimed to be captured while sleeping in a hayloft outside of Benevento, after some British soldiers stepped into the barn to procure some eggs for breakfast. Number two, he claimed to be a decorated *Scharfschütze* (sniper) in Hitler's *Gebirgsjäger* (Mountain Riflemen) unit. No one ever questioned the first story. The second? Well, everyone was about to find out.

"Hey guys, watch Hofstädter give us a week's worth of cigarettes," announced Jennaro confidently to the curious POWs. "*Your* cigarettes!"

Some Germans were not amused. "What do you mean? He can't speak for us. I refuse to give up my smokes . . ."

Hofstädter was undaunted. "Do you want me to shoot that rabbit from here or from the hanging laundry?" he asked Lincoln.

"You said you could hit it from the washline, so hit it from the washline," Lincoln said handing him the rifle after checking the barrel and the clip. The German took the gun and walked to an open area where Maggie had strung up a spider web of clotheslines. Everyone followed with eager anticipation. The loitering complaints over the cigarettes faded away as the prospect of eating rabbit stew became more real.

Looking on from the kitchen window, Big Jack also watched the drama unfold. His curiosity got the best of him, so he stepped out from the back porch and approached the group.

"Guten Tag."

"Hello, Mr. Mueller," said Adam Klein. "It seems Hofstädter is making up tonight's menu."

"Huh? What menu?"

"See that large *Kaninchen* next to your barn? He just ordered it for dinner," said Adam with a chuckle. The other Germans began to laugh, too.

"Good Lord, is that an animal? From here it looks to be a large rock," said Big Jack impressed. "No one can hit that from here. But I do love rabbit stew, so I'll tell you what – if he hits it, I'll cook it."

"That's fine with me," said Lincoln. "But don't get the stove ready just yet, 'cause there's little chance of him nailing it." He then turned toward the German. "Any time you're ready, Soldier."

Hofstädter studied the American rifle and seemed impressed with its weight and balance. "It's not a sniper's rifle, but it will do." Sitting on the grass in the classic raised-leg shooting position, Hofstädter bent his left leg while the right calf lay on top of the left shoe. With his left hand wrapped around the raised knee, he steadied the weapon as he took aim. Just above his head, a large bedsheet flapped about, as if to distract his efforts. He didn't notice or care.

"Pardon me for asking, Corporal," Big Jack interrupted. "But there won't be much left of that rabbit if he hits it square. The only way to save it for dinner is to take its head off. No one is that good."

"Do you mind?" asked Hofstädter as he focused on his target.

"Are we making you nervous?" sang Jennaro with a smile and a laugh.

"No. Not nervous . . . just hungry," Hofstädter snipped, cutting the chatter around him.

The air felt thick, with the crowd of soldiers on pins and needles. Crows in the nearby oak tree tried their best to heckle the German sharpshooter, but he stayed steady and calm.

"You better hit it, Hofstädter," whispered one of the other POWs. "I want to keep my smokes."

"Come on, you can do it!" encouraged another.

Then all went quiet. Even the birds held their breath. The only sound anyone could hear was laundry rustling in the steady breeze.

"What are you waiting for?" pleaded a comrade who could hardly stand the pressure.

"Come on, do it!" said another.

Hofstädter remarked, "I . . . need . . . him . . . to . . . raise . . . his . . . head . . . so . . . that . . ."

BANG!

From a distance the group could see something flip into the air and then lay in a frozen clump.

"He got it!" shouted Adam.

"*Volltreffer!*" yelled another German.

"No way. That was dirt being kicked up," insisted Jennaro.

For a moment everyone stood frozen and quiet, shocked expressions locked on each other's faces, when all at once they screamed and sprinted towards the barn to see the result. Only Hofstädter and Big Jack stayed behind.

"You got it, didn't you?" asked Big Jack smiling.

"Yes."

"Fantastic!" said Big Jack, rubbing his hands together.

The German sniper broke off a tall blade of grass, stood up and squinted his eyes towards the barn.

"So why did you so easily risk giving up your cigarettes? You could have missed," asked Big Jack.

"Well, for one thing I knew I would not miss," said Hofstädter confidently. "And the other thing . . ." he paused momentarily, put the tall blade of grass in his teeth and squinted up at the sun. "I don't smoke."

Big Jack howled. "Well if that don't take the cake! I guess I'll go inside and get a pot ready. You're all going to eat well tonight! This will be a real treat. And I'll be honored to host you for dinner."

Next to the barn, a celebration ensued. Some Germans danced the polka with one another, spinning in circles, arm-in-arm. One of the POWs picked up the rabbit from its hind legs and held it high, shouting to Hofstädter.

"*Guten Appetit!*" (Dinner is served.)

Blood dripped from the headless cottontail. The rifle shot appeared clean, almost surgical. The German holding the rabbit walked towards Hofstädter and held it up over his tongue. Blood dripped into his mouth as he proclaimed, "All hail Hofstädter. Not so much of a storyteller after all!"

"Goddammit," Jennaro said leaning into Captain Lincoln. "I can't believe he did it."

Lincoln was not the least bit upset. "You know what? I'm glad."

"Huh?"

"Think about it . . . Now you and I can go into town for a drink while they stay here for dinner."

"Ooooh, so we both won?"

"We both won."

Lincoln recognized the inestimable importance for these *comrades* and with a wide smile on his face, he allowed the Germans to immerse themselves in the moment. The jubilation flowed like a country stream. It seemed like a lifetime ago they savored any sort of victory. In only a matter of months, the pride of Hitler's Army went from conquering North Africa with the *Desert Fox*, to being captured, dispatched across the Atlantic, then transported by rail to America's Midwest, and ultimately to become field hands on a Wisconsin farm. Few, if anyone, would excoriate their behavior. After all, they finally did something they never thought possible again – savor a triumph over America. Albeit a symbolic win, it revived a sense of dignity within the ranks.

Es lebe der deutsche Stolz. (Long live German pride.)

After another minute of celebratory glee, Lincoln finally called out. "Okay, fellas, settle down. Come on, relax for a sec."

The Germans got quiet, but could barely contain their excitement, feeling as if they were going to burst.

"That was easily the best display of sharpshooting I have ever seen. And because of it . . . we will be late going back to camp tonight. For a feast of rabbit stew will be yours, and your gracious yet humble volunteer chef – Big Jack Mueller!"

At this they all let out a blaring cheer. They surrounded Hofstädter, hoisted him onto their shoulders and carried him back to the apple orchard.

* * *

While visiting Oku in the fields, Maggie and Benny missed the drama of the morning. The Jamaicans were making good progress, and with each passing week they got closer and closer to the farmhouse. On this particular day, Maggie and her son arrived on Big Jack's tractor with snacks and a basket of refreshments. They enjoyed commiserating with the Jamaicans and Maggie felt compelled to keep an eye on things around her farm. Besides, she truly enjoyed her time with Oku.

After providing the crew with sandwiches and engaging in small talk, Maggie reached into her bag. "I almost forgot – I brought you and your team a gift," said Maggie. Then she opened a large brown paper bag and presented an apple pie, perfectly cut into six equal pieces.

"Lemonade . . . cookies . . . and now dis? We are lucky, Miss Maggie."

"You sure are."

Oku proceeded to hand out pieces to his team, and despite Maggie's efforts to remember napkins and forks, they all used their hands to eat.

"It's delicious," said Oku with a big bite in his mouth. "Did you make dis?"

"Ah-huh."

"I'm guessing da apples were picked by dose POWs?"

"Would it matter?"

"As long as I don't start speaking German after eating dis piece." Oku said with a chuckle.

Maggie smiled and turned her attention to the fields. "It appears you are making a lot of headway, Oku. I hope we can get our thresher repaired before your team finishes.

"Well, you can hardly separate the oats without a thresher. What is wrong wit it? Maybe I can fix dat."

"Several things, actually. It needs a new drive belt . . . the fly wheel has to be repaired . . . and the bottom panel keeps popping off . . . My husband Erik said he'd get to it before he left for the Army, but I should have known better."

"I can fix anyting, Miss Maggie. Let me look at it."

"Are you serious?

"Of course."

"I say there's no time like the present. It's in the barn as I speak. We can drive there right now. Your men seem to have things under control."

"Is dat okay? I mean, I heard da German prisoners are near da barnyard. I don't want to cause another problem."

"Oh, don't worry about them. I will make sure they stay away. I have some pull with the guards."

"Indeed, you do."

Maggie smiled. "I also have Benny here to keep them in line. No one will want to tangle with him."

"I'm strong, Oku. Look!" said Benny as he pulled up his shirt sleeve and made a muscle with his narrow right bicep, his favorite way to display bravado.

"I betta be careful, little man. You could harvest dese crops all by yourself and put me out of a job."

Benny giggled as the three of them climbed up onto Maggie's John Deere and she turned the key.

As they slowly drove down the white gravel path towards the barn, Maggie asked Oku about his family and what it's like to live in Jamaica.

"My wife and I have been to-gedda fifteen years. And we have a ten-year-old son named William."

"Do they also work the fields like you?"

"Yes, dey are not far from here actually, picking soybeans down da road."

He went on to tell her how traveling "the circuit" included the northern states in the summer and the southern states in winter.

"It can be a hard life sometimes, but William gets educated, usually in Florida or Georgia during da school months, and I try ta save enough money for my fishing boat. One day I will get dat boat and return to Jamaica for good."

She listened in admiration and they finally pulled into the barnyard. Oku could see the Germans as he stood high on the tractor beside Maggie. They climbed up and down the ladders with satchels around their shoulders, and it appeared they did not see him – or they gave no indication as such from so far away. While he watched, Maggie shut off the tractor and placed a hand on Oku's shoulder as a sign of solidarity. After she and Benny climbed down and walked into the barn, Oku took in a deep breath, jumped off the John Deere and followed behind.

Inside the barn, the large metal thresher stood before them like a tall monument. The color of an elephant and nearly twice as large, this sophisticated piece of machinery was almost always in need of repair. Thankfully, Big Jack knew how to turn the wrench on the behemoth, but at his age he could always use the help.

On both sides of the machine were two metal flywheels with a long, six-inch-wide leather drive belt lying in the dirt. A short conveyor belt which was used to load the dried oats – stalks and all – sat in the front. Riveted to one side was an embossed metal sign denoting the manufacturer: *BELLE CITY. RACINE, WISCONSIN.*

When working properly, the thresher made easy work of separating the grains from the stalks through a system of shakers, belts and a large fan. Driven by a twin flywheel on the tractor, the thresher would separate the dried oats from their stalks and they would then be discharged into a separate holding bin, usually parked beside the machine. In the rear, a large spout or "elephant's trunk," as Benny called it, discharged the remaining stalks that Big Jack used as livestock feed and barn bedding throughout the cold winter.

Normally this enormous piece of equipment stood on four metal wheels, but in his efforts to rehabilitate the monster, Erik raised it off the ground using a set of floor jacks, themselves standing on several pieces of plywood for added stability. While this allowed for complete access to the belly of the beast, the only ones who seemed to appreciate his efforts were the barn mice who found a cozy home in its inner-workings, along with several pigeons who used the gigantic apparatus as a tall perch.

"Now dat is one big sifter," said Oku, impressed. "I believe I may need some help with dis."

"I thought you could fix anything," Maggie said while playfully elbowing him in the ribs.

Slowly they walked around the thresher, studying it like a museum sculpture. As they got to the opposite side, they were startled to see four legs sticking out from underneath.

"Ah!" Maggie chirped, stepping backwards. "Who's under there? Are they dead?"

"It's only us," said a voice from below. With legs kicking and scooching their way out from beneath the machine, out popped Big Jack and, to Maggie's surprise, Adam Klein.

Upon seeing one another, both froze for a split second, then a smile formed on the corner of Maggie's mouth. *Easy girl. Don't be so obvious.* But Adam did not reciprocate. Or did he? Maggie thought she saw a twinge of a reaction to her presence. *Or is he just that cool? Is he happy to see me or not? It's hard to tell.*

Adam stood up first and then helped Big Jack to his feet.

"I asked Adam here to take a look at her and see if he had any ideas to fix the blower," said Big Jack. "He was a watchmaker, you know."

"No, no, to be clear – a watch *salesman*," said Adam.

"And I am a sucker!" said Oku angrily. "Miss Maggie, do I look like a sucker to you? Because every time you offer me a job, dese Germans want to take it!"

Oku's anger snapped Maggie out of the moment. "What? Um, sorry, no . . ."

Adam chimed in, "Please, please, I know we got off on a bad start several weeks ago, but this is definitely more than a one-man job. Perhaps you and I could work on it . . . together."

Oku stared at him, eyes boiling. "I don't need dis!"

As he turned to walk out of the barn, Maggie pleaded, "Oku, wait."

He stopped short of the barn door and slowly turned around, a scowl on his face.

Adam did not give up. "My name is Adam. Adam Klein." He took a few steps towards Oku and extended his hand, which the tall Jamaican refused to take. "Really, that small skirmish a few weeks back . . . let's put it behind us. It wasn't personal."

Oku studied the German and finally said, "You didn't seem like dat when you and your 'comrades' fought us on da side of da highway. You tried to take food from our mouths. Dat's how I see it."

"Surely you can't believe we had any say in the matter. We didn't know you were assigned the same field as us. And regarding the fight . . . it was more duty than anything else. But really, not personal."

Oku studied the German. Taking a deep breath, he seemed to read his mind. Was he really being sincere? Was he right? Maybe it really wasn't personal? After all, if Oku had a beef with any German in particular, it should be the tetchy Heinrich, not Adam. Oku let out a sigh and then extended his hand. "Okay fine, I will take dis leap of fate wit you. You have honest eyes and dat means a lot to me."

"Fantastic!" said Big Jack clapping loudly. "I just showed Adam what needs fixin' on this beast so, Oku, let's you and I get underneath and I'll show you what I showed Adam. You two will get her up and running in no time. I have a long list of other farmers in the co-op who want to use it after us."

While Big Jack climbed beneath the thresher with his new apprentice, Maggie and Adam stood beside one another. Finally, Adam turned to face her and shared an ear-to-ear smile. *There it is!*

"Your father is a good man," Adam said, getting the conversation going.

"Indeed he is. Did he show you what you need to do to fix the thresher?"

"Oh yeah. It was quite easy. Took maybe two minutes. The rest of the time we lay on our backs and he told me all about you."

"Oh-oh. Now you're making me nervous," Maggie said with a smile. "What did you learn? Hope it wasn't all bad."

"Oh, on the contrary," Adam said, rocking back and forth, trying to reminisce. "Let's see . . . I know all about how as a little girl you wanted a pony and instead he got you a goat."

"He said that?"

"Yeah, and how you walked at three months and began to talk at four! That's amazing."

"Oh come on. He said all of that?"

"No," said Adam, pausing momentarily before laughing. "I'm actually making it up. But I would guess that'd be true."

"You are the worst!" Maggie said, punching him in the arm.

"Oh come on. You did want a pony, right? I mean, every girl wants a white pony."

"Sure, that part you did get right. But none of the rest of it."

"Well, I'll figure you out one of these days. It'll be fun trying to put the puzzle pieces together. I guess I have my work cut out for me."

These two swans found themselves floating beside one another sharing a laugh while Benny looked up at them with a sense of bemusement.

"So tell me, Adam . . . what ever became of that friend of yours? You know, the one who took such a liking to Benny here?" asked Maggie, putting her arm around her son.

"Oh, Micah. It's unfortunate, but when we returned to camp that evening, he was gone. His cot was empty, clothes removed. I really did feel bad for him. And for you, little fella," Adam added, tapping Benny on the top of his red mane. Benny just smiled up at Adam admiringly.

"You talk funny," the youngster blurted out.

"Oh yeah? Well on my planet, we have bad teachers, so I blame them. What do you think about that?" said Adam unfazed.

Benny giggled. "You don't come from another planet."

"Oh, he's only teasing you, Benny," said his mother.

The boy giggled and shook his head.

"So, Adam, do you have any children of your own? Or are you married?" asked Maggie casually. She hardly believed the words even slipped out. *Please say no!*

"No, not me," he said half laughing, obviously not upset at her inquiry. "I'm on the road too much for that. Or I *was*. But I would like to settle down one day. Find a *Frau,* raise several children. That would be great. But this damn war . . ." his voice trailed off.

Maggie saw gradated pain on his face as he stared outside into the brightness of the barnyard. *Is there someone back home?* Or perhaps Adam's expression was the realization of dreams lost and the improbability that he was now a prisoner in a land he used to roam so freely. The shocking answer to that question would not reveal itself for several months.

As she studied his expression, she became aware of something she hadn't felt in a very long time – it was an attraction. A slight twinge deep in her solar plexus. That inescapable feeling of want and desire.

He caught her looking deep into his eyes, and she seemed embarrassed, as a child with their hands in a cookie jar. But she could not shake his gaze. She opened her mouth, as if about to say something, then she swallowed the unheard words, teasingly licked her lips, and rocked side to side with a wide smile.

"Sorry for getting so serious, *Frau* Wentworth. I shouldn't share such personal thoughts," said Adam, trying to keep the conversation going.

"Oh that's fine. I really don't mind," she said, half paying attention to what was being said. "And please, call me Maggie, okay?"

He smiled and felt good about the budding friendship. "You know, I really meant what I said to your friend before," said Adam pointing to Oku, whose legs now stuck out of the machine much the same way his did when he and Maggie entered the barn. "I really do not discriminate."

"That's good. But I have to warn you – I do."

Adam looked befuddled.

"I discriminate against people who are selfish, unkind to others and who pass blame when they should take responsibility for their actions."

Understanding her misdirected sarcasm, Adam smiled. "Oh, well, then I don't think you and I will get along too well. I'm all those things . . . and more."

Maggie cracked a crooked smile and said, "Why don't I believe you?"

"Give it a few days."

Each studied the other, and something stirred deep inside Adam, too. Of course he always felt an attraction to her, but this felt more substantial. Those cinnamon eyes, that warm, delicate smile . . . she made it difficult to avert his gaze.

With her feet planted firmly onto the floor of the barn, Maggie blossomed before him and it paralyzed her with both embarrassment and delight. She could tell her allure inspired him, and it felt delicious to think she could do this to a man so handsome. She sheepishly dropped her chin and raised her eyes, then brushed the hair from her face when Benny – who had been curiously watching the flirtations of two lonely hearts – broke the spell with a screech of glee.

"Mommy, the mail!"

Sure enough, off in the distance Mark McCabe's Harley-Davidson could be heard turning the bend.

"Come on, let's go! Let's go!"

Ugh, just when things were getting good. "I'm sorry, but it's kind of our daily routine," Maggie said to Adam almost in a whisper. "I'll be back in a bit. Big Jack will show you what you need to do with the thresher."

"Yeah, he already did, remember? When you walked in, we were underneath it."

"Oh yeah, tsk, I'm losing my head," she said walking backwards as Benny tugged at her arm. "Okay then . . ." she fumbled a little.

"Okay then," repeated Adam with a wide smile.

"Mommy, come on!" insisted Benny.

"I'm coming," she said walking quickly out of the barn. As she stepped into the sunlight, Maggie turned back one last time to look at Adam, his arms crossed, soaking her in. She shrugged her shoulders, as if to say, *I'm sorry to leave, but I have no choice,* then waved him off, and with a smile turned to run with Benny towards the road.

"I'm gonna beat you to the mailbox," said her son, disappearing down the long driveway with a good head start.

* * *

Later that afternoon, while Benny sat at the kitchen table solving puzzles in his *Children's Activities Magazine* and Big Jack prepared the rabbit feast, Maggie sat alone on the front porch swing and held a new envelope in her hands. As she breathed a heavy sigh, it dawned on her she hardly thought of Erik at all those past few weeks. In a strange way, this realization made her feel better about how she'd been coping. However, after thinking about the interaction with Adam earlier that afternoon, she felt ashamed, then acknowledged an underlying sense of guilt, followed by a wave of anger. Some directed at Adam, most of it towards herself.

What am I thinking? I am a married woman! Good Lord. I regress into a high school flirt around him. And why would he lead me on like that? Why would he tell me those stories of wanting to 'settle down one day with the right Frau' *and he wanted lots of children and . . .* she shook her head and let out a heavy sigh. "I have to be careful!" she whispered aloud. Then she opened Erik's letter.

28 August, 1944

Hi all.

Thought I'd take a free moment to play catch up. We've been busy training in the heavy armor division these days and have been doing a lot of tactical field work in tanks. These babies are really something. I like being the gunner and can shoot and reload faster than any of the other fellas in my outfit. Just in the nick of time, too, because guess what? We just found out we're shipping out next week! Rumor is the European theater, but no confirmations yet. Gonna arrive within a month, and then, who knows. I like being in the tanks because they provide the ultimate protection. And they offer the big gun support needed to win this war. I can't wait.

Not sure if I told you, but I'm gonna be part of the 3rd Armored Division, and we're made up of two armored regiments with 230 tanks and 16,000 men, plus some artillery units. Us "tankers," as we call ourselves, get extra portions in the mess, which is a nice benefit.

Okay, gotta run. I'll try to write again soon. Probably from bloody old England. Hopefully, without the "bloody" part. Hello to everyone!

E

Maggie put the letter in her lap and let the words twirl around in her head. Unlike his last note, this one actually sounded upbeat and cheerful – as upbeat as Erik could get, anyways. But something else was conspicuous by its absence – no mention of Benny and his many letters, no mention of Big Jack, and no mention of her. *He really is a son-of-a-bitch.*

As she thought about the assignment, it dawned on her that trekking around in a tank could not be more appropriate for Erik. He would be living in a hard shell . . . Protecting himself from the outside elements . . . He will find safe harbor inside while destroying everything else around him.

How appropriate, too, that such a message would arrive on this particular day. *Is God trying to tell me something? What are the odds?* Maggie actually smiled to herself and wondered why such a note would arrive on her and Erik's fifth anniversary.

* * *

That evening, Big Jack prepared the rabbit stew, along with potatoes and boiled sweet corn. He opened several bottles of homemade hard cider and even prepared a rhubarb pie for dessert. He loved to entertain – and to have guests who spoke fluent German made the night even more special.

While the POWs stuffed their bellies with a full day's worth of nourishment, Lincoln and Jennaro followed through on their plans to roll into Ramsey for dinner and enjoy libations of their own. After getting approval from the camp commander, the two American G.I.s were like parents dropping off their children at a babysitter's house. "We'll be back at 8:30 to pick them up." They trusted Big Jack and Maggie and saw it as a golden opportunity to get some R&R. A true win-win.

Maggie assisted in serving the meal, and if one didn't know better, it looked more like a holiday feast. Throughout dinner, laughter filled the room and stories were shared – most went right over Benny's head – but the youngster hung tough sitting with the group and laughing right along with them.

As the evening began, great respect and admiration were placed upon Big Jack and his family. The Germans felt the connection and they thanked him for the invitation to move indoors on this comfortable summer evening. Even Heinrich Richtor seemed to enjoy himself. Maggie, too, was shown great reverence – a true chore for men who hadn't been so near a woman for months, much less one as attractive. But once the hard cider began to pour, innuendo reared its ugly head and things soon took a turn for the worse.

At one point, Maggie asked Heinrich to pass a tray of sausages. As he handed it to her, she tugged at the platter. Resisting her pull, he said, "Do you really want these sausages? Mine is much better than any of these." A few POWs laughed. Sitting on the far side of the table, Big Jack could not hear the comment, but based on Maggie's disgusted expression he had a feeling it wasn't appropriate.

"What's that? What did he say?" asked Big Jack.

The table instantly got quiet. Henry Elam, a prisoner who sat next to Big Jack leaned over and shouted to the host, "Heinrich said the sausages were delicious." Leery, Big Jack looked at Maggie with one of those *Are you okay?* expressions. She forced a smile, putting her father at ease.

As it happened, her eyes also glanced over to Adam, and he, too, gave her the same protective stare. She pursed her lips and reacted with a simple nod. Adam smiled back, despite having heard the indignity.

Big Jack then refocused his attention and asked everyone which parts of Germany they came from, pointing to the man nearest him and then proceeding around the table in a counterclockwise direction.

While Big Jack engaged the Germans in his little quiz, Maggie stood up, "I'm going to get dessert. Who wants some?"

"Meeeee!" shouted Benny, raising his fork high over his head.

"Meeeee!" mocked Adam, who sat next to Benny. They both laughed.

As Maggie got up to walk to the kitchen, several prisoners turned their heads to watch her stroll out of the room. Adam saw this and slapped one of them across the head. "*Du Sau!*"

"Hey, what's the big deal?" asked the German with the wandering eyes.

Adam let it go and turned his attention back towards the Q & A session Maggie's father had so enthusiastically initiated.

After dinner, Big Jack invited everyone outside to the large front porch while Maggie stayed inside to clean up. The porch was spacious, with more than enough chairs for all of them to sit comfortably, but instead the six POWs took to the stairs and sat together in a tight cluster, as if about to take a family portrait. More cider. More stories. More laughter.

The sun began to tuck itself into the western sky and artfully painted the horizon with shades of orange, red and purple. It made the perfect backdrop as Big Jack and the POWs talked about old Germany.

When the last drop of cider clung to the lip of that empty bottle, Heinrich stood up and said he had to use "the biffy." As he stumbled down the porch steps, Adam watched suspiciously until his drunken silhouette disappeared around the side of the house and into the shadows. Hoping the shifty German wasn't up to any mischief, Adam soon heard the outhouse door slam shut in the shadows, and he breathed a sigh of relief.

Several minutes passed and Adam began to get uneasy. He didn't forget Heinrich's comments at dinner and especially did not appreciate the attention he placed on Maggie all evening.

"Is Richtor back yet?" asked Adam. "I really have to go." With that little lie, he stood up and trotted down the stairs.

"*Dummkopf!* Use a bush," said Otto Vickers.

"Unless that rabbit stew went right through you!" added Henry Elam. They all laughed. Ignoring their teasing, Adam also disappeared around the corner.

"Well, I guess that answers that," Otto said in a chuckle. "Hope you don't shit your pants."

When Adam got to the outhouse, he realized it was empty. Heinrich was gone. *Did he escape into the apple orchard? Maybe he's just smoking a cigarette? Perhaps he passed out.* This thought process was broken when he heard shattering glass off in the distance . . . it came from the rear of the house. The kitchen!

Adam sprinted as fast as he could to the back porch and through the kitchen window he saw Maggie wrestling with Heinrich. The POW had snuck in through the back door and was trying to force a kiss. Grabbing her blouse, Heinrich pulled her close, tearing her sleeve in the process. She resisted and let out a shriek as Heinrich wound back and slapped her hard across the face. Adam entered the kitchen like a lightning bolt. "Heinrich, let go of her!" he commanded and followed up with a hard punch across the back of his head.

His adversary stumbled from the blow, but still held her hands as if in a game of Roman Knuckles. Heinrich turned to face him, all while still struggling with Maggie. "Come on, Klein. Don't tell me . . . you wouldn't want to steal a kiss . . . from such a beauty? I've seen you make eyes at each other . . . for weeks."

"What . . . the hell . . . are you talking about?" said Maggie, struggling to free herself from his iron grip.

"Let go of her!" Adam insisted. While shorter and less muscular than the former SS officer, Adam was driven by adrenaline and incentive. He grabbed Heinrich's right arm and spun him around, so they faced one another. Now free, Maggie slapped Richtor hard across the face!

"Swine!" she snapped.

Letting Maggie go with his other arm, Heinrich aimed his daggers at Adam. He took a wide, drunken swing, which Adam easily avoided.

With Heinrich off balance, Adam charged at him, knocking them both into the kitchen sink. Heinrich's back bent painfully backwards, his head nearly breaking the window behind him. Adam then connected with a hard right hook to Heinrich's jaw. Heinrich tried to counter but fell into Adam, wrapping himself into a bear hug as the two adversaries spun around the kitchen in a clumsy dance. Then, seemingly out of nowhere, Benny walked in.

"Are you guys fighting?" he asked in a high-pitched squeak.

At the sight of the boy, they both separated and pretended all was well. "No, no . . . we're just, ah, playing around," said Adam, half out of breath.

"Right," said Heinrich. "This is us just having fun," he said while pushing Adam hard enough for him to nearly lose his balance.

Crashing into the table, Adam continued, "We will be going now."

They both sheepishly walked out of the kitchen, past Benny and through the interior of the house, towards the front door.

"What's the matter with you?" Adam snapped in a loud whisper as he tried to tuck in his shirt. "Big Jack invites us into his home and Maggie shows you nothing but charmed hospitality, and this is how you show your gratitude?"

"Shut the fuck up, you sympathizer. You make me sick," Heinrich hissed while rubbing his jaw. "You will pay for this, Klein. I swear, you will pay!"

When Adam and Heinrich returned to the front porch, the razzing began. "So there you two lovebirds are . . . We thought you were having a sword fight."

"Shut up," Heinrich popped.

Just then the headlights of the troop transport appeared from the highway. The large truck ground its gears as it drove up the long driveway.

"Looks like we gotta call it a night fellas," said Big Jack. Moans came from the porch and the Germans slowly stood up and stumbled into the barnyard to greet the truck, which came to a hard stop. A cloud of dust floated into the headlight beams, revealing soft, ghostly shapes.

Lincoln and Jennaro jumped out of the cab. "How was the rabbit stew? Sorry we missed it," said the captain.

Sarcastic replies followed. "Not too good . . . You guys didn't miss a thing . . . We should have eaten back at the camp . . ."

Lincoln eyed them suspiciously. "That good, huh?"

"So are all present and accounted for?" asked Jennaro.

"Yes sir!" Big Jack said.

"Where's Mrs. Wentworth?" asked Lincoln.

"Probably in the house cleaning up."

"Well, please tell her goodbye for us. We are late as it is, so we have to run."

"I'll do that," said Big Jack.

"Okay, you guys," said Jennaro to the POWs. "Stop messing around. Get into the back of the truck."

Inside the kitchen, Maggie stood at the sink with her hands in the soapy water, rewinding what had just happened. Being struck by Heinrich brought back memories – *bad* memories – and a twinge began to form deep inside her belly. Embarrassed and angry with herself, her eyes welled up, as the pain of the past begin to creep into her consciousness. Taking a deep, staggered breath she grit her teeth and pushed it down, refusing to let Heinrich cause her any more suffering. Refusing to let old scabs be ripped open.

Instead, Maggie focused on how the incident could have been worse, and how grateful she was that Adam came when he did. Maggie vowed if she got the chance to meet the camp commander again, she would tell him what happened with Heinrich, but she had to do it without bursting Big Jack's bubble. Standing there, she decided not to tell her father about the incident. He loved the German prisoners and she didn't want to poison his perception. Hopefully Heinrich could then be put to work on another farm or in a cannery. One thing was certain, she needed to be more careful around him.

"You okay?" came a voice from behind.

Shocked, Maggie spun around to see Adam filling the doorway. "Oh my gosh, there you go again, making me jump out of my skin."

"I'm sorry. It's just that the truck is here and I wanted to check up on you before we left." Adam then cocked his head sideways as if trying to read her thoughts. *Is she crying?*

Maggie reached for a hand towel and took in a slow, deep breath. "Yes, I'm fine. Thanks for asking. And thank you for coming in when you did. If it weren't for you . . ."

"Oh, no, don't be giving me any credit," he said taking a step closer. "I get the sense that Benny would have been able to beat Heinrich all by himself."

Maggie smiled. "Yeah, maybe. It's just that Heinrich, well, let's just say he reminded me of an old boyfriend."

"Your boyfriend was old? Hmmm, so you liked to date older men? I wouldn't have guessed."

Maggie snickered at the joke. "Oh, you know what I mean."

Adam liked the fact that he could make her smile.

Getting more serious, she continued. "What is it with you?"

"Not sure what you mean?"

"I don't know," she said, her eyes locked on his. "You seem to always be in the right place, at the right time. And I have to admit . . ." She paused momentarily, then couldn't help herself. "I feel comfortable . . . when you're around."

A hint of desire washed over him. He squinted and took several measured strides towards her. Saying nothing more, Adam reached out and placed the back of his hand gently on her cheek. It was warm and soft as he caressed her jawline. His soft touch felt exhilarating and she trembled slightly, tilted her head back and dropped the hand towel at her feet.

Adam then slid his hand to the back of her neck and gently pulled her close. Maggie reached a hand to the small of his back, feeling his strong, sturdy frame. Closing her eyes, she could feel his warm breath against her face. He was close. Very close. She parted her lips slightly, hoping to taste him and feel his mouth pressed against hers, but just as they were mere millimeters apart, Captain Lincoln's voice bellowed through the house, emanating from the front door.

"Goddammit, Klein! Where the hell are you? We're headed back to camp! Show yourself. Where are you, Soldier?"

The spell was broken, yet again.

MOVIETONE Title: ALLIES INTO EUROPE

(Newsreel Narrator): "The capture of Sicily! This was one of the obvious approaches to the fortress of Europe. And when news came of our landings on the toe of Italy at dawn on September the 3rd, the invasion was described by Army brass as "a continuance of our advance."

Another brief pause, and then it was over to Italy to join the Brits, who had established a bulkhead months earlier. That combination was already too much for the Italians. First the loss of their Empire, then the loss of hundreds of thousands of troops, the bombing of their cities, and now the assault on the mainland . . . Nobody was too surprised when Italy threw in the towel.

History may well view the defeat of Italy as the beginning of the end. Our thoughts and prayers are with our forces in the tasks that lie ahead . . . beyond Sicily, deep into Italy, and straight on into Europe."

Chapter Twelve

Reflections

As Maggie sat in the pew at St. Rita's church with Big Jack on her left and Benny on her right, Father Schmidt stood at the pulpit and spoke about the day's Gospel, a reading from the *Book of Mark*.

In the story, Jesus willingly agreed to break bread with a despised tax collector named Levi. For his troubles, Jesus was ostracized by many in the village, especially the Pharisees who seemed to find fault in everything he did during those times. Father Schmidt encouraged his congregation to learn from that story, to be more like Christ and less like those who reviled the tax collector. The message was clear: don't judge others too quickly, or too harshly.

As the priest droned on, his voice slowly faded away . . . Maggie's subconscious thoughts came more into the forefront.

She reflected on Heinrich and wondered if she should think differently of him for what he did at the party. *Why even ask such a question? He's trouble, and will likely cause more. Even Jesus would agree to steer clear of that heathen.*

She then wondered about Adam. It was obvious she had *feelings* for him, and the accompanying "unpure thoughts" made her feel ashamed. *Stop it! You're in church!*

To balance out the guilt, Maggie forced herself to think of better times – like when she and Erik first met at the 1937 Wisconsin State Fair, and how they became inseparable nearly every weekend thereafter. Despite the fact that he lived on his family's farm outside of Wausau, Erik would drive south the 150 miles whenever he could get away and take Maggie to square dances, picnics, on long walks in the moonlight.

After six months of courting, they talked of marriage and lofty dreams. The plan was simple: Erik and Maggie would have a modest wedding, then temporarily move in with Big Jack and Ivy until Erik could take control of his family farm up north. The soon-to-be newlyweds wanted to relocate as soon as possible, but sadly Erik's father, Jefferson Wentworth, was terminally ill, so they would have to wait until after his passing before they could raise their own crops and family.

To complicate matters, Erik's father never liked the plan. Jefferson was a traditionalist in every sense of the word, and he believed a man's largest asset should be passed down to the *eldest* son. That would be Peter Wentworth, Erik's older brother and only sibling. Luckily for Erik, Peter did not need the farm nor did he want it. He had a good job in Minneapolis and had married into Minnesota money several years earlier. That predicament, combined with his wife Betty's distain for "country living" forced Erik's older brother to offer up a secret plan. A blessing in disguise. Or so it seemed.

As an early wedding gift, Peter made Erik a promise . . . Without ever telling their father, Peter pledged to transfer ownership of the farm to Erik after Jefferson died. No muddled probate. No land lease. He would simply transfer the deed into Erik's name so it would be his, free and clear. So much for best laid plans.

Because Erik's father was going downhill fast, Erik and Maggie actually moved up their wedding date in order for him to bear witness to the nuptials. Some thought Jefferson would never live to see his son take his vows, but he showed a remarkable ability to outwit the

Grim Reaper, and hung on with Stage Four Tuberculosis for six months afterwards.

So, the newlyweds had little choice but to stay with Big Jack and Ivy longer than originally planned. Being a relative newcomer to the southern part of the state, Erik learned new ways of farming from Big Jack – classic skill sets that were common in Europe. Erik, in turn, taught Big Jack a trick or two he had learned from his more modern farming practices in northern Wisconsin.

In the meantime, Erik's older brother Peter and his wife Betty temporarily moved from Minneapolis, caring for Jefferson during his final few months. Maybe it was the time up north that changed Peter's mind about the property. Perhaps he decided he liked farming after all. Regardless of the reasons, his change of heart changed Erik's life, and it manifested itself with turbulent vivacity.

The old man wasn't in the ground for more than 48 hours when Erik and Peter locked horns over his *LAST WILL & TESTAMENT* in the law offices of Drifka, Fairbanks & Shaughnessy in downtown Wausau, Wisconsin.

Reading aloud from the Will, attorney Marc Fairbanks officially revealed what everyone already knew: the farm was to be left to Peter, while Erik got his father's timepiece – a gold pocket watch which hadn't worked for as long as Erik could remember. No one was surprised by the bequeathment. All Peter needed to do was transfer the deed and the farm would be Erik's. A mere technicality . . . a simple fix . . . the stroke of a pen. After all, the two brothers had a handshake deal.

But to his complete and utter surprise, Peter changed his mind. The reasons why are still a mystery, but the smart money was on Betty – at least that's who Erik blamed. Having been the *de facto* hospice nurse for Jefferson during those lasts several months of his life, Erik speculated that Betty deserved something for their concerted efforts. The feedings . . . the cleaning of bloody bedsheets . . . the possible exposure to tuberculosis . . . Regardless of the reason, Erik was out,

Peter was in, and there was no legal recourse for the younger brother. Cain and Abel seemed resurrected on that cold, painful day.

"We had a deal, you lying piece of shit!" Erik screamed to Peter at the law offices. "This wife of yours is a greedy bitch who doesn't even like farming."

In defense of Betty, Peter countered with a verbal assault of his own, cutting sharp and deep. "Oh look at my poor, little brother, with his sense of entitlement. Always looking for the easy way out. How about me? I've made something of myself. I became an accountant. But you . . . you've never done a thing in your life worthy of a tombstone etching." The meeting ended with both brothers coming to blows and having to be separated by all three partners of the law firm. From that day forward, the hatred went both ways.

Erik thought he would return to Ramsey with the deed to his own farm in one hand and a long list of dreams in the other. Instead, he came home with his tail between his legs and his identity lost.

Every day since, he became more bitter, more indignant, more depressed. While he went through all the motions of a farmer – prepping the fields, planting the oats, picking the apples, and maintaining all that came with it – Maggie could tell a hole began to burn deep into his soul. It was an incurable cancer that changed the man she once loved, and there was nothing she could do to stop its slow, malignant growth.

Sitting there in the church pew, she breathed a heavy sigh as she recalled Big Jack's common credo over the years: *"If you want to make God laugh, tell him what you're going to do."* Well, He must have had a good chuckle upon hearing their plans, she thought.

Deep down she knew living on Big Jack's farm was a proverbial win-win scenario, despite Erik's reluctance. Maggie did what she could to play the role of both a farmer's wife and a farmer's daughter. Ivy losing her battle with pneumonia two years earlier devastated Big Jack, and Maggie's support turned out to be immeasurable. She watched her father – normally a ballast for the family – teeter on the brink.

Without Maggie's unyielding support, God only knows what might have happened as Big Jack lost his one true love.

Her parents were a good-natured, coltish couple who loved one another beyond measure, so it was vitally important she do all she could to keep her father standing upright and strong. After Ivy's passing, Maggie often caught Big Jack lost in thought, eyes moist, his demeanor quiet, and she knew he was thinking of her. She often wondered what it would be like to feel that way about Erik.

Her husband's deep-seated anger about working the farm had only gotten worse with each passing day, going from a simmer to a rolling boil. In the process, his drinking had also gotten worse. He used liquor to douse the fire deep within. Unfortunately, the choice to numb his pain only magnified hers.

Chapter Thirteen

To The Rescue

A week or two had passed since the *Dinner with the Deutschs* – as Big Jack referred to it – and things settled into an easy pace on the Mueller farm. The harvest had been going so smoothly, American guards Lincoln, Jennaro and Thompson began to ease back on the rules like never before – sometimes dropping the POWs off in the morning, going to the nearby Mill Pond to fish and then returning later that morning for lunch. Despite the fact that both the Germans and the Jamaicans worked their way closer and closer to the barnyard, neither was near enough to provoke the other.

On this particularly hot September afternoon, everyone was present and accounted for. Oku and his team shocked the oats in the nearby field, while Private Thompson and Captain Lincoln stayed with the Germans in the orchard. Inside the farmhouse, Jennaro sat in the parlor with Big Jack and Maggie as they all went through some newly acquired paperwork. About the only person out of place was Adam, as he was asked to tend to Maggie's garden. The chore of the day was adding fresh manure to the soil, an assignment no other POW had any interest in doing. But Adam was fine with it.

As he exited the barn with a wheelbarrow full of compost, Benny bolted out of the front door of the farmhouse, unbuckling his trousers as he ran.

"It's time for poop!" the youngster announced as he sprinted towards the outhouse.

"Tell me about it," said Adam pointing to the wheelbarrow.

Adam laughed at his own joke as he began to shovel the manure into clumps, then carefully hoe it into Maggie's garden. As he worked to avoid damaging any of the roots, he thought about the boy and how close they'd become over the past several weeks. He enjoyed teaching Benny things he had learned over the years, and shared many stories about life in Germany before the war. Like most inquisitive four-year-olds, Benny had hundreds of questions. Everything from, "Why don't boy cows and girl cows get married?" and "Can people float on the clouds?" to "Are your mommy and daddy waiting for you when you go back home to Germany?"

Adam soon came to think about Benny as the son he'd always wanted. Caring, inquisitive, full of joy and a little mischievousness sprinkled in for good measure. That last quality he credited to Big Jack.

After a few minutes of tilling the manure, Adam's thoughts became interrupted by the slam of the outhouse door. With his back still turned away from the boy, Adam remarked, "That was fast. You all better now?"

There was no response.

Turning towards the boy, he repeated, "I said, do you feel bett—" To his shock, he saw a terrified Benny standing face-to-face with an immense and menacing German shepherd.

"Help . . ." the little boy squeaked in fear as the dangerous canine growled in deep, hellish tones.

"*Ach mein Gott!* Benny, don't move. Stand perfectly still!"

"I'm scared."

"Whatever you do, stay where you are!"

Showing its teeth, the stray canine circled the child and barked loudly, foam spraying this way and that. It appeared very sick, its hind legs trembling violently. Trying to draw attention to himself, Adam continued, "Here, *Schatzie*. Here, *Schatzie*. Come here, boy!"

The big dog took several steps towards Adam as he walked backwards, easing himself over to the nearby Army transport truck. Opening the driver's side door, Adam hoped and prayed he'd find one of the American's rifles which usually lay just inside the cab on the front seat.

Success!

The sickly creature barked loudly and moved between Benny and Adam. The boy stayed put, not wanting to attract more attention than needed. Just then, Maggie stepped onto the front porch.

"Hey, did I hear a dog barking? Where on earth did it – oh my God! Oh my God!" she screamed, arms shaking, legs kicking. "A wolf! A wolf. *HELP!!*"

At the same time she screamed, Benny saw an opportunity to make a break for it. But the dog saw him take his first few steps towards the porch, cutting him off, barking fiercely. The boy froze in place once again.

Next, Big Jack and Jennaro came out of the house.

"Hey, what's all the commotion?" Big Jack asked.

"There's a wolf about to attack Benny! Oh my God, do something, Papa! Get your gun!"

"That's not a wolf. It's a German shepherd," said Big Jack, taking in the drama laid out before them. "I heard there was one around these parts that had gone mad, but I never believed it."

"A mad dog? Oh my God!" said Maggie. "Do something!

"Son, do . . . not . . . move . . . a . . . muscle," yelled Big Jack methodically.

"My gun. I need my gun," insisted Jennaro.

"Adam has it," Maggie said pointing to him as he crept closer to the dog from the truck.

"Come on, *Schatzie* . . ." Adam continued, staring down the sick mongrel.

"Adam, what are you doing?" yelled Maggie, now shaking with fear.

"I'm trying to get him to focus on me," yelled Adam back to those on the porch as he inched closer.

Jennaro crept down the steps towards the boy, opposite Adam.

"Slowly, Corporal!" commanded Big Jack. "There's no telling what that dog may do."

Maggie yelled to Adam, "Just shoot him already!"

"I need a better angle," Adam shouted back. "Benny's in the way."

"Oh my God, I can't breathe."

Jennaro crept closer from one side and Adam on the other.

"Please tell me your gun is loaded, Corporal," yelled Maggie wishfully. Jennaro stopped dead in his tracks and a dull pain shot into his gut. He looked back at Maggie with a look of cold fear, the color flowing out of his face.

"Well is it?" she inquired a second time.

"Shit! I don't think so," said Jennaro.

"Have you lost your mind?" cried Maggie.

"Why would we ever use bullets?"

"Corporal, can you walk slowly towards Benny?" asked Adam ignoring their conversation. "I'm going to try to ease the dog towards me so I can get a clear shot."

"The gun is not loaded, Adam!" yelled Jennaro. "Did you hear me? The gun is *not* loaded."

Either it did not register or he was too preoccupied with the drama unfolding before him. "There's no time to waste. He could attack any second," insisted Adam.

"I'm gettin' my rifle," said Big Jack, and he bolted back into the house.

"Corporal, make some noise, try to distract him," said Adam. "And Benny, stay quiet. Do . . . not . . . move, okay?"

Benny only nodded his head.

"Hey, hey, over here! Over here!" yelled Adam to the dog. The German shepherd turned his head towards Adam again and snarled angrily. "Atta boy, come on . . ."

"Adam, what are you doing?" yelled Maggie. "The gun is not loaded. You'll never outrun him!"

"Here, boy!" Adam continued. But the large dog ignored him and focused again on the boy. With eyes red and hind legs quivering, the demonic creature leaned back like a tightly coiled spring, and in an instant lunged at Benny. The child let out a shriek, ducked slightly while raising his arms to shield his face. The dog struck with such force, Benny toppled backwards and landed hard into the dirt. Simultaneously, a shot rang out. With the dog now on top of him, Benny screamed, "Ahhhh! Get him off. Get him off!"

The frightened boy pushed at the dog with all his might, but it was too heavy. Benny then rolled onto his side and was able to push the sick animal away at arm's length. Upon seeing the blood on his arm and on his hands, he screamed, "He bit me! He bit me!"

When Adam reached Benny, he put his boot on the animal's throat, then picked up the boy with one arm and examined him closely.

"I don't want him to bite me. I don't want him to eat me," cried the child, clinging to Adam. Under his foot, the dog lay still, dead.

"Benny, it's okay. It's all over. You're fine," said Adam.

Just then, Maggie arrived and Benny ran to her. "Are you hurt? You're bleeding, oh my God, you're bleeding!"

"It's the dog's blood," said Adam.

Holding up the rear, Big Jack bolted out of the house and approached the group, his rifle in hand.

"Dear God, boy, there's blood on your shirt!"

"He's fine, Papa, it's from the dog. Adam shot it."

Peeking around from behind Maggie's skirt, Benny studied the dead animal, which had a steady stream of froth flowing from its mouth. He could also see blood oozing from an open wound in its side.

"But how did you . . . ?" asked Maggie to Adam, pointing to the gun.

"Yeah," said Jennaro. "It wasn't loaded."

Adam put a hand into his pants pocket and pulled out a carton of bullets. "Glove box."

"The glove box!" Jennaro said, smacking himself in the forehead. "Of course."

Maggie closed her eyes and let out a heavy sigh. "Oh thank God. You saved the day."

"I'll say," said Jennaro, taking the gun from Adam. "Nice shot."

"Well, it's been a while, but I did have some practice the past few years." Pausing for a moment he added, "No offense."

"None taken," said Jennaro with a smirk.

Maggie gave Adam a hug, as did Benny. Big Jack reached out his hand and also showered Adam with praise.

"Oh great," said Jennaro. "This is the *second time* you people used one of our guns. Who's going to use it next? Maybe you, Big Jack?"

"What are you talking about?" he asked.

"Um, nothing," said Jennaro, backpedaling.

"Yeah, nothing," repeated Maggie with a smile.

"You people never tell me anything," said Big Jack in disgust. "But the important thing is that this young man is okay."

"You were so brave," said Maggie to Benny.

"Yeah. He was a mean dog."

"He sure was. Let's get back in the house where it's safe," said Maggie, putting her arm around her son. "And we need to change your clothes."

"The next time I have to poop, I want to bring a gun."

They both laughed and walked towards the farmhouse.

"You boys wanna give me a hand burying this thing?" Big Jack asked.

* * *

Later that afternoon, Adam sat on a bale of hay inside the shady comfort of the barn, took a slow drink of water and wiped the sweat from his brow. It had been a full day full of drama and excitement.

Without notice, Maggie appeared in the doorway as a dark, shapely figure. "Can a lady interrupt a hard-working guardian angel?"

"Of course, come in."

She slowly sauntered towards him, hips swaying. The bright afternoon sunlight illuminated her thin cotton dress, the outlines of her legs silhouetted all the way to her upper thighs. Adam couldn't take his eyes off of this vision of beauty as she swanned closer, her body framed by the sunlight.

"I just wanted to say, I've been inside thinking about Benny . . . and that beast . . . and I wanted to officially thank you for saving his life."

"Hey, it's nothing any guy wouldn't have . . ."

Reaching down, she put a finger to his lips. Adam's eyes filled with confusion . . . and hope.

Maggie kneeled down to be face-to-face with him, cupped his face in her two hands, and quickly pulled him in. Her kiss was hungry and ambitious, tasting both lips at once, then his top, followed by the bottom. Adam was blindsided only momentarily, and quickly reciprocated, placing his hand on her waist. Just as he got to savor her essence, she pulled away, looked into his deep blue pools and smiled. "Thank you." Maggie then stood up and promenaded out of the barn without another word.

Sitting as frozen as Benny had been when face-to-face with the mad dog, Adam sat still . . . then shaking his head, a smile washed over him.

Chapter Fourteen

Fall

Over the next few weeks, life on the farm fell into a smooth, untroubled routine. Big Jack relived his glory days with the Germans by either visiting them in the apple orchard or by occasionally inviting them into the barnyard for lunch. Oku's new row of dried oats stood tall and patient as they awaited the next round with the thresher, which was repaired and working perfectly by now. Maggie immersed herself in the everyday chores of the farm, and did what she could to assist either team of migrants. However, since the run-in with Heinrich, she did whatever she could to steer clear of the tetchy prisoner.

Occasionally, Adam and Maggie would steal flirtatious glances towards one another, sometimes in the orchard, other times during a lunch in the barn, on Big Jack's wooden flatbed or even on the front porch steps. Whenever they were together, they passed the time with tales of life before the war, life after his capture, and all things in-between. The memory of that first kiss floated over them like the ghostly phosphorescence from a camera's flashbulb. Since that day, not a word was said about it, so while Adam and Maggie hitched up a team of horses to the multi-layered collection bin of apples, he decided to bring it up in his own special way.

"So I had the strangest dream the other night."

"Really?" said Maggie as she tugged on several leather straps on her horse's harness. "What was it about?

"Well, there was this guy who just shot a mad, rabid dog, saving a little boy from certain injury, and out of nowhere his mother showed her gratitude in the oddest fashion."

Maggie shifted slightly, almost suspiciously. "So what made it so strange? Did this mother from the dream write him a thank you letter? That would have been odd."

"No. No thank you letter."

"Did she bake him an apple pie? That would have been nice – not strange, but nice."

"Oh no. In the dream, the guy hated apples," said Adam, pointing to the hundreds in the bin before him. "I didn't tell you that part."

"Oh, well, then he must not have ever been to my orchard," Maggie said through a forced laugh. "I suppose if it were me . . . I would have given him something special."

Adam stopped what he was doing and looked right at her. "You know what? She did. That's exactly what happened. And I couldn't help but wonder what it meant."

Taking in a deep breath and getting more serious, Maggie seized the opportunity. "Well, perhaps the mother from your dream was a miserable woman before this knight in shining armor came into her life. And maybe, just maybe, he awoke something that she had forgotten was inside of her."

"I guess I never thought about that," said Adam.

Maggie started to shift her mood, from playful to somewhat chippy. Without knowing it, Adam opened a door to her conflicted thoughts and feelings. "Yeah, maybe you didn't think about that. And maybe you didn't think about how, later that night, that same woman lay in bed for hours, feeling guilty, because maybe she was married to someone who was off at war, and she had torn allegiances and didn't know what to do."

"Maggie, I'm sorry. All I meant to say was . . ."

"All you meant to say was why the hell did this woman kiss him while she was married and miserable, happy and sad, and she didn't have a clue where things were going. Yeah, you're right, it was a very odd dream indeed." Maggie stormed off, back to the farmhouse.

"Okay then," Adam said to himself. "Sorry for bringing it up."

* * *

By this time, everyone had heard the reports about the Allies' continued advances and their subsequent victories in Europe, and Adam knew things looked forlorn for his home country. Sometimes he would think about his house back in Germany, wondering if it was in ruins, and if he could return to the U.S. after the war. The American Midwest made him comfortable. He spoke the language and enjoyed its people.

After a few days of Maggie's obvious frustration, he decided to take things slow whenever around her. While most everyone knew he had feelings for her – his comrades would often razz him for it – he denied the charge with little fervor. "*She's married, for heaven's sake. I would never cross that line.*" They knew differently, of course. Everyone did.

At times he'd catch her looking at him wantonly while serving lemonade in the warm sun, slowly brushing her hair out of her face as she did so, only to look away when he would reciprocate with a smile. Maggie knew she was playing well outside the boundaries but couldn't help it. She loved being the object of someone's affection and relished the attention, but guilt worked its way into the mix every time she cherished a thought about Adam.

On this particular day, with the Germans deeper into the apple orchard, Big Jack and Oku hooked up the thresher to his tractor for another round. Adam, meanwhile, assisted with some simple repairs around the exterior of the farmhouse – odd jobs Erik never got around to doing prior to his enlistment.

Armed with some penny nails and a hammer, Adam had just finished replacing several loose shingles on the backside of the house. "It looks like you got the last one," Maggie said. "Hopefully it'll help make the place less drafty this winter."

"There's one more job I'd like to finish, if that's okay."

"What is it?"

"See that large branch there?" he said, pointing up to the second floor near the back of the farmhouse. "It's scraping against the side. When those November winds begin to blow, that branch will surely burrow a hole clean through the siding if it's not trimmed."

"My Lord, that's really high," said Maggie, a twinge of worry in her voice.

"I saw an extension ladder in the barn the other day. It should work."

"That old thing? It couldn't hold a small child, much less someone like you," said Maggie.

"Oh, I'll be fine," he said with a smile.

Maggie beamed back flirtatiously. *Guilt, leave me alone!*

With that, Adam went to scrounge around in the barn just as Oku and Big Jack exited, pulling the thresher behind them on the tractor.

"Where you two headed?" asked Adam.

"What's that?" said Big Jack.

"He wants ta know where we're going," translated Oku so Big Jack could understand.

"Off to the fields again," shouted Big Jack over the loud idling tractor engine. "You looking for something?"

"I am in need of your extension ladder. Is it sturdy?" yelled Adam.

Big Jack pointed deep into the barn. "You'll have to fish it out of the back. Probably under piles of rubbish. What ya need it for?"

"Your oak tree in the back," Adam said, pointing with his thumb over the shoulder. "It needs a trim."

"Be sure not ta fall," yelled Oku with a laugh as they pulled the tractor and thresher out of the barn, towards the oat fields.

Stepping inside the barn, Adam could still smell the residual exhaust from the tractor as it blended into an odorous cocktail of dusty earth, pigeon droppings, moist hay and manure. Working his way to the farthest corner, Adam's only light source was the midafternoon sun streaming in between the barn boards, which illuminated various pieces of retired farm equipment, including a dilapidated broadcast seeder, an old Sulky plow and the aforementioned extension ladder.

Several pigeons watched the action from the rafters as he muscled the ladder off the ground and out from under a wooden wagon wheel, a large spool of twine and several rusted ten-gallon milk containers. In a thick cloud of dust, Adam picked up the cumbersome ladder, centering his hands in the middle few rungs for balance, and walked it out of the barn and to the back of the house.

As he set it down flat on the ground, Adam studied it more closely in the sunlight. After a thorough inspection, he appeared satisfied by its construction, then balanced it upright, ready for action.

Pulling on the rope, the extension ladder sprouted towards the sky, as if waking from a long sleep. When it reached its full length, he gently rested it against the farmhouse, next to the oak branch. He then placed a foot on the bottom rung before realizing he forgot the handsaw in the barn. With a sigh, Adam returned to fetch it, and just as he stepped inside, he saw Heinrich Richtor approaching from the orchard. *What does* he *want?* They had spoken not a word to one another since the incident in the kitchen weeks earlier, and each seemed coolly suspicious of the other.

Once inside the barn, Adam found Big Jack's toolbox lying next to Missy the cow's flimsy wooden stall. Carrying it towards the door, Adam stopped short to watch Heinrich's next move. Certain Heinrich did not see him enter the barn, Adam tracked his nemesis through a knothole and watched with suspicion as he stopped in front of the outhouse, took a spent cigarette out of his mouth, then tossed it in the grass before stepping inside. Dry stalks of grass smoked a bit from the still-lit cigarette, but the flames quickly dissipated in the breeze. That was Adam's cue to leave.

Upon returning to the back of the house, Adam couldn't help but peek around the corner to keep an eye on his adversary. When the outdoor temperatures rose, the outhouse would get morbidly pungent, which is why most American guards and the POWs would opt to urinate or defecate in the fields to avoid the flies and the stench found in that outdoor latrine. But not Heinrich. *He probably enjoys it.*

Waiting patiently for him to leave, Adam amused himself with corruptible thoughts. Perhaps Heinrich fell asleep sitting on the throne as a brown spider found its way to his scrotum, giving him one of those flesh-eating bites. Better still, Adam imagined Heinrich falling into the hole and suffocating with his head stuck in four feet of shit soup. As quickly as those odious images popped into his head, the outhouse door popped open and his archenemy stepped into daylight.

Looking up to the sky, the cantankerous German adjusted his trousers, then stared at the farmhouse for a protracted amount of time. *Come on, do it! I dare you! Maggie's in the house right now. You could sneak in like you did the last time, and I will surely take you down for good!* But instead, Heinrich took out a fresh cigarette from his front shirt pocket, tapped it several times before he lit a match and headed back towards the orchard. Adam let out a long sigh and returned to the job at hand. Deep down, he didn't want any trouble.

Turning his attention to trimming the tree, Adam opened the toolbox, pulled out the small handsaw, and then took a small piece of rope, looped it through the handle and secured it to his belt. He then put his foot on the first rung and started to scale the summit.

The branch he needed to trim stood a good 40 feet off the ground, near the peak of the roof. As he stepped on the rungs, the handsaw swung back and forth like a pendulum, and occasionally its teeth would nip at the skin on his calf, through his trousers, causing tedious cuts. He decided to slow down his ascent to minimize the oscillation.

On the eighth step, roughly ten feet off the ground, Adam heard a loud cracking sound of the dry wood and he quickly climbed up to the next rung. *Remember that eighth step when you come back down!*

Upon reaching the roofline, Adam had a good angle on the thick limb. Several wasps flew around his head in protest of his unauthorized visit to their neighborhood of honeycombs, which hung precariously under the eaves of the farmhouse. Ignoring the insects, Adam proceeded to turn his body on the ladder a full 180 degrees, so his back faced the house, his heels resting on the rung and his toes pointing outward towards the horizon. He reached for the obtrusive branch and made four downward strokes with the blade to the topside of the limb so as to ensure a nice cutting notch. But before he proceeded with the next stroke, he paused to take in the resplendent view.

With the 200-year-old oak standing majestically before him, Adam watched two squirrels play a game of tag under the shaded protection of the tree's outstretched arms. Several leaves floated to the ground as the squirrels jumped from branch to branch with masterful agility and balance. Some of the oak leaves had begun their annual transformation from green to a light russet, and within a few months snow would eventually rest on its stately branches, the squirrels asleep in their cozy winter nests.

Looking to his right, Adam had an eastern view of the road that passed the Mueller farm and stretched far off into the distance. Just over the treetops, nearly a mile away, he could actually make out the flagpole of Camp Ramsey. He sighed, then turned his head to the left while taking in a western view where different farmhouses, barns and silos rose out of the earth for miles. He could see some of the Jamaicans working in the field closest to him, and a large cloud of dust being kicked up by Oku and Big Jack's tractor as they slowly pulled the thresher deep into the fields. The chalky trail they left behind looked like smoke from a large fire, rising into the sky at a 45-degree angle before dispersing into the soft fall breeze.

Pausing for a long, still moment, Adam took in a deep breath and thought of Oku, and felt good about their relationship. Over the past few weeks, the two had gotten to know one another quite well as they repaired the thresher and talked about their vastly different lives. Adam marveled at the Jamaican's work ethic and personally admired his positive attitude and that perpetual smile. Despite the fact that both men were thousands of miles from their homelands, it seemed Oku could find positives in virtually every situation. Having his wife and son with him certainly helped, Adam thought, but the big difference between them stood out: Oku's hometown would likely not be under a mountain of rubble when he returned.

Adam focused his attention back to the branch, carefully placing the saw blade back in the notch. He began to cut long, even strokes. *Back and forth. Back and forth . . .* He was almost halfway through the four-inch branch when, without warning, the ladder suddenly popped, and then made a loud splintering sound. Adam's heart stopped as he could feel it begin to slip beneath him.

As if moving in slow motion, he dropped the saw with his right hand and tightened his grip on the branch with his left – one split-second before the ladder folded backwards into the house and then crashed to the ground below him. Now dangling in midair by one arm, Adam's body swung to-and-fro like an African gibbon. The pendulating motion torqued his wrist painfully, but he refused to let go. With his mind desperate but too terrified to call for help, Adam tested the elasticity of his free arm as he tried to reach up and catch the branch as his body swung to the left, then to the right. If he could just get two hands on the mighty oak, perhaps he could move laterally towards the center of the tree, then work his way down. Hanging precariously with his left hand, he kicked the air like a bucking bronco as his body swung towards the tree. With a desperate stretch, his right hand found its grip on the branch – *Gotcha!*

Unfortunately, this oak tree was timeworn and apathetic to its unsolicited but well-meaning surgeon, its old wing was too compromised by his lacerations, and ultimately, Adam's body weight was too much of a strain. So, with a loud crack, the tree discharged the vagrant, and with a soft wave goodbye . . . Adam plunged downward.

From 40 feet above, his body did a half-somersault before he saw the ground rush at him – the same way one sees a punch coming, but too late to duck, too late to react. All Adam could do was close his eyes and wait for the impact. With a muffled thump, everything went black.

The resulting injuries were horrific. Adam's body landed hard on its left side, directly onto Big Jack's toolbox, his torso nearly folding sideways like a phone book. His head hit the ground with such force his skull fractured and blood poured steadily out from a deep gash on his forehead. His left femur snapped high, near the hip, his left arm broke just above the wrist and two ribs snapped like dry twigs.

Sorting laundry in her upstairs bedroom, Maggie heard the ladder skate against the entire length of the house and crash hard to the ground. It sounded as if God himself scraped His fingernails on a large chalkboard. In the next room, Benny screamed and ran to his mother.

"What was that?" the child inquired in a panic.

Maggie popped over to the window and could see the ladder – or what was left of it – lying on the ground. Beside the wooden pile of rubble lay a body. She sprang into action.

"We have to go!"

The boy did not hesitate. Both he and Maggie shot down the stairs together. As if the steps were on fire, they tapped each one in quick succession while propelling themselves downward. "Listen to me, Benny . . . Adam's hurt. So I need you to run . . . run to the field . . . and get Opa," Maggie said coolly, but serious. "Get Oku, too . . . Run, Benny. Run as fast as you can!"

They both bolted out the front door and down the porch steps, Benny darting to his right, towards the fields, and Maggie to her left, towards the back of the house.

Turning the corner, she saw Adam's body lying motionless, draped over the toolbox. "Oh my God!" she shrieked as she ran to the somnolent figure before her. Adam bled steadily from a large gash on his forehead. His arm was visibly broken, but thankfully the bones did not protrude from the skin. Although groaning softly, he was incoherent. Kneeling beside him, her adrenaline pumped, and instinctively she pulled the metal toolbox out from under him, all the while praying he would not die.

Adam's body was surprisingly heavy, like a burlap bag of potatoes. As she set the toolbox behind her and Adam settled on the flat grass, he suddenly let out a bloodcurdling scream. Maggie began to cry as she rolled him onto his back. Leaning over him, he coughed hard and a mouthful of blood splattered into her face, onto her neck and blouse. His body then began to tremble violently. She didn't know what to do.

"Adam, can you hear me? Oh my gosh, it's Maggie. I'm here. Please don't die."

Upon hearing her voice, the trembling stopped, but his teeth continued to chatter, like an idling engine. Still in shock, he wheezed but did not speak.

"Hang on. Help is coming."

She talked to him for what seemed like an eternity and tried her best to let him know she was there for him. Soon she could hear Oku and some of his men coming closer with panic in their voices. They seemed miles away, so Maggie jumped to her feet, yelling and waving for them to hurry to the back of the house.

"What happened?" asked Oku, half out of breath. "Oh my God! Is he det?"

"I don't know. I mean, he's breathing but not responding," answered Maggie through wet eyes. "Benny and I were in the house and heard the ladder fall. That's all I know. God, I cannot believe he used this old thing," she said looking at the crumpled mess of wood before her. "It's all my fault! I should have insisted he not use it."

"No!" said Oku sternly. "You cannot take da blame for dis. Deese tings happen. We have to move him very gently. He could have broken his neck. Do you have something flat – like a wooden board? And we need ice."

She mentioned a large, flat board leaning up against the chicken coop, which two of the Jamaican migrants ran to retrieve, while she darted inside to fetch the ice, which thankfully, Big Jack had picked up from the icehouse in Ramsey just a few days earlier.

"Adam, it is Oku," his friend said in desperation. "You fell off da ladder. But we are here now. Squeeze my hand if you can hear me. Go on, Adam, squeeze my hand."

Adam's body shook violently once again, but through the tremors Oku felt his hand tighten slightly.

"Dat is good, my friend. Try not to talk or move. We are going ta take care of you."

They slowly slid Adam onto the large, flat board, just as Maggie returned with a large piece of ice wrapped in a towel. "I have seen dis kind of injury before. He is in shock," said Oku. "We need to put da ice around his head and under his neck, then cover him with warm blankets. And please, someone get a cloth or sometin to stop dis bleeding on his head. Dat's a gusher."

Maggie was no expert but took Oku's advice, quickly embracing the role of a doctor's nurse. They slowly lifted his body and made delicate tracks towards the house.

As they neared the front porch, Big Jack arrived on the tractor with Benny. "That goddamn ladder! I knew I shouldn't have let him use it." Big Jack then instructed them to put Adam in his bedroom on the ground floor.

With two Jamaicans holding him on the board perpendicular to Big Jack's bed, Oku and Maggie carefully slid him over and onto the mattress. Again he let out a shriek of pain as his body settled into the mattress.

"We need someone to call Doc Marshall right away," said Maggie.

"You do it and I'll keep an eye on him," instructed Big Jack.

Upon hearing this, Adam spoke for the first time, with his eyes still closed. "No . . . Maggie . . . stay . . ." he said before coughing up more blood.

"Good God," said Big Jack upon seeing the bright red gore. "Benny, get some towels from the kitchen. Quickly." Like a good soldier, Benny darted out of the room. "Okay, Mags, you may be his only hope for survival. He wants you here, so keep talking to him. I'll call the doctor."

* * *

John Marshall, M.D. epitomized the classic country physician. As a member of the 1924 graduating class from the University of Wisconsin Medical Center, he had planned to become a surgeon in his hometown of Chicago, but early in his career he was presented with the opportunity to gain hands-on experience much faster in a smaller community hospital located in Oconomowoc, about 40 miles west of Milwaukee. He saw this one-year stint as a great opportunity to cut his teeth in the country, and then move on to bigger, better prospects. *If you want to make God laugh, tell him what you're going to do . . .*

During that time, the newly minted physician assisted local icon Dr. Charles Swanson with everything from farm accidents and illnesses to birthing babies and even a bear attack. He worked under Doc Swanson until the local physician unexpectedly drowned while fishing during a rare day off. Most in this farming community believed it to be a heart attack, but because his body wasn't found until several months later, others speculated it may have been murder. The locals loved to fabricate stories, especially in a community intrigued by a runaway pig or a toppled outhouse. Drama was rare in Dodge County. Embellishment was not.

While no one knew exactly what happened to the old physician, one thing was certain: his death forced John Marshall's hand, and he had to decide whether to stay or continue to chase his dream of doing surgeries back in the Windy City. That was 20 years ago.

When Big Jack called Doc Marshall's office, the physician had just finished with his last check-up of the day and had planned on enjoying a quiet evening at home with his wife.

"Hello," answered the doctor's nurse, Mary O'Donoghue.

"Mary, it's Jack Mueller. There's been a horrible accident!" he shouted into the receiver. "One of my Germans fell off a ladder and was knocked unconscious. He's banged up pretty bad. Is Doc Marshall around . . . ?"

* * *

When the doctor arrived a half hour later, he rushed into the bedroom, pushing his way past Big Jack, Benny, a handful of Jamaican migrants, and finally to Adam. The German appeared to be asleep on the bed while holding Maggie's hand.

"I got here as soon as I could. How is his condition?"

"It really hasn't changed since I called," said Big Jack. "He drifts in and out of consciousness, mumbles some things I don't understand, and won't let go of Maggie's hand."

While he examined his patient, he simultaneously inquired into the details of the injury: How far did he fall? Did he land on grass or dirt? Who found him? Did anyone see it happen? And exactly what position was his body in when discovered? He then spoke to Adam while palpating his ribs. "Adam, if you can hear me, squeeze Maggie's hand." Adam did not respond. "Are you in pain?" Again, Maggie shook her head no. "Can you move your feet?" Finally, a reaction. Adam's feet did move slightly. "That is a good sign," said the doctor to the group.

He then opened his medical bag and gave Adam a shot of morphine to ease his pain. He then proceeded to stitch up the gash in his head, all while asking whom it was that took such quick action and wrapped him with blankets and packed his neck in ice.

"It was Oku," said Maggie, pointing to the Jamaican on the far side of the bedroom.

"You did this?"

"Yes, I saw a similar injury in Georgia several years ago."

"Did that man live?" asked Doc Marshall.

Oku paused for a moment. "No, he did not."

"Well, I can say that the next 24 hours will be critical. If you didn't take such swift action, odds are pretty good he wouldn't be with us right now."

"Is there anything you can tell us?" asked Big Jack.

"As far as I can tell, he's got a broken right arm, and judging by the crepitis I heard with the stethoscope, his left hip is most definitely broken, probably from landing on that toolbox you spoke of. I suspect he may have broken a rib or two, but his lungs sound good, so I'm not concerned about a puncture."

"But he coughed up some blood, Doc," added a concerned Maggie. "What could have caused that?"

"There's a tremendous gash on his tongue. I believe that's where the blood came from. Of course, he could also have some internal damage to his spleen or whathaveyou. But all of these things are the least of my concerns right now. It's possible he also broke his back, and there's clearly head trauma, which could be even more problematic. Fatal even."

"He needs to get to a hospital" insisted Maggie. "We should move him straight away!"

"I'm sorry, Maggie, but we simply cannot risk it."

"What?" said Maggie half in shock. "That makes no sense."

"Listen, if his back is broken, the rutted out roads between here and the hospital could paralyze him. Heck, that driveway of yours could be the worst of them all."

"But what if he has a skull fracture? You said it yourself, he could die!" said Big Jack.

"That's true, but if he has a severe skull fracture, the hospital can't do any more for him than we can right here. To be honest, that is my biggest concern. Depending on the severity of the head injury, he may not make it through the night regardless of who watches over him. What we need to do is watch for any clear liquid coming from his nose or if he develops what we call *raccoon eyes* – which could signify blood leaking from the brain. He may also have an intracranial hemorrhage, which most certainly would be fatal. He's got quite a depression on his skull, but hopefully it's not that severe. Like I said, the next 24 hours will tell us a lot." Pausing for a second and looking him over head-to-toe, the doc added, "My goodness, this young man is really banged-up."

"Is there anything we can do?" asked Big Jack.

"I would begin by asking Maggie to stay with him. It sounds like he requested you before, and in my experience, just knowing you are in the care of a friend can make a world of difference to a patient. Hold his hand and talk to him every so often. As a rule, try to keep him comfortable. And I would also suggest . . . everybody pray."

"That we can do," said Big Jack.

"Okay, so the rest of you should probably leave the room while I set this arm."

Oku and the others stepped out onto the front porch. As the screen door closed behind them, they heard a yelp of pain come from the bedroom. They all looked at one another and winced.

At this time, Captain Lincoln and Corporal Jennaro stepped out of their Jeep and walked towards the porch, having just returned from a midday excursion of fishing in the nearby Mill Pond.

"Hey, what's going on? Did we miss another party?" joked the captain. Oku pulled them aside and told them about Adam's fall. They looked at each other petrified, the color rushing out of their faces. *This is going to be difficult to explain.*

"A car's coming," Benny shouted while pointing to the green sedan with a large white star on the door. Lincoln and Jennaro's stomachs jumped into their respective throats.

"This just went from bad to worse," Lincoln said to Jennaro, pulling him aside. "You need to sneak back into the orchard with Thompson, or we're both hitting the stockade."

"Roger that."

Thankfully, Jennaro circled back behind the barn unnoticed. Raymonds stepped out of the passenger side of the car and walked up to the front porch. "Hello, Big Jack," said the colonel while extending his hand. "I have been meaning to stop by and see you. I'm sorry it's taken so long."

"That's quite alright."

"I wish we could have met under different circumstances. I got a call at the camp that there was an accident with one of my prisoners?"

"That's right. He's in the bedroom. It's a sergeant. His name is Adam Klein. He was helping us cut a branch when he fell two stories onto the ground."

The commander turned towards Lincoln, who stood at attention and saluted.

"At ease."

The soldier let down his salute.

"Do you have any further details, Captain?" Raymonds inquired. "Did he fall out of a tree in the orchard?"

Lincoln tried to weave together a coherent story, but thankfully Big Jack chimed in and saved him. "If you don't mind Mark, I can shed some light on this. It wasn't a tree from the orchard but that large oak you see behind the house," Big Jack said pointing towards the roof. "Adam's been . . . er, *Sergeant Klein* has been helping us with some chores around here lately. He helped me repair the thresher . . . he's patched the roof on the barn . . . and one request was to trim a branch from that oak, which he was doing when he fell."

"Did you see him fall?"

"Nobody did. But my daughter Maggie came to his aid immediately."

"Can we go inside and see how he's doing?"

"Sure, but it's not looking good."

With that, Big Jack, the commander and Captain Lincoln walked back into the house through the front door.

"I hope it's alright we had him helping around here," added Big Jack as they stopped in the parlor.

"Well, technically these POWs are to be working on the farms, but *where* on the farm is not clearly defined. So as far as I'm concerned, I really don't care how they help, Big Jack, as long as their hours are logged. Which is true. Right, Captain?"

"Yes, sir," Lincoln said with false conviction.

"So I'm fine with it, Big Jack," said the colonel. "But what happened still makes little sense."

"Hopefully Klein can tell us. If he regains consciousness."

The commander then turned towards the captain. "Tell me, Lincoln, where are all the other POWs? I trust they are in good hands?"

"Yes, sir. Jennaro and Thompson are standing guard in the orchard," Lincoln said, pointing out the living room window toward the rows of apple trees.

Raymonds squinted his eyes as he bent over to spy the orchard. Sure enough, both guards were there watching over the Germans, who stood on ladders with canvas satchels wrapped around their shoulders.

"Okay then. So let's go see this injured POW."

Walking into the bedroom, the commander, Lincoln and Big Jack greeted Maggie and Doc Marshall as the physician wrapped Adam's arm in a cast.

"Hello, Doc," said the commander. "How have you been?"

"Hello, Mark, er, Colonel," said the doctor, showing his respect to the uniform, despite knowing Raymonds for years.

"And hello as well to you, Mrs. Wentworth . . ." Raymonds said nodding.

Maggie looked at him with wet eyes but said nothing. Holding Adam's hand, it struck the colonel as odd she would show such compassion for a man she hardly knew. Breaking the awkward silence, he then added, "So anyone know how he fell?"

"I'm told the ladder was fairly old," chimed in the doctor. "Maybe he could tell us in a day or two, but right now he needs a lot of rest. And I would highly recommend he stay for a while. A move to a hospital in Milwaukee or Waukesha could kill him."

"It's that serious?" inquired the commander.

"I'm concerned he may have severe head trauma and possibly a broken back. If we move him, we risk killing him. What I can say for certain is he's got a broken hip, and some other fractures . . . The bottom line is, he really needs to stay put for a while. A hospital couldn't do much more for him, to be honest."

"That's certainly not standard protocol, but I suppose I can make an exception," said the colonel, "provided it's alright with Big Jack here."

"It's not a problem with us. We'll get this kid back into ship-shape in no time," said Big Jack.

"Listen, I just want him to live through the night," added Doc Marshall impatiently. "Then we'll take it one day at a time."

"Sounds like a plan," said the commander.

"Big Jack, I'm going to need your help with this hip," said the doctor.

"Whatever you need. Are you going to pin it?"

"Heavens no. That's major surgery. Instead, I'm going to have to resort to a rather unconventional method. Something I've only read about, but I believe it'll work."

"Name it."

"I'm going to need a flat piece of wood, about 18 inches in length. We'll have to very carefully remove Mr. Klein's left shoe and nail it to the board. Once that's done, we'll gently slide his foot back into the shoe and nail the board to the bedframe at the perfect angle. I have to align the ankle, knee, thigh and hip. I'll also need some rope, pulleys and weights to maintain enough traction for the two broken bones to stay in place. This will ensure the bone heals in the right spot. Otherwise, he may never walk again."

"I probably have the right materials. I'll go fetch them right now."

"Before you do, I want you and Maggie to understand something. You, too, Colonel." Pausing to organize his thoughts, the doctor continued. "If Mr. Klein makes it through the night, or even through these next few days, it's very possible he'll need to stay on the farm, in this room, for quite some time."

"How long are we talking about? A week? Maybe two?" asked Raymonds.

"More like two or three *months*."

"Good heavens!" said the commander. "To heal a broken hip?"

"Holy smokes," remarked Big Jack.

"I know it sounds extreme, but the predicament is this: If I didn't think he had a skull fracture, or a broken back, we'd probably be able to move him right now. But once we decide to set that hip, well, we're committed. And this all presupposes he makes it through the night. If we get over that hurdle, then we need to focus on healing the rest of his body. And that doesn't even count the time it'll take him to get back on his feet and regain his strength. As you can see, he's got obstacles everywhere, and you need to know what we are up against."

Big Jack rubbed the back of his neck and looked up to the ceiling, as if he was doing arithmetic. "Let's see . . . that will take us to early February, give or take a few weeks. I suppose that'll be alright. To be honest, it gets awfully quiet around here in the winter months, so it'll be mighty nice to have a friendly houseguest. And I could sleep in Benny's room upstairs."

"What do you think, Colonel?" inquired the doctor.

"I can't say any POW has ever stayed on a farm for such an extended period of time . . . if ever! But if you say so, Doc, it'll be okay with me. Of course, I'll need your report to clear it with HQ."

"As I said, we're talking about a best-case scenario here," added the doctor, more serious. "If there is any brain swelling, or if he has excessive internal bleeding, he'll be lucky to see the sunrise."

Big Jack and Maggie looked at each other with viral concern.

"There's one last thing," added the doctor.

"How can this get any worse?" added the commander.

The doctor took a full breath of air. "With patients on bed rest this long, we have to be extremely careful about bedsores and, more problematic, pneumonia."

At the sound of the word, Big Jack turned white.

"I've seen my fair share of farming accidents over the years and have a good sense for how this situation may unfold. Most injuries I tend to are fractures, deep lacerations, occasionally a maiming from various machinery – but broken backs and head traumas – they warranted the most concern."

"How so?" asked the commander.

"Well, only a few homebound patients ever make it through the whole ninety days, and us healthcare professionals have little at our disposal to fight off infections. Now, I have read about clinical trials with a new drug called *penicillin*, but it was not yet available to the masses. Thankfully, there are new approaches to staving off an infection like pneumonia using treatment sessions to clear the lungs and minimizing exposure to germ carriers – namely well-intentioned visitors. And to be honest, I'm quite eager to try these new techniques with Mr. Klein."

Big Jack was lost in a memory. It dawned on him that on that bed, *his bed*, his beloved Ivy passed away from the very same condition. His mind flashed back to the night she took her last breath and the pain of that moment, the sheer grief of dreams ended, and it forced him to bite down hard and take a heavy breath through his teeth. Big Jack looked at the doctor and nodded his head confidently.

"That is an inconvenience Maggie and I will happily put up with."

"Okay, then I'll see what HQ says and keep you posted," said Raymonds.

"Very good," said the doctor.

"If there's anything I can do to help, Big Jack, you just tell me."

"I will, Colonel. Great to see you again."

"So, Lincoln, I'll be headed back to camp. We'll see you at dinner by 1800 hours?"

"Aye, aye, sir."

At that, the commander left the room.

This tragedy had suddenly taken on an entirely new meaning for Big Jack – because there was no way he would let another life be lost on that bed.

* * *

The good doctor decided to spend the night at the Mueller farmhouse and turned in around 11:00. He told Maggie to wake him if Adam showed any drastic changes – good or bad. After getting the doctor a pillow and a blanket, he slept on the davenport just outside Adam's bedroom while she spent the remaining hours putting cold compresses on Adam's forehead and talking to him at length – hoping the sound of her voice mattered.

As the night rolled on, Maggie sat beside him in an overstuffed blue chair with disproportionately padded arms. Big Jack had gotten it as a gift years earlier for helping a local baker repair his roof. Ivy detested that chair, thinking it looked like something out of a comic book, but on that night it served its purpose as a makeshift bed for Adam's very own Nightingale.

As the clocked mingled with midnight, the adrenaline of the day began to wear off, and Maggie curled up in the chair beside him and rested her head on the mattress next to Adam's chest. She noticed his body had a distinctively appealing essence; he smelled earthy, with hints of sandalwood and musk. She thought it odd and wondered if the bouquet wasn't from the plaster of his casted arm or the gauze bandage on his head? Too tired to wonder about it any longer, she decided to say a silent prayer and got as far as "Dear Lord . . ." before succumbing to the night.

* * *

As Maggie awoke with the sun, she sat up in the large chair and stretched her arms upwards. One hand worked its way down to her neck and she tried in vain to work out the stiffness in her shoulders and upper back. She then turned her attention to Adam – still on his back, still asleep, his breathing steady and slow, the jaw half open. *He's alive! Thank God!*

Her eyes then scanned the room for Doc Marshall who, she figured, must have still been asleep in the living room, just outside the door.

Doing her best to be quiet, Maggie stood up, cocked her head, and looked down on this man who, until the past several months, was a complete stranger to her and the entire Mueller family. But who was he, really? Was there more to that carefree flirt who could easily make her laugh one minute and save her son's life the next? Were there more layers to the man who always treated her with dignity and respect and possessed an infectious but corruptible smile? Maggie shook her head in awe at the circumstances and further wondered how it was he found his way to her.

With the soft morning sun sneaking in through the bedroom windows, Maggie leaned in to get a closer look at her patient, first admiring his long, perfectly-shaped Roman nose. His lips appeared full and pink, but very chapped. Upon closer inspection, she noticed a large piece of peeled skin on his lower lip, which hung on by a mere thread. She thought about picking it off, but resisted the temptation. Maggie also observed some dried, crusted blood in Adam's ear and down his neck, obviously from the deep gash in his head, now covered with a large bandage – a faint red stain seeping through to the surface. Whiskers on his cheek and chin revealed the start of a thick, stubbly beard.

Still very close to him, Maggie spied streaks of red hair blended into his sandy mane. *I never noticed that before.* She wondered if he wasn't part Irish. She liked it and believed it made him appear strong and masculine. Maggie continued to hover and could see his eyes moving quickly under closed lids, and she couldn't help but wonder if he was dreaming . . . perhaps about a lover he hadn't told her about? *Maybe he's dreaming about me.* She could only hope.

Without warning, Adam took in a strong, steady breath, filling his lungs with air. Risking embarrassment, she decided to get very close, her lips steadied just above his, and as he surrendered the inhalation with a soft, almost imperceptible hum – she took it in. Feeling his warm breath now in her own chest, she held it in, stood up beside him and closed her eyes. It was as intimate a moment as she'd ever had with Adam, and he wasn't even awake to experience it. Her heart was pounding hard in her chest and, feeling a little ashamed, she wondered if it superseded the wrongness of the act. Still holding his breath in her lungs, Maggie sat down in the chair and realized something she had increasingly been suspecting, but had until then had not let herself truly believe: She was falling for him.

As her bronchioles began to ache for fresh air, she exhaled and felt sad, hollow and guilty. *How could this ever work out between us? What if he dies here in the house? Who am I to wish for such forbidden fruit? I am married for goodness sake*! Maggie knew the war would eventually end and everything would fall back into its monotonous rhythm. So, too, would the pain return . . . The fear would return . . . Erik would return. At the thought of such a life, she couldn't help but bury her head in her hands, while an ache arose deep within the pit of her stomach.

Before she could wallow in too much self-pity, she heard a scratchy whisper. "Where . . . am . . . I?"

Maggie shook off the residual thoughts of what could never be, and jumped to attention, standing over him with a caring, compassionate stare. His eyes darted around the ceiling, then settled on her face as she came into focus. "Well, look who's here," he said softly and with the crack of a smile.

"Are you in any pain?" she asked with genuine concern.

"Yeah," he said softly, making her blush for reasons she didn't understand.

"Do you know where you are? And what happened?"

"Bits and pieces. I was on the ladder, but that's all I rememb—" He winced in pain. "Mmmph, why is my tongue so sore?"

"Yeah, you bit it hard when you landed."

"Landed?" he asked.

"That old ladder you were using broke in half! You fell . . . from the second floor. Nearly killed yourself!"

He paused, looking at her as if to ensure he wasn't dreaming, then looked at his arm. "I have a cast . . . my head aches . . . and I cannot move my leg?" He then tried momentarily to pull at it but felt a sharp pain and he winced once more. "Owww. What's going on? What's with all the ropes and pulleys?"

"Oh no, don't try to move it, please," Maggie insisted. "It's broken. Your hip is broken. Possibly your back, too."

"I don't understand," he said gratingly, the pain intensifying by the second.

Upon hearing the conversation, Doc Marshall entered the room. "I heard talking," he said putting on his wire-rimmed eyeglasses as he walked towards the bed. "Hello there. I'm Doctor John Marshall. You have survived a very serious fall, and I must insist you not move, no matter how uncomfortable you become."

"I hurt all over, Doctor."

"We will try our best to make you relaxed. My nurse is on her way over right now and can assist, along with Mrs. Wentworth here. In the meantime, I am going to give you some very specific instructions and ask you some questions to find out how much you remember about your injury."

Adam understood and nodded, trying to minimize his talking and ignore the pain. As the doctor detailed his injuries and explained the prognosis, Adam began to grasp the reality of the situation and became distressed. Normally playful, even in the most serious of times, Adam acquiesced and listened carefully, nodding his head, biting his lip and letting out several sighs throughout the doctor's assessment.

Maggie could tell he was sinking into a hole of sadness. Doc Marshall, on the other hand, became downright giddy.

"By golly, I can't tell you how good it is to see how alert and responsive you are, and for the most part you seem unaffected by the blow to your head." Looking into his eyes with an otoscope, the doctor continued, "Tell me, Adam, do you remember anything about the accident? Anything at all?"

Adam studied the strange doctor and looked a bit perplexed. "I remember wanting to cut a branch, but I don't recall doing it."

"Don't worry about that now. Odds are pretty good your short term memory will come back slowly. More importantly, we need to focus on getting you healthy. Are you in much pain?"

"I feel like I fell off a ladder," Adam said with a hint of his familiar sense of humor. "And . . . I'm very thirsty."

Maggie gave him a drink of water, which he took from a paper straw in a large glass.

"Why three months in bed?" Adam asked as he swallowed with a grimace, the pain still fresh from the cut in his mouth.

"It takes that long for a hip to heal," said the doctor. "And your back, too, if it's fractured. We have to keep you on bed rest and let your body repair itself. The broken back has yet to be confirmed, but I will know better in a few days as I try to examine your range of motion more thoroughly. The hip – that is indeed fractured. It feels to me like a clean break, so I have high hopes for a nice fusion of the two broken ends, but you must maintain the alignment by keeping your foot in the shoe, and along with some traction, it should heal just fine. Now, my nurse will have a handful of items which should help make your stay at Hotel Mueller more comfortable. She will have more medicine, painkillers and that all-important piece of medical equipment – the bedpan."

"I suppose it beats the outhouse," said Adam.

"Oh no, you won't be visiting there for quite some time."

Chapter Fifteen

The Great Escape

Life in the *"Zeltstadt,"* as the POWs called the densely populated cluster of outdoor tents, was much different from life inside the spacious ballroom. While *"Zelties"* spent most of their free time with the rest of the prison population – either in the open courtyard or inside the old dance hall – the nights in the canvas tents proved inconvenient and uncomfortable, especially when the weather became intolerable. Furthermore, these random housing assignments came to evoke certain socioeconomic stigma within the ranks. Some prisoners saw the tent city as Camp Ramsey's "ghetto," and many jokes were cracked about anyone who had to spend their nights there. The American guards often made threats to the inside prisoners who broke the rules. "*Knock it off! You want to be a* zeltie?"

It was ten minutes after the third whistle, which meant lights-out at Camp Ramsey. Ryan Steger and Oskar Orwig laid in their tent on a cool but comfortable Saturday night in late October, and neither one had any interest in sleeping.

"If this damn war never broke out, what would you be doing tonight?" asked Steger as he lay on his cot listening to the crickets chirp loudly from the thick woods a mere 30 feet beyond their tent – a mere 30 feet to *freedom*.

"Easy. I'd be in a *Gasthaus* with a lovely *Fräulein*," said Orwig, shifting his weight on the cot.

"Ahhh yes. Maybe someone like that beauty who lives in the green house? The one down the road?"

"Oh, yessss. Now she is gorgeous," said Orwig. "Did you know she waved at me last week – twice?"

"You are such a liar!" insisted Steger.

"No, I'm serious. I was sitting in the back of the truck, and as we came up to the stop sign – you know the one right by her house – well, twice she was there and twice she waved."

"How do you know she wasn't saying hello to someone else in the truck? Maybe one of the American guards?"

Orwig sat up in his cot and swung his legs over the edge with an overweight sigh, his outline barely visible in the darkness.

"Look at me," Orwig continued. "I am a man no woman can resist. I tell you, she waved at me, that is certain."

Perpetually perspiring, constantly hungry and a habitual bellyacher, Orwig's diet mirrored that of the other prisoners, yet he actually seemed to be *gaining* weight ever since his incarceration. Other POWs found his body odor so overwhelming, they often joked it could be used as a secret weapon in the war effort. No one struggled more with his foul condition than Steger, the only man who agreed to share his tent – partially out of magnanimity, but mostly out of adherence. The two men had been best friends since grammar school.

"You are so full of yourself," said Steger, the polar opposite of his tentmate. Tall and thin, Ryan Steger's feet dangled over the edge of his cot a good six inches every time he lay down. He had sunken eyes, boney cheeks and by all accounts was addicted to nicotine. For as much as Orwig liked to eat, Steger was equally ravenous about cigarettes. Nearly all his wages were used to buy smokes. Propping himself up by his elbows, the skinny German looked over at the dark silhouette of his friend. "Why would that *Fräulein* want to screw a fat guy like you? She probably knew *I* was in the truck with you."

"Will you two shut up!" came a voice from a neighboring tent. "We're trying to sleep over here."

"Go to hell!" shot back Orwig. "It's a Saturday night for Christ's sake. What are you doing – getting your beauty sleep?"

"Ach," was the only retort from the unseen tent next door, followed by a squeaky cot.

As Steger sat up and spun his long legs over the edge of his bed, both men faced one another. Only the sounds of the crickets and an occasional cough from a neighboring tent filled the night air.

Slowly, Orwig leaned in towards Steger and whispered, "I bet she has a sister."

"What? What are you talking about?" said Steger.

"That beauty in the green house. You want to find out? Let's go find her."

Scratching his head, Steger contemplated. "Are you serious? You want to find her? Now?"

"Why not? It's a Saturday night. The guards are playing cards, the dogs are with them, probably asleep. I bet we could sneak out of here with no problem and be back before morning."

"You don't even know which farmhouse she lives in, or how far away it is."

"*Dumkopf*, you just said it yourself – it's the one we pass every day."

"Well, I don't know where it is from here *exactly*."

"But I do."

"You're crazy."

"Oh come on. What's the worst thing that could happen if we got caught? We're already in the *Zeltstadt*. Maybe they tell us we can't work in the cannery for a week. Is that even a punishment?"

"Or maybe they make us work *two* shifts," said Steger. "And what if the dogs are awake, huh? The guards just need to unclip their leashes and they'd tear us to shreds."

"They won't get us if we're quiet. Besides, the dogs are asleep. I've been paying attention these past few weeks, and they are nothing without their masters."

"So?"

"So, their masters are all playing *Schafkopfen* (Sheepshead) in the main building. The dogs will be with them or in the kennels. Besides, our tent is farthest away. Did you ever notice that? We're on the end! They won't see us or hear us, or smell us . . . I promise you."

"Well, they'll smell you; that's for sure."

"Oh, funny guy," Orwig said sarcastically.

Taking a deep breath, Steger's silence was just enough for Orwig to know he was entertaining the thought.

"Tell me, Ryan . . . when is the last time you kissed a woman? When is the last time you had a big hard-on that only a tall blonde with big tits could satisfy?"

"Would you shut up! God, you're crazy," insisted his friend. He paused for a moment, then whistled in a deep sigh. "Okay, so yes, I hate being here on a Saturday night, or on *any* night for that matter. But to escape . . . ?" The wheels were turning. "Are you sure you know where she lives?"

"Positive!" said Orwig. "It's maybe a kilometer down the road from here. We'd be idiots to get lost."

"She really waved at you?"

"I don't know," admitted Orwig. "Maybe you were right. Maybe it was *you* she waved to!"

"And if the guards catch us outside of our tents, we're dead!"

"Oh come on – we'll tell them we had to take a piss."

"But we have a thunder bucket in our tent. We're supposed to use that."

"We'll tell them it is full . . . full of your shit."

Steger sat quietly, still thinking.

"Come on, we have to at least try," continued Orwig. "I'll give you all my smokes for the next two days!"

With a big sigh, Steger tapped his teeth together mulling things over, then made a counteroffer. "All your smokes for *two weeks*."

"One week."

Steger rubbed the back of his neck and took in another deep breath. "Okay! Let's do it."

"That's my boy," said Orwig, slapping his tentmate on the knee. "This will be so easy you won't believe it. I've been planning it for weeks."

Slowly untying the cloth flaps to their canvas tent, the two men quietly slithered out into the shadows.

"I can't believe we're doing this," said Steger with the excitement of a little boy.

"Shhh!" chastised Orwig. "Keep it down."

A warm half-moon provided them enough luminescence to see the flimsy snow fences directly behind their tent, but it was not so bright as to call attention to themselves from afar. When they arrived at the four-foot tall wooden blockades, Orwig pushed down the fence flat with his large boot and Steger simply stepped across the wooden pickets. Once across, Steger held down the second flattened fence for his friend, and freedom beckoned.

With a few quiet strides they were soon in the tree line and disappeared into the darkness of the woods. They kept looking back at the lights of the camp as they went and couldn't believe how easy it was to simply walk away. At any moment they expected to hear shouting and whistles blowing, and spotlights scanning into the trees and vicious canines hot on their trail . . . but Camp Ramsey slept easy. When they reached a small clearing, they stopped and Orwig whispered to Steger, "I think the road is this way. Follow me."

Not saying a word, Steger followed close behind. From above, an owl announced their presence to the other nocturnal creatures while they trudged through the thicket and across a shallow creek. After five more minutes, they stepped out into an opening and before them stood the county highway. A car raced towards them from a distance, its headlights like two eyes of a monster.

"Get down! Quick, behind that tree!" said Orwig. They ducked low behind a fallen maple as the car shot past, oblivious to their presence. As the taillights faded into the night, they stepped out and stood on the road.

"We need a marker," said Orwig.

"A what?"

"A marker. You know, something to mark the spot we came out of the woods. That way we will know where to enter once we return."

"Good idea. Here, let's roll this tree trunk next to the road. We can remember that."

Together they marked their spot and proceeded down the highway. It took about a mile of walking before Steger started to question his friend. "This doesn't look familiar."

"Relax. It's just up here. I recognized that pond we walked past a few minutes ago."

"That wasn't a pond, it was standing water in a barnyard."

Orwig did not reply. Privately he, too, began to question if they were on the right road, yet they trudged along.

"I'm telling you, that cute farm girl is going to have to wait for another time," said Steger.

"Would you shut up! Just shut the fuck up! Her house is up here. I know it is," insisted Orwig.

Steger kept quiet for a few more minutes, smoking a cigarette as they ambled past two more farmhouses. As they approached a third, he stopped in the middle of the road. "Okay, this is crazy. I think we should go back."

Ignoring him, Orwig kept walking and took a deep breath, secretly hoping to find anything that looked familiar.

"This is a waste of time," Steger shouted while trotting to catch up to his friend. "Why did I let you talk me into leaving? We risked a mauling from the dogs. Risked being shot by the guards. Risked . . ."

Orwig couldn't take it any longer. "Shut up already! Shut up! Shut up! *Shut up!* You are driving me crazy! You sound like a goddamned woman!"

"Well, you are a *dumkopf* who is driving me crazy with this wild goose chase," countered Steger.

Orwig pushed his friend. "You called me a *dumkopf.* Take that back!"

"Fuck you."

"I said take it back!" Orwig pushed again.

"Go to hell!" Steger said, his cigarette popping from his mouth and hitting his roommate's forehead before landing on the ground.

Pausing momentarily, they came at each other on the side of the road, grabbing hold by the shoulders. They stood like two wrestling bears trying to get the other on the ground. Steger hooked his foot behind Orwig's and leaned into him hard. They both fell into the ditch, with Orwig landing face-down and Steger landing on top. Using his leverage, he then pushed his friend's head into the dirt. "You asshole! Why did I listen to you?"

"I wouldn't have asked you if I thought you were going to be such a crybaby!" said Orwig while spitting dirt and grass out of his mouth.

Straddling his friend, Steger grabbed Orwig's shoulder, turned him over and readied a punch. But before he could take the swing, Orwig backhanded him hard across the head, knocking him over and off his chest. "Ahhh!" yelped Steger as he tumbled off and fell deeper into the ditch.

With Steger dazed from the blow, Orwig stood up and assumed the fisticuffs position, arms at the ready, fists clenched. "Get up, you stupid *Kraut*. Come on! I'm going to teach you a lesson."

"What is that?" Steger said as he tried to stand, still a bit dizzy from the punch.

"I said I'm going to teach you a lesson. So get up."

"No, I mean what's that ringing sound?" Steger said, now on all fours. "Do you hear it?"

"Probably the sound of me cleaning your clock."

Ignoring his friend and less interested in the ruckus, Steger got to his feet and walked back to the road in a wobbly upright stance. Something off in the distance held his attention.

"Listen. Do you hear it?"

"What are you talking about?" said Orwig, adrenaline pumping. "There's nothing – " then a soft breeze blew the harmony to his ears, and it came from nearby. "Hey, hey you're right," he said, pointing in the direction they were headed.

"It's polka music!" said Steger, getting his bearings and forgetting about their schoolyard tussle.

Orwig changed his demeanor as well, from anger to anticipation. "Oh my God! Let's check it out!"

They fast-walked farther down the road, brushing off their clothes and trying to smooth down their hair as they went.

"Do you think it's a party at the green house? I'd love to see that *Fräulein.*"

"I don't know, but the fact that they're playing polka music means they are most likely German-friendly," said Orwig excitedly.

As the two came around a bend, they saw a tall barn near the side of the road, light illuminating from the large open door and through vertical barnboard slats, giving the structure a painted pinstripe look. At least 30 cars were parked in the barnyard or on the driveway, and some even spilled out along the shoulder of the road. Loud laughter could also be heard mixed in with the music as they witnessed a couple exit the farmhouse and walk towards the barn carrying what looked like trays of food and bottles of wine. Just then, another man staggered out of the barn door, struggling to unzip his pants as he walked. He stopped next to a tractor and urinated on the large back tire. As Orwig and Steger came closer up the driveway, they could better see inside and noticed people dancing. They were right. A live band played inside, and as the song came to an end, enthusiastic cheers and loud applause followed.

Someone from the band could be heard speaking into a microphone, *"Wir machen fünfzehn Minuten Pause und werden danach wieterspielen."* (We're going to rest for 15 minutes and will be back to play again.)

"Oskar, it's a German party."

"More than that," said Orwig. "Look!"

Inside the barn, they saw a bride in a white dress walk past the wide doorway, her new husband in tow as she pulled him behind her.

"I love weddings!" said Orwig.

"We aren't dressed for such an occasion."

"But we must figure out a way to get inside. I'm starving."

"You're always starving . . . for food. Me? I'm starving for love – and weddings are great places to meet *Fraus*."

"How do I look?" asked Orwig.

"You are a mess. Here, fix your hair," Steger added while grooming his friend. "How about me? Is there dirt on my face?"

Orwig licked his fingers and wiped a smudge of dirt from Steger's forehead. "There you go. Very handsome."

"What are we going to say? I mean, look at our clothes, they have *PW* printed on them. There's no way to lie about who we are."

"Hey, you've heard the many stories of how welcoming these German farmers have been since we arrived, right? Hofstädter is always talking about Klein and how he's staying with that woman and her father."

"That is true."

"Hopefully we will be just as welcome, *ja?*"

"You're right. What's the worst that could happen?"

"We get in trouble. So what. Think of it as a free ride back to camp. You can tell your grandkids about this adventure one day."

Steger nodded his head in agreement.

The two men tucked in their shirts, smiled at one another, took a deep breath and proceeded towards the expansive open door.

As they got closer, two members of the band exited, looked at the two prisoners and smiled. *"Hallo."*

"Hallo," said the two wedding crashers nervously.

The two musicians kept walking, finishing their conversation about a cute farm girl in a yellow dress they had seen dancing moments earlier. Orwig and Steger smiled at one another, raised their eyebrows and proceeded into the barn.

The interior was clean and organized, with strands of lights crisscrossing above 20 round tables – each dressed in bright white linens. The expansive space smelled of perspiration and beer, the air thick with sawdust. A dance floor stood near the entrance, and a lonely concertina, a stand-up bass and simple drum kit waited patiently in the corner. To the right, Orwig found what he was looking for: a long table filled with strudels, cheesecake, fruit pudding and many different varieties of cookies.

"I'm getting me some of that!" said Orwig.

"And I'm getting me some of *that*," said Steger, only he pointed to a table next to the desserts that held bottles of wine and a wooden keg of beer.

As both men went to satisfy their cravings, the chatter among the guests slowly diminished, morphing into hushed whispers. Not paying much attention to the room, and having first made their way to the desserts, then to the drinks, Orwig and Steger slowly turned to face the skeptical assembly. As they stood with two foamy beers in their hands, chewing pastries in their mouths, all eyes settled upon them. A man in back of the barn began to shout as he weaved through the tables.

"Do we know you? You two are not invited guests," his loud voice boomed in German.

Squat and built like a cinder block with short legs, a thick mustache and mutton chop sideburns, the father of the bride made his way to the front to confront the two strangers.

Terrified, Steger looked down at his shoes, wondering how to escape. Orwig, however, smiled at the father, the bride, the groom, and to everyone else in the barn. With a speech that would make a seasoned politician envious, he replied to the father of the bride in an equally loud and commanding voice, also in German.

"Allow me to introduce ourselves," he said, swallowing a Danish and pushing it down with a swig of beer. "My name is Oskar Orwig and this is my dear friend Ryan Steger. We both live in the camp they call Ramsey just down the road from here. We are but temporary visitors to Wisconsin – but our true home, the place we love and miss each and every day is Stuttgart. We both grew up there, we have been the best of friends since *kindergarten*, and prisoners of war for nearly a year. But tonight, we are escapees. It is true. We have escaped from the German prison down the road – but only for tonight – and we are honored to be here at your wonderful party to celebrate love and family and togetherness. Not an hour ago we were in the camp, sharing our tent, when we heard this joyous music and decided we simply had to find out what all the merriment was about. It is with your blessing and shared love of *Deutschland* that we ask for your hospitality."

The tone of the room shifted from suspicion to impressed approval. Several people clapped their hands and many heads nodded up and down as an impressed crowd shifted its eyes to the bride's father, waiting for his reaction. As he staggered towards the two prisoners he struggled with what to say. Before he could ask a question, Orwig held his glass high, and elbowed Steger to do the same. "To the father of the bride," said Oskar.

"And to the wedding couple," added Steger, trying to add to Orwig's great salutation.

The father of the bride, now standing in front of them, studied the two strangers. "You say you are both from *Stuttgart?*"

They both nodded.

"Well, then I have one more question. And this is for my lovely daughter, Mary," the father announced, turning to face her as she stood in the middle of the barn next to a table of relatives. "My love, it is with great respect that I ask, on this, your wedding night – why these two *starke Männer* were not on the guest list?"

The bride simply shouted back to her father with welcoming enthusiasm and a wide smile, "It's because we didn't have the exact address of the POW camp."

The entire barn burst out in laughter.

"There you have it!" said the father with a loud clap of his hands. "It is with our apologies we did not send an invitation. Welcome! Eat, drink, and be merry." The intoxicated father picked up a beer and held it high over his head. "Prosit," he added loudly and presented his beer to Orwig and Steger.

"Prosit," they sheepishly replied.

"Prosit!" yelled the nearly eighty people in the barn, also raising their glasses. With a loud cheer, everyone in the room laughed and toasted the mocked drama. Many stood up from their tables and surrounded the POWs and wanted to learn more about their histories.

But not all in the barn were happy to see the escaped Germans. A table of eight stood from the back of the room, then made their way to the door. Obviously disgusted that two cogs of Hitler's war machine appeared so welcome – and with such open arms – they used expressions like, "Disgusting. Terrible. I want no part in this!" as they departed.

Oblivious to the naysayers, Orwig and Steger smiled ear-to-ear and held up their glasses to the entire room and drank their full mugs of beer in two gulps.

"Hey, hey!" said the farmer father with approval. "Let's get you boys another. My name is Josef Schmich. We have much to discuss."

* * *

Their time at the wedding flew by quickly. 1:00 in the morning snuck up on them and the crowd began to thin out. Both Orwig and Steger did their best to catch up to the intoxicated guests by drinking two beers for everybody's one. Orwig sat at a table with Josef, his wife Anna, their younger daughter Pauline, and a few other neighbors who listened in on the conversation.

Steger, meanwhile, danced with a heavy-set German woman old enough to be his mother. Much shorter than Ryan, the German *Oma's* head rested just above his navel. Both drunk, both leaning on the other, weaving back and forth in slow motion despite the fact the band had packed up and departed 20 minutes prior.

"Did you know I have relatives in Stuttgart?" said Josef while lighting a cigarette and offering one to Orwig.

"My uncle worked as a sheet metal worker," said another.

"How did you get caught?" someone else asked.

Orwig fielded each question in rapid succession. Most in the room were of German descent and all shared a mutual hatred for Hitler but a devoted love of Germany.

"So do you boys have a ride back to camp? If not, you can stay with us," said the mother of the bride.

"Oh, yes, that would be great," said Pauline, the bride's heavyset sister who obviously had eyes for Orwig. "I'll gladly make breakfast."

"I'm afraid that would pose a problem," Orwig said. "We have to sneak back in tonight the same way we came. But we will surely take a ride back to the spot we exited the woods."

"Well, if I didn't see two of everything I would gladly drive you back," said Josef.

"So you see four POWs?" asked his wife. "When did two more arrive?"

Everyone laughed when suddenly they were interrupted by a loud, booming voice in the entrance of the barn. "You think this is funny? Do you even care that these men may have shot and killed my boy?"

The remaining wedding guests turned to see Andy Weber, a neighboring farmer angrily gripping a shotgun in his hands, knuckles white. He had been at the reception earlier but left with a handful of others in disgust. With his words slurred and his body waving back and forth, he continued, "My boy is at the *Siegfried Line* with shrapnel in his leg. And you welcome these pieces of dirt as if they were family?"

"Hold on there, Andy," said Josef playing moderator. "No disrespect intended. We were just being friendly to those from our homeland. They are harmless now. They are prisoners."

"Right, *your* homeland, not mine!" Andy shot back. "*America* is my homeland. I was born here and our soldiers are dying over there. Yet these German soldiers sit drinking our suds and eating our food and, and . . ." He looked over at Steger, who finally stopped dancing with the older woman. ". . . they're dancing with our women! I am disgusted."

"Let's talk about this, Andy. You're obviously drunk, and you don't want to do something you will regret in the morning," insisted Josef.

Ignoring him, Andy raised his gun and pointed it first at Orwig, then over to Steger, then back to Orwig. "You are all alike, you *Krauts*, and I'm here to put things right."

At the threat, everyone scrambled for cover. Chairs were knocked over, tablecloths pulled from tables, glasses of wine and beer mugs crashing to the floor. Andy stepped closer to Orwig and pointed the shotgun in his face, pressing it into his nose.

"You having fun POW?" asked Andy with a clenched jaw.

"I was," Orwig said nervously, not making eye contact with the angry gun toter.

"Let me ask you something. Do you believe there's a heaven?"

"Yes."

"That's good. Because it also means you believe there's a hell."

"Hey, hey, hold on there," interrupted Steger, who had broken free of his *Frau*. "We mean you no harm."

Andy swung the two barrels of the gun towards Steger as he approached. "You guys don't get it, do you? We are at *war!* A war I fight every day while my son is shooting his way to Berlin. And you come in here like nothing's wrong."

"Andy, have you lost your mind!" screeched another voice from the barn entrance. Evelyn, his wife, stood in the doorway, and following her into the barn was Sheriff McGee. Flashing red and blue lights could be seen in the barnyard.

"You called the police?" Andy asked his wife incredulously. "Woman, have you lost *your mind*?"

"Yeah, call me crazy for trying to stop this. Look at you, with that gun in your hand! I *had* to call the sheriff."

"Come on, Andy, that's enough," said Sheriff McGee, now stepping into the barn. "Put the gun down. I mean it. You don't want to go to jail for this."

"Jail? *Jail?* Come on, Dale," said Andy looking at the county's most beloved cop. "These are escaped prisoners of war. I could shoot them right now and be the Grand Marshall of the Fourth of July parade."

"Not with all these witnesses," said McGee. "You'd be watching that parade behind bars. So come on, Andy, put 'er down."

"My boy is over there in the mud, in the filth . . . he's been shot at, he's been getting the snot kicked out of him by these goddamned bastards, and they come in here and enjoy a party? Drinking beer . . . eatin' desserts . . . It ain't right!"

"I don't disagree, Andy, but the law is the law and you can't take it into your own hands just because you're insulted. I understand your anger, but you cannot do this!"

Andy's gaze went up to the ceiling as the gun fell limply at his side. His eyes began to well up. "It ain't right," he repeated. "Tommy is over there, and you know he ain't drinking no cold suds and he ain't dancing with no girls."

The sheriff slowly approached him and set his hand on his shoulder. "It's okay. You hand me that gun, and I'll forget this whole thing ever happened, providing Josef doesn't want to press charges."

Still standing next to Orwig and Steger, the father of the bride shook his head. "That's right, Andy. We go back too far to let this ruin our friendship, providing you don't kill a German here tonight. Really, I understand your grief and it was wrong for me to invite these boys in here."

"So is that an apology?" asked the sheriff.

"Yes. Yes it is. I am deeply sorry. My disrespect was forgetting you were here to celebrate this night with my family."

With a heavy sigh, Andy turned towards the sheriff and handed over the weapon. "I'm so damn tired of worrying, you know? Worrying about my boy. I just want him to come home in one piece. Is that too much to ask?"

"It sure ain't," said McGee, popping the shells out of the chamber. "Now let Evelyn take you home."

Andy's wife approached him and put a hand on her husband's cheek while wearing a sympathetic expression. "Tommy's going to be fine. It'll be alright. Now let's go home." With his head hanging low, Andy let his wife lead him out of the barn.

"So we're all good?" asked the sheriff. "Because I really want to get back to bed and don't wanna be filling out stacks of paperwork."

"Yes, Sheriff. Everything is good," Josef said.

"You two have no idea how much trouble you could have caused," McGee said to the POWs. "There would have been a huge manhunt come sunrise. Do you know what a manhunt would have meant for me?"

"No, sir," they said in sequence.

"It would mean I'd have to work tomorrow. Tomorrow is a Sunday, my day off, and I *hate* working Sundays."

The remaining guests left in the barn all let out a nervous laugh.

Turning his attention to Orwig, Sheriff McGee continued, "You have a good time, son?"

"We almost caught the bouquet," answered Orwig excitedly.

"Oh well, maybe next time. Come on, let's go."

Chapter Sixteen

Making Progress

For the next few weeks, Adam's recuperation was in full force. By this time, Doc Marshall determined he did not have a broken back – to everyone's relief – but because his hip was healing so nicely due to its perfect alignment in the mounted shoe, the country doctor lobbied the authorities to keep him on the farm.

After securing approval, Marshall abbreviated his visits to once a week, and relinquished his expertise to his nurse, Mary O'Donoghue, who stopped by every other day to check on the star patient. However, Nurse O'Donaghue did not share the same enthusiasm for Adam's recovery. Perhaps it was her stillborn disposition, or maybe a deep-seated dislike for Germans, but whatever the reason, the nurse seemed to have perfected the art of the heavy sigh, and when she did speak it was usually a disgusted critique of Maggie's frequent mistakes as a caregiver. To an outsider looking in, she had the bedside manner of a grumpy badger. A reedy woman of close to 45, her thin, expressionless face of stone intimidated Maggie, along with the glow of her classic white uniform: her white, below the knee dress; a white nursing cap; white tights and ankles stuffed into white shoes. Her eyeglasses seemed to always hang from a lanyard chain, but rarely did anyone ever see her wear them.

As much as the doctor hoped to prevent them, the bedsores did indeed begin to form, and they were extremely painful for Adam. Because he was leg-locked to the bedboard, Adam could not easily turn his body off various pressure points, like his buttocks or his left calf. Periodically, Nurse O'Donoghue would insist Maggie lend a hand with personal issues like giving him a sponge bath, changing his sheets, even emptying the bedpan on occasion. When asked, Maggie simply switched from the role of woman with a crush to woman with a cause. She became Adam's Florence Nightingale and enjoyed the responsibility. Adam got over the humiliation quickly, and soon came to appreciate Maggie in ways he could never have imagined. He often thought back to the day of his injury and credited her with saving his life.

Doc Marshall assigned Maggie the daily task of keeping Adam's lungs clear. His new-fangled exercises required Adam to cough as hard as he could for at least one minute, twice a day. The idea was to clear out any fluids or bacteria that may settle in his lazy lungs.

"Do you think this really works?" asked Adam after a hard cough.

"I have to believe so," replied Maggie. "The doctor said it would, so . . ."

"I wonder."

"Oh, so when exactly did you get your medical degree?" Maggie asked sarcastically.

"How do you know if I'm not a doctor?"

"Oh come on."

"What makes you so sure?"

"Of course you would have said something by now."

"How do you know I wasn't keeping it a secret?"

"Oh stop it. You sold watches before the war. You told me yourself."

Adam just looked at her and smiled suspiciously.

"Who are you kidding? There's no way you're a doctor."

"Remember that day in town, when I thought you were shot? I could have performed surgery right then and there."

"You are full of prunes," she said, waving him off.

"Ah-huh. And what do you really know about me?"

Maggie stared into those blue pools and suddenly realized there was a great deal about him she didn't know about. Sure, she knew what he did prior to the war, and that he would occasionally visit America to sell watches, but what about other things like where he grew up, or if he had any siblings? There was much to learn. "Okay, let's play a game," she said.

"What do you propose?"

"How about you say something about yourself – while you cough – and I'll try to guess if it's true or not."

"Oh, I've heard of this game. You call it *'Spin The Bottle,'* I believe."

"You are terrible," she said, playfully punching him in the arm. "This is nothing like that."

Adam laughed. "Okay, okay, I'll play, but only if you do, too."

"No! My lungs are fine. There's no need for me to cough while I tell you things."

"If you don't do it, I won't do it."

"Okay, fine," said Maggie with a heavy sigh. "I guess that's fair. But you go first."

Adam looked up at the ceiling, then let out a loud cough while saying, "I . . . like . . . cabbage."

Maggie laughed. "Okay, I would have to guess that statement is true. All Germans love cabbage."

"Wrong! I hate the stuff."

"What? Really?"

"Yep. Always have."

"I never would have guessed."

"Okay, now it's your turn."

Maggie thought for a second, then let out a cough while saying, "I . . . like . . . to . . . iron."

"Ha! Easy. Nobody likes to iron. So it is definitely false."

"Sorry, but I do."

"Come on."

"It's true. I really do like to iron. Shirts, pants, handkerchiefs, you name it."

"You must have a screw loose."

They continued to play this little game for several minutes. Both learned new things about the other – some silly, like how Adam had never gone fishing; some interesting, like how Maggie had an uncle who went to prison. They laughed numerous times and were having the time of their lives, when Adam suddenly made one comment that threw her for a loop.

"I love your big, brown eyes."

Maggie blushed. "Oh, you can't be serious."

"Are you kidding? How could someone not love them?"

Maggie looked away, a little embarrassed, and felt butterflies in her stomach. She then glanced back and noticed he hadn't taken his eyes off of her. A coy smile formed in the corner of his mouth as the sunlight washed over his features in a way that made him appear statuesque and majestic. Maggie could hardly breathe.

"You're embarrassing me," she said.

"I'm sorry, but it's true. You really are lovely."

She wanted to lean in, stroke his thick brown mane, to feel the stubble of his whiskers against her cheek, then work her way to his lips and lock herself into a delicious kiss.

But as luck would have it, the spell was broken yet again, as Benny rushed into the bedroom.

"What's so funny? I heard you laughing in here. Did Adam tell you a joke, Mommy?"

Far from it, son. Far from it.

* * *

November arrived with a cold and impersonal slap to the face, a disciplinary metaphor to the Muellers who had not yet had their last apple tree picked. Despite the fact that Big Jack and Maggie were shorthanded on the farm, the Germans did their best to make up for lost time, but there simply were not enough hands to finish before the first deep freeze. Oku and his team had already thrashed the last of Maggie's oats several weeks before, so she and Big Jack contemplated asking them to stick around and help in the orchard. Maggie knew no matter how hard she tried . . . vinegar and water simply would not mix, so Oku found work on other farms and would only stop by periodically to say hello or pick up payment for service rendered. As far as the orchard was concerned, it was up to the Germans to finish the task.

During quieter times in the farmhouse, Adam immersed himself into his favorite pastime, reading. Periodically, Corporal Jennaro would grab some of the camp's donated books and deliver them while dropping off the Germans. Adam cherished the written word – especially the American writers – often surfing on the prose of Ernest Hemingway, Margaret Mead and John Steinbeck. Stories of *Davy Crocket* and *Huckleberry Finn* further took him to new places where he escaped the sometimes dreary farmhouse bedroom.

Ever since his injury, the POWs would walk past Adam's first-floor bedroom window each morning, give him a hello-tap on the glass while waving and jeering at their friend, then they'd repeat the ritual in the evening before climbing back into the transport and returning to camp. While it lifted his spirits to know he was in their thoughts, he also wondered about the one person who never waved, never walked past the window, and never said hello when the POWs were allowed to periodically pop in the house. That person was Heinrich Richtor.

One particular morning, Maggie worked in the chicken coop and became suspicious after noticing a hen was missing. Perplexed, she inspected the cage thoroughly to see if one could have possibly escaped.

No sign of a hole. Her mind immediately went to Oku and the rumors about Jamaicans with sticky fingers. *Maybe the bird was missing even before the migrants came to work on the farm and I never noticed.* Maggie wanted so badly to believe this with all her heart, because she had grown close to Oku and refused to believe he or any of his crewmates could be a thief. In fact, the more she dwelled on it, the more ashamed she felt for having such thoughts. But she did promise herself to keep a better eye on everyone – the Germans, the Jamaicans or anyone else who paid them a visit.

Inside the house, one of Adam's closest friends and fellow POW, Henry Elam, had gotten permission to visit. It was a Sunday – the only day Doc Marshall would allow visitors – and one of those rare days of the week the POWs had time off. Big Jack had worked out an arrangement with Colonel Raymonds to have several POWs stop by for these therapeutic visits, which provided Adam the chance to reconnect and get updates on life in the camp. The country doctor protected his star patient and did not want him to catch any infections, so he stringently enforced the "no guest allowed beyond the doorway" rule.

During this particular visit, Henry shared the story about Steger's and Orwig's great escape.

"Those two have never thought twice about risking their lives for the company of a *Fraulein*," laughed Adam.

"They are considered heroes in the camp," said Henry.

"They're probably signing autographs," chuckled Adam.

"The other big story happened in an area cornfield," said Henry. "We were asked to cut down a tree that sat near the edge of the crop line. This thing was long dead and even the slightest breeze could have blown it over, but we still had to take turns sawing at its thick trunk. We were not quite done with the job when out of nowhere a skunk popped out of a hole in the base!"

"Was he living inside the tree?" asked Adam.

"Apparently so."

"Did he spray anyone?"

"He tried, but the little fellow was so scared he didn't know who to aim for. He was surrounded by ten of us and as he ran to get away, so did we. In the chaos, George Bekos, you know him, right? As big as a tree himself – well, he wasn't paying attention to where he was going, and as he ran from the skunk he smashed straight into the tree. That huge thing toppled on top of the skunk! Killed him dead!"

"Bekos was killed?"

"No, *dumkopf*, the skunk! The tree landed on the skunk! I tell you, we should have had George run into that dead tree first off, so we wouldn't have had to spend all that time sawing it."

Adam laughed so hard it hurt his hip.

"Oh, but it gets better," said Henry. "Because there were no guards with us, we decided to have a funeral for the skunk. Made a crucifix out of some dead tree limbs, then told George to hide in the corn patch, beside us. When the American guards finally came to check up on us – around lunchtime – we all sat around the skunk's gravesite and with heads bowed, said prayers and told them about how the tree toppled on *George*. Some of the men were even pretending to cry. We had a real eulogy and everything."

"What did the guards do?" said Adam through his tears of laughter.

"What do you think? They panicked. They said, 'Are you guys crazy? You can't just bury a POW in the field! We have to bring his body back to the camp!' So with much confusion they all grabbed shovels and began to dig out the shallow grave while we sat back and watched. You should have seen their faces when they uncovered that dead skunk! And oh boy, did it smell! Then, right on cue, George walked out of the cornfield as if nothing happened. They looked at the skunk, then looked at him, then looked at all of us before realizing they had been fooled. We all busted up laughing. And George . . . he played the part great. He said he didn't know what was going on, only that he was in the cornfield taking a shit."

"Were they mad?"

"Hell yes, they were mad – at least at first. Then they came to recognize it was a good joke. Soon they began laughing too, by the end of it. They made us bury the skunk again, but it was worth it."

This visit with Henry helped lift Adam's spirits. It was during this trip he also learned that most of the POWs at Camp Ramsey had already shipped out to the lumber mills of Upper Michigan. No more than 50 Germans remained in the local camp.

"Most of the *zelties* are gone. I mean, sleeping in tents during these cold nights would be murder. The only ones left are the officers and the others who sleep inside, like me."

"Is everyone going to leave for winter?" asked Adam.

"No one knows. Rumor is they are going to keep the camp open, and use the rest of us in some canneries and a local battery factory, but no one is sure."

"Don't leave without me, Henry. I'll miss these great stories," said Adam. "You make me miss camp."

"Oh, I don't know. I think anyone would love to be in your shoes. Or should I say, your *shoe?*" he laughed, pointing to Adam's immobile left foot while enjoying his own joke. "Seriously, many speak of you at the camp, and that *Fraulein* who lives here – very cute. Everyone thinks you jumped off the top of the ladder just to be with her."

"Henry, she's married," said Adam, suddenly serious.

"Yeah, I hear he's in France or Belgium or something, fighting for the Yanks. Imagine that, huh? Him there and you here, with his girl. Makes for a real story."

"It's not like that, Henry. Look at me. I am a mess. There's no way anyone would find this broken body the least bit worthwhile. Besides . . ."

Henry jumped in. "Yeah, I know, I know. *She's married.* But you know what they say about 'love and war,' right?"

At that, Adam waved his casted arm at his friend and gave him a half-hearted "tsk," but deep down he knew Henry was right. *I think about her all the time. That smile. Her hypnotic scent . . . a bouquet of lavender and elder blossoms, which fill this room every time she walks in.* Adam recognized that even his pain diminished when she was nearby. Whether handing him a drink of water, changing his sheets, or opening the curtains each morning, he felt lifted to a higher plane – a place where the aches ceased to exist. As she helped with his stretching exercises, he found himself looking at her hair, her skin, and he sometimes imagined kissing that soft neck. The thought of taking his leg out of this immobile shoe and having her share the bed had entered his mind more times than he would like to admit. But then again, each of these fantasies had the same harsh ending: *She . . . is . . . married.*

* * *

An hour after Henry Elam left, Oku stopped by to say goodbye and pick up his final check. During his months on the farm, he and his crew shocked and threshed the oats, brought them to market, and even helped with various odd jobs around the farm, including prepping Maggie's small strawberry patch for winter. In all, the Jamaicans had been working for Maggie and Big Jack for nearly four months.

Following doctor's orders, Oku leaned up against the door jamb to Adam's bedroom at a safe distance. Folding his arms and exposing his bright, white smile, his tall body and wide shoulders nearly filled the doorframe.

"I am glad to see dat you are still alive," said Oku jokingly.

"And I am glad to see that thresher didn't kill you when you used it," retorted Adam good-naturedly.

"Hey, mon, it worked fantastic. Maggie had a great crop of oats, and da leftover stalks are in da barn for her livestock dis winter. I even used some ta cover da strawberries to protect against da winter."

"I wish I could have seen the thresher in action."

"Yeah, too bad you couldn't help us."

"I am a bit hampered by the leg."

Oku saw his sadness and quickly changed the direction of the conversation. "So are you tired a wearing dat one shoe?"

"It's become a part of me, I suppose. But the first chance I get to walk I'm going to go barefoot."

"And look at all deese ropes and pulleys . . . you look like you have been caught in a spider web," observed Oku.

As if on cue, Maggie walked in the room making an excuse to be with these two friends. Both men smiled at one another, marveling at the timing of the *spider's* arrival.

"I think your pillow needs fluffing," she said as she picked up his head, smacked his pillow several times and then tucked it back beneath him. Adam looked at Oku, pointed at Maggie and shook his head with a *Can you believe this?* look on his face.

"Oh, I see how dis works, Miss Maggie . . . You can enter the room, but me? I have to stay in da doorway?"

"She smells better than you," remarked Adam.

"Thank God for dat!" said Oku.

Maggie smiled and didn't say a word as she filled up Adam's glass with fresh water.

"So, when are you gonna get up and walk?" said Oku.

"I hope it'll be soon. I can't stand being here."

"Thanks a lot," said Maggie.

"You know what I mean."

It was always easy for Adam to make friends, but he felt especially good about his relationship with Oku. They had come a long way since the brawl in the oat fields. Since then a mutual sense of trust had grown between them.

"So listen, I wanted ta stop by and say goodbye before we left. My family and I, we will be heading sout in two days. Looking for more work, ya know?"

"Really? You are leaving?" asked Adam, surprised.

"It seems like yesterday that you arrived," added Maggie.

"Our job is done. I hope you and your German friends are no longer upset about having us here. I remember how badly you wanted to cut dose oats," he added with a sarcastic smile.

"You know I was going easy on you and your guys, right?" said Adam about the tussle they had in the fields on that first day.

"Oh yeah, listen to Mr. Tough Guy," said Oku sarcastically. "You can't even fall off da ladder without getting all banged up."

The trio laughed.

"We're just lucky Miss Maggie didn't shoot us all dead," added Oku with a smile, pointing at Maggie.

Looking at the two men, she pointed her index fingers and pretended to shoot two pistols. *"Pshu, pshu,"* she said making the sound effect. Oku and Adam smiled.

"Well, I'm really glad to have met you both," said Oku. "But we betta get outta Wisconsin before it gets too cold."

"I have never seen the south. It sounds nice," remarked Adam, more serious now. "The farthest south I've been was St. Louis."

Oku raised his eyebrows and took a deep breath.

"So do you think you will be back next season?" asked Adam.

"Next spring for sure. We like the berry picking. So if you will have us, Miss Maggie, I would gladly return wit my best crew and attack dose strawberries of yours."

Standing next to him with some towels draped across her arm, she looked at Oku with soft eyes. "You know you are welcome back any time, even though my tiny strawberry patch hardly needs a crew to pick it. But who knows what things will be like in spring? The war may be over by then, too. We all hope so." *One war ends, and another begins,* she thought to herself.

"Hey, dat is not my war. So I am here either way," said Oku loudly.

"And if what Maggie says is true, I may be gone. Maybe back to Germany," said Adam.

Upon hearing these words, Maggie felt a dull ache in her stomach. She had been living in a fantasy these past few weeks, getting used to having Adam in the house. The thought of him leaving did not sit well.

"Well, if I do not see you again, I want ta say it's been a pleasure to know you, Adam," said Oku genuinely.

Adam raised his eyebrows and nodded his head. "Take care of yourself and perhaps our paths will cross again someday. I surely hope so."

"If dey do, I will challenge you to a race. I want to see if dat leg is better than before."

Adam laughed and gave him a wave. Oku returned the gesture. "God bless."

As Oku turned to leave the room, he made eye contact with Maggie and added, "Miss Maggie, may I have a word?"

"Of course, Oku."

They both walked out of the room and into the parlor.

"Uh-oh, sounds serious," chimed in Adam, his voice amplifying from the bedroom. "Fine, keep secrets from me. I've got some secrets of my own. But you can bet I won't share them with the two of you!"

"Send them to *Reader's Digest*," Maggie yelled sarcastically. Oku smiled at the playful nature of the conversation.

They then stepped outside onto the porch. Standing silent, Oku held his hat in his hands and wringed it nervously.

"What is it, Oku? I've never seen you so serious."

"Okay, Miss Maggie, it's like dis . . . one of my workers, Michael – you know him – short, skinny kid . . ."

"Yeah, he's very nice. I like Michael."

"So he told me sometin' the other day and I wanted to share wit you."

"Go on," said Maggie curiously.

"Well . . . As migrants we don't like to rock da boat, ya know, so when we see tings we usually keep dem to ourselves, because it's usually none of our business, and we want ta come back next year, right?"

"What are you getting at, Oku?" asked Maggie, more concerned.

"Okay, so, um, Michael claims dat on da day . . . when Adam fell off the ladder . . ."

Maggie studied him curiously, leaning in.

"He said dat maybe the ladder didn't really break, but it was pushed over."

"What?" said Maggie, stepping backwards from the news. "Did he see this happen or who may have done it?"

"No, he didn't see it happen exactly, but he did see one of da POWs running back towards da orchard very fast just before Benny got Big Jack and me in da fields. He said da German ran like a fox."

"This POW – he could have been coming from the barn," said Maggie, a wishful tinge in her voice. "Or maybe the outhouse."

"No, Miss Maggie. He said it was from da house. From da *back of da house*, actually."

Maggie was dumbstruck.

"Problem is, if dis was true, it would be hard to prove unless Adam saw it, too," added Oku.

"He claims he doesn't remember the fall at all. Small pieces do come once in a while but nothing of this magnitude," said Maggie. "Did Michael see who it was exactly?"

"No, he says dat all you white people look da same," Oku said with a smile, pausing to see if the joke settled in.

Maggie acknowledged the joke with an eye roll, then a look like, *Could you be serious for one minute, please.*

"No, he couldn't tell who it was," said Oku, back on task. "I did ask him dat. All he said was da guy had white hair."

White hair? *Blond hair?* "This is incredible," said Maggie under her breath.

"I could be blowing smoke, as dey say, but I felt you should know."

"Thank you, Oku. This is indeed some news."

"Okay. I must be going to see my wife and son before it gets dark."

"Thank you for telling me this, Oku. And . . ." Maggie paused, "thank you for everything. You really settled into a nice routine around here. Big Jack will miss you, Benny will miss you, and honestly, I will miss you, too."

Oku forced a smile her way, fighting the sadness he had in his eyes. It marked one of the first times she had ever seen such an expression on his perpetually happy face. They stared at each other awkwardly before Maggie stepped forward, wrapped her arms around his broad shoulders and gave him a long hug. "Goodbye."

Oku had never embraced a white woman before, and it made him feel a bit lopsided, but he slowly raised his arms to reciprocate. Maggie had become a true friend as well, and as they separated she put her hand on his cheek and said, "I will miss you."

"Okay den. You are a great boss, yes, but also a great friend, Miss Maggie."

She laughed, fighting back the tears. "Go now, or you will get in trouble with your wife."

"Have you ever seen an angry Jamaican woman? Not a pretty sight, I must say."

Maggie watched as Oku trotted to his truck. Several other Jamaican migrants laughed and razzed him as he ran towards them, having seen the embrace on the front porch. He waved them off and jumped into the driver's seat.

As the large flatbed rumbled down the gravel driveway, a medley of colorful leaves danced in the backdraft. Maggie dropped into the front porch swing and sat in silence, her mind trying to untangle what Oku just told her. *Could someone have actually pushed the ladder over?* It had never occurred to her before. She began to think back and tried to remember if the full crew of Germans had been in the orchard that day. As she cycled through the list in her head, only one blond POW came to mind.

* * *

That night, Big Jack moved the RCA radio into Adam's room so everyone could listen to *The Jack Benny Program,* a Sunday night tradition in the Mueller household. Maggie darned some of Benny's socks in the chair next to Adam's bed, her four-year-old lay on the floor with his box of crayons and a coloring book, and Big Jack perched himself just in front of the radio in order to hear it better, occasionally fine-tuning the dial when a wave of static would float into the room.

One of everyone's favorite parts was when Mel Blanc would say, *"Train leaving on track five for Anaheim, Azusa and Cucamonga."* Big Jack especially would howl every time he heard it. Benny would laugh right along with him, often repeating the final word, "Cuc-a-mooooooonga!" and then laugh again, mostly to himself. Throughout the program, all four seemed to lose themselves in the proverbial theater of the mind. Not many words were spoken, and when someone did chime in, Big Jack would shush them on the spot.

As the radio show ended and the announcer wrapped things up with a plug, *"Lucky Strike cigarettes thanks you for listening . . ."* Big Jack looked at Maggie a bit confused. "You okay, Mags? You didn't laugh once during the entire program."

"I've been thinking about something Oku said before leaving today, and have been wondering how to bring it up."

"What is it?" asked Adam as Big Jack hit the OFF switch, silencing the large radio.

"He told me one of his workers saw a POW running away from the house around the same time as Adam's fall."

"What?" exclaimed Big Jack.

Adam readjusted himself in the bed but said nothing.

"Who? Who was it?" insisted Big Jack. "I'll call the camp commander and . . ."

"Apparently, he didn't get a good look at him," Maggie interrupted.

"I knew that ladder was safe. I knew it!" insisted Big Jack. "Adam, did you see anyone running away?"

Struggling to play back the events of the incident, he shook his head. "I really don't remember. I could picture it happening as you describe, but it would only be my imagination."

"Well, if anything ever comes to mind, tell us right away," added Big Jack.

"Oku mentioned that this person had . . . blond hair," added Maggie.

"Blond hair? But who . . ." Big Jack's voice trailed off and his eyes got wide. He looked at Maggie as if he solved a mystery. After a long still moment, Big Jack followed, "Tell me, Adam, how was your relationship with Heinrich?"

Maggie didn't dare say a word.

"Not bad. But not good, either," said Adam with a heavy sigh, trying to purify his memory of past run-ins with his foe. "He's a hothead, always getting into fights, but I can't think of anything that would warrant attempted murder," he said, wondering if Heinrich could actually be so vindictive.

"I've seen his kind before," said Big Jack. "The things he says around the other POWs . . . Those hard-headed members of the Workers Party who would fall on a sword for a weak cause . . . always looking for a reason to justify their outlets for buried hatred. They feel important by putting others down and standing on the pedestal of a veiled purpose. It's because of people like him your mother and I left *Deutschland.*"

"Germany has certainly seen its share of political strife these past 30 years," said Adam.

"You need – no *we* need to keep a sharp eye on him," Big Jack said looking at Maggie. "I may even mention my concerns to Raymonds when I see him next."

Still lying on his stomach, propping himself up by his elbows, Benny listened to the conversation with interest. "Did a man push you down, Adam?"

"I hope not, Benny. I sure hope not."

The room went silent. It made Maggie feel uncomfortable. She now kicked herself for never telling the commander about how Heinrich assaulted her that night in the kitchen. Yearning to change the subject, she spoke up. "So, Papa, I've been wondering about Thanksgiving? It's only a few weeks away. Any thoughts?"

"Oh right, I forgot to tell you – Art offered me a goose. He said he got two of them from a farmer in Oconomowoc after fixing the guy's roof. So he offered one to me. Whattya think? Want to try a goose this year?"

"Only if I get to make the stuffing," she said.

"That's a deal," he said, now pulling himself away from the story about Heinrich.

"How about it, Adam? Are you up for an authentic American Thanksgiving?" said Maggie as she walked next to him and placed a caring arm on his shoulder. Big Jack took notice, his mouth in a tight nub.

"I've been in America during two Thanksgivings, but we only ate the turkey," Adam said. "I've never eaten a goose before."

Soaking it in, Maggie surveyed the room and felt content with those in her company. It'd been a long time since she felt the embrace of warm intentions, especially in such a caring environment. At that moment, with her solid foundation of Big Jack and her son Benny at her side, as well as a German POW who had become close to all the Muellers, she felt more alive than she could ever remember. She took in a slow, deep breath, smiled and said, "Aren't we just one, big happy family?"

Upon hearing this, Big Jack shot an icy-cold look in her direction. As soon as the words came out of her mouth, she wished she could take them back. Big Jack held the concept of "family" sacred, and while he did like Adam, he also saw the interest in his daughter's eyes. He became increasingly concerned about her attraction towards him those past several months, and by using the word "family," he felt she had crossed the line. Even Adam swallowed hard at this *faux pas* and felt it would be helpful to chime in, "So, um, Benny, I have a Thanksgiving joke for you . . ."

Benny sat up in anticipation.

"If April showers bring May flowers, what do Mayflowers bring?"

Benny just smiled.

Trying to save him, and herself, Maggie played along, "I don't know, Adam. What do Mayflowers bring us?"

"They bring pilgrims, of course."

Benny looked at his mother for validation. Maggie forced a laugh, and of course, Benny followed in line with a chuckle of his own. Big Jack simply smirked while taking in a breath through his teeth.

"Good one, Adam. Good one," said Maggie.

Adam shrugged his shoulders and shared his crooked smile with the room. He knew it wasn't enough to save the moment, but at least the effort to freshen the stale air was appreciated.

"I think it's time this little guy got to bed," added Maggie.

"Ah-huh," mumbled Big Jack, still put off by the earlier comment. "It's getting past my bedtime, too." With that, Maggie picked up Benny and carried him out of the bedroom. Big Jack walked out with her. "See you in the morning, Adam," he said, turning his head back to the bedridden guest and extinguishing the kerosene lantern which sat on the dresser.

"Gute Nacht, Big Jack," Adam said from the dark.

* * *

After Maggie got Benny tucked in for the night, she put on her pajamas and got under the covers. As she settled into bed with Jane Austin's *Sense and Sensibility*, there was a soft knock on her door.

"Come in," she said.

Big Jack poked his head inside. "I saw your light on. Do you have a minute?"

She looked at him, concerned and a bit suspicious. "Sure, Papa. Come in." She then sat upright in bed, fluffing a pillow behind her back.

"I've been meaning to talk with you, Mags."

"Sure, what is it?"

Big Jack hesitated for a second as he stood beside her bed. "You know Adam will leave in a few months, right?"

"Of course," she said with a guilty expression on her face. Big Jack obviously noticed how the young pair looked at each other, and he knew his daughter had feelings for the German POW.

"The thing is . . ." he chose his words carefully. "I hear you two laugh, I watch you wait on him the way you do and . . . well, I'll just come on out and say it." He paused, then continued, "I understand things have not been so great between you and Erik . . ."

Maggie leered at her father in an attempt to look defensive, but something inside her knew he wasn't picking a fight, so her expression quickly softened. *Just hear him out.*

"Marriage is tough. And with Erik gone, well, it can make things even more difficult, ya know? But you have to be true to your vows, sweetheart. You are being watched by God." He paused again, then continued, "I like Adam. I really do. He's quite an amazing man. I see him with Benny, too, and well . . ." Big Jack's words trailed off.

Admittedly, Adam had all the qualities Big Jack hoped for in a son-in-law: He came from the old country . . . he spoke fluent German . . . and most importantly, he was really good to Maggie. Even before the injury, he had watched them together and secretly felt they could have been the perfect match.

"Now, I'm not one to entangle myself in other people's affairs, but I want you to see reality for what it is. Who knows when the war will end, but whether it's today or tomorrow or in ten years, Adam is going to *leave*. And I don't want you to get hurt." Big Jack paused for a second and added, "I love you too much to see that happen."

Maggie put her book beside her and took in a deep breath. She knew this conversation was inevitable, but she had to find her strength. "I love you, too, Papa. And I respect you beyond measure. But I have a few things to say."

Big Jack sat on the edge of her bed, open and willing to hear her side.

"You have to understand, it's been really, *really* hard for me, these past few months. These past few years, even," she said. "God, I have tried to make Erik happy, and it seemed the more I tried, the more he hated me."

Big Jack nodded. He saw it for himself.

"It's that damn farm. Erik thought for sure he would inherit it. He simply could not fathom that we would end up here. He is too proud and too damn stubborn. He drinks all the time . . . he's selfish . . . thinks only of himself . . . And the thought of him coming back . . . argh! I can't think of it," she added with fists clenched and occasionally punching her mattress for emphasis. "The thing is . . ." she continued, "do you want to hear something crazy? I have been sooo happy ever since he left. Really, for the first time in years I have been truly happy. I cannot tell you what a difference it's been. Then Adam showed up. It's not fair. It's just not fair."

Big Jack reached for his daughter and they shared a hug, holding it for several seconds before pulling back – his vibrant baby blues piercing her. "Remember that the Good Lord will never give you what you can't handle. You may not know why this is happening now, but in due time, it'll all make sense." Then wagging a finger, Big Jack raised an eyebrow and added, "But you must remember your vows, sweetheart. Especially now. Before things go too far."

"I can't promise anything."

Big Jack's eyes got wide. "What?"

"I'm sorry, Papa. But I simply cannot make that promise."

"But you're married!"

"I know, I know . . ."

"Think of Benny at least. You must be true for him, if not for yourself."

She closed her eyes and breathed a trembled, shaky breath. He was right. He's always right. But she didn't want to lie, and the way things were going between them . . . who knew?

"Maggie, I beg of you. Think of the scandal. You'll have to move. Probably back to Germany, because like it or not, that young man downstairs is going back and you can't stop it."

"There's something else," continued Maggie, wiping her damp nose on her sleeve.

Big Jack looked at her inquisitively. "What? What do you mean?"

"It's about Heinrich."

Just the mere mention of his name made Big Jack's blood boil. "What about him?"

"Do remember the night you made that rabbit stew?"

Big Jack squinted his eyes, wondering where this was going.

"Well, later that evening, just before the POWs were picked up, he assaulted me in the kitchen."

"What? What did he do?"

"He slapped me . . . and tore my blouse . . . all because I wouldn't kiss him."

"That son-of-a-bitch! I'm gonna . . ."

"Adam came to my rescue," Maggie said, interrupting her father.

"What? Adam?"

"Ah-huh. He took pretty good care of him, too. Benny walked in during the middle of the fight, which stopped it in an instant."

"Why didn't you tell me this before?"

"I wanted to handle it myself. I was going to tell the commander but never got around to it. I thought if I ignored it, well . . ."

"I'm gonna kill him. So help me, Mags!"

"Papa, you *can't* kill him. Maybe talk to the commander about getting him reassigned?"

"What, so he can do this to someone else? Absolutely not!"

"Don't do anything that will land you in jail."

"That goddamned Nazi bastard!"

"Papa, I felt you needed to know. It's also, well, it's another reason why Adam has become so special. Him coming to my rescue in the kitchen that night . . . him shooting that mad dog . . . He's perfect! Don't you see?"

"I do see, Maggie. I get it. But my goodness, he was merely doing what any gentleman would have done," said Big Jack. "Doesn't this news top all!"

"I suppose we have motive now."

"Huh?"

"You know, the story about the ladder – why Heinrich would have possibly pushed it over. That night, after the fight, he threatened Adam. Told him to watch out. That he was gonna get him."

Big Jack sat quietly. Thinking about Heinrich and how much hatred he carried in his heart, he stood up from Maggie's bed.

"Papa," Maggie said suspiciously. "Promise me you won't do anything stupid."

Gritting his teeth, Big Jack nodded. "I won't kill him, if that's what you mean."

"And regarding the other issue . . . I know you're right. And I will be more careful."

He reached for her hand and gave her a reassuring squeeze. He then walked towards the door and, with a soft reply, said, "Good night, sweetheart."

"Good night, Papa."

Sitting all alone, Maggie's shoulders sank and her head hung low as she thought about the houseguest downstairs.

Who am I kidding? This German is nothing more than a stranger in my home and he will be gone as soon as the war ends. My God, he could easily be shooting at my husband right now if he wasn't captured. And what is this, really, but a high school crush? Do I really like this man, or do I like the fact that someone likes me? Come on, Maggie, get your head on straight! Stop this fantasy and face reality! He's going to be shipping back to Germany when all of this is over. This can never be!

* * *

For the next week or two, Maggie did everything she could to swim upstream. Big Jack's lecture allowed her to fight against the strong current of infatuation. She respected him and knew she needed to get some separation – or at least *try.* She ignored the inertia that pushed against her and forced herself to not talk with Adam about his past or any of their mutual interests. When he threw out sticky inquiries, she gave him short replies, disconnecting herself from a segue or a related story. A quiet canyon opened between them. Deep down, however, she desperately wanted to engage. She felt ashamed for storming off when he wanted to talk about their one and only kiss, and she wanted to do it again. She wanted to tell him a joke and laugh with him about something mundane and uncomplicated . . . but instead, Maggie practiced the art of detachment. It was exhausting and unnatural for her.

Adam caught on quickly and recognized the reality of the situation. The look on Big Jack's face that night in his bedroom said it all. He surmised that father and daughter must have had a heart-to-heart, and deep down he knew it would be impossible for this clandestine crush to become anything more. In fact, Maggie's phlegmatic approach to him was a bit of a relief, because Adam finally had some boundaries, he knew where he stood, and the guilt gnawing at his soul would subsequently cease.

Being a realist, he, too, thought, *Why should I invest in a relationship that was headed off a cliff? What am I thinking?* Not surprisingly, Adam's physical pain did not subside like it did when the two playfully flirted. His bedsores felt worse, the pain in his hip seemed to throb more intensely, and he believed he may be coming down with a cold – something Doc Marshall said could be the first domino to something worse. So, he worried alone.

Soon Adam began to reciprocate Maggie's detached approach and kept the conversations to a minimum. He figured this would make life easier for her, too. Maggie no longer helped him stretch or assisted with his coughing exercises, having told Doc Marshall's nurse she would be unable to help, all without explanation.

Each day got a little less emotionally painful for Adam, but *more* painful physically. He had gotten used to the laughter and the innuendo. He looked forward to talking with her and became addicted to her presence. But now, things had become clinical and cold. The only thing left to do was to immerse himself into his reading and try to get healthy as soon as possible. And get back to camp.

MOVIETONE Title: PUSHING THROUGH TO HOLLAND

(Newsreel Narrator): "While the Allies have been getting on well with the clearing of various bunkers and trenches, General Dempsey's Second Army has been driving on towards Southwest Holland. Latest newsreel dispatches show what this jaunt is like.

In this footage, men can be seen going into action in modified Sherman tanks called 'Kangaroos.' Flamethrowers, including 'Crocodiles,' have again been proving their worth during the weeding out and mopping up process, and they have served us well. Mine sweeping trucks are used to clear the roads. Look at that machine clearing a path, saving who knows how many of our boys in the process.

Tanks carrying bundles of wood were used for crossing ditches and wide trenches. Our final image underlines the way things were going in Holland as well as indicating the shape of things to come.

Here a G.I. finds a German flag in the steeple of a ruined church. It looks like his prayers have been answered. Keep it up boys. Keep the fight coming to them and here's to you as you gain more ground.

Chapter Seventeen

Giving Thanks

True to his word, Big Jack roasted the Thanksgiving goose to perfection – golden brown, with crispy skin. The Muellers also prepared sweet potatoes, squash, tomato salad, Maggie's stuffing, and a pumpkin pie – all worthy enough to grace the cover of *Good Housekeeping*.

Just because Adam was "not family" did not mean he had to miss out on the feast. In fact, the dinner was served in his room, with all the food set out on the large bedroom dresser which rested up against a far wall. Maggie propped up a square folding table at the foot of Adam's bed and this makeshift dining table provided more than enough room for Big Jack, Benny and Maggie on each of three sides, with Adam's bed taking up the fourth side, where he sat with his torso propped up by a mountain of pillows.

After settling into their chairs, Big Jack asked everyone to bow their heads as he said grace.

"Sehr geehrter Herr, segne uns alle an diesen Tisch, segne dieses Fest. Wir beten für diejenigen ohne Familie und ohne Essen. Wir beten für die Jungs auf beiden Seiten der Front und bitten um eine sichere Rückkehr nach Hause, vor allem für Erik. Wir bitten auch um Frieden auf der Welt, um ein Ende des Krieges, und die Wiedervereinigung aller Familien, damit

das Erntedankfest nicht nur ein Feiertag, sondern eine Lebensweise ist. Im Namen Jesu sagen wir Amen."

(Dear Lord, please bless us all around this table, bless this feast, and we pray for those without a family and without a meal. We pray for those boys on both sides of the front and ask for a safe return home, especially for Erik. We also ask for world peace, that the war ends soon and all families are reunited, so Thanksgiving isn't only a holiday but a way of living and a way of life. In Jesus' name we say thank you. Amen.)

"Amen," everyone said, and with that, Big Jack's demeanor changed from somewhat staid to playful and loose. "Okay then, let's open some wine!" he proclaimed while rubbing his hands together. "We have much to be thankful for."

Maggie uncorked a chilled bottle of *Liebfraumilch*, and Big Jack walked over to the dresser to carve the goose.

"Adam, you are in for a real treat, let me tell you," said Big Jack. "Eating a goose for the first time is like discovering a new sense you didn't know you had. And this one is done to perfection, if I may say so myself."

It turned out he was right. The meat melted in the mouth like ice cream, and Maggie's Thanksgiving stuffing was worthy of a four-star review. During the meal, they drank much wine and when Big Jack began to feel his liquor, he began to reminisce. On this night he talked about how much he missed *Fasching*, a large German festival from his youth.

"What a tradition," said Big Jack. "Every November 11th at 11 minutes past 11:00 in the morning it would begin, and it was a good few months of Tomfoolery, ending on *Aschermittwoch* (Ash Wednesday)."

"Those were good times," said Adam, his mind drifting back to better days before the war.

"You've heard of it?" asked Maggie.

"Oh yes."

Big Jack laughed. "I could tell you some stories."

"Yes, I could as well. But there is a lady present."

Big Jack shot a warm smile to Adam and winked. Maggie spied that moment and looked on with suspicion. She knew her father was feeling his wine, and as she watched she couldn't help but think how opposite he and Erik were when they drank.

"What did you do there, Opa?" asked Benny about *Fasching*.

Big Jack paused. Then, letting the wine lower his guard, he responded, "Okay, this one will be easy on the youngster's ears. And the lady's."

"Oh yeah, right," said Maggie sarcastically, knowing her father no longer had a filter.

"For an entire week, people in our town would dress up in costumes. Some would dress like clowns – like your Mr. Chuckles, Benny – and we would eat lots of sausage and sauerkraut and wash it all down with good German beer. Needless to say, it didn't take one long to build up a, shall we say, a fermentation tank in the bowels."

"Oh, here we go," said Maggie burying her head in her hands.

"Right, so on this one night, a group of us were in the Great Hall in downtown Düsseldorf," Big Jack continued, laughing at the memory. "It was just after dinner and everyone was singing songs and enjoying stories of the day, when my friend Josef Fritz, a man well known for having the worst *Furzen* (flatulence), pushed the dishes to the side, laid on his back and threw his legs straight up into the air."

"On the table?" asked Adam. "He climbed onto the table?"

"Yep."

Benny giggled up a storm. He only needed to hear the word *Furzen* and he would begin to laugh, regardless of how the story ended.

"Papa, come on now," Maggie said, trying to get him to understand this story may not be appropriate for the youngster's ears. Or for hers.

He ignored her request.

"Oh, it gets better," continued Big Jack. "While Josef is letting out enough foul air to fill a zeppelin, he grabs a nearby candle, puts it up to his *Hintern,* and turned that candle into a blowtorch! There was actually an explosion of fire."

"Lord, help me," said Maggie shaking her head.

"His *Freundin* at the time, who sat on the other side of him at the table, had her eyebrows *singed* clean off! Not surprisingly, she broke up with him that night. And in the process he burnt a hole clean through his leotards!"

Benny could hardly contain himself as he rolled around on the floor holding his stomach. Adam chuckled quietly to himself. All Maggie could do was let out an exasperated, "Oh, Papa. That's terrible."

"Yeah, those were good times," said Big Jack, catching his breath and taking another sip of wine. *"Ein Lebensfeier."* (Celebration of life)

"So how about you, Adam? Any holiday traditions?" asked Maggie. "At least one you could share with a lady?" she added with a smile.

Adam studied her and realized this marked the first time in a long time she actually inquired about something in a sincere manner. He liked it. He missed it.

"Well, I enjoyed *Walpurgisnacht* (Waluburg's Night). It's based on some Germanic folk customs and is dedicated to a legendary seeress. I'm not sure how it all began, but everyone in all the neighboring villages would go into the forest, cut down a tree, strip it of its branches, then paint the trunk in various colors and decorate it with ribbons. In the small village where I grew up, we called it a *May Tree*."

"What did you do with it?" asked Maggie. "Replant it?"

"Oh no. Basically, we set it up like a Christmas tree – for us it was in the town square – then after a few nights we would go to neighboring towns and try to steal their trees. If successful, they would have to buy their tree back with several barrels of beer."

"And what if you couldn't get their tree?" asked Maggie.

"We'd take other things – odd things, like someone's front door or a wooden gate – something they would surely miss. One friend of mine took a cow out of a stable when the owners were gone for the night, then broke into their house and put the cow upstairs in their bedroom."

"That's so strange," said Big Jack.

"As you know, a cow will gladly walk up a flight of steps but not down them. I don't know how they ever got that *Kuh* out of the house, but it must have been some trick."

"So tonight's theme is heavy drinking, passing gas, and grand theft. Thanks, guys," Maggie said, shaking her head. "This is just what my young son needs to hear."

"Ach," said Big Jack waving her off with his hand. "It's harmless fun."

Both Big Jack and Adam held their wine glasses, raised them up, and without a word nodded to one another in a way only those with a shared geography would understand.

"So, Adam, in your story you mentioned a 'seeress.' What is a seeress?" asked Maggie.

"She's a prophet," chimed in Big Jack before Adam could answer. "It's a woman who can foresee the future."

Adam smiled, nodding in validation.

"Humph," was all Maggie could muster. *What a gift that would be,* she thought to herself. *If only I had such powers. The ability to see what will happen with Erik, with Adam, with Benny . . . with my entire life.* She had been doing her best to maintain an apathetic role as Adam's caregiver those past few weeks, but there were times – usually when late night insomnia tapped her on the shoulder – that she acknowledged it was more than a façade and since her talk with Big Jack, Adam was more tempting than ever. It was difficult to ignore the hunger of the heart. *How much longer can I keep this up?*

Chapter Eighteen

Last Day

The Monday after Thanksgiving was quiet around the farm. The sun shone brightly, the air crisp and cold. Most of the trees had dropped their colorful cloaks, and wisps of wind blew leaf piles back and forth in the barnyard, depositing a large pile first against Maggie's garden fence, and then, as if Mother Nature couldn't make up her mind, a pile would get blown to the side of the barn. That game of ping-pong went on all morning.

This particular day also marked the end of the POWs tenure on the Mueller farm. Normally, Maggie had all her apples picked by this time, but with fewer hands to harvest, plus the late blossoms in the spring meant they were flirting with frosty nights. The Mueller orchard consisted of two varieties of apples: Winesaps and Pink Ladies. Both were a hardy fruit that could be picked as late as November. But the remaining crop was being tested for its mettle and permanence so late in the season.

Just after breakfast, Corporal Jennaro pulled his truck into the barnyard for the last time, stopping in the same spot he'd parked for months. By now, the POWs knew the drill: Each hopped out of the truck and walked towards the house to tap hello on Adam's bedroom window, then they followed the American guards into the orchard. On this day, however, Jennaro went to the front door with a clipboard in hand.

Maggie heard his knock and was surprised to see him.

"Morning, Mrs. Wentworth," he chimed.

"Hello, Corporal. Can I help you?"

"Actually, yes," he said, his warm breath condensing into a thick vapor in the crisp air. "As you know, today is our last day, and I need your signature on some paperwork."

"Certainly. Come inside. It's as cold as the Dickens out there."

As they moved into the kitchen, Jennaro plopped himself into a chair as Maggie poured him a cup of coffee and looked over the forms. "So, will there be any help for our winter pruning?" she asked.

"Not sure yet, but the good news is we're keeping roughly 30 Germans in camp. The other 200 or so are going to lumber mills up north and to the battery factory in Milwaukee. Most are already gone. The place is like a ghost town."

"30 POWs left? That's not many."

"I wish I had a say in the matter. I'd have them pruning your farm next week."

Pausing for a moment, Maggie looked off in the distance as a reminiscent expression washed over her face. "You said some Germans are going to Milwaukee?"

"That's right."

"Ever been there? I like that city."

"As a matter of fact, me and some of the fellas were there a few weeks ago." Hesitating for a moment, he continued. "I think I met a girl."

"You *think* you met a girl? You weren't sure if she was a girl?"

Jennaro blushed slightly. "No, I mean yeah, of course it was a girl, but it's just that I may see her again."

"Is she a local?"

"Ah-huh."

"Oooo, sounds like the stuff of fairy tales," Maggie teased.

"Oh, cut it out. It's just a date is all."

"You be good to her, you got that?" instructed Maggie, dispensing motherly advice to someone nearly her own age. "We Wisconsin girls are true. You treat us right, and we'll treat you right in return."

"I'll heed your warning," chuckled Jennaro.

"Is she Polish or German or Ital—"

"Italian. She's Italian," he interrupted.

"Then you know what I mean, right?"

"Oh yeah. I'm Italian, with seven older sisters."

"My goodness. Seven? You have my condolences," added Maggie with a smile.

"She's so beautiful and tender and funny and . . ." Jennaro caught himself and realized that perhaps Maggie was right. Maybe this was a fairy tale.

"Someone you could take home to your mother, perhaps?"

"That's true."

"See? See what I'm saying? You have fallen under the spell of an Italian Wisconsinite. Lord, look out for the fireworks. What's her name?"

"Rosa."

"That's very pretty. I bet she's as beautiful as her name."

Jennaro smiled bashfully.

Suddenly, Maggie felt a mix of emotions. She thought about the early days with Erik, the good days, contrasted with the weeks prior to his departure. Her heart experienced the sweet and sour flavors of love.

"So anyways," said Jennaro, "I'll take that paperwork before we leave for the day. I think there's a spot on the last page for you to request a Continuance of Labor. You and Big Jack know how many Germans you'll need to prune the orchard?"

"I figure four or five would do the trick. Maybe sometime after Christmas?"

"That's great. Just have Big Jack sign it, too. I'll turn in the paperwork today."

"I'll do that. He's in the barn setting up the team of horses to grab the last remaining apples. You have no idea how much the pruners will help."

"Oh, and there's one more thing before I forget. A lot of the soldiers would like to have an opportunity to say goodbye to Adam today, being our last day and all. Would that be alright with you and Big Jack?"

"The Germans or the Americans?

"Actually . . . both."

This news surprised Maggie. Of course, she knew a mutual respect had developed between the Allies and Axis Midwesterners – a brothers-in-arms camaraderie – but never would she have expected the guards to become close enough they would want to say goodbye to an *enemy* soldier. Snapping out of the thought, she said, "Of course. They are all welcome. They just cannot go past the bedroom door. Doctor's orders."

"They know the drill."

"And good luck with the last of the harvest. Big Jack will be taking those remaining apples to market tomorrow. Hopefully none of them froze last night. It was very cold."

"We'll cross our fingers."

* * *

Around midmorning, the POWs worked in the back of the orchard. With most of the trees picked clean, the Germans lost their focus and began lollygagging and playing practical jokes on one another. As always, Jennaro and Private Mike Thompson were assigned to watch the POWs, and occasionally one of them would bark, "Quit screwing around! Get back to work!" For a time the Germans would refocus, but like the last day of school, they soon started up their shenanigans again.

It looked as if they had gathered the last of the apples and filled the large metal collection bin when Big Jack strolled into the orchard bookended between Suri and Bucky, his two workhorses. With a leather strap in each hand, he arrived to hook up the team to the large wagon.

"So we ready to take these apples to market?" Big Jack asked as he approached.

"I don't know, a lot of these look like they caught some frost last night," said Jennaro. "They feel pretty spongy."

"Cross your fingers. The sugar in those there Winesaps help them survive below freezing, but not below 28 degrees," said Big Jack, his voice trailing off. "If they did freeze last night, they may fetch a good price if used for applesauce or cider."

Big Jack then positioned his team of horses to the front of the metal bin, steam projecting out of their nostrils, a thick froth dripping from their mouths. As he began to hook them up, both horses seemed particularly edgy, but Big Jack calmed them down with a few pats on the neck and several carrots he kept hidden in his pocket. He first secured the Dutch collar, tightened some leather buckles and attached the double-neck yoke. While preparing the team, he noticed a phlegmatic Heinrich standing nearby smoking a cigarette.

"Heinrich, would you help me for a second?" Big Jack asked almost too politely. "I need you to hold these reigns steady."

Heinrich cocked his head, dropped his eyebrows and breathed a heavy sigh.

Big Jack pressed him further. "Come on, you're obviously not doing anything, so give me a hand."

"Get someone else to be your slave," he quipped, not even making eye contact.

"Hey, Richtor, snap to it," ordered Jennaro, who stood nearby.

The disgruntled German dropped his satchel to the ground, tossed his cigarette and sauntered toward Big Jack. "I hope your apples go rotten. Hypocrite."

"Excuse me?" said Big Jack, anger building up inside him.

"You heard me."

"Hypocrite, you say? Listen, Heinrich, don't be confused but my Germany is long gone. America is my country now. And we're fighting a war *your* country started. So don't call the kettle black!"

"A pretender then? Perhaps that's more appropriate," Heinrich said in German, taking a half-hearted grip on the horses' reigns. Jennaro tried to follow the conversation, but the language barrier proved too much.

"You and that daughter of yours – along with Adam Klein," Heinrich said with distain. "He follows her around like she's a bitch in heat."

Big Jack continued to tighten the straps on the yoke, his anger forcing him to pull hard at the leather pieces, as if wanting to snap them in two. But he showed a forbearance few would have been able to muster.

"Klein should have died falling from the ladder," Heinrich added.

There it was! The opportunity Big Jack had been waiting for. "Oh? You know something about that fall, do you, Heinrich? Something you might want to share?"

"Why, I have no idea what you are talking about," Heinrich said sarcastically. "*Verpiss dich!* (Fuck you!), and your family of traitors."

The American guards standing within earshot did not react to the insult, but Big Jack understood it loud and clear, and he could hardly contain himself. *You son-of-a-bitch! If I was younger . . . I wouldn't think twice about pounding you to a pulp.* As it turned out, he took in a slow, deep breath and had another plan.

"I'm sorry you feel that way," said Big Jack, biting back on his rage. As Heinrich held the horses steady, Big Jack hooked up Suri to the wagon and then walked around to Heinrich's side to secure Bucky. As he took the reins from the German, he made a suggestion. "Tell you what, Heinrich, why don't you show me how good you are at hitching horses to a wagon. Can you do that, or were you a city boy your whole life?"

Heinrich's ego got the best of him and he took the bait. "I know how to hook up a team," he boasted. "I can do it in my sleep." With that, the German walked over to Bucky's side and stepped behind the ornery horse. As he did so, the large workhorse reared up on her hind legs and let out an agitated whinny. Then as she came down, planted her front legs into the dirt, and before Heinrich could step out of the way, she bucked violently. Her kick knocked Heinrich's body backwards hard – as if being shot out of a cannon – into the heavy metal wagon and then onto the ground.

Sitting in the dirt, he let out a strange gasp while holding his chest as he struggled to breathe. The horse had temporarily knocked the wind out of him and likely broken a rib or two in the process. As Heinrich gasped for air, his legs straddled the front-left wheel of the apple container, which brimmed with hundreds of pounds of fruit.

"Holy smokes!" said Jennaro, running to Heinrich's aid. But before he could pull the POW out from under the agitated horses, Suri and Bucky whinnied loudly, then lurched forward with the cart in tow. The metal wheel rolled up and settled directly on Heinrich's crotch. He let out a gritty scream his relatives could likely have heard back in Germany.

"Oh Gott, weg damit. Sie es jetzt!" (Ahhhhh! Get it off! Oh God, get it off!)

The other Germans watched in horror as the front wheel rolled repeatedly up and down his groin, pinning him down with no way out.

Finally, Big Jack pulled the horses backwards and far enough and Heinrich became free from the crushing weight of the wagon. As Jennaro and Thompson grabbed his arms and dragged him out of the cart's path, they could see blood pooling on his pants. Heinrich cried out in pain.

"I know it hurts," said Jennaro. "But you have to let me see the injuries."

As Jennaro and Thompson unbuckled his trousers, they could see Heinrich's white boxer shorts soaked in blood and his scrotum – or what was left of it – actually dangling out the sides of the underwear, looking to have the consistency of raw meat.

"Holy Christ!" exclaimed Thompson upon seeing the extent of the injury. "We need to get him to a hospital, fast!"

"I don't want to die. Oh God, I don't want to die!" the German cried.

Some of the other POWs saw the disfigurement and quickly turned away. One ran to the base of an apple tree and vomited.

"Come on. Give me a hand here!" insisted Jennaro.

But many of the other Germans shrugged.

"Come on, we have to move this man!" Jennaro insisted.

"I can get my truck," said Big Jack with feigned concern.

"I don't think there's time for that!" said Thompson. "Everybody, empty your satchels! Come on, put them down on the ground, in a row. Let's go! We can lay him on top and carry him back to the truck in the barnyard. Move it!"

The other POWs did as requested, and the American G.I.s placed Heinrich on top of the bags. On a count of three, everyone picked him up using the makeshift stretcher and carried him out of the orchard. With three Germans on one side and three on the other, they had an eerie similarity of pallbearers.

As they left the orchard, Heinrich's yelps of pain slowly faded towards the barnyard. Jennaro looked back at Big Jack as if to say, *You did this on purpose, didn't you?* In response, Big Jack simply shrugged his shoulders.

Weeks afterward, rumors circulated that Heinrich made a full recovery and went back to work at a different POW camp. Others said they heard he committed suicide in the hospital. The one thing everyone agreed on: they were glad he was gone.

Chapter Nineteen

Special Delivery

Throughout that week, Maggie kept herself busy doing mundane, everyday chores around the farm. She'd milk Bessy twice a day, then feed Suri and Bucky. She washed clothes by hand, baked bread, canned and preserved pork and beef and even made soap from bacon fat. One morning, while gathering eggs in the chicken coop with Benny, her son pointed out something which had been on her mind, but she never verbalized it to anyone else before.

"I miss Oku," he said out of the blue.

Maggie stopped gathering eggs for a moment and looked at her son. "You know, honey, so do I. It's been kind of quiet around here. More quiet than I would have ever thought."

"Where did he go?"

"Oku and his family went to the south, where it's warmer."

"I wish it was getting warmer here," he said rubbing his elbows.

"I thought you liked snow? Santa likes the snow."

"I guess. But why can't we have snow and have it be warm?"

"Sorry, it doesn't work that way," his mother said with a smile.

As they gathered several more eggs, Maggie's thoughts floated away to what lie ahead for her family. She realized once the snow did fall –

which could happen any day – several months of solitude and isolation would surely follow. Winter on a farm became a quarantined life of chores, recovery and preparation for spring. Time to repair equipment, mend old clothes, play Schafskopf (sheepshead) with friends, and basically enjoy life as best one could.

However, this winter would be different. Because not only was Erik dispatched, but also Adam would be his proxy, and the thought of living under the same roof with the handsome German for a few more months . . . well, that changed everything.

After cleaning the chicken coop, Maggie and Benny moved to her withered garden where they extracted distending stalks from the cold earth. As she cut her tomato plants at the base, Benny would pull them out of the garden, much to the chagrin of the entwined weeds and tall grasses which tethered themselves to the perennials. Periodically, Benny would find a green tomato lying in the dirt, and with much excitement add it to his collection.

When finished in the garden, she moved inside and did more laundry, dusted the living room and, because Doc Marshall's nurse called to say she could not make her regularly scheduled visit with Adam, Maggie had the opportunity to do something she hadn't done in weeks – help him with his daily stretches.

"I'm sorry to say, I have some bad news," said Maggie as she stepped into Adam's bedroom soon after lunch.

The injured POW looked up from his book and smiled as her essence filled the entire room.

"Apparently Nurse O'Donoghue cannot make it today," said Maggie. "So you'll have to settle for mean old 'Nurse Maggie' to help with your exercises."

"If that's 'bad news,' you have to promise you'll give me bad news every day."

Now it was Maggie's turn to smile.

She approached his bed, stood beside him and slowly reached for the ankle of his good leg. The mere touch of her hand sent a wave of warmth up the spine. It had been far too long since the two of them were alone, and that physical touch made Adam feel like he was plugged into an electrical outlet, his batteries recharging at lightning speed.

Maggie bent the knee up to his chest, then down again, then continued the topic. "Is this the way Nurse O'Donoghue does it? It's been a while since I helped."

"No, not even close."

Maggie paused for a moment, concerned. "Does it hurt? I hope not."

"Oh, it's fine. It's just that if you want to do it the same way she does, you'll need to grunt, mumble to yourself, smell of bad breath and fart every so often."

Maggie laughed. "Oh my goodness."

"Where is she, anyways?"

"She called to say she had to assist with a breach birth."

"Ha, I'm sure the newborn baby heard she was coming over, so he turned himself around in an effort to stay inside. 'No, not Nurse O'Donoghue! Please, let me stay in here where it's safe!'" Adam said, pawing his arms at the air.

They both laughed.

"Nurse O'Donoghue was probably a breach, too," Adam added. "I'm guessing all of her species came into this world breach babies."

Maggie smiled. *Oh my God, that sense of humor!*

After they recovered from the laughter, their eyes locked in longing. "So, Maggie, I have something to tell you. It's been eating me up lately."

Maggie blinked several times and studied that gorgeous face. Just being this close to him sent her heart into overdrive. She could actually feel it pounding in her chest.

"I've missed you. I've missed this," said Adam, letting go of a heavy sigh.

Maggie's face washed itself in a wave of warmth. Her breath quivered and she nodded her head. "Ah-huh."

"Is there any way things can go back to, you know . . . the way they were?"

Without saying a word, she stepped closer to the front of the bed, placed her hand on his forehead, and she brushed his hair back. Adam smiled and reveled in feeling her touch. They were reconnecting again and it felt so good, so necessary. The bond was real. Both could feel it. These two were meant to be together, and they stared into one another's souls.

Suddenly, out of nowhere, the gravely sound of someone clearing their throat could be heard from the doorway. Turning to look, Maggie saw Big Jack standing behind her. Stoic . . . cold.

"So, when you're done here, Maggie, I need your help in the kitchen."

She gave her father a sour look, then nodded.

As Big Jack stepped away, Maggie turned to follow. "I better go. Sorry."

Before she took another step, Adam quickly reached for her hand and snapped her back towards the bed. "Hey, you're forgot something."

"What's that?"

Without saying a word, Adam pulled her to him, and his lips landed squarely on hers. Maggie's mouth was soft, like silky rose pedals, and she smelled delicious. He cupped her face in his free hand and they held the kiss for what seemed like forever. When he released his grip on her arm, she stood up, dizzy and a bit cloudy.

"Will that suffice as payment for services rendered?" Adam asked.

Tucking her hair behind her ears, Maggie smiled and simply said. "Why yes. In fact, I may owe you some change the next time I see you."

She smiled, gently rubbed his arm, and walked out of the room in slightly staggered steps, as if she had one too many glasses of wine.

* * *

Later that morning, Maggie prepared a peanut butter and cucumber sandwich for Benny while Big Jack worked on the opposite side of the kitchen cleaning their wood-burning stove, one of their main sources for heat for the winter. Maggie carefully arranged her son's plate by adding carrots and a dab of homemade applesauce. But before she brought it over to the table, she looked out the window and noticed a bright red Cadillac approaching up the driveway. Sporting a white hardtop, thick white-walled tires and polished chrome bumpers, it appeared to have recently been driven off a showroom floor. Everything about the automobile reeked of money and status.

"Papa, do you recognize that car?" Maggie inquired.

Big Jack put down his pliers, walked over to Maggie and cocked his head to have a better look out the window.

"Can't say I do. Looks like a '42 or '43. She's a beaut! Wonder what they want."

As the car came to a stop, the driver stepped out and paused for a moment. Standing tall, he looked about 45 and was finely dressed, with a light brown overcoat and a matching top hat. A woman about the same age emerged from the passenger side. Also impeccably dressed, she donned a thick wool overcoat, black Mary Jane pumps, white gloves and a red felt medium brim hat.

Then the car's back door opened, but no one came out at first. These two strangers in waiting – still looking at the house, then looking back at the open car door – were not willing to approach the farmhouse until this mysterious VIP stepped out from the back seat.

Maggie and Big Jack could see someone still inside, but this person seemed to postpone their exit, as if to hide his or her identity. As everyone waited, the occupant slowly emerged, stepping out of the shadows.

Maggie leaned over the sink and squinted her eyes. "Is that Audrey? Oh my gosh, it is! I wonder who she's with."

"Is that her husband's car?" asked Big Jack. "Either that, or she has some fancy connections."

Without saying anything more, Maggie grabbed her coat off a kitchen chair and stepped outside. Big Jack stayed put, watching from the kitchen window. As the back door slammed shut behind Maggie, an uneasiness crept into Big Jack's belly. Based on the body language of Audrey and the two strangers, he had a sense this was not a visit to show off a new car.

Audrey gave Maggie a less-than-enthusiastic hug. The four stood in the front of the car having a chat, the large Cadillac's hood ornament visible between them. From the time she had walked up to her friend, Maggie's body language changed from excitement . . . to confusion . . . to fear.

Handshakes were shared as Audrey did most of the talking. Maggie listened intently as her best friend opened her purse and took out a folded piece of paper. She held it in her hand and offered it to Maggie, but she refused to take it. Her arms went behind her back, her shoulders slumped down and she shook her head from side to side as if to say, *No, no, no.* Audrey appeared agitated, giving the paper a shake.

Slowly, Maggie reached for the note, not once taking her eyes off of Audrey. She then turned to look at the kitchen window, knowing Big Jack would be watching, and sent him a look of helpless sorrow. Something scared her to her core, and he swallowed hard as a witness.

Meticulous in her movements, she gently unfolded the piece of paper, read it momentarily, and stumbled forward into her friend with a loud howl. Audrey reached to steady her, as did the two strangers. Despite the support of three people, Maggie fell to her knees.

"Big Jack! Big Jack," Audrey yelled looking in vain at the farmhouse, hoping he could hear her pleas.

* * *

Sitting in the parlor, Maggie sunk into her couch, motionless and numb. She was flanked on either side by a set of tall windows, the outdoor sunlight diffused by floor-to-ceiling lace curtains. In the corner, beside the couch, stood a black parlor stove, next to that sat a wooden storage trunk full of folded blankets and thick comforters. Resting in Maggie's lap was a Western Union telegraph.

Adam promised to keep Benny in the bedroom to distract him while the family dealt with this pressing situation. The two strangers from the Cadillac turned out to be John and Kathy Murphy, two business owners from nearby Pewaukee. Kathy sat across from Maggie; her husband John stood at his wife's shoulder; Audrey sat beside her dear friend on the couch, compassionately rubbing her back, as Big Jack paced the floor digging for clues.

"Okay, okay, so I understand the meaning of the telegram," said Big Jack. "But tell me again how you happened upon it."

"Certainly, Mr. Mueller," said John. "As I said before, it came to our drugstore just this morning. This was supposed to be an exciting day for us. Our Pewaukee location was the first of our twelve stores to get a Teletype machine, and everyone was in attendance, including our Western Union representative." Pausing, he took a deep breath before continuing. "So anyways, we invited all the employees to the back of the store. I really don't know how they all fit in that little office. My wife Kathy was the one who thought it would be good to have our oldest employee, Mildred Wilson, turn on the machine."

"Just get to the story, John," interrupted Kathy.

"Right. So the Western Union machine chugged a few times, then the first notice came across the wire and you would have thought we'd won the World Series. 'Hello,' it read. Everyone let out a loud cheer. Then another line came across reading: 'There is a casualty to announce.' Well, at that, everyone went silent." John's voice trailed off.

"I recognized the last name 'Wentworth,'" said Kathy, folding herself into the conversation. "And then I saw the township of 'Ramsey' and wondered if it wasn't you, Maggie. The thing is, Audrey and I have known each other for several years – ever since her husband sold us a life insurance policy – and she just goes on and on about you, so I remembered the name. I had hoped to actually meet you one day, but under much different circumstances." Swallowing hard, Kathy continued, "Well, once this news came across the wire, we believed it was not the sort of message a delivery boy should make to your doorstep. So we decided to contact Audrey and agreed to accompany her to your farm."

Maggie sat motionless. *Is this all a bad dream?*

"Could you have the wrong Erik Wentworth?" asked Big Jack wishfully.

"I asked our Western Union rep the exact same question," said John. "He said it was virtually impossible. That is your address on the telegram, with Maggie's name printed on the front. And we're told the Western Union contract with the War Department is extremely accurate. I wish I could give you a glimmer of hope here. I suppose the only thing we can do is pray Erik is in a hospital or at a POW camp someplace. The fact that her husband is missing in action gives one some hope, right?"

Maggie listened while everyone talked about Erik as if she wasn't even in the room. As they carried on, she began to realize that for all the shock and all the pain that came with this news, she didn't feel as sad as 20 minutes earlier. Perhaps her collapse outside wasn't so much from sadness as it was from shock. In a weird way, she felt sure Erik would still return home one day, and as the minutes passed, she felt less and less upset.

After more back-and-forth discussion, Maggie finally spoke up. "Do you know when we will be contacted?"

"I'm sorry," asked John Murphy. "Contacted?"

Maggie held up the telegram. "It says 'further details will follow.'"

John Murphy shrugged his shoulders. "I suppose that's a question for the War Department."

"Hey, I know the camp commander at the German POW camp just down the road," said Big Jack, excitement in his voice. "Maybe he can shed some light on this subject. I'll run down there this afternoon."

"There's a German POW camp nearby?" asked Kathy. "My word, I heard they were thinking about doing that but I didn't know they already arrived."

"They've been here for nearly the entire summer," said Big Jack. "Most have left for the winter, but some may be coming back to prune my orchard. We're even hosting an injured POW in the next room. Nice fellow, actually."

Kathy's eyes got wide as saucers as she popped out of her chair. "What? A German soldier? He's in your *house?* Right now?"

"It's a long story, but he was working in our fields and sustained a pretty severe injury."

"Is he guarded? Aren't you afraid? Where are the Americans to watch him?"

"He's harmless," said Big Jack.

Kathy looked unconvinced. She glanced over to her husband and then at Maggie. She took in a long breath. "Good heavens."

At that moment, they could hear a loud giggle from behind the closed door next to the parlor. Upon hearing Benny laugh, a sharp pain bored into Maggie's stomach. If Erik never comes back, will the boy even remember his father? She began to feel guilty, but also confused. *Is Erik dead or isn't he? What does it mean if he's "Missing-In-Action?" What if he's in a German POW camp?* Yeah, he was a son-of-a-bitch, but she didn't want to see him die for his sins. Some days she felt otherwise, but now – nearly six months after he shipped out – there seemed to be a thin layer of compassion. *Why is this happening? Did God strike him down for all the pain and suffering he bestowed on those close to him? Or was it to see how I'd react to the forbidden fruit in the next room? Why did I let him kiss me just a few hours ago? Why did I kiss him in return?*

Maggie had so many thoughts, so many emotions. How could she tell Benny the news? Should she tell him at all? She took a deep breath and pushed down the pain, locking it in her special safety deposit box, right alongside all those other volatile emotions she hid from the rest of the world.

As the parlor got silent, Audrey picked up the telegraph from Maggie's lap and read it once again to herself, shaking her head as she did so.

Washington, D.C.
Nov. 29, 1944 14:23 PM

MRS. MARGARET WENTWORTH
10 COUNTY ROAD C, RAMSEY, WI

The Secretary of War desires me to express his deep regret that your husband, Corporal Erik G. Wentworth, is missing in action and presumed dead in Belgium. Additional information will be sent when received.

THE ADJUTANT GENERAL

In the bedroom, Adam had encouraged Benny to build a tower with Lincoln Logs so he could cock an ear to the conversation. After hearing the bulk of the discussion, a wave of emotion washed over him, too. There was pain . . . confusion . . . guilt . . . anger . . . sadness . . . Feelings that cycled through his heart in the same sequence over and over again. Finally, one emotion settled into his conscience: *Hope.*

Chapter Twenty

The Ghost of Christmas Present

As Audrey and Maggie drove along the busy streets of downtown Milwaukee, gentle snowflakes began to fall, landing on the windshield and instantly melting into tiny water droplets. With a flick of a switch on the dashboard, Audrey quickly wiped them away, only to have them replaced with hundreds more.

Looking out the passenger side window, Maggie felt guilty for taking this overnight trip, even though it had been planned for months. She thought about Adam and how he'd been acting since the news of Erik's disappearance. She could tell he did his very best to tread lightly with her, keeping to himself and rarely engaging her in deep, meaningful conversation. The emotional distance between them had never been so cavernous, she thought . . . and so painful.

Deep down, she knew this trip would be beneficial. Besides, Audrey prepaid for everything, and her best friend would simply make her life miserable if she backed out.

"I'm a little worried about these flurries. What if there's a big storm and we get snowed in? What will Big Jack and Benny do?"

"Oh for heaven's sake," scolded Audrey. "We haven't even checked into the hotel yet and you're bringing me down. Everyone will be fine.

Big Jack's got it all under control. He raised you, didn't he? So he can certainly take care of Benny and Adam for one night."

"Two days," corrected Maggie.

Audrey gave her a look.

"I know, I know," said Maggie, a little embarrassed and slouching into her seat. "But you have to understand, it's hard to leave them. Benny and Big Jack, I mean."

Audrey twisted her mouth and gave Maggie a suspicious look and wondered if she secretly included Adam in that thought. "Hey, darlin,' don't take this the wrong way, but at least you have Big Jack and Benny *and Adam* to talk to. Me? I'm the wife of a traveling salesman, though I may as well be his widow." She caught herself, cringing at the insensitivity of her bad joke. "Oh dear . . . I'm sorry. What I mean is, Bob is home maybe three nights a week, if I'm lucky. Selling insurance takes a lot of travel."

Maggie let the insensitive comment pass and breathed out a heavy sigh. "Where is he this week?"

"At a conference in Dayton. Last time he called, he said he'd be back in a few days. So . . . you and I have some time to play, and I plan on making the most of it. Besides, we'd only be sitting at home tonight listening to Danny Kaye on the radio if we weren't here."

She's right. How could I even consider turning down such a great birthday present? Audrey had promised to take me on this overnight getaway months ago and it would be rude to not make the most of it.

"I'm sorry," Maggie said. "Let's have some fun. Lord knows we deserve it."

"Now you're talking."

"So where is this famous Pfister Hotel, anyway?"

"Um, look outside your window."

As Audrey pulled her car up to a stop in front of this historic landmark, they both looked at one another and smiled.

Audrey put the gearshift into PARK as two valets opened their doors. "Good afternoon, ladies. And welcome to the Pfister Hotel," said a short man with a pencil mustache. "I am happy to take your car and any luggage. It is my pleasure to serve you."

"Our intention is to be served," said Audrey, letting out a loud laugh as she stepped out of her blue 1940 Buick. Maggie forced a laugh as well, beginning to feel a little better about the trip.

As they walked through the front doors and into the lobby, the flamboyance and beauty of the building's architecture and décor was overwhelming. Constructed in 1893 by Charles Pfister, the Romanesque Revival hotel featured an ornate three-story lobby, a massive fireplace and a grand marble staircase. Unlike other buildings of its time, the Pfister Hotel offered electricity throughout, a built-in sprinkler system, and its very own emergency power plant.

"Reservation for Stanton," chirped Audrey to the front desk attendant as she and Maggie stood beaming with anticipation.

"There will be two of you?" asked the counter attendant, a handsome man in his late forties, dark hair greased back, tight collar, starched shirt.

"That is correct," Audrey said.

"Will you be needing any transportation to restaurants, shows, or shopping this evening?"

"We are going to see a play at the Pabst Theater at 7:00," chimed in Maggie proudly. *"A Christmas Carol."*

"Oh, it's very good. I saw it last week," the attendant said. "I can have a taxi waiting for you, or if you prefer, we can also do a nice horse-drawn carriage. It's a splendid way to arrive in style, if you ask me."

"But it's snowing," Maggie said.

"Yes, but the carriage is fully enclosed. And plenty of blankets are inside, heated bricks on the floor to keep you warm. It's quite cozy."

"What do you think?" Audrey asked Maggie.

"Let's do it. You only live once, right?"

"I'll make all the arrangements. In the meantime, your room is ready. I will ring the bellman."

* * *

As they stood outside their hotel room for the unveiling, the bellman inserted the key, turned the handle and revealed a whole new world – something foreign to a farm girl who only knew of manure, chicken coops, dirty barns, early mornings and a chronically sore back. This type of palatial chamber only existed in magazines or on the silver screen. About the only thing missing was the angelic chorus, but in Maggie's head their harmonies were deafening.

Two full-sized, four-post beds were positioned in the center of the expansive room. The comforters alone were nearly as thick as Maggie's mattress at home. Linens of rich satin and finely woven cotton sat neatly folded on a shelf. The wallpaper consisted of hundreds of velvet shapes, forming a *fleur-de-lis* pattern. The crown molding was ornate and stained dark, bringing out its rich walnut grain. The floorboards were nearly 12 inches wide and they, too, matched the crown molding above them.

The bellman set the suitcases down and opened the Venetian blinds to illuminate the accommodations. Maggie spun in a circle looking up at the ceiling, then walked over to the window and asked him, "What direction is this? Is this east?"

"Yes, ma'am. That's Lake Michigan over there," the bellman answered with a pointed finger.

"Oh my gosh! It looks like an ocean."

"Yes, ma'am," he repeated, more interested in getting his tip than playing the role of tour guide.

Steering Maggie away from the window, he showed her where the towels were kept, how to use the phone, how to draw a warm bath and how to control the in-room thermostat – a feature neither of them had ever seen in a building before. Maggie was in heaven. Audrey sat on the edge of her tall bed – both feet dangling off the sides, not even close to touching the floor – and she watched her friend delight in the excessive pampering.

Next, the bellman pointed to several extra pillows and a bed warmer in the closet. He then bent over and handed Maggie a porcelain spittoon. "Just in case," he said.

She didn't know if she should be insulted or if he was trying to be funny. She was literally on overload. This beautiful hotel . . . the energy of the city . . . and someone to wait on her hand and foot . . . it was all so surreal. She couldn't help but share a wide smile.

"If there's anything else you need, just let us know. We are dedicated to making your stay a pleasant one." The bellhop put his hand out looking for a tip. Maggie grabbed it and shook it, as if to say goodbye.

"You have been so kind," she said.

Confused, the bellman looked to Audrey for help. She laughed out loud at her friend's *naïveté* and then, awkwardly walking her buttocks off the tall mattress and plopping her feet onto the hardwood floor, approached the bellman and handed him a nickel. He nodded in gratitude, first to Audrey, then to Maggie, before leaving the room.

"Oh!" said Maggie. "He wanted a—"

"Welcome to the big time, sister. Things are a little different in the city."

Maggie slapped her forehead. "I am such a dope!"

"No worries, darlin'. We're gonna set this town on fire tonight. By the time we leave, everyone will be giving *us* a nickel just to be seen with us."

Both stood quietly for a moment when Audrey went to her suitcase. "I have something for you. I have been meaning to give you this for some time now."

"Another gift? Why? This trip is plenty."

"Oh, it's nothing really, just something I made."

She pulled out a small cigar-sized box and handed it to her friend. Maggie stared at Audrey and then at the present. She methodically removed the bow, then the wrapping paper, and slowly opened the top to reveal a Blue Star Service Banner. The small flag featured a lone blue star in a field of white – the same type of banner displayed in the homes of soldiers throughout America. The more servicemen, the more stars.

"It's incredible, Audrey. And you made this?"

"Ah-huh. You must be the only wife of a serviceman without one," she added. "You can put it in the front window of your house when we get back to Ramsey."

"I really don't know what to say."

"Say, 'Thanks, Audrey,' and I'll be happy."

Maggie looked at her friend and wondered if she could detect the mixed emotions. She was holding a gift Audrey so thoughtfully took the time to make, yet she wasn't too certain about paying tribute to a perpetrator who was now MIA. But she put on the happy face and said, "It's so thoughtful. Thank you." Staring at her friend, she took her hands in hers, looked her straight in the eye and added, "I really, *really* need this weekend. And I want to apologize if I ever came across as ungrateful."

"Happy belated birthday, hon. I'm just so happy you decided to come. I know things have been tough, especially lately. So you deserve a little fun."

They hugged each other, and as Audrey let up, Maggie wouldn't unwind her coiled embrace. It felt so good to have such a friend, someone she never wanted to lose.

"I'm so lucky to have you."

Audrey squeezed her again, and when they finally separated she changed the subject. "So, which bed do you want?"

"The one nearest to the window," said Maggie. "This view is breathtaking!"

"It's all yours. Now let's unpack and get ready for a great Saturday night."

* * *

6:30 PM. Both women looked radiant as they stood atop the large marble staircase overlooking the hotel lobby. As they descended in slow motion, these two country VIPs could have easily been mistaken for true royalty, thanks to Audrey's remarkable aptitude as a seamstress. Outside on the street, a horse-drawn carriage awaited.

Audrey glowed in a perfectly sculpted gold dress with long pleats, a chiffon stole, elbow-length white opera gloves and a small crown hat. Equally elegant, Maggie donned a black velvet drop waist dress with V-pleats running from the waist through the bodice. Also one of Audrey's creations, it featured padded shoulders and fit Maggie's slim figure perfectly. She, too, had white crocheted lace gloves and topped off the look wearing a matching black pillbox hat, complete with a thin-laced veil.

To protect themselves from the cold evening, Audrey wore a full-length white wool evening cape, with beautiful brocade trim. It featured a round neckline, fitted shoulder seams and was lined with white satin.

Complementing her ensemble, Maggie donned an extra-long capelet made of wool which had a small rounded collar and hidden arm flaps.

There was no mistaking it – these two shining stars owned the night, as evident when they walked to their carriage, a Marine donning his Dress Blue uniform grabbed his heart and said, "Aren't you two dolls a knockout!"

Laughing, they waved him off.

The ten-minute carriage ride to the Pabst Theater felt a little rugged on some of Milwaukee's cobblestone streets, but it was still enjoyable and *sui generis*. At one point, Maggie leaned over to Audrey saying, "We deserve this, right?" Audrey nodded her head, knowing if she said even one word her voice would crack.

As the two stepped out of the carriage near the main entrance to the theater, an usher met them holding a large umbrella to protect them from the light mist, which had been flurries hours earlier. The soft drizzle varnished everything with a rich luminescence as streetlights reflected on sidewalks and automobile headlights danced off the cobblestones in the road.

"Are you here for *A Christmas Carol*?" the usher inquired.

"Indeed we are," said Audrey.

"Well, step right this way, ladies," he proclaimed before walking them to the main entrance.

As the two luminaries stepped into the magnificent theater, Maggie was again in awe of the surrounding architectural details and noted how the venue shared a similar *savoir-faire* of their grand hotel. After checking their cloaks in the main lobby, they walked up a staircase of Italian Carrara marble, Maggie could hardly contain herself, turning to Audrey, "It's magnificent."

Built by world-renowned beer baron Frederick Pabst, the theater utilized the traditions of European opera houses and the German Renaissance Revival halls. The intimate yet opulent venue featured a drum-shaped seating arrangement accommodating 1,300 patrons comfortably in a wash of plush reds and soupy maroons. Before them stood an impervious velvet curtain framed by a proscenium arch of hand-carved golden leaves. Floating overhead and fighting for attention hung a two-ton glass chandelier made of Austrian crystal, its precarious presence giving patrons a certain incommodious chill as they warily settled into their seats. From the theater itself to the patrons who mingled about, the room radiated glamour and affluence.

Finely dressed couples made up the majority of the crowd – women in long gowns, older gentlemen in tuxedos – and various servicemen in pressed military uniforms escorting wives, girlfriends or new acquaintances. Maggie and Audrey in particular turned heads from the moment they set foot inside the theater. As others filed into the grand hall, whispered murmurs could be heard as everyone set their gaze on this pair of country girls from Ramsey, wondering who they were and why both were not walking the red carpet at the Academy Awards.

They were then shown to their seats – first row center – complements of Audrey's husband Bob who had received the tickets as a sales perk.

"Oh my Lord," breathed Maggie to the usher, trying her best not to act impressed. "Are we in the right seats?"

"Indeed you are, ma'am. Enjoy the show."

Soon the lights dimmed and the performance began. Maggie lost herself in the costuming, the live music, the special effects and the outstanding acting. She was particularly taken by Dickens' storyline about Ebenezer Scrooge – a man who got a second chance at a better life and to make good on his past mistakes. She couldn't help but think of Erik and wonder – if he wasn't dead – could he, too, receive the same kind of salvation? Could he change like Scrooge did?

* * *

By the time the house lights came on and the applause subsided, Maggie and Audrey retrieved their cover wraps and followed the current of patrons outdoors and into the chilly December night. Looking up, Maggie noticed the change in the weather. "It stopped raining. I can even see a few stars."

"Well then let's walk to dinner," suggested Audrey. "It's maybe four or five blocks. Besides, getting a cab right now will take us forever."

With arms locked and bodies snugged tightly together, the two dignitaries walked lock-step to Karl Ratzsch's, one of Milwaukee's premier German restaurants. Once again, Audrey pulled out all the stops – having made dinner reservations two months prior – all in an effort to ensure this evening would be memorable and complete.

The restaurant was a throwback to the city's early German heritage. As if stepping through a wayfaring portal, the exterior *fachwerk* was classic Bavarian – the white stucco and a dark brown trim making up isosceles, obtuse and equilateral triangles throughout the facade.

Inside, the main dining room was warm and dusky, with Renaissance, Baroque and Neoclassicism reproductions gracing the walls; like Gottlieb Schick's *Frau von Cotta*, *The Fall of Phaeton* by Johann Liss and *The Crucifixion* by Matthias Grünewald. Single candles centered on each table illuminated the patrons who shared the intimate space with oversized European beer steins and porcelain statues methodically placed on shelves throughout the dining room. A zither player wearing lederhosen and sporting a thick white beard sat comfortably in the corner singing romantic German love songs. *Big Jack would love it here,* Maggie thought to herself. It was *Gemütlichkeit* at its finest.

After settling in at their table and enjoying the first few sips of a chilled bottle of Riesling, Audrey ordered the stuffed pork chops, Maggie the sauerbraten. They each lit a cigarette and talked about the hotel, the play and how they needed to do this again, sooner rather than later.

"So tell me, Mags," said Audrey, reaching for Maggie's hand, more serious now. "How are you handling the news about Erik? You rarely talk of him."

Having just finished her first glass of wine, Maggie's head got light and her lips got loose. "Oh, I don't know," she said, tapping a white tip of her Chesterfield into the ashtray. "I try not to let myself think about where he is or if he's really dead. In fact, some days I don't think about him at all. Isn't that odd?"

Audrey froze for a moment, took a long drag from her cigarette, then collected herself. "Really? Gosh, if Bob went MIA I would be a mess."

"Yeah, it's strange. But honestly, since he left I have been much happier. Benny, too. I feel less like I have to walk on eggshells, you know? And if Erik never comes home," she paused and sucked more nicotine into her lungs, "well, I don't want to think about that."

Curious to know more, Audrey cocked her head slightly and studied her friend. She half expected Maggie to talk about the sleepless nights and the challenges of not having her husband around. Instead, Audrey followed the path of the conversation and took a contrarian's point of view.

"Wow. Okay then. So . . . I have to ask you about the day he left to go to basic training . . . You were obviously cross. Remember how we talked in your kitchen?"

Maggie nodded.

"It's none of my business, but was there more to it than him leaving?"

"Well, yes!" Maggie snapped loudly, turning heads in the dining room. She had a flashback to the ugly days – the abuse and the pain. Feeling her wine, she leaned in closer, talking more softly as to not disturb the other patrons. "Audrey, you know how everyone in town hates him? Well, they have good reason!"

"For that drunken temper of his? Yeah," whispered Audrey as she stamped out her cigarette in a crystal ashtray.

"No, I mean, yeah. But . . . there's more to it."

Audrey's curiosity escalated. She leaned in closer.

"He used to be so kind, so understanding," Maggie continued in a loud whisper. "But when he lost the farm to his brother, well . . . something broke inside of him. My husband hasn't been gone for six months – as far as I'm concerned, he's been gone about three years, and he has been a bastard of the worst order."

"Hon, you don't have to talk about this – "

"Oh yes I do!" insisted Maggie. Pausing for a moment to take in a slow, measured breath, Maggie continued with confidence, and it felt great to get things off her chest. "Audrey, the truth is, he was abusive. That bastard would hit me. He would *punch* me! Kick me! He gave me shiners, bruised ribs – and I would hide them. Once he nearly broke my neck. Argh! I can't stand the thought of him returning and us repeating the cycle."

Dumbfounded, Audrey's eyes locked onto Maggie as she moved her head side to side in disbelief.

"You know what else? He wrote us three times since he left. Three *goddamned* times! He doesn't love me. I thought he'd at least write Benny, but no. Nothing. Just three lousy one-page letters. Can you believe that?" Maggie said with damp eyes.

"Oh, hon, I didn't know. Really, I am so, so sorry." Audrey then reached for a handkerchief in her purse and passed it to Maggie. "I shouldn't have brought it up. I apologize."

"It's alright," said Maggie, dabbing at her eyes. "Everyone knew he was trash except me. Now I know, too, right? The crazy thing is, I would *defend* him all the time. God, what a fool I was. Did you think I was a fool, Audrey?"

"Not at all. You are the most kind, most sincere woman I know, so don't get down on yourself. You are not a fool! Let's put all that behind and make this weekend about *us* and better tomorrows."

Maggie raised her glass. Audrey did as well, and together they toasted to friendship and carefree times. At least for one night.

During the rest of the meal, Maggie talked about other subjects . . . like Benny and Big Jack . . . and they shared some stories about some of the American guards. Audrey carried on about the challenges she faced having a part-time husband. It was a therapeutic conversation shared over a wonderful dinner and a few more glasses of wine. After dessert, they each had a glass of liqueur. Then Maggie brought up Erik again.

"You know, I don't miss him in the least."

"Not one bit?" said Audrey.

"Who needs him? He poisoned my home. He poisoned my life. Really. And I am happier now than ever before."

Audrey smiled nervously.

As Maggie put her glass to her lips to take another sip, she let the words slip out, "If only he was like Adam."

Audrey's eyes got big and she set her snifter hard onto the table. "Um, what did you just say?"

"Nothing."

"Oh yes you did," she said through a throaty chuckle. "I heard you."

"No you didn't."

"Ha! You sly girl. Let's talk about this."

Maggie giggled, uncertain. "For Pete's sake, Audrey. There's nothing to talk about."

"I know when you are lying, and you are soooo not telling the truth right now."

Maggie took another sip of her drink, hiding her smile behind the glass. She didn't know if it was the alcohol talking or if deep down she felt relieved at the idea of discussing her innermost feelings about her houseguest.

Twirling her glass and leaning back in her chair, Audrey smiled. "Well the plot doth thicken, does it not?"

"What?"

"You have feelings for him. *I knew it* the day you met him in the town square."

Maggie just smiled, embarrassed. "Oh you're making that up."

"No I'm not. By golly, I should have foreseen this the moment you both met behind that flower pot."

Knowing her retorts were futile, Maggie acquiesced, "Well okay, here's the thing . . ."

Audrey leaned forward.

"He's incredibly kind. He's always helping me. And he makes me laugh. Big Jack *loves* him, too. The list goes on and on. And you should see him with Benny! He's a natural with that boy."

"Oh . . . my . . . God . . ." said Audrey with her jaw on the floor. "You are smitten, my friend."

"Of course, nothing will happen. He probably hates me now, since I have been such a pill this past month. It's just nice to have a man around the house who is so caring. Is that such a crime?" she added with slightly slurred speech.

"I'm guessing what's on your mind is the real crime."

"Oh good heavens, Audrey. I'm a married woman!"

"Ah-huh," Audrey teased while taking another sip and opening her gold cigarette case to grab another smoke.

Maggie let out a heavy sigh. "It's just that having Adam in the house all the time, well, it's getting so he's become part of the family, you know? I have to tell you, I have tried really hard to be mad at him. Get this – I blamed him for Erik's MIA notice, do you know that? Then I blamed myself. Then I blamed both of us and decided to stop talking to him altogether. We even got into an argument the other day, and the whole time I kept thinking I really wasn't mad at him at all, but instead I was mad at, hell, I don't know, *everything*. All of it. My life, his life, the fall off the ladder . . ."

Audrey sat speechless.

Fueled by truth serum on the rocks, Maggie continued to spill her emotions at the table. "Big Jack talked to me about it," Maggie added.

"Really? My gosh, what happened?"

"He was very upset after I said we were all 'one big happy family.'"

"Oooo, I can only imagine. He's a real traditionalist."

"Yeah, it was not pretty. He basically said I shouldn't get too close to Adam. But it is tough, ya know? Tough, tough, tough!"

"Maggie, be careful," cautioned Audrey, reaching for her friend's hand. "Big Jack's right. This could get out of control and then – BAM! – Erik's back and the Germans are gone and that's that. Or Erik isn't back but Adam is *still* gone. Hard to see this one having a happy ending."

Sighing heavily, Maggie knew she was right. "So? So what is wrong with enjoying the company of a man who is tender and honest and good with my child? I deserve that, don't I? As long as nothing happens, right?"

"Do I need to answer that?" Pausing a moment, Audrey put her hands in her lap and studied her friend. "Just don't do anything you'll regret later is all I'm saying."

Maggie dropped her head, took in a deep breath, then looked back at Audrey, "Well tell me this – do I at least have your permission to get drunk tonight?"

"Only if I can join you."

"You already is, um, are . . ." Maggie slurred. They both laughed hard and asked for the bill.

They left the restaurant around 10:30 and decided on a nightcap. They planned to walk back to the hotel a mere three blocks away but also wanted to stop for one last cocktail at the first bar they found en route.

Walking east along Mason Street, the wobbling starlets giggled, spoke of their youth and the many changes over their years together. As they passed a particular alley, they heard a heavy door burst open and crash hard against galvanized steel garbage cans no more than 20 feet from where they stood. Loud music spilled into the cold night air as a man stumbled out the door and fell to the ground in drunken hysterics. He staggered to his feet, let out another hearty laugh, and then proceeded to walk in the opposite direction, disappearing into the shadows of the alleyway while singing "I'll Be Home For Christmas."

A weak light bulb hung above the door, illuminating the alley like a small candle. The silhouette of a large doorman stepped into view, then with a long reach he grabbed the heavy steel door and proceeded to close it, but just as he pulled it towards him, he paused for a moment and looked directly at Maggie and Audrey, who stared back in awe. They could only make out minimal features. Maggie noticed he had a very large nose and possibly a thick mustache. The darkness didn't help.

He tipped his hat and then closed the thick steel door, muting the loud music and laughter which emanated from inside.

Maggie and Audrey looked at one another and smiled.

"That sounded like a fun bar," said Audrey. "Want to go in?"

Still buzzed and a bit plucky, Maggie gave it some thought. "I guess, but what kind of place has its main door in an alley? Seems kind of shady."

"They're playing Christmas songs, Mags. I'm sure it's fine."

"Okay, you're right, let's do it. We did say we'd stop at the first tavern we saw – and that would be it."

They headed down the dark alley, still arm-in-arm, and with the help of the dim light they could see a small, unassuming wooden sign screwed to the Cream-City brick building. It read: THE KING'S THRONE.

"See. It's got a name. So it's gotta be legitimate," Audrey said. She then grabbed the door handle and gave it a confident pull. But her body snapped back and she nearly lost her balance. The door was bolted shut.

"Maybe it's a private party," said Maggie, starting to backpedal.

Without saying a word, Audrey knocked hard. Maggie started to get nervous and pulled her friend close.

At eye-level, a small rectangular peephole suddenly slid open, and they could see two eyes and part of a nose studying them.

"Hello," sang Audrey, waving a hanky playfully towards the peephole. "We're from out of town and heard this was a good place for two ladies to get a drink."

The set of eyes stared at them for a moment, blinked twice, and the small door quickly slid shut.

"Why did you lie?" inquired Maggie. "We've never heard of this place. Now we'll never . . ."

Suddenly, the handle jiggled, then clicked, and the door swung open. The tall doorman stood before them like a Goliath.

"Welcome to The King's Throne," he said with a deep but friendly voice. "There is a two drink minimum and all we ask is you not dance on the tables."

Maggie and Audrey smiled at one another and without saying a word stepped inside a cramped foyer. The heavy steel door closed hard behind them, echoing into the night. Before them stood a tall flight of stairs which led to the second floor.

"The refreshments and music are right up these stairs," the doorman said while settling back into his chair.

As they methodically took one step at a time, these two fish-out-of-water could hear the Christmas music getting louder while the smell of cigarettes and sweet liquor got stronger.

Once at the top of the stairwell, they stepped into the doorway. Maggie turned towards Audrey and said, "It's really dark in here."

"Our eyes will adjust."

Illuminated mostly by candlelight, there was a long bar on one side and intimate booths opposite. At the very back of the room, a cluster of patrons sang "White Christmas" in time with the piano player. The club seemed fueled by laughter and merriment, and that's exactly what they wanted – especially Maggie.

The King's Throne had a good crowd on that Saturday night, and lucky for these two, they found the last two available seats at the end of the bar, near the top of the steps. With no coat rack visible, they draped their cover capes on the backs of their tall barstools.

"What can I get you two lovely ladies this evening?" asked a handsome bartender dressed in a white silk shirt, dark vest and tight bowtie.

"Manhattan for me," said Audrey.

"I'll take a Brandy Old Fashioned," added Maggie.

As the bartender mixed their cocktails, Maggie dug into her purse.

"Oh no you don't," said Audrey. "Your money is no good tonight. This weekend is my treat."

"You mean I'm not even allowed to buy just one drink?"

"Nope."

Maggie sighed and then turned to get a better look at the room, her eyes slowly adjusting to the dimness.

When the cocktails were placed before them, the two best friends held them up, each with one elbow on the bar. "To us," toasted Audrey.

"To us," echoed Maggie. The glasses clinked.

They both took a sip, breathed a long sigh, and then for nearly a minute didn't say a word. While the Christmas songs played from the other side of the room, the ensuing silence between them seemed like it would never end. Audrey sat still, thinking about the news of Erik's abuse and Maggie's admitted infatuation with Adam.

Maggie, on the other hand, stirred the ice cubes with the stem of her maraschino cherry, trying to decide if she told her friend too much.

Finally, Audrey broke the silence. "Wow! That sure was a great play, wasn't it?"

"Yeah, terrific," Maggie said, somewhat relieved by the topic. "Better than any movie I've ever seen."

Again, silence. Soon the ice jiggled in Audrey's drink. "Boy, that went down in a hurry. Want another?" she asked. "I think we have time."

"Good Lord, slow down, Audrey."

"I guess I'm thirsty."

"And soon you'll be really drunk. Or more drunker-er."

They both laughed.

Getting serious for a moment, Maggie placed her glass on the bar and swiveled her barstool to face her friend. "I want to tell you something . . ." She paused, taking Audrey's hands into her own. "I need to thank you for not being judgmental."

"Whatever do you mean?"

"You know what I mean. I told you a lot of things tonight. And I want to thank you for not thinking less of me."

"I understand – I think," said Audrey, trying to share her true feelings. "Listen, you know I'm here for you. I will always be here for you regardless of what happens in your life. But I have to confess something as well." She paused for a deep breath. "I really can't say

I knew about what was going on with you and Erik, but I did have my suspicions."

Maggie snapped back her head a little. "You did? Really? Were things that obvious?"

"To me, yeah, sometimes they were. Little things, like the way he'd boss you around or lose his temper at the drop of a hat. But you mean the world to me, hon, and I want so bad for you to be happy."

Maggie looked at her and smiled, eyes getting wet.

"You will get through this. And when Erik comes back maybe things will be better, like they were years ago. Adam will be gone and you can start life anew. You have to keep the faith."

"*If* he comes back," said Maggie softly, more to herself. "That Western Union telegraph also said, '. . . *missing in action, and presumed—*'"

"Don't say it, hon." Audrey squeezed her hands hard and wore a twisted expression on her face.

"This is why I love you so much," said Maggie. "I have to admit, holding that secret about Erik had been *killing* me. I simply had to tell you, and I'm so glad I did."

Audrey gave her a loving smile and then turned towards the bartender and ordered another round.

"Okay with you? We can sleep in tomorrow. Church isn't until what, 11:00?"

With that Maggie breathed a heavy sigh. "Yes. And I may even have another after that," she said, slapping the wooden bar top with confidence.

"It's my pleasure to oblige," said the bartender, pulling their empty glasses towards him.

Maggie smiled at her friend, rubbed her shoulder and then looked down towards the end of the long bar.

"It's hard to tell, but there seems to be a lot of men in here, don't you think?"

Audrey leaned back in her chair, stretched her neck and looked down towards the chorus of singers. "From what I can see, it appears you would be correct. But it's so dark."

"Well, they obviously haven't seen us come in yet or we would be beating them off with a stick," said Maggie with false bravado.

They both laughed, finally feeling more like themselves.

"You know, while the bartender makes us these drinks I'm going to powder my nose," said Maggie. "Care to join me?"

"Are you afraid some of these fellas might spoil your good name?"

"No, I hope they would spoil *both* of our good names," Maggie said with a chuckle.

Audrey opened her purse and pulled out a small compact. "Actually, I'm fine! Besides, you're a big girl, and I don't want to give up these last two seats to whoever else may walk in, so go ahead without me."

"Okay, just don't be upset if I return with a few good options."

"You are naughty!"

Maggie laughed and proceeded to walk towards the back of the bar searching for the ladies' room. She made eye contact with several men, smiled politely – and they in turn smiled back. But there was something insoluble about these patrons . . . their body language felt cold, almost hollow. She couldn't quite put her finger on it.

As she got closer to the piano, she passed more men sitting alongside the bar rail to her left and in dark booths to her right. Most were paired up as couples and all talked very closely, as if making top secret business deals. She began to notice other things, too, like a hand placed on another man's knee; one fellow rubbing his friend's shoulder; another man stroking a friend's hair . . .

As she neared the back of the room, a handsome younger man, barely 20 years old, let out a loud laugh as he sat perched on his barstool facing someone who appeared to be twice his age. It seemed the older fellow just revealed the punch line to a joke, and what happened next caused Maggie's heart to skip a few beats.

The younger man stepped off his bar stool, threw his arms around his male friend and kissed him passionately on the lips. Maggie froze in her tracks.

Oh my God! This is a homosexual bar! I've heard about them but never thought I'd ever see one!

Maggie didn't know if she should proceed to the restroom or bolt back to Audrey. She took one step back, then one step forward, then another step back. *Don't make a fool out of yourself! Just pretend this is no big deal.* So Maggie collected herself, and decided to carry on toward the restroom, but before she could proceed, the kissing couple separated and turned directly to face her.

The young man smiled at Maggie, a bit embarrassed. "Oops, I could get in trouble for that," he said through a high-pitched, intoxicated chuckle. She did not reply. She could only force a smile and then turned to look at the recipient of the kiss. Were her eyes playing tricks on her? Was she seeing this correctly? She stepped back with jaw agape and tried to focus. She was not imagining things – she knew this man. Despite the dark environment, the recognition hit them both at the exact same moment.

"Bob?" Maggie said in shock. "Oh my God! *Bob!*"

"Maggie? Oh good Lord!" he said in a panic. "Maggie?"

She just stared, frozen.

"This isn't what it looks like. I can explain. Um, let me tell you . . ."

"You're supposed to be in Dayton! Audrey told me you were in Dayton – "

"Audrey? She's *here?*"

"But wait – you're in Dayton . . ." Maggie repeated more to herself than to him.

"Uh-oh," said the younger man playfully, not realizing the severity of the situation. "Someone's in troooouble," he sang while pulling on Bob Stanton's necktie.

"I can, um, explain," added Bob, ignoring the young man. "I, um, ah . . ." Before Bob could formulate a lie, Maggie turned and shot back towards Audrey, who had just handed the bartender money for the second round of drinks.

"We have to go," Maggie insisted.

"Holy smokes! You look like you've seen the ghost of Christmas past. Come on, I just bought us another round."

"We have to leave, *now!*"

"Whoa. Okay, okay," Audrey said. "Did someone make a move on you? Who was it? I'll take care of this guy and show him he can't mess with my girl!" she added playfully, fisticuffs upright and at the ready.

Audrey took a step towards the back of the room, but Maggie grabbed her friend's arm forcefully, spinning her around and nearly pushing her towards the door.

"Oww, you're hurting me. I was only kidding. Jeez."

"Let's . . . go . . . *now!*"

Audrey looked at her with intense confusion. "Okay, okay, I'm leaving. You can tell me about it outside. It must have been some kind of pickup line."

Maggie nearly ran down the stairs, turning often to look back at Audrey. "Hurry. Come on!"

"What's your problem?"

Maggie kept walking and soon met the doorman at the bottom of the stairs. Ignoring him, she pushed hard on the door but it would not open.

"Um, let me help you, ma'am," said the doorman, moving methodically. He slid a large metal hasp to the right, unlocking the metal door.

"Goodnight, ladies. Feel free to come again."

"I'm not sure I'm allowed to," said Audrey, catching up.

Once the door closed behind them, they stood alone in the cold and dimly lit alleyway. The laughter, the singing, the murmur of conversation all muted in an instant. The night silence enveloped them.

Audrey stared at the exit while putting on her cape and trying to best assess the situation. She then looked at Maggie who paced back and forth in the alley, lost in her own world.

"What the hell?" snapped Audrey, her voice echoing, the steamy breath floating out of her mouth.

"I have to make sense of things," said Maggie to herself. "How drunk am I?" She started replaying the scene in her head. *Maybe that wasn't Bob. Perhaps it was someone who* looked *like Bob. But no . . . he used my name!*

"Hellooooo! Do you mind telling me what just happened up there?"

"I can't talk about it. Oh God, I can't believe it."

"What in heaven's name are you saying?"

"We have to go," said Maggie, taking a step towards the street. "Let's head to the hotel."

"No!" insisted Audrey. "I am not budging from this alley until you tell me something. My God, woman, you walk in like you own the place, tell me you want *three* drinks, maybe more, and then without notice you announce your departure. You have to give me something! Did you even make it to the bathroom?"

Maggie stared at her friend, pursed her lips and a deep sense of sorrow filled her eyes. This woman, her best friend, the sister proxy who pulls her up when she's feeling down, who virtually kidnapped her to ensure she had a fun weekend, who makes her son quilts and even sewed the elegant dress she wore at that very moment . . . this Rock of Gibraltar, without whom she would be entirely lost . . . cannot know.

How can I say your husband is a homosexual? My God, that will kill you to know this. Is that why you don't have children? Do you even sleep together? Oh dear Lord, do you already know? Maybe you already know. What am I thinking? There's no way you would know such a secret. And I am not about to be the one to tell you . . . Say something! Anything!

"Well? What gives?" snapped Audrey.

Maggie took a heavy sigh and said. "Audrey, I don't know any other way to say it so I'm going to come right out with it . . ."

Audrey cocked her head and twisted her mouth. "Okay . . ."

"That bar . . . it is . . . was . . . a *queer* bar."

Audrey stared at her for a tick. "What?"

"It's true."

"That place? Noooo . . ." Audrey growled in a deep voice.

"I'm serious. I saw two men kissing one another. Like really kissing. I don't think I've ever dreamed of kissing another man as passionately as that."

"You mean that . . . that place was . . ." Audrey began to laugh hysterically. "Oh my God! *OH MY GOD!* No wonder they kept it locked. The secrecy to get in . . . and the little door . . . the peephole!" Audrey paused for a second then slapped her knee, adding, "For the love of Pete, we got in because that doorman thought we were . . ." Audrey started laughing even harder. "What a story that will be."

Maggie felt sick. For the first time in her life, she lied to her best friend. She felt ashamed, yet somewhat relieved she pulled it off with such believability. But was it really a lie? She did indeed see two men kiss. That was true. She simply didn't share the details.

"I want to go back to the hotel," said Maggie.

"Wow. A homosexual bar," repeated Audrey, ignoring Maggie and still reeling from the prospect. "That is *unbelievable*."

"Can we just go?" begged Maggie.

"What? Really?"

"Yeah, I'm tired."

"Well, I guess we did have our one last drink."

"Yes we did."

"Okay, hon. A deal's a deal. The hotel's just a block away. Let's the two of us take a nice *roooomantic* stroll on this cool evening," joked Audrey, putting her arm around Maggie.

"Stop it!"

"Wow, you really were put off by that place. I mean, when you think about it, what's the big deal? It's not like we had anything to worry about, right?"

Maggie stopped walking, turned towards Audrey and got serious. "It is a big deal! You know that, right?"

"My gosh, darlin.' You are acting like you saw President Roosevelt in there or something." Audrey sighed and smiled. "Don't let one stop ruin your weekend. You have to admit, this was one hell of a night, right? We wanted fun and adventure, and I would say we found it."

"More than I wanted," Maggie said quietly to herself as she began walking again. "Let's go. I'm really cold." With arms wrapped tightly against her chest, as if to give herself a bear hug, Maggie proceeded down the sidewalk carrying the weight of a new, even heavier burden. *How long was it, maybe an hour? I confess one secret, then am burdened by another.* Time to suffer in silence, yet again.

* * *

That next morning, they barely arose in time for Sunday mass at St. John's Cathedral. As they nursed their hangovers and walked to the church a few blocks from the hotel, neither one spoke of the previous evening's finale. They talked about the play, the VIP treatment, the marvelous dinner . . . but not a word about The King's Throne.

Maggie could not get the image of Bob kissing that younger man out of her head. Despite being intoxicated, it was burned on the inside of her eyelids, and each time she closed them – even if merely blinking – she would see it again and again.

As she knelt in her pew, she wondered if or when she should share the news. Being a homosexual was a sin – at least that's what she had been taught. *How could I ever tell Audrey? And what might Bob say or do the next time he sees me? We spend Christmas Eve together every year – and that's a week away!*

As she pondered these things, Maggie turned her questions over to God in the form of prayer. She asked why men are attracted to men. She pondered why so much pain exists in the world. She wondered if the Western Union telegraph wasn't a shot across the bow to wake up from her fantasy. She didn't have the answers. *"Well, Lord . . . it worked,"* she said in her head. *"I have no interest in Adam anymore and I'm sorry my heart went wandering. You must think I'm such an idiot. I'm so, so sorry."* Maggie bowed her head and prayed for forgiveness.

After Mass, as they walked back to the hotel, the sun seemed especially intense. It was as if God pointed a brilliant flashlight in Maggie's face as she walked. *Okay, enough already! You've made your point.*

"Are you hungry?" asked Audrey as they sauntered south down Jefferson Street, unaware of Maggie's mindset.

"Actually, I'm famished. I need some eggs."

They enjoyed their late breakfast in the hotel restaurant and checked out of the historic destination around 1:30. It would be an hour-long ride back to Ramsey, but to Audrey it felt like it would take several days. She only hoped she could keep her eyes on the road and her headache didn't cause her to go into a ditch.

As these short-term city girls drove back to their country lives, Maggie rested her head against the passenger side window and absorbed its cold, therapeutic tactility. It's not as if she never got drunk before, but nary sleeping a wink made things worse. Looking out the car window as they sped down the highway, she could see naked, hibernating trees fly past in the desolate countryside, along with tall brown grass and snow-covered farms. Maggie's eyes soon got heavy, and in no time at all she fell into a deep slumber.

In what seemed like less than five minutes, the car pulled into the barnyard and the rocking of the pitted-out driveway jarred Maggie from her dream.

"We're here," said Audrey, snapping the car into PARK.

"What? Oh my gosh. I must have fallen asleep," Maggie said, clearing the fog.

"Um, yeah. About 45 minutes ago."

"I'm sorry, Audrey. I guess I wasn't much of a traveling companion."

"Don't worry about it. With this hangover, I wouldn't have been much in the mood for chatting anyways."

Just then, Benny came bolting out of the house wearing no coat, only denim jeans, a T-shirt and untied shoes.

"Mommy, Mommy!" Maggie could hear him through the glass window of the car.

"Isn't that adorable?" remarked Audrey.

"He really is the love of my life."

Audrey smiled back, thinking about the stories shared from the night before. She was happy Maggie had Benny. He kept her level-headed and gave her purpose.

The boy used all his strength to pull the door open, and he jumped into Maggie's lap. "Welcome home!"

"Look at you. And where is your coat? It must be 20 degrees out."

"I'm not cold." Giving her a hug, he added, "I missed you."

"Me, too. How'd you and Big Jack do last night?"

"We played games and listened to radio shows."

As Maggie climbed out of the car and got her suitcase out of the trunk, she walked over to the driver's side door as Audrey rolled down her window.

"Thank you for the great birthday present," said Maggie.

"What a weekend, huh?" replied Audrey from behind the wheel.

"I'll never forget it," said Maggie with a hint of sarcasm in her voice.

"Now it's time to start thinking about Christmas," said Audrey.

"Ha! Don't remind me. I'm not ready at all," said Maggie, thinking about how to handle her holiday get-together with Audrey and Bob. "Thank you again."

Audrey blew her a kiss and drove down the driveway, her car bouncing on frozen ruts in the gravel.

As Maggie turned to walk to the house, Benny tried to take the suitcase from her. "I can carry it, Momma."

"Are you strong enough?"

"Yep," he said as he half-dragged the suitcase in the snow towards the farmhouse. "I have muscles."

After a few steps, it became obvious it weighed too much, so her son paused for a moment. "Momma, you sure have a lot in here. How do you carry it all?"

You have no idea.

MOVIETONE Title: THE BATTLE OF THE BULGE

(Newsreel Narrator): "Facing the brief but furious German counter-offensive in Belgium, the Christmas season proved to be a tough one for many of the Allied forces. Here we see American soldiers pushing on through in brutal winter weather. Snow has no beauty on the warfront for the men who must do the fighting. These soldiers helped turn the tide and pushed the German forces back. Digging out artillery from under a blanket of snow proves once again that war waits on no weather. Before long the big guns are ready to go into action to pound the Hun.

"Then the platoon moves forward to hunt out enemy snipers. Rifles, machine guns and bazookas do the job. Many storm troopers are counted among the prisoners taken, looking far from Hitler's conception of supermen.

"Some of the bitterest fighting took place in Landen, in Belgium. Losses were heavy on both sides, but nothing could stop the slow and steady Allied advance. Evidence of the struggle is shown in these pictures of wrecked equipment.

"Troops move into the still-burning town of Beringen. Retaking this key point meant a safer and surer advance. Here, too, is bloody testimony of the battles which raged. These casualties tell their own story, while the number of German prisoners testifies to the fact that victory was ours. And from the east and from the west, the Allies close in for the kill."

Chapter Twenty-One

What Is A Lie?

"Hello, Mueller residence."

"Oh, Maggie, I'm so nervous," said Audrey in a panic over the phone. "It's as if he just slipped off the face of the earth. He's nowhere to be found."

"Wait. Back up. Who are you talking about?" Maggie closed her eyes and mouthed the words, *Not Bob . . . please not Bob.*

"Bob, of course."

Maggie felt as if someone punched her in the stomach, the air running out of her lungs.

"He was due back three days ago. Lord, I don't know what to think anymore," she said, her voice pitched high, the panic even higher. "Maggie, you won't believe this, but when I called Northwestern Mutual's home offices, in downtown Milwaukee, they said there were never any meetings in Dayton. His secretary said he was making calls throughout the state all week long! What is going on? Oh my God, do you think he's having an affair?"

The phone felt like it weighed a hundred pounds. "I'm sure there is a logical explanation. Maybe they don't have an updated schedule at the office."

"Even if that were true and he really was in Ohio, he'd be back by now. At least he would have called. I can't stand not knowing where he is."

"Do you want me to come over? I can be there in 20 minutes."

"No, thank you though. I have an appointment with a bride-to-be from Sussex and then a fitting with Mrs. Franz after, so maybe it'll do me good to stay busy. Golly, I hope he calls soon. I just had to tell someone."

"At least let me drop by tomorrow, okay?"

"Sure, that would help. I'll call you if I hear anything."

As Maggie hung up the phone, she stood in silence and wondered about the irony . . . now she and Audrey both had husbands who were MIA Except Maggie understood Bob was alive. Erik? God only knew.

"Maggie! Maggie!" came the call from Adam down the hall. She shook off the thought of Bob and darted into Adam's bedroom.

"I'm sorry, but can I ask a favor?" he asked, half in pain, half laughing.

"What is it?" she said, confused and curious at the same time.

"I'm embarrassed to say, but I have the most horrible itch just above my ankle and I can't reach it. I tried to use my book but it fell on the floor."

"Where is it? Right here?" she asked rubbing a spot on his lower shin.

"Ahhhhh, yes. Oh my God, that's it."

Maggie was amazed at how easily she could put romantic inclinations aside when she and Adam were apart, but when in the same room . . . all those pleasure points were triggered again, as if a warm breeze enveloped her and a switch jump-started her heart. Trying to shake the thought, she turned her attention to his white, almost hairless lower leg. It had seriously atrophied over these past two months, with the calf muscle the size of a forearm. She wondered how long it would take for him to regain full strength.

As she rubbed the skin, a sad cloud began to settle overhead. She missed their talks – about life, the war, about her day-to-day activities on the farm and his past life as a German salesman. Perhaps she was too aloof these days, blaming herself for Adam's predicament – which deep down, she knew was silly – but maybe, just maybe it was a sign from God. *"Hands off the forbidden fruit!"* She felt guilty for stepping over the line before, but then again, she didn't. *Where's the harm if I inched back, ever so slightly – providing I never crossed that line again*? Besides, she really needed to talk to someone, *anyone*, about Bob Stanton, so she thought that moment would be as good as any.

"Can I ask you a question?" she said, stopping the scratch.

As if waking from a wonderful dream, Adam opened his eyes, looked at her with that infectious smile and simply replied, "Of course."

"I have a situation that I have been struggling with and, well . . ."

"I'm all ears."

"Okay, so if you had a secret that affected a good friend . . . I mean a *really big* secret, and you didn't tell them about it, would that be the same as lying?"

"Hmmm, moral dilemma, huh?"

Maggie nodded.

"Did this friend come right out and ask if you have any information pertaining to this secret?"

"No, not like, 'Tell me what you know.' Nothing like that."

"Okay. Well, I suppose it would depend on whether or not they needed to know the secret. If they would benefit from the news in any way, then yeah, I guess I'd say it's a lie if you didn't share the information. But if it had absolutely no upside and they really didn't need to know, I guess you would be doing them a favor by keeping it to yourself. And in that instance, I would say, no, it's not a lie."

Maggie sat for a moment on the edge of Adam's bed and pondered the perspective. "Problem is, it's kind of both. While it would be great if she never had to find out – a 'what you don't know can't hurt you' situation – in the long run, I believe it is something she needs to know. But my God, it'll kill her to know the truth."

Adam twisted his mouth to the side of his face as he listened to her logic and let her continue.

"I mean, why is it I had to stumble upon this? God, I wish I didn't have to carry this burden."

"You're obviously conflicted, and that tells me there are both pros and cons to sharing this secret with her. So my advice would be to sit with it for a little while longer."

Maggie gave him an embarrassed look, as if she told him too much already.

"What?" asked Adam.

"How do you know it's a she?"

"You just said, 'It'd kill *her* to know,'" said Adam.

"I did? Oh, gosh . . ." Maggie buried her face in her hands.

"Don't worry. The point is, you should listen to your heart. It always knows what to do in these situations. The challenge is letting yourself listen."

It was great advice. *It buys me some time and perhaps Bob will come home soon and tell Audrey the truth himself. That would be ideal, because then I wouldn't have to do it. But in the meantime . . . Audrey is living in pain and I feel absolutely terrible about it.*

"Thank you, Adam. I think you're right," she said. "I'll sit with this for a bit longer and then decide what to do."

"I hope it helps."

She looked deep into his eyes. Those pools of blue nearly reached out and grabbed her, pulling her in for a swim. He picked up on it and smiled – which made those cute dimples form in that rugged face. Maggie wanted to give him a hug, but she knew that would only lead to a kiss, which could lead to . . .

She remembered their last kiss . . . how his mouth was soft, and full, and alive! She could hear her subconscious scream at her to stop the fantasy before it went too far. Like an internal game of tug-of-war, she told herself to not let this attraction get the best of her, then momentum would shift, and she would savor ever second of it. *Get out! No, stay! Get out now! Don't you dare. Kiss him . . .*

One second she was caught in a riptide, and a second later she was released. She thought of Big Jack's watchful eyes, how he's been studying the way she'd been acting around Adam, and could not bear to think of him catching her in a moment of intimacy. She took in a deep breath and mustered up all the energy she had to take that first step towards the door.

"Thank you. Thank you for your advice, Adam," she said, her steps quickening, carrying her briskly out of the room as fast as she had entered.

Adam sat still, a bit confused, and upon her exit he responded quietly, "Sure, and thanks for scratching my itch."

Chapter Twenty-Two

The Holiday Surprise

"It's snowing! It's snowing!" yelled Benny as he scampered up the stairs to Maggie's bedroom. A wave of panic washed over her. She could hear the 'clop-clop' of his shoes as she sat on the floor wrapping all of her Christmas gifts. Having her son find out there's no Santa Clause . . . no reindeer . . . no elves . . . no magic in this most holy of days for a youngster would be a disaster. With little time to hide the presents, she grabbed the comforter off her bed and threw it over the rolls of wrapping paper, the Scotch tape, her scissors, the various ribbons, and of course, the numerous gifts, a split second before the door flung open.

"It's snowing!" Benny announced as he bolted into her bedroom, out of breath. He paused momentarily and looked at the quilt on the floor. "What are you doing to that blanket, Mommy?"

"Oh, I'm, ah, sewing a tear in it."

Satisfied with the answer, Benny slid over to the window and turned his attention back to the outdoor flakes. "Santa must be getting his sleigh ready."

"Well, it is Christmas Eve, so that makes sense," said his mother.

"I don't think I'll be able to sleep tonight."

"I'll tell you, it's easier to sleep when you have a good lunch. Are you hungry?"

Maggie had a lot of wrapping yet to do, so leaving the thick blanket on the floor, they walked downstairs to find Big Jack in the kitchen, himself rustling through the cupboards.

"I think we're out of bread," he said.

"I didn't hear you and Benny return. You are back sooner than I thought."

"Yeah, well, we're efficient. So you hungry, Benny?"

"Ah-huh!" he said with enthusiasm. "Can I have a bacon and pancake sandwich?" the youngster proclaimed with excitement.

"I guess we could do that," said Big Jack, rubbing Benny's hair like he was doing a static electricity experiment. The boy giggled.

"If you two are okay, I'm gonna head back upstairs. I'm fixing . . . a . . . hole . . . in . . . my . . . quilt . . . so I better get back at it," she said to Big Jack as if it were a secret code.

He understood, smiled and told her the two of them would be fine, adding, "Hey, Benny, go see if Adam wants lunch. I'll make some of these great sandwiches for him, too."

"Okay," he said, hopping off his chair and trotting out of the kitchen.

Maggie looked at Big Jack and said, "He almost walked in on me."

"Sorry about that. We got things done in a hurry today."

"Well, I still have a lot of wrapping to do, so keep him downstairs, okay?"

"Got it," Big Jack said sheepishly. "Oh hey, I ran into Art Kreiter in town, and he told me the POWs are all but gone."

"What? All of them? Did they forget about the guy in the next room?" asked Maggie.

"I said we were hoping to get a handful to prune the orchard next month, but he heard they all shipped out."

"That can't be. Last time I saw Jennaro, he said they were keeping a skeleton crew."

"Maybe I'll stop by and see if Raymonds is still there. Someone's gotta prune those apple trees this winter."

"Right."

"I'll go after lunch. I can take Benny with me if you want."

"Um, yeah."

* * *

Later that afternoon, as Maggie put a bow on her last Christmas present, a loud knock could be heard at the front door downstairs. She thought it strange she didn't hear a car pull up, as it would be the second time in a few hours someone showed up unannounced. She stood up and peered into the barnyard, but did not see a vehicle. The knocking came again.

"Okay, okay, I'm coming," she shouted as she curiously trotted down the stairs to the front door.

There in the entrance stood a stranger wearing a full red beard, deep, sunken eyes, with a drop of clear mucus hung on the tip of his nose. He was cold, the body shivering, his overcoat covered in snow. It was Bob Stanton.

Instinctively she exclaimed, "Bob? Oh my God! Come in from the cold," she said all without even thinking about the circumstances surrounded their last meeting.

"Is Big Jack home?"

"No, he and Benny ran an errand. Where's your car?"

"I parked on the side of the road about a half-mile down. I saw Big Jack's truck leave but I wasn't sure if it was him or you."

"Well it wasn't me. Now get in here!" she commanded like a mother dispensing an edict to a child.

Looking down at his shoes, he stepped past her, his familiar limp carrying him into the living room. She studied him dispassionately as he stopped next to the davenport and placed an arm on the backrest for support. With his back to Maggie, Bob bent over and began to cry. She took in a heavy sigh, closed the front door and approached.

At this point, the full weight of that night in Milwaukee landed heavily on her shoulders. While she was quite drunk at the time, that kiss between Bob and the younger man became etched in her brain as clearly as if it had happened five minutes earlier. At first, she hesitated to even place her hand on his back, but then her motherly instincts got the best of her and she rubbed his shoulder for a moment, brushing snow off his coat in the process.

As his pain poured out, she didn't say a word. Between staggered breaths and sniffles, she could hear him whisper a few undecipherable words, so she leaned in to hear more clearly. "I'm sorry. I'm so sorry," he repeated over and over again in a half-whispered, half-squeaky voice.

After he drained out the pain, Maggie stepped forward to face him. "Take off that coat, sit down next to the parlor stove. I'm going to make us some hot coffee."

She returned with two cups and sat beside him next to the Christmas tree. "So, here we are."

Bob held the coffee in his hands, feeling the heat from the earthenware mug warm his frozen palms and fingertips. He continued to stare at the cup as steam floated up towards his nose.

"I don't know what to say. What do you want me to say?" Maggie said. "The floor is yours."

After a few more breaths, he finally spoke. "I hardly know where to begin. I suppose I should start by saying I'm sorry. I'm so, so sorry, Maggie. I have been a wreck ever since that night. I haven't eaten. I've hardly slept. I haven't gone to work . . ."

"*You've* been a wreck?" Maggie snapped. "Have you even thought of calling *your wife* and telling her you are at least okay? She's every bit as upset as you are. I was over there yesterday and she's really confused. She called your office, you know."

For the first time since arriving, Bob looked directly into Maggie's eyes, and an expression of fear overcame him.

"That's right. She knows there was no conference in Dayton or wherever you told her you were going, and she's a real mess."

Maggie realized she sounded preachy, set her coffee mug down and leaned forward, a bit more sympathetic. "Listen, Bob, that woman loves you. At least you owe her the courtesy of a phone call. She thinks you're dead for crying out loud!"

He nodded his head in agreement, then asked her a most pressing question. "So, did you . . . you know . . . ?"

"Did I what? Did I tell her? Did I tell my best friend her husband was caught kissing another man?" She paused briefly then continued, "No, I didn't. And I have to say, this has been causing me some sleepless nights as well. My God, Bob, what the hell happened to you? When did you, like, when did you change, or convert, or whatever it is you people do?"

"It's not like that, Maggie," he said, eyes glued to the floor again. "The thing is, I've battled with this my whole life."

"Oh fiddlesticks! You got married for crying out loud! I mean, not that it's any of my business, but you and Audrey must have had, you know . . . with each other . . . where . . . well my goodness, Bob, I've seen you kiss her!"

Bob licked his lips and forced a cough at the uncomfortable air which settled into the room, then added, "I'm sorry you saw me that night."

"So am I. By golly, Bob, why the hell do I have to be burdened with this secret?"

With his eyes fixed on the floor, he took a deep breath and gathered his thoughts. "I felt maybe as time went by I'd change, you know? I mean, look at Audrey. She's beautiful. And if she couldn't make a man feel something, then I don't know who could."

"But it never went away? Those feelings?" Maggie asked, now more sincere. "I really don't understand it the way you do, I suppose."

They both sat in silence. Maggie felt as if her brain were a small rubber ball, her thoughts ricocheting off the walls of her skull.

"So when you went to the military . . . your injury . . . is that related?"

Bob nodded his head in shame.

Not willing to let him off the hook, Maggie sat in silence, her eyes burning into him. Bob looked up at her and read her body language. She wanted to know more and wasn't going to budge until she got her allowance.

"It's like this . . ." Bob sighed. "There was another man in my company who, well you know, let's say we became really close friends . . ."

"All guys become friends in the military. They're your brothers-in-arms."

"Well, let's say there was more to it than that."

"Did you two get caught the same way I saw you in Milwaukee?"

"Not exactly. But we might as well have been. This other man, his name was Kirk . . ." His voice trailed off again.

"What? So what happened?"

Bob hesitated, knowing he had to show all of his cards. Letting out a slow breath through his teeth, he continued, "As it turns out, Kirk kept a diary. And I don't know, maybe the other guys in our barracks sensed something, I can't say for sure, but one night, when we were on guard duty, one of those fellas read his diary. When we got back, well, it got ugly."

Maggie studied his face. Bob glanced up at her. His eyes still watering, the tip of his nose wet again. She handed him a handkerchief.

"They beat you? Both of you?"

"Yes."

"What about your platoon leader or commanding officer?"

"Who do you think encouraged it?"

"My God," she gasped.

"I was the lucky one. Kirk will never walk again. Me? Well, I'll have this limp my entire life, so they say."

"Somebody must have said something. At the nurses station or the camp hospital?"

"It was filed as *Injuries Sustained In Training.*"

Maggie sat silent for a moment. "So when you saw the doctor at the Army base, did he know? I mean, could he tell?"

"You mean could he tell if I was queer?" Bob said sarcastically.

"Sorry, I just don't know about these things." Hesitating for a long, still second, Maggie pressed the question. "So did he?"

"No! No, Maggie! For Pete's sake, you can't just look at a person and know such a thing," he said angrily.

"Well now I know, I guess. Sorry." Another stretch passed as she collected herself, then continued with the questioning. "So what if you tell a doctor here in Wisconsin? What if you tell him you're like this? Can they fix it? I mean, you had to have changed at some point, right? So maybe you can change back."

"Maggie, I don't expect you to understand this, but I've had these feelings ever since I was a teenager. And I think they will always be there. I've tried. Lord knows I've tried everything I could to change."

"What about Audrey? You have to tell her."

Bob looked at Maggie with a painful expression. For several years now he'd had the perfect cover, the perfect job for a homosexual man in the 1940s. On the road . . . living out of a suitcase several days a week . . . visiting *clubes homosexuales* and learning the underground codes for admittance . . . going where he pleased . . . doing what he pleased. But now the word was out. At least, with his wife's best friend.

"I feel so bad you know this, Maggie. I truly wish you two wouldn't have been in the bar on that particular night, at that particular time. Lord knows how you even found it, or how you got in."

"Dumb luck, I suppose," Maggie said with an eye roll.

"This news will absolutely devastate Audrey."

"But she has to know. You can't keep living this lie."

Bob didn't respond. He sat his coffee mug on the end table, looked down, buried his face in his hands and began to weep once again.

"My life is over," he said between sniffles. "The Army should have killed me when they had the chance."

"Now stop that! Stop it, Bob. You can't think that way. There has to be a way to deal with this. It's a choice, right? I mean, that's what I hear. So you just have to choose to change back. Just tell yourself that you'll do it – and you can do it." Maggie tried to talk herself into the simplest of answers. Simple for her, anyways.

"I think I should get going. I'm sorry for bothering you, Maggie," he said, still sniffling but gaining composure.

"Wait, don't leave before you call Audrey, okay? Call her now. You can use my telephone. Come on, Bob, please, I'm begging you. Don't leave without calling her."

Bob took a deep breath, while putting on his coat and said, "I know, you're right, Maggie. I have to let her know. I just need to figure out a way. I will do it, though. I promise."

Maggie didn't respond. She stood, watching him limp towards the front door. His entire demeanor changed, from pure sadness to a calm confidence. Talking to Maggie seemed to have helped him formulate a much-needed plan of attack. He grabbed the door handle, then turned back towards her. "Maggie, I'm sorry for this burden. I always want to be friends. Wish me luck."

She studied him, curious to know how that conversation would go. Letting out a puff of air, she looked at him and said, "Okay. I'm sure she'll be contacting me. But let her know tonight!"

"I will," he said as he stood up and scratched his beard. "And I won't tell her you knew."

Maggie looked relieved, thinking she would be read the Riot Act if Audrey ever found out she knew the secret. The fallout was sure to be devastating, and Maggie would be the only person Audrey could depend on. While this made her feel like a traitor, it was the best she could hope for, given the circumstances.

"Okay, Bob," was all Maggie could muster.

Bob went outside, onto the porch, and as the front door creaked to a close, she quickly stepped forward, "Bob, wait. There's one more thing . . ."

He pushed the door open a crack and leaned his head into the house.

"Merry Christmas."

"It's Christmas?" he asked, startled.

"Christmas Eve, anyways."

Looking at his feet again, Bob drew a heavy sigh and added, "Thanks for the coffee," then closed the door.

Maggie stood there momentarily when the realization hit – Adam's bedroom door! It had been wide open the entire time. Hoping he was napping, she slowly crept towards his room and as she peeked into the doorway, she found him not only awake, but looking at her with big eyes.

"Now *two* of us know the secret," he said.

* * *

While in a deep sleep, Maggie dreamed she was in the bed of her pickup truck, as Benny stood above her and the Dodge rumbled down a bumpy road. The mystery driver seemed to go out of his way to hit every pothole and every speed bump he could find. Each time he hit one, Maggie's body bounced with such force she was nearly sent airborne. Benny laughed and kept jumping up and down repeating, "I love Christmas! It's Christmas time! Get up, Mommy, it's Christmas morning!"

Maggie woke from this strange dream to find Benny bouncing

with excitement not in the bed of a pickup truck, but on her bed in the farmhouse. In one hand he held Mr. Chuckles, waving him around left to right, and in the other he had a small Christmas present. The boy's favorite holiday had arrived.

She sat up and grabbed him by the waist to stop the trampoline effect. "Good heavens, child! The sun isn't even up yet. And where did you get that gift?"

"Santa brought it!"

"You know, waking Mommy so early in the morning is naughty. If Santa hears about it he may not bring you any other gifts."

"But I saw the tree. There's a gazillion down there!"

"Really? Well maybe they aren't for you, ever think of that?"

"I know they are, 'cause I saw my name on a bunch of them."

Maggie couldn't help but smile at her son's checkmate.

"Can we open our presents now?"

"It's not even 5:30," she said, glancing at the clock on her nightstand. "Let's wait for Opa to get up."

"He's already awake. Adam, too."

"How do you know?"

"I woke them up," the boy giggled.

"Alright then," Maggie said, sitting up in bed and stretching her arms high. "I guess it's a Hobson's Choice."

Downstairs, the Christmas tree sat with a finely stacked pyramid of presents – many more than Maggie had put under there before she went to bed. "Wow, Santa sure was nice, wasn't he?" she said looking at Big Jack suspiciously as he sat on the couch with a cup of coffee in his hand and a coy smile on his face.

"He sure was!" Benny exclaimed, his fingers quivering with excitement. "Can I start opening some?"

"Tell you what, Benny," said Big Jack, chiming in, "let's do something first, just so Adam can take part in the fun."

The boy studied his grandfather.

"You and your Mommy help me move Adam's bed so he can see out of the doorway. Unless you don't think you're strong enough to help . . ." he goaded playfully.

"I'm strong enough. Look at my muscles," Benny boasted, flexing a bicep.

"That's really not necessary," came a voice from the bedroom. "I feel awkward enough as it is, being here on Christmas Day."

"Hush!" yelled Big Jack from the living room. "Everyone deserves to enjoy this day. Besides, I think I saw a present for you under the tree."

"Santa sure is nice," said Benny.

"He sure is," said Maggie with her eyes focused on Big Jack. Her father winked.

Once they moved his bed into view, they were ready to dig into the gifts. Despite Adam's hollow protests, it became obvious he enjoyed being able watch from the bedroom door.

One by one they took turns. Most of the presents were used or homemade. *The best kinds!* Thankfully, Benny didn't know the difference and Big Jack didn't care.

Among the many gifts, Benny enjoyed a 3D View-Master. Big Jack received a fry pan and a five-gallon kettle. Maggie got a box of Burpee seeds, which included watermelon, cucumber and zucchini. And Adam opened a copy of *The Grapes of Wrath*, by John Steinbeck.

When all the gifts had been opened, everyone sat quietly, pleased with their bounty. A moment later, Benny surprised everyone by making a proclamation. "Oh, wait! I forgot one!" Skipping over to the couch, he put his hand under the seat cushion and revealed a flat present, giftwrapped in bright red paper.

"What on Earth . . . ?" asked his mother, amazed at her ingenious son.

"It's for Adam."

Maggie pressed her hand to her heart in awe.

"That's a fine-looking wrapping job," said Big Jack. "Let's all go in the bedroom together so he can open it."

Benny marched in and proudly presented the gift to Adam, who was truly touched by the gesture. Tearing off the wrapping paper, he revealed a small homemade book.

"It's a coloring book," Benny said in a quiet voice, suddenly a bit embarrassed. "Adam told me he liked them, so . . ."

Twelve pages full of line drawings, each representing all that was familiar to the youngster. Sacred observations, which included illustrations of the family's two horses, Suri and Bucky as they stood majestically in their stalls; a smiling image of Benny's favorite clown, Mr. Chuckles; a likeness of the U.S. Army's "deuce-and-a-half" truck, complete with German POW stick figures climbing out of the back.

"Is that my friend Oskar?" asked Adam, pointing to an illustration of a heavy-set stick man behind the truck. Everyone laughed.

Another page of the coloring book featured a likeness of Oku and his team of harvesters – complete with sickles and drawings of them standing beside various shocks of oats.

But it was the drawing on the last page that evoked the most emotion in the room. Benny had illustrated the barnyard, complete with farmhouse, their John Deere tractor, his tire swing, the chicken coop, the barn . . . and there in the foreground stood a man and a woman holding hands, both wearing grins extending ear-to-ear. It looked like a child's rendition of Grant Wood's *American Gothic*. Only less frowns and more fun.

"How nice, Benny," said Adam. "You drew a picture of your mommy and daddy. And the entire farm is very accurate. I will cherish this always."

Benny looked confused and in an innocent high-pitched voice said, "No, that's *you*, with Mommy."

"Me?" said Adam nervously.

"Ah-huh. After you heal your leg." Benny then walked to him and gave him a kiss on the cheek. "I'm happy you are here."

The room went silent. Perhaps Benny had already forgotten about his father, after all, the glossy eyes of this child didn't miss much of the goings-on at the farm. Not between Maggie and Adam, anyways.

A bit uncomfortable, Big Jack stared at the floor. Adam looked out the window at the sunrise. Maggie stroked her cheeks with each hand. The only sound anyone could hear was the wind and light sleet which tapped against the glass. Benny, oblivious to the sensitivity of the moment, broke the silence by saying, "Remember, Adam, when you color Oku's picture, you shouldn't use a black crayon because then you won't be able to see his face too good. Use a brown one."

This snapped everyone back into reality. Maggie smiled and gave her son a hug. "I love you," she said. Big Jack seemed accepting of the little boy's gift and nodded his head in approval, but he couldn't help feel somewhat upset with himself for not recognizing the youngster's astute perceptivity.

Adam, however, was more reserved. He forced a smile towards Benny and thanked him for the coloring book. Maggie studied him and saw someone who didn't know what his future held. She recognized conflict in his eyes, an expression of deep-rooted pain on his face. She felt sad and broke the reverie by announcing, "My goodness, look at the time. We best be getting ready for 7:00 Mass. Papa, could you help me push Adam's bed back?"

After they repositioned his bed on the other side of the room, Maggie and Benny headed upstairs to get dressed for church. As their footsteps rhythmically echoed up the stairs, Big Jack stayed behind. He approached Adam, who remained pensive while looking out the bedroom window, trying to decide if he should be embarrassed, ashamed or proud.

"He's a special boy. *Ein liebevoller Junge.*"

"Yep," said Adam, still looking into the frozen apple orchard and obviously troubled by something.

"You know, his father was a farmer just like me, only he came from Northern Wisconsin. Benny loved his dad, but with each passing day, I think he loses a small piece of him. Soon, all he'll have is a photograph or maybe a letter."

"Do you think he'll come back?" asked Adam, his eyes focused on the outdoor view, his heart elsewhere.

"Hard to tell. By now, if he was in a POW camp or even a hospital, we'd probably know."

Adam turned to look at Big Jack, studied his face and wondered about his motives. A sudden wave of anger arose from deep within, as if all the pain of being a POW, all the pain of losing his country, all the pain of the injury had culminated into a tight ball of fury. He began to rant in German. "What do you want from me, Big Jack? Huh? You know, I didn't ask for this. I didn't ask for any of it."

"Huh? What are you talking about?"

"I was perfectly happy selling watches and traveling America's Midwest and even picking apples. So what the hell happened? Here I am, half-paralyzed, dealing with painful bedsores, living with a former German and his daughter and her little boy, and I can only sit here day after day thinking about the pain I feel, the pain no one knows about, and then I start to think I'm losing my mind."

"Whoa, hold on there, Adam. I'm not sure what's gotten into you, but . . ." He was cut off.

"I didn't ask for this!" shouted Adam, now in a near frenzy. "I didn't ask to stay, and I'm sorry to put you and Maggie out like this. I really am. So it's time I leave. I need to get out of here, okay? Yes, that is what I'll do. I'm getting out of here and out of your hair and out of everyone's life!"

His anger started to boil over. As he sat up in his bed, he pulled at his foot, reached for his shoe and unlaced it. He then untied the two ropes which were tied to traction weights. They fell on the floor with a loud BANG! "I cannot stay here any longer!"

"Adam, stop it! What are you doing?" said Big Jack, confused and a bit in shock. "I didn't mean to offend you."

"I have to get out of this *fucking* house! Don't you understand?"

"Adam, stop it!" Big Jack insisted as he tried in vain to prevent him from undoing the laces in his shoe and releasing the harness around his waist. "You must leave your foot in there. The doctor said so!"

"He can go to hell! I'm fine!" His anger was now white-hot. Pain and frustration blazed in his eyes. With that, Adam released his foot from its leather cast, spun his body ninety degrees and, for the first time in over two and a half months, flung his legs over the edge of the bed and tried to stand. Fueled by incentive, adrenaline and pain from distant memories, Adam actually stood upright, at least momentarily, then when trying to take a step towards the door, he went off a cliff. He hit the floor hard, and shrieked in pain as Big Jack ran to his aid.

Lying face-down on the floor, Adam pounded his fist and shouted in German, "Why did I have to come to this place? This farm?"

"What's wrong, Adam?" asked Big Jack, confused and desperate.

"Don't you see? I miss *meine Frau.* I miss my Henry." His anger turned to tears and he began to sob. "They are dead. They are both dead!"

"What are you talking about? Who is dead, Adam? Who died?" asked Big Jack in a soft voice, kneeling next to him, a hand on his shoulder.

"My wife. And my son!" he said, still pounding his fist on the wooden floor.

Big Jack was astounded. *You had a family? My God, you never spoke of them before. Why did we not know this?*

Always a sucker for tears, Big Jack felt a wave of great compassion wash over himself. As Adam let the pain pour out, Big Jack heard a squeak from behind. He turned to see Maggie standing in the doorway. She, too, was crying. She had heard it all.

Just then Benny arrived from upstairs, wearing only a pair of dress slacks, otherwise shirtless and barefoot.

"Did Adam fall out of the bed? Is he hurt?" asked Benny.

Through her tears, Maggie could only nod her head. "Yes," she said, trying to hold it all together. "He is hurt."

* * *

The week passed quickly and no one had spoken about the incident that Christmas morning. The idea of peeling off that scab didn't appeal to anyone in the least, and the consensus was if Adam wanted to talk about it, he could bring it up. So the subject sat dormant.

That is, until New Year's Eve.

Maggie had invited Audrey to spend the night with the family. She hadn't seen much of her best friend since their trip to Milwaukee, and couldn't stand the pain of cradling a lie as Audrey suffered. While Bob promised to tell Audrey everything just one week prior, he never did. In fact, he never returned home, and he never called. *One more husband missing in action.*

The group had a nice dinner of ham, fried green tomatoes and an apple pie for dessert. As was the Mueller family tradition, everyone always welcomed the New Year twice – first by East Coast time, then by Midwest time. Just before 11:00, they would turn on NBC radio and listen to the countdown from New York City.

As the night progressed, they tuned in to Guy Lombardo and shared copious amounts of Big Jack's hard cider. With Adam's bed once again positioned in the doorway, he could listen in and occasionally take part in the celebration carrying on in the adjacent living room.

At one point, the subject of Bob came up and Big Jack couldn't help himself. Fueled by liquor and a genuine curiosity, he rarely kept quiet when there was an elephant in the room. "So, Audrey, any word? About Bob, I mean?"

"Papa!" scolded Maggie. "That is a private matter."

"What, he's been here every New Year's for as long as I can remember. So I'm just wondering is all."

Audrey looked at her friend, then at Big Jack, and nonchalantly said, "Nothing new. Except I've taken to praying more Hail Mary's than ever before. My only hope is he's in a hospital with amnesia or something and no one knows who he is." She paused for a moment and added, "Not knowing is hard. It's been almost a month!"

Realizing what she said, Audrey reached her hand for Maggie's. They both squeezed tightly. "I pray for Erik, too," said Audrey, which was true.

"What about the police? Do they have any leads?" asked Big Jack.

Audrey pursed her lips and shook her head.

Maggie had a sick feeling in her stomach. Not only had she kept the news of the Milwaukee encounter from her friend, she hadn't mentioned a word of his recent visit on Christmas Eve. It hurt so much to see a friend in such straits, but it pained her also to say nothing. *Bob, where are you? My God, you said you'd go home and tell her everything. I can't be the one to do it!*

Then out of the blue, Benny chimed in and said, "Adam fell out of his bed the other day."

Breaking out of her spell, Audrey looked at Maggie as if she had an entitled privilege to know everything that happened in the Mueller farmhouse.

"Really? You didn't tell me about that."

"Yeah, it's true. He had an accident," Maggie replied. "Doc Marshall came out, looked him over and said he was okay. Said his hip was healing so well he may be able to put some light weight on it, maybe in a week or two. But for now, he's still gotta keep it in that shoe."

"Are you okay?" Audrey shouted to him from across the living room and into the doorway where Adam lay.

The German smiled from the doorway and gave her the thumbs up, adding, "I'd be much better with another splash of this cider."

Big Jack stood up and walked the bottle to his houseguest. "You wanna know something, Adam?" Big Jack said, half slurring his words. "My cider improves with age. The older I get, the more I like it."

Adam chuckled at the joke and shook his head.

As the evening wore on, they played cards, sang songs, and at one point Big Jack noticed Adam teaching Benny how to make a paper airplane. At that, he couldn't contain himself.

"So, Adam, last week, you mentioned a boy. Your son. Can we ask you about it?"

In the middle of making the airship, Adam stopped folding the paper and gave Big Jack a heavy sigh. Maggie normally would have stifled her father, but curiosity had consumed her as well. Audrey's eyes got as big as saucers, and she simply said under her breath, "My goodness. 'Tis the season for surprises."

"So it seems," said Adam having heard Audrey. "But it's okay. Really, I am fine talking about it now. I tried to keep it a secret for way too long, even from my comrades, but I suppose it's been burning a hole inside of me. In many ways, I *want* to tell you."

Everyone got up, moved some kitchen chairs around his bed and sat in a half-circle with ears at the ready.

"His name was Henry," Adam began. "He was the most adorable four-year-old you'd ever seen. His mother's name was Olivia. She was tall, dark-haired and a great cook. Almost better than you, Big Jack," he said with a half-smile. Big Jack's chest puffed out.

"We were married almost five years. I worked at a local jeweler and learned the trade from Edwin Wallschlager, one of Germany's greatest artisans. Olivia worked at the local bakery and helped teach Sunday school."

"How long ago did you lose them?" asked Maggie delicately.

With pain in his eyes, he nodded. "1938. So what's that, six years ago? We were living in Munich at the time, and there was a rally in the town square for the Social Democrats. Secretly, Olivia was a *Wandervogel* member, even though they were outlawed and disbanded a few years earlier. Always fighting for human rights . . . an end to corruption in Germany . . . she hated to see the violence between

Hitler's Worker's Party and the communists' Red Front. So one day . . ." Adam paused to gather his thoughts, then continued. "One day, she went to a rally with Henry and things got ugly. Hitler's storm troopers got into a fight with some from the Red Front. There was pushing and shoving, and then . . ."

Adam paused again and took in a slow breath. "Olivia had always been about sovereignty for Germany, and she felt very strongly about it. Her father was involved in national affairs his whole life and had passed the passion down to her, I suppose. She was educated at the best schools and some teachers even encouraged her to go into politics. But this was a time of the Three K's: *Kinder* (children), *Kirche* (church) and *Küche* (kitchen), so a woman in such a position would have been unheard of, and she knew it. But she was tough and opinionated, never backing down from an argument."

"She sounds like someone I'd like," said Audrey, forcing a smile.

Adam's eyes lit up. "Yeah, she was terrific. The night we first met . . . I saw her crack a beer stein over the head of a man who was harassing her in a *Wirtshaus*. She was a waitress there and this guy wouldn't let up, so she let him have it. I said to myself, 'I have to meet this girl!'"

Everyone laughed, both at the story, but also to dilute the pain in the room. Adam continued, "Besides her spunk . . . she was gorgeous," he added with a smile, looking off in a distant place. Maggie grabbed a handkerchief out of Audrey's purse and dabbed the corners of her eyes.

"So anyways, when she went to this rally with Henry, the pushing and shoving between the storm troopers and the Red Front grew into a full-blown riot. First, rocks were thrown, then bottles, followed by . . . gunfire. In all, ten people were killed. Olivia and Henry were among the casualties."

"Oh Mein Gott," said Big Jack.

"Were you in Germany or in the U.S. at the time?" asked Audrey.

"I had business in Aalen, a city not too far from home. When I got the phone call at my hotel, I rushed back and luckily got to her bedside when she . . ." his voice trailed off. He swallowed hard and took a trembling breath.

"Adam, we really don't have to talk about this," said Maggie.

"No, really, it's okay. I've been wanting to tell you this for months. Please, I think I have to share the story."

Everyone sat still as he went on.

"Little Henry . . . he died in the street after catching a bullet in his temple. When I first arrived at the hospital, I had to identify him in the basement morgue. It was the hardest thing I've ever had to do. Then I went upstairs to Olivia's room . . . she was shot in the back, probably running away from the riot with little Henry, and as she lay there falling in and out of consciousness, she begged for my forgiveness, saying she should have never taken him there. Problem was, she didn't know he had died. So when she asked me about his condition . . ." Adam's voice cracked a little, but he found his composure and continued. "I lied. I knew by the severity of her wound she was not going to make it – and I guess I didn't want her final thoughts to be bloodguilt. At least she could pass to the other side thinking her son was in a good place. Was that so wrong?" Letting out a heavy sigh, Adam added, "She knew her condition was bad, too, because she made me promise I would raise him right, believing it was important he learn living in freedom is worth sacrifice. Only she didn't think it would ever be so real." Adam's eyes began to well up. "She died later that night."

"In one day, your life was gone," observed Audrey sympathetically.

Taking a deep breath, Adam echoed the remark, "In one day, my life was gone."

The room fell silent, and everyone felt great compassion for the German, more than on the day he nearly died from the fall. Maggie buried her face in her handkerchief and walked to his bedside. She bent over and hugged him. Audrey stood behind her, also rubbing her eyes with a hanky. On the other side of the bed stood Big Jack, arms crossed and head nodding up and down in approval. Benny watched and tried to make sense of it all.

In the next room the Midwest clock stuck midnight and Guy Lombardo's band played "Auld Lang Syne." 1945 was officially upon them.

Chapter Twenty-Three

Time Heals

Big Jack was not an active participant when babysitting, and Benny had figured that out long ago. During those occasions when Maggie asked him to watch her son, the youngster usually spent his time drawing and thumbing through *Children's Activities Magazine* while Big Jack read the *Saturday Evening Post* or took a nap. On this particular Saturday afternoon, he did both – falling asleep on the couch with the magazine on his chest.

Because of the war, everyone had to ration gasoline, so it marked the first time in weeks Maggie went into town for groceries and various sundries. She loved making these trips and always looked forward to visiting old friends and catching up on the gossip of the day. In her absence, Big Jack snored away in the living room while Adam sat in his bed engrossed in reading *The Red Badge of Courage.*

Checking in on Adam, Benny ever so gently opened the door to his room.

"Hi, Benny! Come in, please," said Adam.

The child was nervously spinning a gold pocket watch in his hand.

"What have you got there?"

"It's a old clock."

"Does it work?"

"Naw," he said sheepishly. "But look at this!" Benny pressed the winding stem and the metal side snapped open, exposing the clock face and its nearly perfect crystal dome.

"Well how about that," said Adam acting like he'd never seen a timepiece like this before. "That's quite something."

Benny pursed his lips and nodded his head several times, proud of himself for discovering the amazing feature on the watch.

"Would you mind if I took a look at it?"

"Okay. But don't break it."

Adam smiled at the thought of breaking a broken watch. Holding it oh-so-gently by its gold chain, Benny lowered it into his palm as if it were a baby dove. Adam bobbed his wrist up and down, getting a sense for its weight and balance. It had been many years since he held such a timepiece. Impressed, he massaged its gold back and rotated it in the palm of his good hand. *This is far from being a toy. In fact, this is a quality heirloom. An original Patek Philippe. In good working condition, this Swiss timepiece was worth a fortune.*

"It's a hunter-case design," he told Benny, who cocked his head with curiosity. "Watches like these were used by railroad men who made sure the trains ran on time. See here . . ." Adam opened the spring-hinged metal lid again. "This piece opens at the 9:00 position, and the winding stem is at the 3:00 spot. It's the standard for most train conductors throughout the country."

Benny did not understand a single thing he said, but tried to absorb this new information as best he could. "And look what the time says," said Benny, pointing to the clock face and enjoying his turn to impress Adam. "It says 8:30. It stopped ticking at 8:30."

"You're right," said Adam with a smile, realizing he needed to simplify his discussion for the young mind. "Let me show you something else . . ." Adam then showed Benny how the other side of the watch also hinged open, revealing an engraving with the letters: *JTW.*

"I didn't know it did that!" the boy said, awestruck.

Adam wondered whose initials they were, but before he could ponder the question further, Benny snatched it out of his hands.

"It has two doors?"

"It does indeed. Want to see how they work?"

Around this time Maggie had returned from her errands and came into the house through the back porch. "Hello, I'm back," she announced, setting some groceries down on the kitchen counter. She listened for a response. In a distant room she could hear Benny laughing. As she went to investigate, she quietly approached Adam's bedroom, passed a snoring Big Jack on the couch, tip-toed closer and finally peeked around the doorway to see the tutor with his young student.

"Do you know how they told time before there were watches?" Adam asked him.

Benny shrugged.

"One way was to use a sundial. Here, grab that broom over there and bring it to the side of the bed." As Benny walked to retrieve it, Adam did his best to reposition his body so as to see better. He winced a bit as he shifted his weight.

Maggie's first instinct was to step into the bedroom to help make him more comfortable, but she didn't dare spoil the moment. The midday sun streamed into the bedroom and Adam told Benny to stand the broom vertically in the middle of the light. He then explained how the edge of the bed was the same as 12:00 on the watch and the shadow of the broomstick was the hour hand, which made the current time roughly 11:00 AM. Benny looked at him, astonished. He peered at Adam as if he had just shown him the world's greatest magic trick.

Maggie brought her hands to her chin in amazement. Not so much at the demonstration but at the connection they were making with one another. She felt a tingle in her stomach. *Who is this man?* She even brushed aside the subtle guilt. *Don't bother me right now. This is too good.*

"How did they tell time if there were no watches?" asked Benny.

"Years ago, they didn't have them. Or they couldn't always use a sundial. So often they used an hourglass. Do you know what an hourglass is?"

Benny shook his head. "No."

"Basically, an hourglass had sand in it and that sand would flow through it every hour. Some other places in the world would tell time by burning candles, and they would melt at a certain pace. Have you ever heard of a place called Egypt?"

"Ah-huh. They have the big triangles. I draw those."

"Right. The pyramids. Well, in that country, thousands of years ago, they used something called a water clock."

"What's that?" said Benny enthusiastically.

"Picture a tall container filled with water . . . and there was a little hole in the bottom."

"It would leak," Benny said.

"That's right. You know how a clock ticks, well a water clock dripped instead of ticked. As the dripping water filled up a small container, there were markings on the side that told them the time based on how much water was inside. Isn't that something?"

Benny seemed a bit muddled, but tried his best to hide it.

"Now let's have a look at that watch again," Adam continued, referring back to the gold timepiece.

Maggie didn't notice the heirloom when she first peeked in the room. However, the image of Adam holding the old watch snapped her out of the moment and she felt uncomfortable. So she stepped in the bedroom, as if she had just arrived.

"Hello, you two! Hey, what have you got there?"

"Opa gave it to me," said the boy, fibbing about its origins.

"Opa, huh? You've been snooping around my jewelry box again, haven't you young man?"

"Maybe."

Maggie smiled. "How about I hold onto that for you?" Adam handed it to her, suspicious of her interest. It wasn't hard to read Maggie and he could tell a story came with the watch. He knew every engraved timepiece had one.

"Mommy, did you know they used to tell time with dripping water?"

"Really? That's fascinating," she said, smiling at Adam.

"Come help me unpack the groceries and you can tell me all about it."

"Alright!" he proclaimed and skipped out of the room. Standing near the doorway, she turned back towards Adam and said, "Thanks for entertaining him. He thinks the world of you."

"It's my pleasure. He's a great young man."

Maggie took the compliment to heart. "Oh, and before I forget, Doc Marshall's coming over today. He's going to work on your leg. He thinks you can get on your feet soon."

"Will you be helping?" Adam asked, aware she had been maintaining a bit of a hands-off approach to his rehab those past few weeks.

"Well," she paused, adding, "if that's alright with the patient."

Adam smiled ear-to-ear.

Just then, the sound of an Army truck could be heard pulling up to the house. Maggie looked out the window and recognized Corporal Jennaro. Bundled up in a long G.I.-issued wool overcoat, a thick hat and heavy boots, he stepped out of the truck and trudged through the six inches of snow that had slowly piled up over the past few days. She greeted him at the door.

"Corporal! Come in! Come in!"

"Thank you, Mrs. Wentworth," he said, clapping his mittens together. "Brother, let me tell you, it's cold out there."

"Hand me your coat. Step over here by the parlor stove where it's warm."

As he unbuttoned the overcoat, she noticed he had an envelope in his hand.

"What have you got there?"

"New information about the pruning, and I need your and Big Jack's signatures."

At the sound of the front door closing and Jennaro's voice booming, Big Jack awoke and sat up on the couch.

"Well, hello there, Corporal," he said.

"Hi, Mr. Mueller. Happy belated holidays."

"And to you as well." Big Jack struggled to find his glasses, then stood up to greet the American guard.

"Would you like some hot coffee?" asked Big Jack. "Mags, get him some coffee, would ya?"

Maggie gave her father a sour expression.

"Actually, that'd be nice," said Jennaro, rubbing his hands together quickly, then placing them above the black stove. "I swear, that truck's got no heat."

Maggie hung his overcoat on a tall pedestal rack near the front door and walked towards the kitchen. "Make yourself at home. I'll be back in a sec."

Jennaro then cocked his head slightly to glance into Adam's doorway. "Hi, Sergeant," he said with a friendly wave from across the room.

"Hello, Corporal," Adam said with reciprocated friendliness. "How are things at camp?"

Jennaro walked to the doorway, stopping short of entering the room. "Things are quiet. My goodness, nearly all you Germans have left. No more than maybe 15 give the place a heartbeat these days."

"I heard you were shut down. Thought maybe you forgot about me."

"Ha! Not just yet. And we wouldn't leave without you."

"So who's still around?"

"Let's see who you'd remember . . . There's Elam, Hofstädter, Orwig, Kästner . . . know any of those fellas?"

"Of course. Tell them I say hello, will you please?"

"You can tell them yourself. A handful of them will be back here in a few days to prune the orchard."

"What? Really?" said Big Jack happily as he stepped into the conversation.

"That's right," added Jennaro. "That's why I need your signatures. It got approved."

"Well I'll be," said Big Jack, slapping his knee. "There's just no way I can prune those trees myself. And it has to be done when they're dormant."

"I'd help, but I'm kinda tied down," said Adam.

"Yeah, I can see," said the corporal, pointing to the ropes and pulleys. "But for how much longer?"

"They say I'll be doing some standing very soon. Maybe later today."

"I bet it's been tough being like that all this time."

"Yeah, I feel like a prisoner."

Jennaro pointed at him, acknowledging the joke.

Maggie returned with the coffee. Benny followed her. "I see you boys are getting reacquainted."

"Just talking about your orchard, Mrs. Wentworth."

"Maggie. Please call me Maggie."

"No, ma'am. Can't do it."

Maggie was about to get after him when Big Jack jumped in. "Let's look over that paperwork and get you a few John Hancocks."

As they walked to the couch, Jennaro waved goodbye to Adam and then he looked at Benny, who smiled and then stuck out his tongue at the corporal. Playing along, Jennaro did the same. Benny then picked his nose. Jennaro reciprocated. Next, Benny turned his eyes inward towards his nose, looking cross-eyed. The corporal followed suit. Then Benny let out a loud fart. And Jennaro let out a loud laugh, "I can't top that, kid."

"Come on, boys, let's get serious," said Maggie as she tried to read the new contract.

Together they went through the paperwork which spelled out the schedule and the names of six German POWs who would be doing the pruning. Some of them happened to be good friends of Adam's. She was happy about that.

"I'll be back in a week then," said Jennaro, folding the paperwork in half and stuffing it into his back pocket. "How long do you figure it'll take them, Big Jack?"

"If the weather cooperates and we don't get hit too hard with snow or a stretch of bitter cold, maybe a month or two."

"Okay. I'll add that to the form. And if for whatever reason you feel the conditions are too severe, just call the camp on any given morning and we'll reschedule."

"Roger that, Corporal," Big Jack said with a smile. "The sooner the better, to be honest, because there really aren't any tall snowbanks in the orchard yet. At least from what I saw. I haven't been in there for a while now."

As Jennaro got up to leave, he shook hands with Maggie, Big Jack, and even Benny, who smiled at him again and let out a second loud fart.

"Benny! That is uncouth!" Maggie snapped.

"Oh, that was good," said Big Jack proudly.

"Don't encourage him," Maggie insisted to her father.

"Ach! You don't think the corporal has heard such things?"

"I don't care, Papa. It's in bad form," said Maggie.

"Really, Mrs. Wentworth, it's fine. I'm not offended."

"Well I am," Maggie said.

Chapter Twenty-Four

Kiss The Bed Goodbye

Bookended by Doc Marshall on his right and Maggie on his left, Adam sat on the edge of the bed, cautiously optimistic. With his legs dangling off the edge of the mattress and his arms wrapped around their shoulders, the three counted together.

"One . . . two . . . three . . ."

On a silent "four," they popped him up as he put light weight on his injured leg for the first time since his failed escape attempt on Christmas morning.

"Boy, that's worse than I expected."

"Are you in much pain?" asked Doc Marshall.

"No, I'm talking about the floor. It's freezing."

"Funny guy. So tell me about the pain. Any pain?"

"Actually, it's not the hip so much, doctor, but my knees, my ankles and these thigh muscles. However, it's a pain I can deal with."

"You'll get stronger each day. I've seen it before. Today we are only going to take a few steps, and that's all," insisted the doctor. "Tomorrow you can take more with Maggie and my nurse. Before you know it, you'll be skipping down the road singing Dixie."

"It feels good to stand," added Adam. "I must admit."

"Well, you've made great progress, son. All your cuts have healed . . . we got that cast off your arm now . . . your ribs are tip-top. I'm very happy with the progress."

"Me, too," said Adam, his chest puffing out a little.

After walking him from one side of the room, then back to the bed, the doctor asked, "So any other concerns?"

"The bedsores. They're pretty bad. Any thoughts about those?"

"Actually, yes," the doctor said. "Now that you can keep your foot out of the boot, you can roll onto parts of your body that are free from the sores."

"Halleluiah!" proclaimed Adam.

"Yeah, I also have a paste I can give you for those. It's proven to be more efficacious than the castor oil or the carbamide."

"What is it?" asked Maggie, equally curious.

"It's made from pectin, Ringer's solution and urea. We apply it to the ulcer and then let it air-dry. It not only helps to heal the sore, but also, as it hardens it acts like a protective layer."

"Like a second skin!" proclaimed Adam.

Sitting him back on the bed, Doc Marshall reached for Adam's ankles, lifted his legs and helped swing him back into that familiar position. He winced, lay back on his pillow and took a deep breath. Doc then looked him over, head to toe. "It seems you gained some weight?"

"I blame this one," Adam said, pointing to Maggie.

"Hey, blame Big Jack. He does most of the cooking around here," she said, giving Adam a playful punch on his shoulder.

"All things considered, you're a lucky man, Adam. I've seen people never get out of bed after a month, much less 90 days."

"I must have lived right."

"That and you didn't get pneumonia, which could have been devastating."

"Maybe it was his coughing exercises," said Maggie proudly. "I helped him with those."

"I suspect they did help. But we also tried to keep people away from you and that may have made a difference, too," said Doc. "As for your strength, your legs have atrophied quite a bit. But don't worry, as soon as we get you up and you start walking in the next few weeks, your muscle mass will return and so will your strength."

Adam looked at Doc Marshall with hope and thanks in his eyes. "Words cannot express my gratitude, Doctor. You saved my life."

The physician laughed. "I didn't save your life. *You* saved your life. That's how medicine works. If I can help get your body to a point where it can heal itself, then I've done my job. But the person you should be thanking is yourself."

The doctor looked at his watch and realized he was late for an appointment. "My goodness, look at the time. I've gotta go." Grabbing his coat he continued, "Remember to not overdo it, Adam. Stay off those bedsores. And tomorrow my nurse will come by to help. We're going to get you walking in no time!" Adam felt a lump in his throat and could only nod, then swallowed hard. Doc smiled at his patient, glanced over to Maggie and said goodbye.

Adam loved the prospect of being mobile again. Several times over these past three months he questioned whether or not he'd ever stand upright. But now he had true validation. He took a deep breath and looked up at Maggie.

"Well?" she said.

"Well?" repeated Adam. "We did it."

Maggie nodded proudly and gave him another pillow.

"The doctor was terrific. But you . . . you were my Florence Nightingale," said Adam as he looked deep into her eyes.

She took the compliment and held it to her heart. Standing in front of Adam, Maggie felt delighted to have played a role in his recuperation, and she beamed before him. Losing sight of the moment, she took two steps forward, bent over, and gave Adam a hug. "I'm very proud of you," she said into his ear.

He hugged her back and simply whispered, "Thank you."

As each loosened their respective grip – which nearly cocooned them into one – they gazed at one another wantonly. The invisible wall between them seemed to crash down at their feet. Maggie took in a trembled breath, held it a moment, and without saying a word leaned in with a kiss.

Adam did not reciprocate at first. "Are you sure about this?"

She pulled back slowly and paused for a long second. "Big Jack and Benny are running errands in town, so . . ." With that, she dove back in, hungrier than before. Adam couldn't stop himself any longer. Feeling the softness of her lips, he welcomed her exploration. They were both caught in the current and there was no pulling out.

Maggie's eyes glazed over as Adam gently caressed her cheek with the back of his hand while kissing her without severance – just as he imagined it in his dreams. His hand then moved to gently stroke the side of her neck and softly comb her long brown mane with his fingers, all without losing the rhythm of the moment.

Waves of heat washed over them. Their kisses became more energized, and they savored one another as if biting into an ice-cold peach on a hot summer's day.

As things heated up, Maggie placed a knee on the edge of the bed . . . and in one smooth motion climbed on top, hiked her skirt up just enough to straddle him while molding her body against his. Adam periodically tapped the tip of his tongue against hers as a playful tease. Maggie began to slowly grind against his hardness, and it sent chills up her spine – and his.

"God, is there any way we can make this work?" she whispered into his ear.

Between kisses, Adam said, "I don't know . . . but we can make it work today . . . and maybe tomorrow . . . and the next day . . ." his voice trailed off. Cupping her face in his hands, they both stared at one another. In Maggie's big brown pools shined hints of happiness, hints of pain.

"Oh, Adam. What are we—"

"Shhhh!"

With more passion and aggressiveness, Adam tasted her neck as the rough stubble on his cheek scraped her soft collarbone. He worked his way downward, and as his hands reached up to the front of her blouse, he pulled hard – the buttons flying this way and that – before he buried himself into her chest, his tongue dancing in circles on the raised tips of her exposed breasts. As pleasure washed over her entire body, Maggie let out a moan followed by an exhaled whisper. "Oh . . . God!"

All sounds around them disappeared. The farm, the house, that room . . . it was as if everything enveloped these two soulmates in their own bubble. Maggie couldn't get enough of him as her hands trestled around Adam's shoulders, feeling the ripples of his upper back. Her kisses found his mouth once more while he pulled her hips tight against his trousers. Adam became more delicious with each second, and she ate him up. She moaned as her grinding became more pronounced.

"Yes. Oh yes," she said – perhaps out loud, perhaps in her head – she couldn't be sure.

After a tremble, Maggie fell into him, her body drained and exhausted. The wave of lust and sweat and sin quickly retracted, rolling themselves back into the sea. Worse still, an unseen chasm worked its way between them, leaving Maggie cold and exposed. Lying on top of him, guilt had once again paid her a visit, and soon reality came into full view. She lay frozen on top of Adam, then sat up and looked into his eyes. At first, she looked right through him, not at him.

"Um, Maggie, are you alright?"

She didn't respond.

"You look like you're going to faint or something," he said, genuine concern on his face.

As Adam came back into focus, Maggie took in a staggered breath and stared at him suspiciously, as if she needed someone to blame for the momentary lapse of judgment. Sitting on the edge of the bed, she pulled the blouse over her shoulders and replied softly, "I don't feel too well."

Breathing a heavy sigh, Adam pushed himself up in the bed, then spun around to sit beside her. Maggie reached for his hands and studied the palms, much the same way a fortuneteller would inspect the hands of an unsuspecting client. As she did so, her fingers wrapped around his like a vine. Adam's digits were thick and strong. Despite the steeled life on the farm, Maggie's fingers were long, creamy and delicate. Sitting on the edge of the bed, Adam squeezed his grip, rested his forehead against hers, closed his eyes and took in the amalgamated essence of this female farmer whose selfless epithet changed by the day, the hour, by the minute . . . all depending on the needs of those around her.

His nose took in a subtle but earthy resonance of leather and straw from when she worked in the barn earlier that morning; there was also a savory trace of rosemary, sage and thyme from this homemaker's kitchen; and the most overt yet pleasant of all, he perceived the ladylike notes of white lily, jasmine and honeysuckle – fragrances which reminded the world that beneath those many layers lived a resplendent beauty with whom he had fallen in love. As they disentangled their grip, Adam wrapped his arms around her in a tight hug, cupping her head to his shoulder. He could feel her body shudder with a pulsating rhythm. Her crying caused him to squeeze her even more. "It's okay," he whispered into her ear. "It's going to be all right."

She let out a loud sniffle and pulled away. "Oh God," she said in frustration, looking down at the floor and wiping her nose with the back of her hand. "How can this be happening? You're going to have to leave, and if Erik comes back I . . ."

With sadness in his eyes, Adam forced a smile in the corner of his mouth. "I know, I know . . . It's difficult to understand any of this. Life comes at you fast, and oftentimes there's no way to predict what's next. I mean, look at us. Think about where we were several years ago. Several *months* ago," he said, pausing for a moment. "I had a family and a good job, then blinked, and they were gone. Before I knew it, I was in the army, then the African desert, and now – I'm here, with you. While we can try to understand it all, the truth is, no one knows what will happen next. So let's not overthink this, Maggie. Maybe, just *maybe*, things will change in our favor. If the war ends and it turns out you are alone, perhaps I can return to America and we can try to make this real."

"I don't know about anything anymore," she said with sorrow in her eyes. "I'm sorry about this. I don't know what came over me."

"Please, do not apologize. I'm the one who led you on. I should be the one saying he's sorry."

Reaching for his hand again, Maggie squeezed it and added, "I am so confused about Erik. All I ever hear is when things go this long, without word from the Red Cross or the Army, a missing soldier is most probably . . ." Finally she said it, "He's probably dead." She dropped her head. "And I feel so guilty about it all. Sometimes I think he's missing because of me. Because I let my guard down, and started to fall for you."

"That's ridiculous."

All Maggie could muster in response was a sigh.

Adam put his index finger under her chin and coaxed her to look up.

"What? Why are you smiling?" she asked.

"If you want to blame anyone . . . blame me. I'm the one who set his sights on you, from that very first day."

Maggie took another cleansing breath. "Oh, who are we kidding? Even if he is dead, you will still have to go back to Germany, and here I'll sit, wondering whether you're alive, and what you're doing, and who you may be with. I can't bear the thought."

"I could come back, you know."

Maggie buried her head in her hands and began to sob.

He wrapped an arm around her and rubbed her back. "It will all be okay. Trust me."

Maggie stood up, wiped her eyes, and turned to face him. "God, look at me. I am such a mess." She then reached her hand up to his face and stroked his cheek, feeling the stubble from a three-day beard.

"I need to be alone for a while. I need to think things through."

"I understand."

She cinched her blouse together where the buttons used to be and exited the room.

Chapter Twenty-Five

Pruning

Over the next few weeks, Adam's rehabilitation continued on schedule. With the help of nurse O'Donoghue, Maggie and even Big Jack, Adam got on his feet and slowly began to walk with the aid of crutches, occasionally going solo from one side of the bedroom to the next. With his leg no longer locked into a boot, his bedsores finally began to heal as well.

During this time, he and Maggie would occasionally steal a kiss, but usually Big Jack or Benny were nearby, so a coquettish smile, bashful eyes, a simple touch here and there would have to do. With each day, they waited for the universe to unveil its next secret.

The winter of 1945 was shaping up to be quite mild, with the largest snowstorm not measuring more than eight inches. The POWs had been back on the farm for almost a week, pruning the apple orchard at a steady pace. The days became quite routine: Jennaro would drop them off, sometimes leaving the orchard for several hours, then come back for lunch inside the farmhouse with Maggie and the small group of Germans. Then back to the fields until roughly 4:00 PM.

On this particular morning, Jennaro sat at the kitchen table with a hot cup of coffee while Maggie stood opposite making vegetable soup. Benny sat beside the corporal drawing on scrap sheets of paper.

"So, Corporal, why is it you have no place to go today?"

"What do you mean?"

"Well, you usually drop off the POWs and leave. I'm curious . . . do you go back to camp? I can't believe your commander would allow them to be unsupervised in this cold weather."

"Private Thompson's in the orchard with them."

"You know what I mean. Let me say it another way: what do you do when you leave?"

"Um, I go into town sometimes, and other times I have to pick up supplies from other camps in the area," he said, taking a slurping sip out of his cup.

Maggie stopped peeling her potatoes, spun around and looked at him suspiciously.

"So what's her name?"

"Huh? What?" Jennaro said, refusing to make eye contact.

"Do you think I was born yesterday? It's that girl you met in Milwaukee a few months back, isn't it?"

He studied her, his knee bouncing up and down quickly as he sat in the chair. "You know I could get in huge trouble if anyone found out."

"Corporal, it's me. Steel trap," she said pointing to her lips and making a twisting motion.

Jennaro glanced over at Benny, who was lost in his project.

"You think he's going to care?" said Maggie cocking her head towards her son. "Come on, give me some dirt."

He paused and then confessed, "Okay yeah – it's her."

"I knew it!" said Maggie with a clap of her hands. "What's her name? Rita? Rhoda? I forget."

Unable to stop himself, Jennaro shifted in his chair, his knee still restless. "It's Rosa. And yes, she actually lives pretty close – in Pewaukee.

Her father is ill and she is the only caregiver. So I go over there and help out."

"Aren't you the saint?"

"I don't mind. I get to help him, and spend time with her, so . . ."

"That sounds pretty serious."

"Maggie . . ." he paused again, then leaned forward in his chair, "When do you know you're in love?"

"What did you say?"

"No, really. I think I'm in love."

"Not that. I mean, yes! That's big news, but you called me Maggie."

"I did?"

"Ah-huh. You must be losing your mind over this girl."

"Jeez, you're right. I'm sorry, Mrs. Wentworth."

"Don't apologize. We women tend to have that effect on men when they fall head-over-heels. And if it is love, wow, congrats."

"Well, you're married, right?"

Maggie gave him a twisted look.

"I'm sorry, that was rude. With your husband missing and all."

"It's okay."

He continued, a bit embarrassed. "So tell me, when did you know it was, you know? I mean, I can't stop thinking about her. I'm making mistakes at the camp. I'm dreaming about her. I smell my shirts whenever I leave her. Just the other day, I almost went off the road because I was smelling her perfume on my collar. I'm risking a huge punishment by going to her house all the time. If my C.O. found out about me sneaking over there . . ."

"Corporal, you just answered your own question."

"Huh? What question?"

"You, my friend, are in L-O-V-E."

Jennaro smiled at the validation.

"I'm very happy for you. I hope she treats you well."

"Oh, she does."

Maggie smiled too, genuinely delighted for him. But in an odd way the conversation forced her to reevaluate her own feelings towards Erik, trying to recall if she ever felt this same way. Perhaps it was due to the passage of time, but those memories seemed to have faded, if they had existed at all. But when it came to Adam . . . well, she could relate.

"So I have to get her a birthday present," said the corporal. "And I thought maybe I'd get your two cents, seeing as you're a woman and all."

"Thanks for noticing."

"You know what I mean."

"So here's what I do know . . ." Maggie said, turning her gaze toward the ceiling. With a far-off look in her eyes, she recited, '*Love is, above all, the gift of oneself.*'"

Jennaro looked at her, confused, "Is that Shakespeare or something?"

"No, it is Jean Anouilh Ardele. You should read some of his works. Quote him every so often and your future wife will be impressed, if she isn't already."

"My future wife? Wow, you think?"

Breaking the moment, they heard yelling from outside. Both looked out the window and saw two of the German POWs sprinting fast towards the farmhouse.

"Oh-oh, this doesn't look good," said Jennaro, grabbing his coat from the back of a kitchen chair.

Gary Hofstädter and Henry Elam stepped through the backdoor, white as ghosts and scared to death.

"You have to come! You have to see!" said Hofstädter, out of breath.

"What are you talking about?" said Jennaro.

"There's a body! We found a body!" said Elam.

"What?" said Maggie.

"In the orchard?" followed Jennaro.

"Yes!" they said in unison.

"My God!"

"Benny, where's Big Jack?" asked Maggie.

"In the barn," said Benny, a scared look on his face.

"Okay, so I'm going to get him to come to the kitchen and watch you. Stay here, Benny."

Her son began to cry, "Momma, don't leave. I'm scared."

"It's okay, Opa will be right here."

"Don't go!"

"Mrs. Wentworth, I have to go with the POWs. I'll meet you there."

"Okay. I'll be right behind you."

With that, Jennaro bolted out the door and ran into the orchard with the two Germans. Maggie grabbed her and Benny's coats and hastily put them on. Together they ran to the barn and found Big Jack pounding out a large dent in a plow blade.

"Papa, can you stay with Benny? I have to run with Jennaro into the field. They found something."

"Huh?" he said, confused. "What is it? Why is Benny crying?"

"They found a dead man," Benny said chiming in. "I'm afraid."

"Please, Papa, stay with him. I'll come back as soon as I know what's going on."

"Does the corporal have his gun?"

"Yes. No. I don't know. I'm sure someone does."

"You'll be keeping me on pins and needles, but okay. Go. *Go!*"

Maggie bolted out of the barn, her coat unbuttoned and open to the cold. As she ran, she occasionally stumbled on the frozen ruts of mud which had been formed by her tractor in the warmer months. A sprained ankle seemed imminent, so she sacrificed speed for purpose and arrived shortly after Jennaro.

The cluster of Germans appeared subdued at the large maple tree before them. It had rooted itself more than a hundred years ago at the edge of the orchard. Unlike the apple trees next to it, this tree didn't yield fruit – but held something else: a man with a rope around his neck hung from one of its biggest branches. He swung gently in the wind, his long overcoat flapping in the breeze.

"Ahhh!" shrieked Maggie. "My God, he's been hung."

Everyone turned to look at her. Jennaro approached. "You shouldn't be here, Mrs. Wentworth. I'll take care of this."

"What?" Maggie said, attempting to compose herself. "No, no, it's okay," she continued, reestablishing her gumption. "I thank you for your concern, Corporal, but this is my farm and I am responsible for everyone on it. Dead or alive."

"Okay, but I have to warn you – it's not pretty."

"Was he murdered?" she asked as she cocked her head to get a better look at the suspended corpse.

"I have no idea."

Maggie walked slowly towards the body, which faced away from her approach. She thought it strange his feet floated no more than two inches off the ground, as if his death could have been prevented had he been a little taller. The corpse swung in the soft but icy-cold breeze, the feet occasionally scraping against an exposed root, then coming back to center when the wind would subside.

"It's odd he's so low to the ground," she said advancing slowly.

"I'm guessing he's been hanging there for quite some time and the rope simply stretched," said Jennaro.

Maggie hardly heard the corporal's voice as she focused on the body. As she stepped closer, a light breeze picked up and the dead man's left foot caught a large fieldstone, which caused it to turn 180 degrees directly in front of her. At that moment Maggie came face-to-face with a horrific sight. One of the eyes of the corpse was gone, revealing a hollow socket. Dried blood streaked the cheeks and the tip of the chin. Several black crows in a nearby tree chimed in with loud protest at what they believed was their discovery. She noticed, too, that half of his right ear had been gnawed away, perhaps by a squirrel or a mouse. But as horrific as this sight was, Maggie noticed something else which terrified her even more: the thick, orange whiskers of an unshaven friend.

Her eyes grew wide and she lost all composure, letting out a blood-curdling scream. “Oh my God, no! No, no, no!” she yelled as she stepped backwards, tripping and falling to the ground. Jennaro and two of the Germans ran to her aid.

“Do you know this man?” asked Jennaro, kneeling beside her. “Do you know who this is?”

“Oh my God, oh my God, what am I going to tell Audrey?” Unable to stand, Maggie remained seated on the frozen ground. “What am I going to say?” she repeated, hitting Jennaro’s thigh.

“Who is Audrey? Who is this man?”

“His name is Bob. Bob Stanton – and I killed him. I *killed* this man. I should have made him stay, but I let him go. Good Lord, I let him leave. Why? *Why?*” she shouted, now pounding the ground.

“It’s okay, Mrs. Wentworth. You didn’t do this. This was not your fault.”

She curled up in a ball and sobbed.

“Someone cut him down, please,” ordered Jennaro. “Come on, grab one of those pruners and cut the rope would ya? Let’s get him back to the farm.”

At that request, Hofstädter took pruning shears and with little effort snipped the rope. Like a piece of strong timber, the body fell over, tall and stiff, like a toppled mannequin from a Marshall Field’s window display. The knees did not buckle and the arms did not move. When Maggie saw this she let out another shriek and buried her head in her hands.

“I’m sorry you had to see this,” Jennaro said to her softly. “I didn’t know you were friends.”

Now on the ground, the corpse rocked back and forth slightly and finally settled on its back. Henry Elam loosened the noose from around the neck and pulled it over the head. Bob's overcoat opened slightly and Hofstädter noticed something.

"Es gibt einen Brief in seiner Tasche," he said pointing to the coat pocket.

Maggie looked up slowly. "What? A note?"

In broken English, the German looked at Maggie and repeated. "*Ja,* in the pocket!"

Hofstädter pulled it out, stood up and walked it over to Maggie, holding it like a valuable artifact.

With bare hands shaking, she struggled to take it out of the envelope, then finally slid it out and unfolded the letter. All she could bear to read were the words, *My dearest Audrey . . .* she then looked up to the cold, cloudy sky and wailed.

* * *

Sheriff John McGee's voice could be heard over all others. "One at a time, please. I'll get everyone's statements, just stop talking all at once!"

Maggie rested on the davenport in her living room, numb to all the commotion. Standing nearby: Big Jack, Jennaro, the POWs, Father Schmidt from her church and Adam, who stood with the aid of his crutches. Benny knelt beside his mother, stroking her arm.

"Can I get you something to drink, hon?" asked Big Jack. "Some tea, maybe?"

"Sure," she said with a soft voice and a sigh.

"I've got it, Mister Mueller," said Jennaro as he walked to the kitchen to put a kettle on the stove.

"Are you feeling well enough to issue a statement, Maggie?" Sheriff McGee inquired, his notepad at the ready.

"Oh come on, Dale, give her a minute, would ya?" said Big Jack.

Maggie sat up tall and sucked air in through her teeth, rubbed her eyes with ferocity, then stroked her forehead, trying to make sense of it all.

"Has anyone called Audrey yet?" she asked.

The room got quiet. All eyes went to the sheriff.

"I dispatched my deputy to her home. She will arrive shortly," he said. "I'm terribly sorry, Maggie. I know you were close to the Stantons."

Maggie looked at the floor and could only nod her head. Her thoughts went back to the day Bob visited, and she tried to remember what he said before departing. Something about how he would tell Audrey the truth? Should she have seen through his pain? Could she ever have imagined he would take his own life? Hundreds of questions.

"Okay, tell you what, folks, let's give Maggie a little time and we'll all go into the kitchen," said the sheriff. "I'll take your statements in there."

Everyone left the living room except for Big Jack and Benny. Adam proceeded to his bedroom, but Maggie asked him to stay. Big Jack sat down next to his daughter and put a comforting hand on her shoulder, Adam stood behind the elder statesman and bit his lip.

"I'm sorry you had to see such a thing," her father said.

Maggie shook her head in shame. "You know, I could have stopped it, Papa. I could have made him stay here and call Audrey."

Big Jack looked perplexed. "What? He was here? Bob was *here?"*

Maggie looked at Adam, then at Big Jack. "Yes."

Big Jack turned around to look at Adam. "Did you know about this?"

"I overheard some things."

"Why doesn't anyone tell me what's going on in my own house? So when was this?"

"Christmas Eve. He was upset and confused and . . . I should have made him stay."

"Did he and Audrey have a fight? Is that why he never came home?"

Looking up at Adam, Maggie wore a pained expression. She didn't want to relive the sequence of events that happened that night in Milwaukee, but she knew she had to tell her father. "No, Papa, there's much more to the story."

"Well, I'm not going anywhere."

"Benny, dear. Could you go into the kitchen? What I have to tell Opa is not best for your ears."

"Oh shucks," he said, before walking into the next room.

"So what happened?" asked Big Jack.

"Oh Papa, I'm so torn."

"I'll try to give you my advice once I know what it is."

Feeling the memory pull at her, Maggie's eyes grew sad and tender. She took in a slow, deep breath and began to tell him what she saw that night at The King's Throne. Adam remained silent but stood by for moral support. Big Jack's demeanor went from being confused, then horrified, to angry . . . and then sad.

As Maggie wrapped up her abbreviated version of the story, the second squad car pulled up to the farm. Deputy Sheriff John Kurchen stepped out one side, Audrey the other. Walking with a sullen and lethargic expression, it was obvious she had been given the news.

McGee greeted them at the door and they entered the living room. Maggie popped up off the couch and walked briskly to her friend. They embraced without a word. Tears streamed down their cheeks. Audrey let out a soul-shredding cry and the pain spilled out of her. With her mouth buried in Maggie's shoulder she tried to speak through the tears. "He was such a good man. Why would he do such a thing? I don't understand any of it."

"I know. I know," Maggie said softly.

When they separated, Audrey's nose dripped and she sniffed loudly. "Oh God, look at me." Big Jack handed her his hanky, which she used to blow her nose.

After a long, still moment, she said, "May I see him?"

A silence covered the room like a soft cloud. Obviously uncomfortable, the sheriff continued, "Audrey, he's been out in the orchard for several weeks – as near as I can tell – and while the severe cold preserved him, some things happened over the course of time which, well, changed his appearance a bit."

"I don't understand. What kinds of things?"

McGee struggled for the words. "Oh Audrey, this is so hard. Let's just say the birds and some rodents found him first. You may have a hard time recognizing him."

At this, Audrey's eyes got large and she found hope. "Oh my God, if that's true . . . maybe . . . maybe it's not him. Maybe it's not Bob! Is that possible?" She looked around the room for some support, but most eyes looked away. "Isn't there some hope? If he's hard to recognize, how do you know it's him?"

"Audrey," Father Schmidt said, pausing as he stepped into the conversation. "His wallet was in his trousers." Hesitating again, he added, "And there is a note."

"A note?" Audrey's tiny flicker of hope extinguished before their eyes. Her shoulders sunk and her head dropped.

"I'm so sorry," the priest added.

In a soft voice, she asked, "Can I read it?"

"Sure. Let's go to the barn and you can read it there," said Maggie. "He's in there, too."

Audrey suddenly seemed to find strength from deep within. She looked at everyone in the room, gritted her teeth and simply said, "Okay. Let's get this over with."

"We don't have to do this right away. We can wait until you're ready," said Sheriff McGee.

"No, I've waited long enough. I'm tired of waiting."

Father Schmidt looked at her with sad eyes.

"Why do people do that? Why do people take their own lives, Father?"

The priest took a deep breath. "Many reasons. We don't always know what they are or how bad the pain must have been. And while it may not make sense now, one can only hope clarity will come one day soon."

Upon hearing this, Maggie swallowed hard.

"Let's go to the barn," Audrey ordered with commanding authority. She stood tall and prepared herself for the inevitable.

* * *

Bob's body lay on the cold, dirt floor, covered by a wool blanket. On one side stood Big Jack, Sheriff McGee and Father Schmidt; on the other, Audrey and Maggie. The sheriff slowly pulled back the blanket to reveal Bob's head and upper chest. While most were aghast at the grisly sight, Audrey looked unfazed, squinted her eyes, and to everyone's surprise kneeled down to study his face. She looked at him closely, with very little emotion, like a county coroner trying to determine a cause of death. With her breath billowing out of her mouth like smoke from a cigarette, Audrey reached for his chin and tried to turn his head to face hers, but she struggled due to the combination of frozen tissue and rigor mortis. She seemed particularly focused on the open eye socket.

After a few more seconds, she said matter-of-factly, "Yes, that's him. He had that mole on his temple and this scar on his neck." She then let out a blowing sigh. "Please, cover him up."

Father Schmidt draped him with the blanket and glanced at Maggie with a look of confusion. *Why so matter-of-fact? No emotion?*

"You said there was a note?" said Audrey coldly.

"Yes. I have it right here," said the sheriff. "I didn't want you to read it inside with so many people around."

The sheriff put his hand into his overcoat and pulled out the tri-folded piece of stationary from the 40 Winks Motel in nearby

Brookfield. Audrey unfolded it slowly as she wandered to the other side of the barn. Reading the letter, she stopped beside Suri's stable and propped herself up against the gate. Maggie looked at Big Jack, who studied Father Schmidt, who turned to look at the sheriff, all four holding their breath, waiting for a reaction.

After a minute or so, Audrey tipped her head high and let out a long, steady sigh. The chill in the air caused her breath to float effortlessly over her head, dissipating just in front of the horse who watched her curiously while chewing some oats. With her arms hanging at her side, shoulders now sunken, Audrey's fingers loosened their grip on the letter, and it gently floated to the ground. She then wrapped her arms around herself – the way one does when getting a strong chill – bent over and vomited into the horse's stall.

Maggie ran to her aid, put her arm around her friend and guided her out of the barn. They walked slowly towards the farmhouse. "You're gonna stay with us for the next few days," Maggie said while handing her a handkerchief.

Audrey didn't say a word. As Father Schmidt and the sheriff followed them back to the house, Big Jack turned towards the stable and went to retrieve the letter. Four cats who lived in the barn lapped up the vomit from the floor next to Suri's stable.

"Get outta here!" he snipped in disgust, trying to kick the felines away. Alone now, Big Jack opened the half-folded note and held it up to the light of a kerosene lantern which hung on a barn post nearby.

My dearest Audrey:

Let me begin by saying I'm sorry. I'm sorry for the grief you will surely feel as you read this. I'm sorry for the confusion. I'm sorry for the anger you will eventually feel. I want you to know that none of this is your fault and you never did anything wrong. This is all my doing. I was living a lie, and could no longer do so.

I am a homosexual. I always have been. Perhaps you knew. I wanted so badly to change. But in the end, I couldn't do it. I tried with you. I tried in the Army. I tried at work. When traveling out of town I even saw various doctors to help me change. This burden . . . will be with me always.

It is my wish you find a good man, a loving man. Someone who can make you happy and give you the children you so desperately desire. Children who may one day see a world of tolerance and acceptance. You deserve nothing less.

I hope you won't miss me too much, my darling, for I am not a man. Not the one you think you married, anyways. I wish so badly I could have been better for you. Because you deserve better, Audrey. I love you now and will love you for all eternity.

Bob

MOVIETONE Title: ALLIES OPEN FINAL DRIVE ON GERMANY

(Newsreel Narrator): Without expressing definite optimism, Allied leaders say the final curtain is about to fall on the European War. The crossing of the Rhine has spelled the doom of Nazi hopes of victory.

The Germans put their faith in the Sigfried Line, but as we took key fortresses and smashed through, it was the beginning of the end.

The Allies have taken more than a million prisoners since our invasion of France. In the course of our rapid advance, forced laborers were freed from manufacturing centers that we reduced to rubble. Allied strategy called for the leveling of towns if it meant saving the lives of our boys.

In these pictures, supreme commander Eisenhower joins General Simpson, commander of the Ninth Army, on a tour of what was once part of the Sigfried Line. This is one of the first places where we cracked the shell of Nazi resistance and brought the Hun to his knees.

The speedy push of the Allied Army has caught the Germans by complete surprise – they have admitted – and when G.I. Joe passes through town without a chance for a 'howdy,' the civilians can only stand by and watch.

As the American troops pushed on, they freed countless numbers of Russian and Polish prisoners who were forced laborers under the German heel. When they have received medical attention and decent food, these folks are all smiles. Look at these G.I.s . . . they can make friends at the drop of a Nazi.

We have the opportunity to stamp out evil like this. It's up to us to supply the final punch that will mean peace in this war-weary world.

Go get 'em boys! And come home safe!

Chapter Twenty-Six

Coming Attractions

Going to the movies provided a whimsical escape for Maggie and Audrey. The suspension of disbelief seemed a subtle, yet essential coping mechanism for both women. And on this Saturday night in mid-March, both retreated to their sanctuary of the movie house in downtown Ramsey. It provided an excuse to get away from the farm and step away from a life of uncertainty – to a world that fostered dreams and took both of them to faraway lands and into the arms of exotic lovers.

These diversions had an undercurrent of hope that ran well below the surface of their respective lives. *What would it be like to kiss Clark Gable? Is Tahiti as beautiful as it looks on screen? Maybe one day we can find out.*

Visiting the Uptown Theater nearly once a month filled a void in their lives. For Maggie, being in the arms of an exotic stranger from another country was closer to reality than she could have ever hoped. These silver screen dreams also allowed her to breathe underwater. On this particular night, she and Audrey had invited someone else to join them in their private retreat: Adam.

Over the past few weeks, Maggie's star patient had made incredible strides in his therapy. Even Doc Marshall could not believe how quickly he was progressing. Adam moved freely around the house with the help of crutches and had even ventured into the strawberry fields a few days prior, with Maggie by his side.

It had been several months since Big Jack gave his *"stay true to your vows"* speech to Maggie, but with no word and no updates from the Army brass about Erik's MIA status, he started to believe his son-in-law was most likely dead. So he became more comfortable with his daughter's relationship. Adam made her happy. Adam made Benny happy. Adam made . . . Big Jack happy.

Until death do us part. That verse had been replayed in his head ever since his daughter first showed an interest in the POW. He wondered if such a relationship could actually work, or if it represented just another Hollywood ending.

Being in the movie theater that night marked the first time Adam left the farm since his fall. It was a big night for Audrey, too, because she had not yet ventured out in public since Bob's funeral, nearly a month earlier.

Adam had gotten approval from the camp commander to visit the movie house with Maggie and Audrey, but only after some coaxing from Big Jack. Six months prior, this would have been unheard of, but during the spring of 1945, many POWs had become commonplace on the streets of Ramsey. Those who had earned privileges for good behavior were granted trips into town more frequently than ever.

They could go into ice cream parlors and get a scoop of vanilla, visit a dime store for a deck of cards, walk into a bar and buy some suds – and most amazingly of all – they would pay for these goods and services with the money they earned as American laborers. While some of the town residents did not approve of these visits, most tolerated the Germans and knew if the recent newsreels were accurate, the European end would be coming soon and America would be swapping soldiers in no time. Besides, money is money, and privately, even the most critical believed it didn't matter where the money came from.

As the three moviegoers sat in the dark near the back of the theater – Adam with his crutches propped up in the vacant seat beside him, Maggie in the middle and Audrey on the end – they viewed the latest newsreel about the Allies' advance toward Berlin. As they watched in silence, each felt a stabbing pain in their guts.

Maggie seemed convinced at any moment Erik would appear on screen in one of the *MOVIETONE* news clips as a wounded American in a liberated army hospital. Perhaps he'd be on a bed, look at the camera with that crooked smile of his and giving the thumbs up as if to say, *Look at me, Mags. I'm banged up a little, but alright. I'll be back on the farm in no time.* A hollow pain formed deep in her stomach.

As Adam viewed the footage, his throat burned. The devastation of his homeland seemed ubiquitous. *Could this really be Germany, or was it just American propaganda?* Looking at the footage of bombed-out cities, dead bodies on the side of the road, and fellow POWs who wore expressions of stone disturbed him deeply. The captured German soldiers on the big screen appeared shell-shocked and numb. It was as if they were looking right at Adam and telling him to stay put. How could he ever return to *Deutschland?* What would life be like without his home, without his wife, without his son, without . . . Maggie.

Audrey, too, had mixed feelings. She knew she wouldn't be the only widow in the county. In fact, she'd be one of thousands in the state who lost loved ones during that horrible war. As she watched the newsreel of American G.I.s carrying flowers in the streets of liberated European cities, she wondered if maybe one of them would come home, marry her and give her that family she'd always wanted.

The main feature that evening was *To Have And Have Not*, a film starring Hollywood mainstay Humphrey Bogart and a stunning newcomer named Lauren Bacall. It was about a tough charter-boat captain in Martinique who fell for a beautiful pickpocket. As it turned out, she stole more than his wallet. Bogart and Bacall had true chemistry, and it showed on the big screen. Maggie believed she and Adam could have been in the same movie – a chance meeting, in the backdrop of war, fighting against all odds to be together. Several times during the film, Adam would nonchalantly reach his hand across the armrest for hers. They would squeeze tight, occasionally rub a wrist or an arm, then return it to their respective laps. During one particularly romantic interlude between Bogart and Bacall, Maggie slowly leaned forward and looked at Adam's face as he watched, and she wondered if he shared her thoughts. She knew the answer. *Why did Audrey have to tag along?*

* * *

As they left the theater, it was obvious Adam was in pain. "Are you alright?" asked Maggie.

"I'll be fine."

"I noticed you shifting your weight throughout the film. I should have given you the aisle seat," said Audrey.

"Thank you, but the only way for me to get stronger is to push through a little pain. That's what Doc Marshall says."

Walking back to Maggie's pickup truck on Main Street, a group of teenagers approached. The two boys and three girls looked to be high school upperclassmen, based on the young men's letterman jackets, and they were likely headed for the town malt shop for some root beer and grandstanding on this cool but pleasant Saturday night. One of the boys, a tall, physically fit young man playfully tugged at one of the girl's long ponytails.

"Stop that, Billy. Or I swear I'll . . ."

"You'll what?" he said in a mocking voice. "You'll tell your mother?" He then let out a loud laugh.

As Maggie, Audrey and Adam passed the group, the brash boy inadvertently kicked Adam's right crutch, knocking it out from under him. Adam dropped like a rock, crashing with full force to the sidewalk. Both boys immediately came to his aid.

"Hey, I'm sorry, fella. Should have been watching where I was going. You veterans deserve better," said the boy as he bent over to help Adam get up.

"That's quite alright," said Adam. "I'm not too good with these things. Still getting used to them."

Upon hearing his subtle German accent, the boy recoiled in disgust as he realized his mistake.

"What the hell? You're a goddamn *Kraut*?" said the boy, instantly releasing Adam and letting him fall to the ground a second time.

"I am a German, if that's what you mean?" said Adam trying to get up from all fours.

"What's your problem?" insisted Maggie. "Have you no heart?"

"What's my problem? What's *your* problem, lady?" barked the teenager.

"Yeah, what's your problem?" repeated the second boy, a pint-sized carbon copy of his friend who felt more compelled to impress the three girls than he did to interrogate Adam.

"Come on, Bobby, give it a rest," insisted the girl with the long ponytail. "Can't you see he's injured? He's got crutches and stuff."

"Forget that. This here is a genuine German soldier, ladies. How's it feel getting your ass whooped over there, huh, Adolf? Piece of shit probably shot at my brother. He's on his way to Berlin right now!"

"Your brother got shot? I thought he was a cook," said the other boy.

"Shut up!" said Bobby, pushing his friend and looking perturbed at having his bombastic tale revealed. "Even so, this guy could have shot him at any time."

"I assure you, I don't believe I ever took a shot at your brother," said Adam diplomatically as he stood back up with the aid of his crutches.

The energy turned increasingly negative and Audrey could feel it, so she stepped in and tried to shut down the conversation, but only added fuel to the fire. "What the hell are you guys doing, huh? Trying to show off in front of these girls? Yeah, you're real tough – knocking over an injured man on crutches."

"Why don't you all just keep walking and go on your merry way," Maggie added.

"Shut your face, *Kraut*-lover!" said the bigger boy to Maggie.

"Don't talk to her like that," said Adam, now getting angry.

"What you gonna do about it, Heil Hitler? I'll talk to her any way I darn well please. This is America. Home of the brave, land of the free!" At that, the teen put his arm around Maggie and in an obvious flirting voice added, "So, what in the world are you doing with a guy like this? I can show you how American boys have fun."

"Stop it!" insisted Adam. "Show her some respect."

"Wanna do something about it, Franz? Let's go – you and me!" he then pushed Adam, who stepped backwards but didn't fall.

"Stop it, Bobby. He's got crutches!" insisted the younger girl.

Ignoring her, Bobby went into hot pursuit, "I'll show you how we do things here in Amer—"

Before he could finish his sentence, Adam took the blunt end of his crutch and jammed it hard into the Bobby's stomach. The boy buckled over, letting out a hollow "*Awhoogh*" sound. Pulling it back and spinning it clockwise, Adam then came at the teen with an uppercut. He fell backwards and landed hard on his seat. A bit dazed and shaking it off, he brushed his chin and, upon seeing some blood from his lip, Bobby bounced back. "You son-of-a-bitch!" exclaimed the bully teen as he jumped up and stepped towards Adam.

He took a swing, but caught air as Adam ducked. The boy swung a second time, and again Adam ducked. Frustrated, the teen came at him harder, but Adam bobbed and weaved like a prize-fighter. Having cornered Adam against the plate glass window of the General Store, the teen gritted his teeth and took another swing, this time successfully finding Adam straight in the gut, then the jaw. Still on his feet, Adam tried to retaliate with a left-cross, but his hip was not yet strong enough to provide the push-off he needed to deliver the punch, and he lost his balance. The teen took advantage, hitting him again, and Adam crashed to the ground a second time. Bobby then began kicking Adam in the ribs.

"Stop it!" yelled Maggie, trying unsuccessfully to pull the larger teenager back.

"Are you crazy?" insisted Audrey.

"Hey, Bobby, come on, you've given him enough," remarked the other boy.

Bobby turned towards them with fire in his eyes and said, "What, are you a bunch of *Kraut*-lovers, too? I'm just teaching Hitler-boy a lesson."

In that instant, as he talked at his friends, a Graf's Root Beer bottle crashed over his head and Bobby fell hard to the ground, unconscious.

"I told him to stop it," said Maggie, holding only the broken end of the bottleneck. "Now let's go home."

Everyone froze, looking at Maggie in amazement. She had taken down this thug with a single stroke. Maggie, Audrey, and even the young ladies helped Adam to his feet and walked him across the street to the pickup truck. Lines like, "He's such an idiot . . . I apologize for him . . . He deserved it," came from the high school girls who took a sympathetic liking to Adam. One even declared to her girlfriend, "He's kinda cute."

* * *

The next day, as Adam read *Life* magazine on the living room davenport while holding an ice bag to his black eye, Benny walked by spinning the gold watch he had displayed weeks earlier. Adam couldn't help but notice the way Benny twirled it, almost as if to say, *Look what I found.* His technique worked.

"That looks familiar."

"I found it again."

"You *found* it again? Well, that's great," said Adam with a smile, knowing full well the little boy had been snooping around in his mother's jewelry box again. "Does it work yet?"

"Naw. But I like to pretend it does. Look, it says it's 8:30," Benny said, forgetting he pointed that out the first time he showed Adam the pocket watch.

"You know, I've been thinking about that watch . . . I'll bet we can fix it," said Adam as he set the magazine in his lap.

"You mean it?"

"Well, I'll have to take a closer look at it. But if we could repair it, maybe we give it to your mother for her birthday. It's coming up soon, I believe."

"A birthday present? Okay!" said the youngster with enthusiasm. "Can it be a secret?"

"Yes, Benny. It'll be our little secret."

The youngster then held the watch in front of Adam. "Don't break it."

Adam smiled. *You are way too cute.* "I used to own tools that would allow me to fix watches like this one. But maybe in this instance we can improvise."

"How do you know how to fix them?"

"I worked for a company that made watches. Before the war."

Benny tried to understand but only gave him a smile.

"Depending on what's wrong, I may be able to do it with a paperclip or a sewing needle. Do you know what those are?"

Benny nodded softly but obviously did not know.

"Does your mommy have a desk? You know, a place she keeps the mail and pays the bills?"

Benny led him to a drawer in the kitchen. Inside were neatly organized stacks of envelopes with strings tied around each bundle. Next to the stacks: small glass jars holding everything from thumbtacks and rubber bands to – *voilà!* – paperclips.

"Here's what I need," Adam said.

"That's a paperclip?"

"Yes. That's a paperclip. And here's a push-pin cushion. One of those pins could come in handy as well."

As they sat down at the kitchen table, Benny watched Adam lay the watch flat on a clean hand towel. "I don't want to lose any pieces," he said to the youngster, who looked confused about what was going on.

Tipping the pocket watch on a 45-degree angle, Adam opened the back cover and pushed the paperclip straight through the hinge that held it in place. In an instant, the back cover separated from the body of the watch.

"You broke it!" proclaimed Benny.

"No, no, this is how we fix it. Trust me."

Adam then put the watch in the palm of his hand and twisted hard on the backside of the timepiece. His hands trembled for the effort, as if to open a tightly sealed Mason jar. It took a few tries, but on the third attempt he got the metal cover to turn.

"Here we go," said Adam with a wisp of relief.

Adam laid the watch down flat on the towel and, using his thumb and index finger like a pair of needle-nose pliers, he slowly turned it counterclockwise until it separated from the body of the watch. With the help of a sewing needle, he methodically separated the cover from the base with the skill of a surgeon. Benny let out an impressed, "Whoa. What are those?"

Adam was in his element. "These are springs and gears," Adam explained, pointing to various parts of the watch with the sewing needle. "This is called the escapement. Here is the fusee. And this is the mainspring. Now, I suspect a small piece of that spring popped off and that is the reason the clock is not working."

Benny leaned in so far, he ended up in Adam's lap. So curious, in fact, that Adam could hardly see what he was doing. With the boy's uncombed and matted hair tucked tight under Adam's nose, it gave him pause. Adam recognized the smell: a scented potpourri which finds its way to little boys' manes via farm fields and hay barns, through wood-burning stoves and mothers' hugs. And it instantly sent him back to another place, another time. He couldn't help but think about his boy, Henry, and the times he would hold him and kiss him and smell his hair, often as he carried the sleeping child to bed.

Adam pulled in a staggered inhalation through his nose and then tried to hide it from Benny by faking a cough. The youngster paid no mind and continued to study the metal gears. Adam closed his eyes and savored the memory. It had been years since he'd felt the nurturing inclinations that came with parenthood. Subconsciously, he found himself sliding his arms around the boy and he began to squeeze him gently. Upon feeling the embrace, Benny turned his head, looked up towards Adam and smiled. With that, the boy turned his attention back to the watch.

"Can we fix it now?" Benny asked.

Adam sniffed hard through his nose, snapping out of the memory, and as he did so he felt a strange tingling in his stomach. It felt warm, and it filled him with energy and love. For the first time since before Henry died, Adam felt like he mattered in the life of a young boy, and it felt wonderful.

"Yes, let's fix this old watch, shall we?"

By delicately manipulating various components with the steadiest of hands, Adam reattached the spring, let Benny help him reassemble all the pieces, and when it was put back together, he said to the youngster, "Wind it up."

Benny held the watch in his left hand as if holding a fragile piece of crystal, and with his right thumb and index finger, slowly clasped the pendant and began to twist. "It's clicking! It never clicked before." Benny looked up at Adam in amazement, then turned it faster and with more vigor.

"Don't overdo it," Adam said with contained caution.

Benny stopped and put the watch up to his ear.

"It's ticking, too! I hear it ticking!" With a push of the thumb on the pendant, the metal casing sprung open to reveal the watch face. Benny stared at the watch, speechless, then at Adam, and back to the watch again. "Mommy is going to love this present," he said as he listened to the ticking sounds once more.

"Let's make sure we tell your mommy you helped fix it."

He nodded his head proudly. "I did!" he proclaimed proudly. "Can I tell Opa about it?"

"Can Opa keep a secret?"

"Yeah, he never told anyone about the time we ate only ice cream for dinner when Mommy went on her trip, so I think he can keep a secret," said Benny, not realizing he just divulged a secret.

"Yes, you can tell your Opa," Adam said with a laugh.

"I'm going to show him right now. He's outside."

"Please, take it easy with that watch," added Adam. It made him nervous such a valuable timepiece could easily be dropped or scratched if Benny was not careful.

"Okay. I promise." The boy grabbed his spring jacket, pushed open the screen door and darted off into the barnyard. Adam sat alone in the kitchen, looked around at the room and thought of Henry. Tears pooled in his eyes.

Chapter Twenty-Seven

Closing Time

Colonel Raymonds and Big Jack each held a glass . . . and held their gaze.

"Prosit," toasted the commander.

"Prosit," repeated Big Jack as they clinked glasses of brandy and swallowed each shot with one quick gulp.

"You know I'm not supposed to drink on the job," said the commander from behind his desk.

"Tell your generals a German made you do it. They'd love that," Big Jack joked as he slowly filled the shot glasses one more time.

"That's the problem. I'm supposed to make sure the Germans do as *I* say," the commander snickered. Forgetting how obsessed Raymonds was about keeping clean quarters, Big Jack inadvertently set his glass on the leather-top desk, causing the colonel to twist his mouth to one side and promptly reach for a small coaster. "So speaking of Germans, I hear your favorite prisoner Sergeant Klein has made great progress."

"Doc Marshall is calling him his 'miracle patient,'" said Big Jack.

"Well, that's one of the main reasons I invited you here, Big Jack. I wanted to let you know I'm gonna need him back."

"Who? Adam?"

"If you mean Sergeant Klein, then yes."

"Wow, I guess so," said Big Jack with a slight degree of longing in his face. "That young man has almost become part of the family. He's really connected with my grandson Benny, and he's doing lots of little things around the house to us help out."

"I believe it. Even the guards here think the world of him. But the reality is he's been there longer than we thought he would, and it's time I get him to work KP in *my* house for a while."

Big Jack was taken aback a bit. But deep down knew this day would come.

"Hey, if he's as good a babysitter as you say he is, perhaps I could have him watch some of my guards," said Raymonds.

Big Jack laughed at the sarcastic notion, then took a smaller sip from his glass.

"I wanted to tell you in person so as not to spring it on him unannounced."

Big Jack studied the commander, cocked his head slightly and took in a deep breath. "Yeah, you're right," he said, exhaling. "It'll be pretty quiet without him in the house. It's been mighty nice having another fella around to help. He's up-and-about now and basically walks with a limp, that's about it."

"Tell me," said the commander leaning forward, more serious now, "how's your daughter holding up? I try every day to get news about your son-in-law and no one knows a thing."

"She's doing remarkably well, considering the circumstances," said Big Jack. "With each passing day she's putting Erik behind her, as if she knows he's no longer with us."

"Well, tell her not to give up hope. That can help carry a person through some pretty choppy waters."

"I will," he said, thinking such a statement would probably cause more harm than good.

"All I can get from HQ is he was in Belgium, pushing towards Berlin. It sounds like he was in a tank and there was an ugly firefight with German Tigers. Apparently our boys got hit pretty hard. Tigers are capable of destroying our tanks even from a great distance, but this battle happened up close, and . . ." the commander paused, then regained his composure. "Big Jack, they tell me there were casualties. *Unidentifiable* casualties, they call it. I'm so sorry. The good news is, no dog tags were found. So perhaps he escaped? Or was taken prisoner," his voice trailed off.

Big Jack took in a slow breath and rubbed the back of his neck.

"I'll be frank. In my position I hear a lot of things, not just from HQ but on a local level too, you know? And if you don't mind me saying so, that son-in-law of yours had a bit of a reputation. I'm told he was a drinker, got into a lot of fights . . ."

Trying to avoid eye contact, Big Jack shifted in his chair, then reluctantly addressed the topic. "Yeah, well, everyone has their demons, I suppose."

The commander could sense his pain at the memory and offered up some good news. "Tell you what I can do for you, Big Jack . . . I can grant Klein visiting privileges once he returns to camp."

Big Jack seemed to perk up at this notion. "You can give the POWs permission to leave?"

"Yeah. We're actually being encouraged to allow more and more POWs to go into town and spend their money, thereby helping out the local businesses. They buy things at the confectionary, the bakery, even in area taverns. Seems for the most part they are being accepted by the townsfolk with open arms."

"That's a hell of a thing," said Big Jack.

"Tell me about it. This past Sunday I had ten prisoners go to church with me, and afterwards, I couldn't get them out of there because they were mobbed like movie stars. And get this," Raymonds added with enthusiasm, leaning forward in his chair, "one of them discovered he has an uncle living over in Johnson Creek! I mean, what are the odds?

We got the two of them together a few days ago. They haven't seen one another in fifteen years, but here they were, together again, and it took a war to do it. I'm amazed by things like that."

"That is incredible," said Big Jack, still thinking about what life would be like without Adam. "I guess I can get my bedroom back?"

"Huh?"

"I'm just thinking about Adam and how he's been recovering in my bedroom for all these months. I'll get it back."

"Well there you go! No more steps to climb. That's good news."

"Ah-huh," said Big Jack half-heartedly. The colonel picked up on it and leaned forward.

"Listen, Big Jack, you know if it were up to me I'd let Klein stay. After all, he is technically helping out a local farmer, right? It's just that HQ has been asking me about his progress, and to be honest, it's a rare thing to have a POW stay at a civilian's home. Unheard of, really. My district includes Illinois, Wisconsin, and Michigan's Upper Peninsula. There are forty camps in Wisconsin alone, each one holds between 150 and 600 prisoners and not one is staying with a civilian. HQ asks me about him at least once a week."

"I suppose he will be leaving soon anyways, if all the reports about the European war are correct."

"I have every indication they are. This war in Europe could be over by July, I hear. Maybe sooner."

"Wow. And what's the plan with the POWs?"

"They'll be sent home, of course."

"So how do I go about keeping Klein on the farm when this whole thing is over?" joked Big Jack.

"Ha," snorted the commander. "That's a good one. Maybe you could kidnap him. That'd be your best bet."

"Yeah, that'd be quite a trick," said Big Jack. Realizing he shouldn't push the issue, he continued, "So when should we expect you to come get him?"

"Let's see here," Raymonds said, looking at his calendar. "The best I can do is push it one more week, but that's it."

"Sounds like a plan." Big Jack extended his hand to his friend. "I know you've gone above-and-beyond, Mark, and it is most appreciated." As they shook hands, Big Jack added, "Thanks for letting him recover at the farmhouse. You know Doc Marshall believes he could have died had we tried to move him."

"Yeah, well it seems to have worked out best for everyone."

"Yep. See you soon, Colonel."

With that, Big Jack turned towards the door, and Raymonds noticed the bottle still on the desk.

"Hey, Big Jack, you forgot your bottle of brandy."

"Keep it. It's a gift."

Chapter Twenty-Eight

Auf Wiedersehen

"Why do they need him there? He's helping us right here!"

Maggie used all the arguments a little girl would use after finding a puppy on her way home from school. About the only thing she didn't say was, *"Finders-keepers!"*

Big Jack explained that Adam may continue to work the farm, especially during the upcoming planting season, but he is only going to *live* back at Camp Ramsey. "He'll still be around and may even get visiting privileges on weekends."

Adam seemed nonchalant about it all. Perhaps he was trying to hide his pain, but literally shrugged when Big Jack shared the news. "It'll be good to see my friends again," he admitted. Maggie studied his response, knowing full well the news didn't sit well with him, either.

The week went by in a blur. Maggie spent as much free time as she could with her pet POW, finding excuses to help him walk in the barnyard, climbing the stairs, even venturing to the highway and back on numerous occasions. He soon traded the crutches for a cane, and as they found themselves in Maggie's small patch of strawberries on one particularly warm spring day, both reminisced about the past few months, trying not to feel sad about it being his last day on the farm.

The strawberry patch sat very near the highway, and whenever Maggie worked there, friends and neighbors would often pass by and honk their car horns. This particular day was no different. As she stood with Adam, she would wave and provide a brief editorial about those behind the wheel and what piece of gossip affixed itself to each car.

"That's Mr. Strause. He grows the biggest tomatoes in the county."

"Mr. Arban. He went to prison for robbing a bank when he was 18."

"Mrs. Neery. She once brought a dessert made of cow chips to a picnic. The woman hosting was a town rival."

Then to her surprise, a truck full of Negro migrants drove past. Like the cars before him, the driver honked and waved to Maggie and Adam.

"What the hell? Is that Oku? I think it is!" said Maggie excitedly.

"I'm not sure. It could be him," said Adam.

"He did say he'd be back for the spring season. That went fast."

Adam was transfixed. He couldn't help but notice how the sunlight wove its way in and out of her gleaming brown hair, accentuating subtle red highlights, how her eyes and lips glistened in the sun, how the curves of her waist, her breasts and her shoulders formed a sculpture worthy of an art museum. He admired how integrated she had become into this farming community, and he felt happy to even know her.

Maggie raked the frost-protective hay off the strawberry patches with little effort, while carrying on about growing up in this community of immigrant farmers. She also shared a memory of a winter blizzard that kept them in the house for a week due to eight-foot-tall snow drifts. Adam felt good as she spoke, despite the aching sensation that came with knowing he needed to return to camp later that day.

"Can I ask you something?" he said.

She stopped raking, wiped her forehead with the gloved hand and leaned up against the butt-end of the handle. "Of course."

"Do you believe the news reports? About the war, I mean?"

Maggie's disposition went from carefree to guarded. She took a second or two to answer, measuring her reply. "Everything seems so upside down these days. The newsreel footage says one thing. Then we hear last week President Roosevelt died of a stroke and some guy from Missouri I've never heard of has taken his place . . ."

"Truman."

"Huh?"

"Truman. His name is Harry Truman," said Adam.

Maggie cocked her head and wondered how he would have known such a thing, then continued on. "If you forced me to pick an answer, I suppose I would have to say yes, I do think the war is coming to a close. In Europe anyways."

"Does it make you happy or sad?"

She hesitated. "It terrifies me. I know that sounds crazy, but it really does. I lay in bed at night wondering if my husband is dead or alive. I wonder what his son will do without a father. And I wonder about you. I *worry* about you, and what it will be like to return to Germany. And I wish . . ." she paused again and then laid her cards on the table. "Adam, you already know this, but I wish you could stay. Or at least, I wish you could return when all the European dust settles. If Erik is alive – I don't know – I have terribly mixed feelings. I wonder if the army has changed him. For the better, I mean."

"It was tough? Before the war, I mean?"

"You have no idea."

"If you ever want to talk about it . . ."

"Maybe someday." She looked off into the distance and perked her mouth into a tight nub. "All I can say is it was a marriage made in heaven, but it quickly went to hell. And I don't know if an angel will grace this farm again or the devil. If Erik is alive, and if he comes home the same person, the war will *not* have ended. At least not for me."

"Did he ever hurt you?"

Maggie looked away. "It's best not to talk about those days. The past is in the past. I have learned when it comes to love and life, I can't change what's already happened." Pausing for a second, she added, "But I will tell you this . . . if he does return, and nothing changes, perhaps I could get a divorce, and you and I could start over . . ."

Adam put a finger up to his mouth, gently conveying a sense of silence. He took a step towards her and gently cupped her face in his hands. "Maggie, if I could make it happen, I surely would. But this is so much bigger than us. If I can return, and if you want me back, I will be here. But there are no guarantees. I, too, lay awake at night thinking about you and I feel so torn inside. Am I an adulterer for wanting you, for wanting this, or am I just a hopeless romantic? I'm a man who believes in fate, and I wonder each and every moment why I was led to you." Adam bit his bottom lip momentarily. "Know this, Maggie Wentworth . . ." he paused again, looked deep into her eyes, and said, "I have fallen in love with you, and whether it's right or wrong, I don't regret it. That would be like feeling guilty for enjoying the scent of a flower or the taste of fine wine or watching a beautiful sunrise. I refuse to feel bad about it. I'm sure it is wrong, and I may have to take it up with God one day, but know this: I understand what it's like to live with dreams lost. So please, let's you and I at least hold on to hope, okay? If your husband returns and your life settles into a pattern of tolerance, and if I become but a pleasant memory, well, we can hold on to that. On the other hand, if things go back to the way they were *and you want me back*, I will do everything I can to return. I have to believe perhaps one day there will be a reunion. Until then, there will be good days and there will be bad days, so cling to that hope to get you through those bad ones. I'm being realistic, and honestly, the odds are not in our favor. But the fact there are odds at all . . . means we have a chance."

Tears crawled down Maggie's cheeks. "My God, how do you do it?"

"What do you mean?"

"You're always so optimistic!" said Maggie, wiping her tears on the sleeve of her shirt. "You lose your family, you get captured, you're sent to America as a POW, your home is likely in ruins . . . time and again, when faced with things that would crush most men, you just seem to roll with it. Bad luck doesn't faze you."

"I met you – so I wouldn't say it's all bad luck."

That's all he needed to say. Without caring if another car drove past or if Big Jack or Benny saw them, they stepped towards one another. As they stood there and kissed one another, Maggie let go of the rake and it fell into the strawberry patch. She couldn't help but think *this* was the goodbye she should have had in front of all those friends and neighbors almost a year ago. *Look everybody! I am giving the man I love a goodbye kiss. He is the one I will truly miss. He is the one whose return I will long for.*

But no one saw them. No cars drove past and no well-wishers stopped by. It was just the two of them kissing, in a strawberry patch – perhaps for the very last time.

* * *

Colonel Raymonds climbed out of the passenger side of the olive green Chrysler, a large star painted on the door. Corporal Jennaro turned off the ignition and exited from the driver's side. The sun, which shone so brightly just an hour before, had disappeared behind a thick wall of gray clouds off in the horizon. As they walked towards the farmhouse, Big Jack and Benny stepped off the porch to greet them.

"Well, I didn't expect to see you today, Colonel," said Big Jack.

"What can I say, things are relatively slow at the camp, and with most of the POWs working in the Oconomowoc canneries, I felt I'd get out of the office and see our star patient, Sergeant Klein."

"What's a patient?" asked Benny. "And who is Sergeant Klein?"

"A patient is someone who was hurt or sick and they are trying to get better," said Big Jack. "And Sergeant Klein is Adam. His full name is Adam Klein."

"It is?" asked the youngster in a high-pitched voice.

The commander looked down at Benny, shook his head and chuckled.

"He's in the house with Maggie packing up some of his belongings . . . books, magazines, things like that," said Big Jack.

As if on cue, the front door opened and they emerged. Maggie held the door as Adam came out dressed in the clothes he'd been wearing for the past several months. They were Big Jack's. In one hand he had a bag, in the other his cane. Based on the way he walked, it seemed the cane was of little use these days. His strength had nearly returned to normal and he used the walking stick more out of habit than anything else.

"Well, well, look at this fine young couple," said the commander.

Big Jack cleared his throat.

"Hello, sir," said Maggie as she walked a few steps in front of Adam. They shook hands, and the colonel noted the firmness of her grip.

"You sure have come a long way," the commander said to Adam. "You look good."

"I feel very good, sir," he said.

"It shows," said Raymonds. "You're walking quite well. Hey, Jennaro, take his bag, would you?"

"Yes, sir," said the corporal, shooting half a smile towards Maggie. She smiled back.

"So are you ready to return to your humble abode?" the commander asked Adam.

"I can hardly wait. Do you still have Meatloaf Night on Wednesdays?"

The commander let out a loud howl. "Oh, not quite. But the good news is every Saturday is now called 'Spamerday.' You'll love cooking for us."

Turning serious for a moment, Adam addressed the commander, "Cooking, sir? No work on the farms or in the canneries?"

"Not until you can walk without a limp. I don't want to slow down your progress. And there's a lot you can do around the camp, trust me."

Adam looked disappointed as the reality of the situation sunk in. He knew there would be restrictions on his time after returning to camp, but he had become spoiled these past few months; he could come and go as he pleased – from the barn to the fields or to simply relaxing on the front porch swing. It became easy to forget he was still a prisoner, and this reality nearly knocked the wind out of him.

"Don't look so sad, sergeant. You'll like the changes. We have a movie night now, some of the boys have started a small orchestra, and we're even issuing day-passes on Sundays, so if you don't cause trouble, perhaps you could earn one or two."

Adam nodded as Jennaro closed the trunk of the car.

"I'd offer you some lunch, but it sounds like you have everything in order back at camp," said Maggie.

"You better believe it. Right, Jennaro?" said the commander.

"That's correct, sir," Jennaro said.

"Well, we best get a move on. Smells like it's going to rain," said Raymonds.

"May showers, right sir?" asked Jennaro.

"Do you mean May *flowers?"* asked the commander sternly. "It's April showers, they bring May flowers."

"Oh, right," was all Jennaro could muster.

"Okay then, we best be on our way."

At that announcement, Adam turned to face the family for his formal goodbye. Over those past months he had come to know and love them in ways he would never have imagined. He had gone from the sands of Africa to the fields of Wisconsin, and in the process not only became part of a family, he had fallen in love with a farmer's daughter – and her little boy. It became the perfect sequel to a life he believed would never be repeated. He had a large lump in his throat as he extended his hand to Big Jack, who nodded his head with a pinched expression. Adam then put his hand out for Benny, who took it momentarily, then fell into his thigh, squeezing him hard. "Don't go! I want you to stay!"

Adam leaned over and rubbed the child's back. "Oh, I will try to stop by for a visit. This isn't the last time you will see me."

"Promise?" asked Benny.

Adam's gaze moved to the commander. "I promise."

He then turned towards Maggie. She gazed at him with sorrowful longing. He had not yet left and she already missed him. With wet eyes, she curled her lips between her teeth and bit down hard. So as to not make a scene in front of the commander and to minimize any suspicions, Maggie held out her hand for him to shake. "Sergeant, all the best to you," she said with a cracking voice.

Adam desperately wanted to hug her, to hold her, to kiss her. With the tension in the air obvious to everyone, even Raymonds squinted his eyes as if to say, *It's okay if you hug the man. It's common knowledge you have become friends.* But Adam played along and took her hand in his and said, "I am forever in your debt. I couldn't have done it without you, Mrs. Wentworth."

A lone tear dripped down her cheek, but she maintained her composure. Tightening her stomach muscles, she mustered out the words, "It was my pleasure."

Adam then opened the back door of the car and stepped inside.

"Okay then, I'm glad this all worked out," said the commander. "I'll let you know about any future visits."

"Always good to see you, Colonel," said Big Jack.

"Likewise."

They drove down the gravel driveway. Big Jack stood next to Maggie and put his arm around her. She sniffled several times as he rubbed her shoulder. He felt sad for his daughter – he knew she was in love. Privately, he, too, hoped for a way to make such a thing work. With no news about Erik, and based on the violent tank battle the commander described a week earlier, Big Jack felt fairly certain Erik was dead.

As they stood on the driveway, Benny took off in a futile attempt to catch the car as it went down towards the highway. "Bye, bye, Adam!" he shouted waving his arms.

Through the back window they could see him waving back at the "family." When the car turned left onto the main road, a gentle mist of rain began to fall, and the car drove out of sight.

Chapter Twenty-Nine

V-E Day

For the next few weeks, life around the farm settled into customary routines for Maggie and Big Jack: making pies, baking bread, feeding the livestock, prepping the fields, maintaining equipment, scrubbing floors, emptying chamber pots, making butter, splitting wood, cleaning the chicken coop . . . the fabled practices deemed necessary to properly manage a rural "corporation." Long before the POWs were ever part of their lives, the pace and the convention of it all felt familiar.

When not tending to her to-do list, Maggie spent nearly all her free time with Audrey. They sewed together, baked together, saw movies and leaned on each other for support. They occasionally laughed, mostly cried, and questioned life's purpose. Over coffee or tea, the two talked at length about being single once again. For Audrey it was the loss of one man. For Maggie . . . two.

That spring of 1945 proved to be very wet, and finding time to plant the oats became a challenge for Big Jack and Maggie. Practically speaking, oats need planting when the soil is dry enough to till – and early enough that they can flower before the hotter months. But . . . Mother Nature had put things on hold for the time being.

During this time, Adam visited only once, with three guards Maggie had never seen before. Frustrated, she desperately wanted some alone time with Adam, but it became impossible. Those guards were like chaperones at a high school dance, their eyes constantly scrutinizing her every move. She couldn't help but wonder: *Did Colonel Raymonds see something he didn't like when he picked up Adam?* Maybe if she had hugged Adam, the commander wouldn't have thought twice. Perhaps the informal handshake gave him the opposite impression? Regardless, that first visit ended after a half-hour, when one of the new guards announced he had to get back to camp. It had been an unbearable tease.

Thankfully, the second visit couldn't have been timed any better. Scheduled for Maggie's 26th birthday, Adam was supposed to arrive soon after lunchtime and stay for dinner. Maggie couldn't think of a better present.

She got up earlier than usual that day, but instead of spending her time doing chores in the barn or prepping her vegetable garden, she focused on cleaning the house – dusting in places that didn't need dusting, tidying up rooms no one would ever see, then tidying them up a second time. The more she tried to coax the clock to tick faster, the slower it moved. Then at 9:00, the phone rang.

"Oh my God, Maggie, turn on the radio! Turn it on!" yelled Audrey on the other end, nearly too excited to speak.

"Why? What is it?"

"The war. It's over! Germany has surrendered! I'm coming over!" With that, the line went dead.

Instead of matching her best friend's enthusiasm, Maggie calmly hung up the phone and quietly murmured to herself, "And so it begins."

Snapping out of it, the true meaning of the call began to sink in. Worldwide, millions of lives had been lost, thousands of them Americans – possibly her very own husband. The significance of this moment became monumental, and the reality hit her right between the eyes, her excitement now matching Audrey's.

"Papa! Papa, come quickly. Benny, you too! Where are you guys? I have incredible news!"

Benny's footsteps came closer as he as he ran down the stairs. Big Jack was busy painting the porch railing outside and couldn't hear her plea. "Benny, go outside and get Opa! Quickly," she said to her son as he arrived.

"What's all the fuss?" asked Big Jack as he came inside holding a paintbrush.

Without saying a word, Maggie gathered everyone in a tight circle, took a deep breath and proclaimed, "That was Audrey on the phone. Germany has surrendered! The war in Europe is over."

"What? How does she know?" said Big Jack with all the enthusiasm of a child who had just learned Christmas would be coming a second time in the year.

"She heard it on the radio."

"Ach mein Gott!" said Big Jack in awe. *"Ich habe von diesem Tag geträumt."* (I've dreamed of this day.)

"It's V-E Day, Benny!" she said.

"What does that mean?" asked her confused son.

"Victory in Europe. We won, Benny!" said Big Jack. "We won the war your father went to fight. We won the war against that son-of-a-bitch Adolf Hitler! It's over. Oh God, it has ended, finally! Just yesterday at Mass, I prayed for this day to come. Finally it is here!" Big Jack had tears in his eyes and hugged Benny, inadvertently leaving a white mark on the back of the child's blue shirt with the paintbrush he still held in his hand. He then looked up at Maggie, who also had pools accumulating in her eyes, but for other reasons. Stepping to his daughter, he hugged her tight, whispering, "Everything's going to be alright. Whatever happens will be for the best."

She nodded but didn't speak.

"Benny, let's turn on the radio," said Big Jack excitedly. He set the paintbrush on an old magazine and the two of them powered-up the RCA.

Virtually every station played news of the surrender along with patriotic songs. It was official. The war in Europe had come to a close.

In no time at all, Audrey pulled up and bolted through the front door without even knocking. "Maggie! Maggie, where are you?"

The two friends met in the kitchen with a tight hug. "Could you have picked a better birthday present?"

"I think I'm numb."

For Maggie, the fog would finally begin to lift, revealing a better view of her future. She was ready, and frankly, tired of the waiting game. *This really is a cause for celebration!*

Throughout the day, various well-wishers called the farmhouse, most to say happy birthday and to remind Maggie she got the best present in the world. She expressed her gratitude . . . and agreed.

Twice the phone rang, and both times a stranger said to her, in a whispered tone, "It's your birthday."

"Um, that's right. And to whom am I speaking?"

"Doesn't matter," was all the voice replied.

"Hey, what is this?" replied Maggie. "Who are you? Stop calling over here!"

"Who was that?" asked Big Jack.

"I wish I knew. Some creep, I think. But he knew it was my birthday."

"Some joker," said Big Jack. "Let me answer the phone the next time it rings."

Maggie nodded.

A few minutes later, the phone rang again. This time Big Jack picked up the receiver. "Listen, buster," said Big Jack in defense of his daughter. "I don't know who you are or what you're doing . . ."

"Big Jack?" the caller replied. "It's Raymonds."

"What? Oh, sorry, Mark. I thought you were someone else. We've been getting a few strange calls today and . . ."

"Sorry to disappoint you. If you'd like, I could call back and pretend I'm someone else."

Big Jack shook his head, realizing how trivial he must have seemed. "I apologize. You must be pretty ecstatic today with the news and all."

"The Armistice is great, great news for all Americans. Many sacrifices have been made, both at home and abroad. I don't have to tell you that."

"He's calling to cancel, isn't he?" said a worried Maggie standing beside her father tapping her feet. "I knew it! I just knew it."

"So I'm calling to confirm our plans. For today. I thought you may be wondering about it. We are a go!"

Big Jack smiled at his daughter and winked. A wave of relief washed over her. Maggie's excitement finally matched everyone else's.

* * *

That afternoon, Adam arrived an hour early, and to her pleasant surprise he walked in the door with a familiar face: Corporal Jennaro, with no other guards in tow.

"Greetings! Greetings," said the friendly American guard. "It is a big day!" Maggie could smell celebratory alcohol on his breath as he gave her a hug. Over these months he had become close to the family, and they gladly welcomed him into their circle.

"It is a big day indeed!" she said to him.

"Maggie, now that this war is over, I am one step closer to proposing to Rosa. What do you think about them apples?"

"I'm very happy for you, Corporal," she expressed with a charmed smile.

"Darn tootin'," he slurred. "That Italian honey is gonna be mine soon and I can't wait to ask for her hand. Now we just have to take care of business in the Pacific and it'll be the bee's knees."

Upon seeing Jennaro and Adam, Big Jack came up and welcomed them with firm handshakes. Looking at Adam specifically, he shook his hand and said, *"Keine Feinde mehr."* (Enemies no more.)

"Keine Feinde," repeated Adam.

For much of the afternoon, the talk of the war's end overshadowed the original purpose for the gathering – and that was fine by Maggie, one who preferred to stay out of the limelight.

The intimate group of guests that evening included Adam, Audrey and Jennaro. Big Jack had cooked a beef stew with sweet potatoes and uncorked a bottle of his homemade hooch. After dinner, everyone settled in, rubbed their stomachs and praised the cook. When the sun had about settled into the horizon, Benny asked, "When are we going to give Mommy her presents?"

Everyone looked at one another as if they had completely forgotten the purpose of the gathering.

"And her cake!" added Audrey. "My goodness, I feel terrible we talked so much about Europe and not about the guest of honor."

"Please don't worry about it," said Maggie humbly.

After singing and serving cake, it was customary for Big Jack to present his gift first. After disappearing into the barn for a few minutes, he returned with a one-foot square box wrapped to perfection, of course. Everyone could hear whimpering and whining sounds coming from inside the package. Maggie's eyes got big. Benny's eyes got bigger.

"I think I know what it is, Mommy! Open it!"

She brought her hand up to her chin and looked at her father. He beamed with pride, pointed at the box and nodded, as if to say, *Go ahead, open it.*

With Benny's help she ripped the wrapping paper off the top of the box, then gently lifting the lid, marveling at its contents. "Ohhhhh . . ." Her shoulders dropped and eyebrows raised.

"I knew it. I knew it!" yelled Benny happily. "It's a dog!"

Unable to contain himself, the youngster reached inside and pulled out a yellow Labrador puppy. "Hi, little buddy."

"Oh, Papa. He is so cute!"

"Can we call him Butch?" asked Benny.

"Well, I don't know," said Maggie. "Lift him up, Benny." Her son held the puppy up high and she looked under its back legs. "Oops, seems we've got ourselves a girl dog, Benny. Maybe a girl name?"

"A girl dog? Oh." Thinking for a moment he said, "How about Lily?"

Maggie paused. "Yeah, Lily is a nice name for a dog like this."

"He looks like a Lily," said Benny. "He's a good girl!"

Everyone laughed at the gender miscue and let it pass.

Setting the dog down on the floor, Benny pet her softly. "Hi, Lily, how are you? I'm Benny." The puppy licked his face while urinating on the carpet.

"Oh Papa, I don't know what to say," said Maggie, standing from her chair and giving her father a big hug.

"I have to admit, it's been a long time coming, ever since we had to put Max down two years back."

"Where did he come from?"

"The Skrochs had a large litter recently, and I couldn't resist the chance to get another lab on this farm."

"You are the best!"

After embracing her father, Audrey gave Maggie a package decorated with chiffon and lace. "This is for you. I hope you like it."

Maggie cocked her head and smiled. "I am so curious."

"Maybe it's another puppy," exclaimed Benny. "The box is the same size."

Maggie took her time peeling off the beautiful packaging and slowly lifted the top to reveal a ladies' hat, complete with a laced front and polished suede on the sides.

"Oh . . . my . . . gosh. This must have cost a fortune! It's gorgeous!"

"Naw, not that much," said Audrey, obviously lying.

"Now all I need is to find an occasion to wear something so fancy."

"Look inside," said her friend.

With a confused expression, Maggie momentarily stared at Audrey, then peered in the box again to uncover an envelope beneath flowering tissue paper. She took it out, glanced back at her friend, and then towards the group.

"Come on, open it!" said Jennaro, about as excited as Benny when he heard the whimpering dog.

Maggie slipped a finger under the glued flap, slid her hand across the top and revealed two tickets. As she read them, her eyes got wide. "Chicago?" she breathed.

"What?" said Big Jack.

"Chicago!" sang Maggie. "Oh my gosh, it's two train tickets to Chicago!"

"We need another weekend of fun, don't you think?"

Despite a sudden flashback to their last getaway, Maggie smiled and said, "Thank you, Audrey. Thank you so much. We'll have a grand time, I'm certain of it."

As the two women embraced, Benny remembered his gift and pulled at his mother's dress.

"My turn, Mommy. My turn."

He presented a very small box wrapped in the comic section from the Sunday *Milwaukee Journal.* "It's from me . . . and Adam."

Maggie looked up at Adam who feigned confusion.

"Hey, this was all Benny's doing," said Adam.

"Why don't I believe you?" Maggie said with a smile.

She then peeled off the paper and revealed a small tin box which had the words LIPTON'S TEA printed on the side. "Oh how I love tea. Thank you, Benny. Thank you, Adam," she said while setting the box down playfully, knowing full well there was something else inside.

"No! Mommy, that's just the box I used. It's not tea."

"It's not?"

"No. There's something else inside."

Giving Adam a wink, she picked it up again and slowly opened the container. "Whatever could it be if it's not tea?"

Benny looked up at Adam and smiled ear-to-ear while excitingly tapping his little fingers on the table. As she reached her thumb into the tin box, Maggie revealed a gold chain, which her eyes followed down to a spinning gold watch. Everyone in the room was awed. She recognized it instantly. "Well isn't this nice. Your father used to have one just like this. Thank you, Benny. And thank you, Adam," she said in forced praise.

"No, Mommy, that *is* the old one."

"It is? Well, thank you just the same."

"Come on, Mommy . . ." the youngster could hardly contain his excitement. "Put it up to your ear."

"Huh?" asked Maggie, genuinely confused.

"Do it," added Adam smiling like the young boy.

Maggie looked at him from across the table. When she put the watch to her ear she let out a shriek, "*Ahh!* It's ticking. Good Lord, it's actually ticking! This watch has been broken for probably forty years! How on Earth . . .?"

"Adam did it! And I helped," said Benny proudly. "We used a clipper!"

"A what?"

"A paperclip," said Adam, correcting Benny. "And a few other makeshift tools."

"That's all you needed?"

"We had to improvise."

"I can't believe it. I'm amazed. "

"You have a real treasure there."

"What? This old thing? It's a piece of junk," Maggie said, her statement sounding half like a question. "I mean, it is . . . right?"

Adam laughed. "Oh on the contrary. That is an original *Patek Philippe.* It's Swiss. One of the best watches in the world. I wish I could have sold them."

Maggie's eyes met Big Jack's, shock on both their faces.

"You'd need a proper appraisal, but if I had to guess, I'd say this watch is worth perhaps a few thousand dollars."

"What? Oh my God! What?"

"You're joking, right, Adam?" said Big Jack.

"Oh not one bit. And that might be a conservative estimate."

Maggie looked at her father, back to Adam, then rolled her head back and laughed out loud. "Oh Erik, you *idiot!*" she yelled to the ceiling. "You are such a fool!"

Jennaro and Adam had no idea what she was talking about, but let it go, believing it to be a private matter. All Big Jack could do was bury his head in his hand and shake it back and forth. "My God," he said to himself. "Will wonders never cease?"

Oblivious to the bombshell that just exploded, Benny gave her a hug. "So you like it, Mommy?"

"I love it!" she said, putting her arm around her little boy. "Your grandfather would be so happy it's working now."

"Grandfather?" asked Adam.

"Yeah, Jefferson Wentworth. These are his initials, JTW," she said, opening up the gold cover on the back of the watch. "Jefferson Thomas Wentworth."

"I wondered about those," said Adam. "And he passed it on to his son, Erik?"

She nodded. There in her hand, Maggie held more than a watch. It was a lesson. A moral. A message passed on by Jefferson Wentworth to his son, and yet, the heir was too stubborn, too short-sighted, too reckless to understand that his father gave him the best gift of all. A watch that was worth almost as much as Erik's lost farm – perhaps more!

"I'm sure Erik will be glad it's fixed," said Adam.

"Truth be told, Erik hated this old watch, for many reasons I won't go into now. Thank you, Adam and Benny – it's a great gift."

"You're welcome," said Benny, now with his attention back on the puppy.

* * *

After everyone had filled up on birthday cake, Maggie and Adam found time to sit on the front porch swing while everyone else stayed inside to enjoy some of Big Jack's card tricks. He was especially proud of his parlor games.

Hundreds of random twinkles lit up the barnyard as fireflies called attention to themselves in hopes of attracting a mate. Not coincidently, Maggie's own features glowed as well due to the light of setting sun, a fireball coating the entire farm in hues of red and orange.

"You look so good," said Adam with a warm smile. "How are you doing?"

"I'm hanging in there. Staying busy helps me keep my mind off of things. Off of you," she said wantonly.

Adam held her hand, then turning his head briefly towards the front door to see if anyone would see them, and then leaned in for a kiss while Maggie turned her head slightly to accept. They held the kiss for several seconds while laughter emanated from inside the house.

Maggie pulled back and looked into his eyes. "I miss you so much."

"It's been hell to not be here. Thankfully, I have been busy with garrison duties, KP time, and basic cleanup. I keep wondering if I'm being punished for living the high life with you these past several months."

Maggie squeezed his hand tight and looked deep into his crystal blue eyes. "About the news today . . . I don't know what it all means."

"Let's not talk about that, okay? I would much prefer to focus on right here, right now, and not speculate about such things. Is that alright?" Maggie nodded her head in agreement, her large brown eyes staring into his soul. "Benny seems great. I miss that little fellow, too."

"That boy sure thinks the world of you. All I ever hear is 'Adam this' and 'Adam that,' and all the things you taught him. I can only imagine how much fun he had helping you repair that watch."

"We had fun. I love his passion for new things. It makes me see the world differently."

They both squeezed their hands tightly, with fingers intertwined.

"Did you know he corrected me the other day when I was peeling carrots? He said, 'Momma, you should not peel the carrot towards you, always away.' Did you tell him that?"

"Of course. I mean, who peels a carrot towards themselves? You could have cut off your finger doing it that way."

Maggie could only shake her head. "You are something else."

"What? I'm only trying to dispense good advice."

"Understand this: That young man remembers everything he sees. And I believe he has a real sense of whether someone is good or bad. It's very intuitive for him."

"That is a gift."

"Although I must say, he's liked you from the start, so maybe he's not that good at reading people after all," she joked.

Adam gave her a pat, and Maggie pushed him back. They both giggled, stared into one another's eyes, rested their foreheads up against each other and their lips met one more time. It was a refreshing kiss, like drinking ice-cold lemonade on a hot July day kind of kiss. These two thirsty lovers swallowed each other up, not letting a drop hit the ground. As they separated both let out a sigh at the exact same time, which caused them to giggle once more.

* * *

Later that night, after the party settled down and Benny was tucked into bed, all the guests sat in the parlor to relax. "So when do you have to go back to camp, Corporal?" asked Big Jack. Maggie shot her father a look of anger, hoping to milk all the time she could with Adam.

He looked at his watch, his eyes trying to focus. "Probably an hour ago," he slurred followed by a loud laugh.

"I think we know who's going to drive," insisted Audrey, looking at Adam.

"Oh, that's fine, I'm" *hiccup* "good," insisted Jennaro.

Everyone rolled their eyes.

"Now with the war in Europe officially over, what is the status of the POWs?" Big Jack inquired. "Have you heard anything?" Maggie had been dying to ask the same question all night long.

The drunken corporal had consumed plenty of truth serum and apparently felt confidential information could now be shared for public knowledge – especially among friends. "All I know is we may be pulling up stakes soon. That's what they tell me. Probably getting ready to ship the POWs back to Germany. Hey, all I want to do is to bring my wife to New York and introduce her to my mother."

"I didn't know you were married," said Big Jack.

"He's not," said Maggie, chiming in. "Not yet, anyways."

"Nope. Not yet, Big Jack, but preeeetty soon," the corporal sang. "She's gonna be my darlin' darlin.'"

"So when are we closing the camp?" asked Adam, trying to stay on topic.

"Huh?" asked the drunken soldier, swaying a bit in his chair.

"When are we supposed to leave?"

"Oh, well, they have been talking about it for months . . . waiting for the official word, I guess. Could be in a week or two, or a month. Who knows with the Army, right?" *Hiccup.* "And I'm just a corporal, so . . ."

"Are you sure about this?" asked Big Jack. "I mean, some farmers still need the help. There's no way all those boys will be back from Europe in a few weeks. There's also the fighting in the Pacific."

"Yeah, they talked about that. But I guess they'll be using POWs from Camp Cedarburg. So the farmers around here should be covered with other POWs. That . . . Big Jack . . . includes . . . you!" he sang, poking a finger in Big Jack's chest playfully.

Maggie and Adam looked at one another with fear in their eyes.

Could it be? Could Adam be shipped out with the rest of the prisoners so soon? Was Camp Ramsey to shut down within a week? They had every reason to believe the drunken corporal.

Maggie then looked at her father with longing in her eyes, "Papa?"

He knew her concern. "I'll try to get a better sense of where things are when I meet with Raymonds in two days. We're gonna have lunch together."

"More like a Last Supper," added Audrey.

"Okay, so we should probably get back to the camp," announced Jennaro. "Now where did I put the truck? It was in my pocket a minute ago."

"Do you mean the *keys* to the truck?" asked Big Jack.

"Yeah, they're gone."

"Oh no," said Maggie pointing to the keys in his hand. "Let Adam drive."

"Nooooo, I'm fine," he slurred in retort.

"Tell you what, let me pilot us back to camp, then we'll stop about a quarter mile down the road and switch spots. That way you'll be the one to pull us in. How's that sound, Corporal?"

"Okay, but just don't be messing with my gun again. You people are always using my gun."

Adam laughed. "Don't worry, I don't think we'll see any more rabid dogs tonight. Pink elephants maybe, but no mad dogs."

Jennaro thought about the joke for a second, then elbowed Adam a few times. "Ha! That was a good one. I like you, Klein, you know that? You're a good egg."

"And I like you, too, Corporal," said Adam, half playing around with him.

"You know we're no longer enemies, right? So maybe you can come to my wedding. I'll invite you."

"I would be honored," Adam said as he led the drunken American towards the front door.

"Good night, everyone," said Jennaro, waving his arm high into the air, his back to the group.

"I'll see you both out," Maggie said, following them into the barnyard.

As they walked to the truck, Jennaro kept talking about his dream wedding. "You know, you both could come. I think you two would be good for one another. I know these sorts of things. I have a keeeeen sense," he added while tapping his temple.

Maggie and Adam looked at each other and smiled. As they got to the truck, they poured the corporal into the passenger seat, and he then promptly laid his head onto the dashboard. Adam and Maggie then walked around to the driver's side and stared into each other's eyes. "Please tell me this isn't goodbye," said Maggie. "I don't think I could take that right now."

"I doubt it. I'll try to get another pass in a week or two. Hopefully there will still be a POW camp."

"Big Jack will get to the bottom of it. God, I can't imagine you just disappearing overnight, without notice."

"I'll be alright. Don't worry. The good news is the war has ended, Maggie. Think about that. It's actually over. And now we will see what happens next. As scary as it all is, this is what we've been waiting for, right?"

"What if he comes back?"

Adam looked into her eyes. "The odds are not in his favor, but time will tell. And you'll deal with it then."

"You are so carefree about these things. That's so admirable."

Adam looked at her and leaned in for a kiss. Maggie hesitated and pointed to the inside of the truck. "What about him?"

"Oh, he won't care. Or even remember."

She smiled and they held the kiss for what seemed like several minutes. Breaking the spell, they could hear Jennaro inside of the truck singing "Paper Doll" by the Mills Brothers.

They both smiled and embraced in a long, tight hug. Maggie buried her head in his chest and caressed his back as they held each other tight. "I don't want you to go. I just want you here, the way things were a few weeks ago."

"I could get back on that ladder," he said playfully. "When we pulled up. I noticed the roof needs some repairs."

"Don't even kid about that," she said, punching him in the back.

They separated and Adam climbed into the truck. As he did so, he rolled down the window and blew Maggie a kiss from the driver's seat. "Goodbye . . . and happy birthday."

"Thank you. It was one of the best ever." She then stepped away from the truck as Adam turned the ignition and drove away. In the distance, Jennaro could still be heard singing.

Chapter Thirty

The Storm Front

A week came and went, and all appeared quiet at Camp Ramsey. Maggie had driven past the prison at least once a day since her birthday, looking for signs, looking for clues. Boxes being packed into trucks . . . fewer prisoners than normal . . . All seemed normal each time she crawled past. Of course, each time she hoped to get a glimpse of Adam in the yard. No luck.

That morning, Colonel Raymonds called to cancel his lunch with Big Jack, saying he had to be in Chicago "for official business." That didn't sit well with her, and it only roused more suspicions.

"You're leaving again?" said Big Jack. "We're supposed to be rationing gas!"

"This is important, Papa!"

"I know, but . . ." Big Jack could only sigh. "You go past there once a day. Sometimes twice!"

"I have to!" she insisted. "They're closing up. I can feel it."

With a heavy sigh, he stopped fighting her, because deep down he believed his daughter may be right.

Without saying another word, she grabbed the keys to the pickup truck and bolted out the door. As she approached County Highway CC, she looked to her left to see any oncoming traffic, and in doing so failed to look to her right. Pulling out, she nearly hit a man who was walking along the side of the road. He wore a top hat and U.S. Army overcoat, and he was hunched over while she passed by. At first she was startled by the sight of a pedestrian on the road, but even more surprised that someone would dress with a thick army coat on such a warm summer day. "I'm sorry!" she shouted out her window as she passed. "I didn't see you."

The stranger didn't respond. He kept his eyes on his shoes and kept walking on the gravel median. There was something about him that made her nervous. Was he a hobo watching the farm? Hoping to get one of her chickens? She told herself to keep an eye out and be careful of strangers. There were reports of various veterans who came home with numerous psychological issues. "Shell-shocked" was the term often used to describe them. But just to be safe, she told herself to mention it to Big Jack upon her return.

Once she arrived at the camp, Maggie parked on the highway and saw familiar sights beyond the gate – Army trucks sitting in the yard, American soldiers playing with the guard dogs – and she heard periodic laughter emanating from behind the fence, but in her gut she could sense the exodus was near.

Only a handful of the prisoners had returned from their winter assignments, so if ever there was a time to close the camp, it would be soon. Knowing there wasn't much she could do, Maggie put the car in drive and headed back home.

That evening, the wind shifted, the temperature dropped and the animals got restless. A storm seemed imminent. So Maggie and Big Jack locked down the barn and spent the evening playing cards with Benny. Just prior to bedtime, thunder could be heard rumbling off in the distance. Benny became increasingly nervous. "Those are the night monsters, Mommy."

"No, no, you remember, it's only angels breaking rocks." That comment put him at ease. Somewhat.

"Would you lie down with me tonight?"

"Of course, sweetheart. Speaking of which, it's about that time, so we should probably get you in your pj's."

They went through all the nightly routines, which included the reading of a bedtime story in her old rocking chair, saying prayers, and on stormy nights, lying with him until he fell into a deep slumber. Maggie paid particular attention to his breathing. *I think he's asleep . . .* Suddenly a loud crack of thunder shook the house, and he clutched for his mother's arm.

"It's okay. Mommy's here," she whispered while rubbing his back.

After several minutes, she could tell by his steady breathing that he had finally dozed off, and he stayed that way even after a few more loud thunder strikes. Slowly and methodically, she unclasped his little fingers, sat up in the bed, and looked back at her sleeping son one more time. Her solar plexus tingled at the sight.

After tip-toeing down the stairs, Maggie saw Big Jack's bedroom door was closed and his light was out. For a brief moment, a wave of sadness washed over her as she recalled how Adam had spent those past several months in that very same room. To her, it had become Adam's room, not Big Jack's, but over the past few weeks, reality found its center, and everything seemed to be back in place. It was as if those past few months were nothing more than a dream.

Snapping out of it, Maggie decided to stay up awhile and read her book. As she walked into the kitchen to get a drink of water, she noticed a light emanating from the barn. *What's Big Jack doing out there? I thought he went to bed.* The rain fell steady, so she grabbed a light jacket, stepped out through the back porch and sprinted across the barnyard to investigate.

Upon opening the door, she saw a man standing in the shadow of the large thresher, which Big Jack had recently lifted up off the ground in order to make some new repairs. The large metal behemoth balanced precariously several up on three floor jacks.

"Papa? Are you okay? I thought you went to bed."

The man turned and stepped into the light. It was not Big Jack.

"Hello, Maggie."

"Adam! Oh my God!"

She rushed into his arms. He shivered while holding her tight.

"You are soaked to the bone! Did you get a ride here or . . ."

"Maggie, I just had to see you."

"Why? I mean, what's happening? How did you get here?"

Adam hesitated and stared deep into her eyes. "They're closing the camp. We're shipping out tomorrow morning."

"What? Oh my God, tomorrow? No! It can't be!" She hugged him tighter and wrapped herself around his soaked shirt and his strong wet arms. "Please tell me it isn't true."

"I'm afraid so. That's why I had to sneak out. I couldn't bear the thought of not saying goodbye. I don't even know where we're going. Some say Britain. Some say Canada."

Maggie began to cry as he held her even tighter. "They will be looking for you. And they will know where to come."

"I don't care."

As the lightning and thunder increased with intensity, they hardly noticed. The rain poured down hard and sounded like a freight train on the roof of the barn. A backdraft of water sprayed off the ground and through the open double doors, the cool mist settled on Maggie's bare legs. With each thunderous clap and each wave of pouring rain, their inhibitions washed away.

As they tasted each other's lips, Adam pulled her tight, molding himself to her body. Their hearts beat as one, pounding through their chests in perfect harmony. Releasing herself from his mouth, she nibbled on his ear, his neck, then she dove into that divot in his throat. He tasted the way a man should – a fusion of salt and dust and rain. Her hands explored his broad shoulders, his slippery wet back, the small of his back, then his buttocks.

"We shouldn't be . . . doing this," he panted.

"You're right," said Maggie, kissing him with more passion.

She was no longer afraid. Not anymore. At that moment, nothing else in the world mattered but those two souls in need of each other. As their bodies melded together, Maggie felt his thickness grow between them as a wave of heat washed over her body, every nerve ending on fire.

Adam cradled her head in his hands as he pulled her into his mouth, both tongues dancing with each other in an erotic ballet. Their breathing became heavy and deep, him taking in her exhalation, and she his. Adam slid a hand up the back of her blouse and stroked the silky-smooth skin of her lower back. Then, moving slowly forward, he gently teased the raised tips beneath her silk camisole. Maggie moaned aloud, her knees went weak, and if not for his strong arms, she would have fallen to the floor.

Another crash of thunder exploded above them, the heavy mist from the rain seemed to sizzle on her bare calves, like being sprayed onto a hot iron skillet. Adam's free hand pulled down the zipper on the side of her skirt, and with a twist of his thumb and forefinger, he released the clasp on the waistband. As if on command, the skirt fell to her ankles, and with a few more slight-of–hand maneuvers, her slip and cotton underpants soon followed.

Reciprocating these efforts, Maggie's hands slid up and down Adam's strong back, pulling at his soaking-wet shirt and peeling it off like a second skin. Her hands were soon on his belt, and with a quick discharge of the buckle, his trousers surrendered to her desire.

Kissing her neck, his tongue glided down across the soft line from her ear to her shoulder, all while his fingers magically released every button on her blouse. With little effort, Adam picked her up, and she wrapped her legs around his waist like a morning glory to a trestle. With Maggie secure in his arms, Adam glided to the nearby flatbed wagon and gently laid her naked body onto a soft bed of straw. She presented herself like a porcelain statue, her skin the color of whipped cream and reflecting the blue hues of the lightning, along with the warm glow from an oil lantern hanging just above their heads.

Floating above her like an angel, Adam supported himself mere inches above her pulsating body. With each lustful breath, Maggie's hips rocked upwards to find him, while a hand stroked his thickness beneath his cotton boxer shorts.

A coy smile washed over his face. "You are a vision."

"I can hardly breathe."

Adam traced a line downward from her breasts, circled her bellybutton, then his fingers gently massaged her inner thighs in soft, measured strokes.

"I love you," he said.

She closed her eyes and floated away as he set her body on fire with every touch. Reaching up, Maggie gently caressed his lips with the back of her fingers. His eyes locked onto hers before their mouths snapped together like a magnet to metal.

She moaned out loud and felt as if she was suspended in midair, her body floating on an invisible cloud. Adam's tenderness was evident in his eyes. Looking closely, she saw them moisten, tears forming in the corners, as if he was saying goodbye to his past, and hello to a new, uncertain future.

"I will come back. I promise," he whispered in her ear.

"Don't talk about that. Just take me."

There was no turning back. With his warm breath on her neck, she was ready for him. In a moment, their bodies became one.

Maggie's entire body vibrated, his hips slowly pulsated up and down in perfect rhythm. Maggie let out a soft moan and lost all sense of time, where she was and how she got there. She wanted this – more than anything she ever wanted in her life.

As their lovemaking became more fervent, and more aggressive, their bodies intertwined while fingernails scraped the smalls of backs, shoulders, buttocks and calves. Their bottled up emotions manifested themselves in waves of passion brought on by a mutual yearning, but also for all the pain each had been forced to endure those past few months . . . those past few years.

Sliding his hand to the small of her back, Adam pressed hard, cementing himself to her body as he rolled onto his back . . . all the while staying deep within her.

Now it was Maggie's turn to ride the wave. She pinned Adam's arms above his head, her hands locked to his wrists as she rocked back and forth, faster and faster. He seized the opportunity to nuzzle and nibble her flesh. She moaned in pleasure with each flick of his tongue, with each soft kiss.

Floating above them, the violent storm – *the night monsters* – shook the heavens, and an entire year of longing, of waiting, came to a crescendo.

Reaching up to grab Maggie's hair, Adam pushed himself deeper as she arched her back and wailed. She then fell on top of his chest and dove into his neck, kissing every inch. Then, like a carnivore, she bit his flesh – drawing blood on his earlobe even, which tasted delicious in her mouth.

Adam didn't notice. His hands were everywhere, like a goddess with ten arms. Touching, stroking, pinching . . .

Maggie's skin felt alive and burned to his touch, tingling in strange new ways.

As if climbing a mountain, these two intoxicated lovers could finally see the summit. Together they increased the pace, the breathing getting faster, the pleasure increasing by the second. As if on cue, a ground-shattering rumble of thunder above the barn made the ground quake and their bodies quiver.

Exhausted, Maggie let all her weight fall onto Adam's chest, his arms molding her to his body. They could feel their hearts beating through their chests. Both were drained, but at the same time, energized.

Chapter Thirty-One

The Storm After The Storm

The robust storm outside soon transformed itself into a gentle shower, and not another clap of thunder could be heard nearby or even in the distance. Still naked, these two swans laid on their sides caressing, kissing . . . and crying. Small cues slowly brought them back to reality – be it a whinny from a horse's stall or a few cold raindrops falling through the leaky roof – both lovers filled the night air with heavy sighs, the unbridled passion transforming itself into a stillborn sadness.

"Please come back to me," Maggie said.

"I'll do everything I can," he whispered.

With that, they kissed again and again, staring deep into each other's eyes. After nearly an hour in the wagon, they realized they were on borrowed time. "You better get back. I'll drive you to camp," said Maggie, a tear dripping down the side of her cheek.

"Thank you," he said looking down, wiping the trail of water with the back of his index finger.

They both took in a deep, cleansing breath, when Maggie finally sat up in the bed of straw. "How can I find my clothes in here? They are all over the floor."

Stepping out of the wagon, Adam reached for the lantern and held it up to illuminate her strewn about garments. One by one he gathered them up, shook them off as best he could, and watched as she added layers onto her porcelain figure. Adam marveled at every small detail: how she buttoned her blouse, how she zipped up her skirt, how she threw her hair back and pulled it into a ponytail. Still in the wagon, she gave him a show, and when she finished, she looked at him and said, "You better put your clothes on, or you're likely get a cold."

Adam had just buckled his trousers and had begun buttoning up his shirt when Maggie noticed a lone figure step into the doorway behind him. She jumped to the back of the wagon and let out a shriek, "Papa! Oh my God!"

Adam whipped around to look, trying desperately to think about what to say to the man who had become a bit of a father figure to him those past months. Before he could make out exactly who it was, a booming voice filled the barn.

"Maggie? What and the *hell* is going on in here?" Only this voice was deeper than Big Jack's, and much younger.

No, it can't be! It couldn't *be. Is this a ghost? An apparition? Am I dreaming? Oh my God, it simply cannot be him. How could he have returned without anyone knowing? We never received a telegram. No phone call. It's not possible. But then again, this is his way. If Erik came back, this is exactly how he would do it. The devil has returned, and he wants to collect for my sins.*

Wearing a tattered and worn Army-issued dress uniform, Erik Wentworth stepped into the light of the barn for the first time in a year. He carried a thick Army knapsack on his shoulder and dropped it onto the floor of the barn. While thinner than when he left, he still sported a strong upper body, muscular arms and a narrow waste. His cream-colored garrison cap sat crooked on his head, thick strands of wet hair dangling from underneath onto his forehead. A soaking wet, untucked khaki shirt stuck to his chest, a loose dress tie dangled from his neck.

Water dripped from the end of his nose. He had been in the rain for quite some time, looking as if he just fell into a lake while wearing a beat-up and weathered uniform.

"I said what in the hell is going on?" he barked again.

"Erik? You . . . you are dead," Maggie's voice squeaked like a child's.

"Sorry to disappoint you, Mags. Unless I died in that goddamn *Kraut* hospital and nobody told me about it. You know, the Belgian hospital I've been living in these past *six months?* You knew about that, right? How I escaped my tank after a huge firefight, and how I got caught by the fucking Germans, my arm and my leg filled with shrapnel?"

"We never heard a thing," said Maggie, voice trembling. "I'm serious! All we knew was you were missing in action. Everyone told us you were dead."

"Well it appears you may have been too busy to read the telegram that said I *wasn't* dead," he added sarcastically without taking his eyes off Adam.

"We never received a thing! That's God's honest truth." Pausing for a moment, she added, "Why didn't you call? Why didn't you write? Why didn't we hear anything? And who knows you're back?" She tried to divert his attention away from what had just happened with Adam.

"I didn't tell anyone. My plan was to *surprise* you," he said loudly to his wife, anger beginning to emerge. "That is, after I got to keep an eye on things for a while first."

"Oh my God! You were the one calling the house."

"Well, that was when I could find a phone. Otherwise, I was camping out in the woods. Getting reacclimated to good old Wisconsin, you could say."

"So you've been spying on us? Your own family? My God, it was you who I almost ran over today!"

"And right now . . . I bet you wished you had."

"You really are a twisted person, you know that?"

Erik smirked at the comment, let it go and turned his attention to Adam. "So if you will stop trying to change the subject, Mags, let me ask . . . who the hell is this guy wearing half a shirt, no socks on his feet, and why is he in the barn in the middle of the night . . . with my *wife?*"

Maggie picked up on a few slurred words and said, "Oh God, you've been drinking."

"That's right, darlin'. I found a friend who doesn't cheat on me and his name is Johnny *Fuckin'* Walker." Erik then pulled the nearly empty bottle out from his coat and held it up high. "If I knew you were having a party I would have saved you some, but it appears wine would have been more appropriate for this romantic setting. Maybe I should have brought some candles, too, huh?"

"I can explain," said Adam, doing his best to hide his German accent, something he had had plenty of practice doing during his time as a salesman.

"No, let *me* explain," said Erik, stepping towards Adam with motive and meaning. "You two were playing hide-and-go-seek. Then when that got too boring you decided to play strip poker instead. Am I right? Huh? Am I?"

"It's not like that," Adam said, struggling to draw Erik's wrath towards himself and away from Maggie.

"No? Okay then, I guess that leaves only one other conclusion – and that is you were both *screwing in my barn!*" He shouted while poking Adam hard in the chest for emphasis.

"Erik, please," said Maggie. "I thought you were dead. We all did. We didn't mean for this to happen."

"You know, Mags, I figured you'd go for Tom Kettles or Jack Webster, or some other 4F loser, but this guy . . . this guy is a stranger. Tell me, Mr. Stranger who has been rollin' in the hay with my wife, what's your name?"

"Adam, you should leave," said Maggie. "This is between us now."

"Adam, huh?" Erik said as he circled the German, sizing him up head to toe. "I see you've met Eve, the keeper of the sweet and oh-so tempting fruit. Eve, the evil bitch who shows no loyalty." Having walked his way over to the wagon, just a few feet from Maggie, Erik quickly spun around, grabbed Maggie's arm and aggressively flipped her over the side railing. She fell out of the wagon and landed hard on the floor of the barn with a dull thud.

Maggie felt a searing shot of pain. "Oh God, my arm! You bastard!"

"What the hell is the matter with you, treating a lady like that?" barked Adam, taking a step closer to Erik with his fists clenched.

"Oh, but Adam *this* is no lady. She is a cheating wife bitch, and this is how you treat a lying, cheating, good-for-nothing bitch!" He bent over and broke the empty bottle of whiskey over her head. Maggie screamed, blood poured.

Furious, Adam stepped forward and took a swing but missed.

"Oh no you don't," Erik said while placing his leg just behind Adam's . . . and with a strong push, Maggie's lover fell backwards onto the dirt floor of the barn.

"Go on. Kill me," Maggie spat at Erik with her face in the dirt. "I'd rather be dead than be with you again."

"Oh, that can be arranged. Did you forget Uncle Sam taught me how to take a life in the name of honor? Only tonight, it is *my* honor I defend." Erik then picked up Maggie by her hair and cocked his arm back to take a swing. Adam lurched forward to stop him, but it was too late, and Erik's closed fist landed on her face. The blow resulted in a loud pop, the sound of her nose breaking. Maggie's body flew hard into the side of the metal thresher. She hit it with such force the large machine wobbled on the three support jacks, which precariously supported its two tons. Maggie let out another cry of pain and curled up in a ball.

"*Scheißkerl!*" barked Adam as he took another swing. Despite being nearly the same size, Erik was in better physical shape, and even drunk he managed to bob sideways and avert a swing, an uppercut and a left cross. Adam felt like he was fighting a ghost.

Erik then lifted his leg and kicked Adam hard in the chest, knocking the wind out of him as he fell onto the dirt floor of the barn. He laughed at his wife's lover who lay gasping for air. Then, after a substantial delay, Erik's drunken mind finally registered Adam's last remark.

"Hey, wait a sec! Are you kidding me? Was that *German* I just heard before?" As Adam finally found his breath again, Erik stood above him, cocked his head sideways and asked, "Holy Christ, are you a POW? And to think, I was concerned about niggers." Erik sneered, and his cocky smile quickly turned to rage. His eyes got red, and he bit down on his bottom lip.

But before he could act upon this new level of hatred, Adam dove at his knees and tackled him hard, landing on top of him. *"Stirb, du Drecksau!"* Straddling Erik, Adam hit him square in the face once, twice, but before he could land a third punch, Erik kicked his leg upwards and caught Adam in the groin. He fell sideways with a strained exhalation, yelling out, "Aaaaaah!"

Erik then got to his feet and circled the German, who laid on the ground before him in a ball. "Are you telling me my wife was having *relations* with a German soldier – while I was over there fightin' other Germans? Goddamn! I can't think of anything worse." Turning towards Maggie, he shot, "What if I was in the Pacific? What then, Mags? Would you be screwing a Jap?"

"Go to hell," she muttered, kneeling on all fours with blood now flowing freely from her nose and from a gash above her eye.

"Too late!" Erik said, taking one giant step over to her. Looking down at his wife with cold hatred and great distain, he wound back and kicked her hard in the chest, cracking two of her ribs. All the air left her lungs, followed by desperate gasps of air. He then kicked her in the face, nearly knocking out a tooth. The blow flipped her over like a rag doll and knocked her unconscious.

Upon seeing this, Adam found renewed strength and came at Erik with adrenaline and purpose. They both crashed up against the broken thresher with such force it wobbled dramatically, nearly tipping over onto Maggie. In a raving frenzy, Adam punched Erik in the stomach, causing him to buckle over in pain, then quickly followed with a knee to Erik's chin, slamming him backwards and knocking him off balance. Then he swung at Erik several more times, each punch connecting hard and square on his face and jaw. Erik's nose broke after the first punch and three front teeth popped out with the others. Erik floundered, but Adam wanted more.

Ten feet away, the woman he loved lay beaten and bruised – quite possibly dead – and a glance her way further fueled a barrage of kicking, swinging and punching. He had never felt such rage, such hatred. The ferocity with which Adam fought was unchartered territory. He felt as if nothing could stop him. Defenseless, Erik yelped in pain with each body blow. Now lying on his back in the dirt, with Adam straddled over him, Erik's fingers opened and closed tightly as they scanned the dirt floor for something to grasp. A brick, a rock, the handle of a shovel . . . anything at all. Miraculously, in the middle of the beating, Erik's hand found the end of Missy's single wooden yoke, which leaned up against a pillar. Instinctively he closed his grip around its end and swung hard at the air, hoping to blindly hit any part of his attacker. His second swing connected, crashing against Adam's right temple, knocking him over and leaving him nearly unconscious.

As Erik struggled to get his bearings, he staggered to his feet and stood over the German. Dizzy, with blood pouring from his nose and mouth, Erik spat red onto Adam and kicked him in the ribs. "I'm . . . going . . . to *kill* you, you fucking *Kraut* bastard. Just like I did all your friends back home."

Erik took the yoke and raised it over Adam, who tried to find his bearings as he knelt on all fours. Taking a golf swing, Erik hit him once across the skull, flipping him over onto his back. Then, like a human pendulum, he swung the yoke in the other direction with such force, the blow rendered Adam unconscious. At the same time, Maggie came to and could see the love of her life was about to be killed. Helpless and weak, she crawled closer towards him, but could only watch as Erik steadied himself, then raised the wooden yoke high above his head for what would have surely been a fatal blow. "You ungrateful bitch," he said, pausing momentarily to look at his wife.

But before he could drive the yoke down into its intended target, a stranger blew into the barn door like a strong gust of wind. Putting a shoulder into Erik, this apparition drove him hard into the broadside of the thresher. Still balancing precariously on the three jacks, the giant machine rocked backwards, paused for what seemed like a few seconds, and then it reversed direction. The forward momentum of the thresher proved too much for the supports, and the jack in the nearest corner buckled, followed by the other two in quick sequence.

Dizzy and somewhat confused, Erik took several half-hearted swings at the mystery man who had come to Adam's aid. Behind him, the metal behemoth landed hard on its front edge while making a terrible crash, followed by an ear-piercing screech. Instinctively, Erik spun around and raised both arms in a futile effort to stop its advance – but he may as well tried to stop a two-ton boulder from rolling down a mountain.

As the thresher tipped sideways, Erik's body was pushed backwards, and as he helplessly pressed his hands up against its cold metal his feet slipped out from under him, landing him face-first into the dirt. Erik made a desperate attempt to crawl out of the way . . . but it was too late. The metal machine settled hard onto its side, and Erik's head became pressed beneath its massive weight. His body twitched several times, then moved no more.

A thick pool of blood poured out from under the thresher, then soaked into the dirt floor of the barn. Amazingly, his body from the neck-down remained untouched and exposed, only his head and part of the right shoulder were hidden from view. The enemy . . . was dead.

Badly beaten and extremely dizzy, Maggie crawled over to Adam – who lay unconscious mere inches from being crushed himself. She checked to see if he was dead. Putting her ear to his mouth, she heard him breathing, or more precisely . . . panting. *Oh God, he's still alive! But is he dying?*

She then looked up at the stranger who had come out of nowhere to save her . . . to save Adam. Standing next to the tipped-over thresher, this silhouette was tall and athletic. With blood dripping from her forehead and into her eyes, Maggie wiped her brow and tried to place the face, but it was too dark, and she was too disoriented to focus. All she could muster were the whispered words, "Thank you. Thank you."

Stepping towards her, this knight-to-the-rescue simply said, "Dat is okay, Miss Maggie. I'm sorry I wasn't here sooner."

Chapter Thirty-Two

The Aftermath

"Don't move, dear. You've been through a significant trauma," whispered a woman dressed in a nurse's uniform. "Lie still."

As Maggie blinked her eyes, the white tiles of a ceiling came into focus. With her head propped up on pillows, she adjusted her gaze slightly and could see several figures standing beside her. The faces quickly became familiar: Doc Marshall . . . Colonel Raymonds . . . Sheriff Dale McGee . . . and the most welcome sight of all, Big Jack. All held vigil in her hospital room. A smile briefly twitched across her face, followed immediately by a grimace. It hurt, but she was safe, and that's what really mattered.

"Papa?" she whispered.

"There there, honey. Shhh . . ." he said, resting a hand on her shoulder.

"Where am I? What happened?"

"You're in the hospital, dear. Try to relax."

"Where's Adam? I need to see Adam," she insisted as the events from the night before began to flow back into her mind. She tried to sit up, but a sharp pain pierced her side.

"Maggie, be calm. You have a separated shoulder, a broken nose, several broken ribs, and God only knows how many stitches," said Doc Marshall, now standing beside her on the opposite side of the bed.

"Sweetheart, I'm so sorry I wasn't able to help you," said Big Jack with sorrowful eyes.

"And please don't worry about Sergeant Klein," added Colonel Raymonds. "All we care about is you right now."

"What happened? I mean, how did I get here? And where is Adam?" she repeated through the gauze which covered half her face.

Sheriff McGee leaned in. "Maggie, I don't know how to tell you this, but . . . Adam Klein is dead."

Maggie could not believe it. "No, oh no. He can't be! I saw him last night. He loved me . . ."

"He loved you?" snipped the commander, incredulous. "And he showed it how – by nearly beating you to death?"

"What?" she said, confusion numbing her pain.

"We found him in the barn, Mrs. Wentworth," said the commander. "And it wasn't last night – it was *two nights ago!*"

Big Jack bent over towards her and held her hand. "She obviously doesn't remember the details, gentlemen, so can we give her a break? Maybe come back in a few hours?"

"I have my orders to ship the remaining POWs to Upper Michigan *today!*" insisted the commander. "I'm already a day late. I cannot wait any longer. There is a great deal of paperwork that has to be signed, and *Cause of Death* certificates need to be submitted and God knows what else. HQ is breathing down my neck."

"How about you leave the Death Certificate paperwork with me and I'll mail it to you tomorrow?" suggested the sheriff. "Just give me a forwarding address. I'll sign what you need and pass it on to Doc Marshall for any medical reviews."

"I'm happy to do that," chimed in the doctor as he placed a cold washcloth on Maggie's forehead.

"That's not exactly proper protocol," said the commander, somewhat appeased. "I suppose I could agree to do that. To be honest, it would help immensely."

"It's not a problem at all," insisted the sheriff.

"But I can't leave without knowing what will happen to the body," added the commander.

"Oh God!" said Maggie, through her tears. "His body? His *body*? Is he really dead? Papa, please tell me it isn't true."

"I'm afraid so, my dear. Adam died in the barn." Big Jack gave her a consoling squeeze to her hand. She began to cry.

"Do you need the body? Going to send it back to Germany, perhaps?" inquired Doc Marshall to the commander, rather insensitively. "If not, I can arrange to have him buried in an empty plot in the graveyard. We could do that, if it's easier."

"I think that would be best," said the commander. "There's no way the military would pay to send him home. Do you think any fallen G.I.s are gonna get to come back?"

"My God! Listen to you," interrupted Big Jack, exasperated. "Have you people no decency? Any respect?"

Maggie's grief subsided briefly as more memories of the night started to return, and in a moment of clarity, she inquired. "Wait! Wait a second . . . What about Erik? Oh my God! What happened to him? He's back! I saw him!"

"Mrs. Wentworth, I have tried every day to find out if he is alive or not and I can tell you we have still not heard a thing. Now that the European fight has ended, maybe we can . . ."

"Who do you think did this to me?" she interrupted, shifting her gaze to the various bandages and sutures covering her body. "I swear I saw him. My memory is a little fuzzy, but this much I know – Erik is the one who beat me! Not Adam!"

The men stared at each other, then turned sympathetic gazes towards Maggie.

"Oh my gosh, you think I'm making it all up? You think I dreamt it!"

"We'll come back later," said the sheriff. "Maggie, please get some rest." With that, he turned to walk the commander to the door.

"I feel bad to leave on these terms, Big Jack, but I really have to get back, load up the trucks and head up to the U.P. before it gets dark," said the commander from the doorway of the hospital room. "Mrs. Wentworth, I'm so, so sorry you sustained such a brutal beating. We're all happy to see that you are okay and still alive. Goodbye. And I promise to call if I ever hear anything about your husband."

"You aren't listening to me! He was here, on the farm, in the—" But Big Jack's light hand on her arm signaled for her to dial it down. She gave him a look of utter surprise but acquiesced to his touch.

"I'll leave with you," the sheriff said. "I have to get back, too." Turning towards Maggie, he continued, "Darlin', I can't tell you how happy I am you survived. I'll see you later, okay?"

"Good luck in the Upper Peninsula," Big Jack said to the commander. "And we'll talk later, Dale," he said to the sheriff.

The sheriff and commander left the hospital room, their voices trailing off as they walked down the hall. Maggie looked up at Big Jack with tears dripping down her face. "Oh Papa, it wasn't a dream, was it?"

"Shhhh . . ." Doc Marshall soothed with a forced smile. "I just gave you a shot that will help you rest."

Big Jack studied his daughter's face, hardly recognizing her. One eye was nearly closed due to swelling; a bandage covered fresh stitches on her forehead. Her arm was wrapped in a sling, and under her translucent hospital gown he could see medical wrapping around her ribs. A sense of guilt washed over him for not being there to help. As he leaned in to kiss her forehead, he could tell the medicine was taking effect. Her eyes floated upwards as she quietly whispered the word, "Adam." With her eyes shut, a tear pooled in the corner, then dripped down to her ear. With a long sigh, she quickly fell asleep.

* * *

Maggie spent two more days in the hospital before returning home. As she stepped out of the pickup truck into the barnyard, Benny and Audrey bolted out of the farmhouse to greet her.

"Mommy, Mommy!" yelled Benny.

"Careful, son," cautioned Audrey, more reserved but just as relieved to see her best friend in one piece. "Your mommy needs to take it easy for a while."

Big Jack opened the tailgate to grab a small overnight bag and hand it to Audrey. "Could you take this inside for me? I need a moment with Maggie."

"Of course," said Audrey.

"Benny, can you carry something, too?" asked Big Jack. The youngster gladly came to the back of the truck. "Here, open your arms."

The boy did as asked, and Big Jack proceeded to scoop up several bundles of twined flowers and hand them to Benny. They included everything from roses and daisies to tulips and chrysanthemums. "What are all these for?" the boy asked.

"It seems your mother has a lot of friends," said Big Jack.

Ever since the news got out about Maggie's beating, word spread like wildfire, and of course, the real story quickly evolved into a country tale that vaguely resembled the truth. What began as, *"Did you hear Maggie Wentworth was found beaten in her barn?"* soon became *"Did you hear how an escaped POW robbed and beat Maggie Wentworth?"* and within no time it transformed into, *"Did you hear about the* group *of POWs who escaped and killed the entire Mueller family?"* Big Jack, too, received plenty of calls these past few days from well-wishers, many whom were genuinely relieved just to hear his voice on the other end of the phone.

"Come on, Benny, let's take those flowers inside," said Audrey.

"But I want to stay with Mommy."

"It's okay, Benny. Do as Audrey says. I'll be right there," said his mother.

As Benny and Audrey went into the farmhouse, Big Jack looked at his daughter and said, "I need to talk to you."

"Papa, I am so confused. Being back here. Knowing Adam is dead. All I want to do is cry."

"That's what I have to talk with you about."

"I know, I know, you're gonna repeat what the doctor said . . . that I dreamed everything . . . Erik wasn't really here . . . Adam manifested himself into Erik as he tried to kill me . . . But I tell you, Papa, it seemed so *real*. The thresher fell on Erik. I saw it! Adam did not do this to me."

"Are you okay if we go into the barn? It may help"

"I don't think I can go back in there. At least not for a while."

"Please, sweetheart. It's important."

Maggie looked up at the tall red structure and hesitated. "I don't know."

"I realize it's difficult, but I want to show you something. It may help explain a few things."

Maggie studied her father for a moment. He rarely asked for favors, so she agreed.

As they stepped inside, nothing seemed out of the ordinary. Suri and Bucky were secure in their stables and Missy the cow chewed hay while tied to a rope. Most obvious though, was the large thresher . . . it stood on the three support jacks, just as it had been for several weeks awaiting Big Jack's latest round of repairs.

"What the . . . ? This thing tipped over! Did you put it back on the supports? And this spot, right here, this is where Erik almost killed me. I know you don't believe me, Papa."

Her father looked at her with sorrow in his eyes.

"I don't know how to convince you just how real it was. I wish you would believe me."

"But I do," said Big Jack.

Maggie snapped a look at her father. "What? What do you mean?"

"I believe you."

"But . . . what? Why now? Why didn't you say so at the hospital these past few days?"

"I couldn't risk it in front of certain people. At least not yet."

"Okay, I'm going to lose my mind here any second. What are you talking about?"

"It's important others *not* believe your story, Mags. At least not for a few months."

"I don't understand."

Taking a deep breath, Big Jack continued. "I'm saying I believe Erik was here. And I believe he beat you within an inch of your life."

"Obviously *somebody* did it. And what about Adam, huh? Next thing you'll probably tell me is he's with the rest of the POWs in Upper Michigan."

At that moment, someone shuffled into view from around the corner. Maggie turned and her eyes got wide. Standing before her was Adam. She screamed, jumped up and down, and ran to embrace him. "You're alive! Oh my God, you're alive!" She proceeded to kiss his lips, his face, his neck. He winced occasionally, but never would he have asked her to stop.

"It's alright. I'm here. I'm here," he said gently.

Big Jack stood by with an ear-to-ear smile on his face. Maggie turned to look at her father, then with an expression of awe, back at Adam.

"You are hurt!" she said, examining his swollen face.

"*You* are hurt," he said, looking at her bruises, the two black eyes and the sling that held her arm.

"Oh my gosh, we are a sight, I'm sure," she said. Taking a step back, she looked him up and down. "But wait a sec – you're wearing . . . is that Erik's uniform? I mean . . . how is this possible? What's happening?"

Then without notice, Oku stepped out from the shadows as well. "Hello, Miss Maggie. I hope dis isn't a bad time." He then let out his trademark laugh as she ran to him and hugged her migrant friend with her one good arm.

"It was *you*! You were the one! I remember it now. Oh my gosh, I remember it all! You fought Erik. You pushed him into the thresher, and it tipped over, and . . . You were the one who saved our lives."

"Oh, it was noting," Oku said modestly.

"But how did you get here? Did you come with Adam that night?"

Oku looked ashamed. "Well, I, um . . ."

Maggie saved him. "You were stealing my chickens! You crazy Jamaican!" she said with a painful smile, giving him a playful punch in the chest.

"Dat's not entirely true. I was *replacing* a chicken."

Maggie tipped her head, trying to make sense of the remark.

"I mean, I did take a chicken from you, dat is true, but it was back in da fall. We simply had no food, so I swore to my wife I would return it. And on da night of da fight . . . I snuck into your chicken coop to *replace* da bird."

"I can't believe this," Maggie said with her hand covering her smile. "So while you were in the chicken coop . . ."

"I heard da fight. It was bad, Miss Maggie. Dat man was da devil himself." Upon saying these words, Oku made the sign of the cross.

Maggie could hardly believe it. She looked at Oku, then back at Adam, then to Big Jack. Shaking her head, she remarked, "Okay, can someone please start from the beginning?"

"I'll try," said Big Jack. "So late that night, I was shocked to see Oku at the foot of my bed. He shook me awake and told me I had to come out to the barn. He looked like he had seen a ghost. When I got up and stepped into the barn, well, I couldn't believe my eyes, either."

Maggie walked to her father and put a hand on his shoulder.

"There lay Erik," he continued. "Or what was left of him." The memory of the moment gave Big Jack pause. He took a deep breath, let it out slowly and went on. "My goodness, I didn't even know for sure who it was until Oku showed me his wallet. His head was completely . . ." He winced at the memory.

Maggie let out a slow exhalation.

"We took care a you first, Miss Maggie, den Adam," Oku interrupted. "Both a you were in bad shape, but I knew you'd live. We got some ice from da kitchen, made some butterfly bandages . . . and made you comfortable until da sheriff got here." Oku paused for a second. "You really don't remember any of dat?"

"No. Nothing. Nothing at all."

"It happened as I say."

"So what about Erik?" Maggie asked. "You never told me about Erik. What happened to his, um, body?"

"It was Big Jack's plan, actually," said Oku. "I can't take any credit."

"I guess I couldn't help myself," said her father humbly. "After taking care of you two, we quickly exchanged Erik's clothes with Adam's. I told Adam he would have to hide in the loft for a few days, I then sent Oku home, swearing him to secrecy, and then . . . I called the police."

"Hey, who's gonna believe me anyways," chimed in the large Jamaican, followed by his self-deprecating chuckle.

"By the time Sheriff McGee arrived, the crime scene said it all. On the ground, underneath the toppled-over thresher, was a man dressed in POW clothing. Somehow, that giant machine crushed him during the fight. That's the story I'm sticking to."

"Wasn't the sheriff suspicious?"

"All he saw was a dead man lying on the floor . . . a man who was reported missing earlier that night by the guards at Camp Ramsey. He just put two and two together. And when he saw how beaten you were . . ."

"So now what? How are we gonna explain Adam?" she said, gently placing her hand on the small of her lover's back.

"You mean Erik?" said Big Jack.

"Huh?"

"This ain't 'Adam' no more, sweetheart. It's *Erik*. At least in the eyes of the surrounding community – and the military – who just shipped out."

Looking at Adam, Maggie recalled, "Oh my gosh, nobody from the area knew Erik was back. I remember that now. He said he wanted to 'surprise us.' So in that coffin, buried in the cemetery . . ." Maggie's jaw dropped as she came to realize the brilliance of the plan.

"That's right, it's escaped POW Adam Klein," said Big Jack. "At least, that's the official story."

"Do you really think we can pull this off?"

"I don't see why not. Think about it, Mags – the war is over, the POW camp is closed, and all the Germans are headed back to Europe, or they will be soon. So we'll just ask Adam to stay out of sight for a while and then after a few weeks or so, everyone will simply say, 'Hey, look who's back. He must have gotten approval to return to America.'"

"What if Colonel Raymonds finds out? What if Sheriff McGee finds out?

"Don't worry about McGee. He already knows!"

"What? He's a policeman. He will surely—"

"Mags, he never liked Erik to begin with. The public drunkenness . . . the fights with the locals . . . but the kicker for him was seeing you and the bruises and . . ." his voice cracked slightly. "Well, he's on board with this plan. And the colonel will be too, if he ever finds out. Which my guess will be never."

"But people in town? No one will be fooled into thinking Adam is actually *Erik*. They know what Erik looks like."

"Like I said, we'll wait it out a few months, and then they'll just think Adam has returned. And Erik . . . well as far as everyone knows, he's still MIA You said yourself, no one knew he came back."

"But everyone thinks *Adam* tried to kill me. They will wonder whose dead body was buried in the gravesite. If it's not Adam, they'll wonder who it is."

"Apparently it was someone else – a *different* POW. They'll believe your word, of course. You know how stories spread in this county. People will just chalk it up as another unsubstantiated rumor. And Sheriff McGee will back us up. Besides, the simple truth is they all love you, Mags. Our tight-knit German community will probably find this to be a cause for celebration."

Maggie turned towards Adam. He smiled and said, "Didn't I tell you we'd find a way?"

"You did. You always said that."

Just then, Audrey stepped into the barn. Maggie looked at her friend and smiled. Audrey smiled back. "So how's this for a surprise?" she said to Maggie.

"You knew?"

"Well, as of a few hours ago. Big Jack told me everything."

"And you think this will work?"

"All I can say is, it's worth a shot," said Audrey. "I know I'd be all for it if I were in love the way you two are."

At that, Maggie walked over to Adam, kissed him, and then rested her head on his shoulder.

Adam put his arm around her, and with a painful smile he made eye contact with Big Jack.

Maggie's father took a deep breath, extended his right hand to Adam and said with a smile, "Welcome to the family, son."

MOVIETONE Title: JAPAN SURRENDERS AT LAST

(Newsreel Narrator): "Here sits the USS Missouri in Tokyo Bay. On this morning of September 2nd, 1945, the drama of surrender has reached its climax. In a ceremony which lasted only 20 minutes, the fate of Japan was sealed forever. The 11-man delegation was photographed by cameramen perched on every vantage point of the great battleship, all to record this meaningful event for posterity.

On behalf of Emperor Hirohito, Foreign Minister Mamoru Shigemitsu signed for the Japanese government. Japan accepted unconditional surrender according to the provisions of the Potsdam Declaration. With the news came much celebration and moments of relief throughout America in cities like New York, Chicago and San Francisco. After many years of war, first in the Pacific, then in Europe and now concluding off the shores of Japan, peace is finally here. Think of the anxieties and the grief and the horrors of universal war. Those days are behind us now.

In all of the Allied land, this is a time of great rejoicing, and people everywhere pray this is a lasting peace for generations to come.

Afterword

"Daddy! Daddy!" shouted Benny enthusiastically as he bolted through the front door of Ramsey's only jewelry store, his wet shoes leaving footprints on the hardwood floor. Following close behind was Maggie, shaking off of a rain-soaked umbrella.

"My goodness. It's raining cats and dogs out there," she said, a bit overwhelmed by it all. "Ugh."

"Yeah, it's been doing that all day," said Adam from behind the counter. Craning his neck to get a better look at the rain through the storefront windows, he added, "I hope you didn't step in a poodle."

Maggie froze as she was removing her raincoat and then gave him a twisted expression.

"Sorry, I couldn't resist," Adam said, backpedaling.

"One more of those and I'm going to stand in the street holding the umbrella as high in the air as possible. Maybe I'll get lucky and get struck by lightning."

Adam smiled at his wife's quick wit.

"It would put me out of my misery of having to endure such horrible puns," she added.

Adam laughed.

"I miss you," said Benny as he ran behind the counter and hugged Adam.

"And I miss you, too," said Adam, wiping the wet hair away from the youngster's forehead. "I know I've been working a lot lately."

"That's okay," said the six-year-old understandingly.

"So, tell me . . . to what do I owe the pleasure of a visit?" Adam asked as he stood behind a glass display case of wedding rings, gold bracelets, oversized dress clips, sweetheart bracelets, brooches, pendants, and of course, watches.

"We were just running a few errands," said Maggie, "and thought it might be a good idea to pop in and say hi."

Adam looked at her admiringly. "I must say, you are the prettiest customer I've had all day."

"Has the rain kept many people away today?" she asked sympathetically.

"Not at all. I've actually been quite busy."

"I'm sure most of the ladies in town come in here to see you. You're such a charmer."

"Oh hardly," said Adam modestly. "In fact, all of my customers today have been men."

Maggie smiled, leaned over the glass case and gave him a kiss. "Lucky you."

"Yuck," said Benny as he looked up at his parents. "Kissing is yucky. I'll never do that!"

Ramsey's newest Main Street merchant had much to be happy about these days. Sales had been rising ever since Adam opened the business six months earlier. After purchasing the old storefront – which had previously been occupied by the town butcher – Adam had been working nearly six days a week, and some Sundays, just to keep up with the demand. After installing the display cases, putting in new lighting, adding a coat of fresh paint and stocking up on inventory, he'd drawn customers from as far away as Chicago to the *little jewelry store that could.* The word was getting out about a remarkable new artisan who once worked for a top horologist in Europe. Of course, none of this would be possible if it weren't for Erik's old pocket watch, which he and Maggie sold at the Chicago Auction House several months earlier for a whopping $3,000!

Klein's Jewelers sat in the heart of Ramsey's downtown. A green awning brimmed the two glass storefront windows, each with hand-painted lettering which read: JEWELRY • WATCHES • REPAIRS. Neighboring businesses included a barber shop, a building and loan, a bakery, the town's only drugstore, Hotel Ramsey, a florist, a bowling alley and pool hall. Since the end of the war, business was booming for all of these merchants, but especially for the only retailer in the area who sold wedding rings.

"Hey, Benny, take a look at these new watches I got in this week," said Adam while pointing to a wicker basket next to the cash register.

"Whoa!" said the youngster with great enthusiasm. Benny always liked to play with the old watches. Maggie smiled as her son enthusiastically dug into the pile of metal timepieces.

"So, Maggie, I want your advice on something," said Adam, his focus now on her.

"Sure. What is it?" she asked. Maggie was always willing to assist with his affairs. He trusted her opinion and felt she had a good acumen for business.

"What do you think of these freshwater pearls that came in the other day?" He then opened a cigar boxed lined in black velvet. Inside were at least 30 different earring designs. "I can't decide if people will think they are too old-fashioned."

"Oh Lord, are you kidding? I love pearls! But that's just me," said Maggie as she looked at the jewels with an enthusiasm that matched Benny's affinity for the old watches. "I know these young couples today are going for fancier things like diamonds or emeralds, but give me a pearl any day! Classic and elegant."

"So you really feel that way?"

"Goodness yes."

"I'm glad to hear that, because . . . I was going to give you these later tonight." Adam then presented her with a separate box, wrapped in red wrapping paper. "Happy Anniversary, darling!"

Genuinely moved, Maggie brought her hand to her chin. "You remembered!"

"Of course. How could I ever forget our wedding date?"

Maggie opened the small box and let out a gasp upon seeing a pair of earrings. She clipped the pearls onto her earlobes, looked at her reflection in a countertop mirror, and marveled at the new gift.

"I love them . . . and I love you! Thank you!"

Adam glowed at her approval.

Again they kissed.

"Big Jack is making a big dinner tonight. Should I wear them? We can see if he even notices."

"You wear them whenever you want."

"Good gracious, they must have cost a fortune," she said as she clipped them off her ears and held them in the palm of her hand. "Can we afford these?"

"Trust me. I know a guy."

"You know a guy, huh?" said Maggie with a smile.

"Yep."

"How lucky for me."

She then walked around the counter and held Adam's hands in hers. Gazing at him lovingly, her eyes pooled slightly. She kissed him again, then hugged him tight, her head resting against his chest. "As long as we are giving one another our presents a bit early today, I have one for you, too."

"You do?"

"Yes."

"And you brought it with you?"

"I did indeed," she said, her eyes locked on his. "Like you, I was going to wait to share it, but . . ." Maggie went up on her tip-toes and whispered into his ear. She then pulled back and smiled wide and proud.

"What? Really?"

Maggie could only nod her head up and down excitedly.

"Whew-hoo!" yelled Adam. "When?"

"The doctor says in about seven months."

"What? What is it?" asked Benny, his attention off the box of watches.

"Well, honey," said Maggie, "it seems you are going to have a little brother or sister, sometime around Christmas!"

"Really? There's a baby in your tummy?"

"That's right."

The boy pondered the news for a moment. "That's neat." He then went back to looking at the watches.

Maggie laughed, kissed Adam again, and simply said, "I love you."

"I love you, too, *Frau* Maggie."

As they held their embrace, both stood cheek-to-cheek, looking out the storefront window. They noticed the rain had stopped and the sun was fighting for attention in the afternoon sky. In the distance, a rainbow began to form.

Acknowledgements

First and foremost, I'd like to thank my remarkable parents. To my mother, Mary E. Hanneken, for planting the seed for this wonderful story back when I was a teenager, and then again for fact-checking the manuscript after I finished the first draft. (Mom, you smoked Chesterfields? Nice!) Back in the 1940s, she worked in the medical clinic at Camp Grant – a U.S. Army facility located just outside of Rockford, Illinois – and she often spoke of the German POWs who lived in that *stalag*. Through her storytelling, she humanized a group many think of as having horns on their heads and pitchforks in their hands. Speaking of fact-checking, a very special thank you also goes to my father, Clemens B. Hanneken, for painting a detailed picture of life on his pre-war country farm, and for teaching me the difference between a seven-oat shock and a five-oat shock.

Of course, my deepest appreciation goes to my editor Sam Stoeger, whose arm-twisting and numerous recommendations made these characters so real, I feel as if I got to know them personally. Sam is a lover of good stories, a voracious reader, and a wonderful advocate for quality writing. I couldn't have done it without her. Furthermore, D.J. Herda helped immensely, especially in the early part of this journey. It's always good to have a Sherpa available when venturing into unfamiliar territory.

The good folks at Ten16 Press have been nothing short of spectacular. Their support and optimism for this project was evident from Day One, and it continues to thrive. In particular, I'd like to give a shout-out to Shannon Ishizaki, Kaye Nemec, Lauren Blue, Kaeley Dunteman, and Jenna Zerbel. I couldn't have done it without all ya alls.

To my dear friends, Melanie Roach, Pam Ford, and Pamela Ferderbar, your perspective and advice meant more than you will ever know. Clara Meinen, I can't thank you enough for arranging for me to attend "Thresher Day" on your West Bend farm. Seeing an old-time thresher in action made me truly appreciate its engineering. Laurette Perlewitz, you continue to impress and amaze, as the cover art for this book instantly conveys the plotline like no other book I've seen in recent memory.

I further owe a huge debt of gratitude to Betty Crowley, who researched and wrote the fascinating book *Stalag Wisconsin*, which served as a great reference for me. Her many interviews with German POWs and American guards helped to preserve this quiet piece of history. It gave me an added sense for what life was like inside a POW camp, as well as on the American farms and in the factories where the German POWs worked. It is a terrific book and I highly recommend history buffs jump in with both feet.

Derek Buyan was a helpful resource for me with the German translations. His attention to detail helped me in so many ways. I may even ask him to read the audio version of the book in the future. Danke, Derek!

Speaking of influential writing, Francisco Jiménez's *The Circuit: Stories from the Life of a Migrant Child* is a must read for anyone who wants to get a better understanding of what life was like for family migrant workers in the 1940s. It further gave me a unique perspective of life as a migrant worker in America and is a fantastic book to read.

The Milwaukee Public Library provided wonderful historical references, especially for the simplest of tidbits, like daily weather reports during the years 1944–1945, and for the classic MOVIETONE clips played in countless theaters during the war.

Appropriately, I would like to thank Greg Fredericks, Mark Miner, and all other academics who taught me, inspired me, and gave me the confidence that something good can come from putting pen to paper. Speaking of believing in oneself, I would be remiss to forget my sister Anne Hanneken, M.D., who pumped me with 1000 cc's of confidence and made me believe I could actually paint vivid pictures with a pallet of 26 characters.

As long as I'm referencing physicians, I feel the need to thank my uncle Dan Miller, M.D., who regaled me with firsthand stories of his life as a country doctor. A renaissance man who practiced medicine for nearly seventy years, he was an anesthesiologist by trade, but could have just as easily worn the hats of numerous medical disciplines. Back in his day, country doctors had to be masters of many specialties and he was no exception.

Dr. Hull Cook's amazing assortment of stories from the book *50 Years A Country Doctor* became a wonderful resource for me as well. His collection of memories and anecdotes were a helpful reminder that "doctoring" in the first half of the 20th century was markedly different from "doctoring" today, and they confirm the notion that real life really is stranger (and in some instances, funnier) than fiction.

For nearly three years, I did a lot of my writing while taking the Amtrak to work between Milwaukee and Chicago, so I am indebted to the American Track Corporation for adding a Quiet Car on the back of every roundtrip route to the Windy City. Thank you also for hiring an Amtrak conductor whose name I do not know – and never dared to ask – as she put the fear of God into anyone in that Quiet Car who uttered even the softest of syllables. The risk of being verbally ostracized and thrown off the Hiawatha Line someplace between Kenosha and Buffalo Grove proved too much for me. Admittedly, her efforts to muzzle us commuters was a Godsend.

I would also like to thank Stan. Who is Stan, you ask? Does this mystery man have a last name? I'm sure he does but I will likely never know it. You see, a black-and-white, wallet-sized photo with the words "Stan – 1944" written on the back was given to me by Gina Ferrise (another friend and muse) after I told her I was writing this book. Gina found Stan tucked into the pages of an old book, and she thought he'd be an inspiration while I wrote. Stan's hometown is unknown. The photographer is unknown. The location of the photo is unknown. But what is known is his old photo sat in my wallet for several years as I crafted a story I'm certain he would have enjoyed. Thanks for motivating me, Stan!

Saving the best for last, I dedicate this book to my amazing wife Mary, the writer's equivalent to Mikey from the old Life Cereal commercials. "Hey, Mary! She likes it!" She's one tough critic, so when she likes something it's usually quite good. I am also forever grateful to my three children, Sarah, Kevin, and Kyle. If not for them, this story would have been written sooner, but thankfully I made the time to attend school concerts, track meets, and coach youth basketball. Over that time, I watched them grow and prosper with no regrets. As far as I'm concerned, this little story waited to be unveiled for seventy-five years, so a few more wouldn't hurt, right?

Hopefully, you feel it was worth the wait.

Made in the USA
Monee, IL
22 December 2021

86835375R00223